ABOUT TRICIA STRINGER

Tricia Stringer is the bestselling author of the rural romances *Queen of the Road, Right as Rain, Riverboat Point, Between the Vines, A Chance of Stormy Weather* and *Come Rain or Shine*; three historical sagas in the Flinders Ranges series, *Heart of the Country, Dust on the Horizon* and *Jewel in the North*; and several contemporary novels, including *Table for Eight, The Model Wife* and *The Family Inheritance*.

Queen of the Road won the Romance Writers of Australia Romantic Book of the Year award in 2013 and *Riverboat Point* and *Between the Vines* have been shortlisted for the same award.

Tricia grew up on a farm in country South Australia and has spent most of her life in rural communities, as owner of a post office and bookshop, as a teacher and librarian, and now as a full-time writer. She lives in the beautiful Copper Coast region with her husband Daryl. From here she travels and explores Australia's diverse communities and landscapes, and shares this passion for the country and its people through her stories.

For further information go to triciastringer.com or connect with Tricia on Facebook or Twitter @tricia_stringer

TRICIA STRINGER

Something in the Wine

mira

First Published 2019
Second Australian Paperback Edition 2021
ISBN 9781489281029

Published by
Mira
An imprint of Harlequin Enterprises (Australia) Pty Limited (ABN 47 001 180 918), a subsidiary of
HarperCollins Publishers Australia Pty Limited (ABN 36 009 913 517)
Level 13, 201 Elizabeth St
SYDNEY NSW 2000
AUSTRALIA

® and TM (apart from those relating to FSC®) are trademarks of Harlequin Enterprises (Australia) Pty Limited or its corporate affiliates. Trademarks indicated with ® are registered in Australia, New Zealand and in other countries.

A catalogue record for this book is available from the National Library of Australia
www.librariesaustralia.nla.gov.au

Printed and bound in Australia by McPherson's Printing Group

For Kelly

CHAPTER
1

Keely Mitchell peered at the numbers on the overhead panel and stopped beside 19B. A man was already in the aisle seat. His head was back and his eyes were closed. She paused. His relaxed face had the most freckles she had ever seen, and it was topped by wisps of faded gingery hair. If he'd had a straw hat, he would have made a good scarecrow. Pressure against the pack on her back reminded her of the passengers queuing up behind her, waiting to find their seats. She had to get past the scarecrow to reach hers.

A loud laugh erupted from the group of young men who were seating themselves a few rows ahead. She had noticed them in the airport bar before the boarding call came. They were a happy crew sharing jokes over their drinks – a sharp contrast to Keely's bored brothers and fussing parents. Her mum had asked her several times if she'd packed spare cash and, to Keely's horror, underwear in her backpack in case her bag was lost, and her dad kept checking departure and arrival times and reminding her of the time differences.

"Are you going to sit down, love?" a plaintive male voice asked from behind.

The scarecrow man opened his eyes and Keely flushed as she felt his piercing gaze sweep over her. She pointed at the seat beside him. "Excuse me. I'm in the middle."

He stood and she ducked her head, barely missing a collision with his shoulder. She struggled past him and fell into her seat. Her pack dug uncomfortably into her back.

"I'm sorry." She turned away from him to ease off her pack and hide her embarrassment. She felt a hand tug the last stubborn strap over her wrist. Clutching the bag to her chest, she turned awkwardly to face him.

"Thanks," she murmured.

"There's not a lot of room on these planes, is there?" He grinned and his face creased into hundreds of tiny lines. Keely glanced at his wiry frame and then looked over the backpack to her long solid legs. The space allowed would be fine if all of the passengers were his build.

"It's a long time since I've flown," she said.

His weathered appearance made it hard to judge his age. She thought he was probably in his sixties but the twinkle in his ice-blue eyes made him seem younger.

"Would you like me to put your pack up top for you?" He pointed to the overhead console.

"No, thanks," she said.

"They won't let you nurse it."

"I'll put it at my feet." She leaned forward but was interrupted.

"Excuse me, I need to sit there."

They both looked up. A woman dressed in a tight t-shirt and clinging designer workout pants loomed over them.

Keely hugged her pack tightly as they both clambered out to let the woman in. The faint smell of stale sweat wafted from the newcomer as she settled into her seat then immediately tugged out a pen and magazine. Keely sat back down, dismayed to see a muscular arm already covering the divider between them. The woman opened to a large crossword and began to work; Keely edged away.

"This is going to be a cosy flight." A low voice murmured in her ear.

She turned and looked directly into the face of the man who sat beside her. In her attempt to avoid contact with the woman she had almost leaned her head on his. Once again she felt her embarrassment burn across her cheeks.

"I'm sorry." She jerked upright.

"It's a long way to Perth. If we're going to be this close we may as well introduce ourselves. I'm Euan Levallier." He held out his hand and a smile crinkled his face again.

Keely disentangled her own hand from her pack and gave his a quick shake.

"I'm Keely Mitchell."

"Are you going home to WA or visiting, Keely?" He said her name with a hint of brogue that reminded her of her Irish grandfather.

"Oh...visiting," she replied, but the thought of escaping forever was momentarily intoxicating.

"Have you been before?"

"Only to Perth. When I was a child my grandparents lived there."

"You'll find it's changed since then. Are you planning on travelling further?"

Keely hesitated. He asked a lot of questions. She wasn't good at confiding in strangers. "Yes...Perth is just the starting point. I plan to head north from there."

"South is better."

"Is it?"

"We have everything in the south; great wine, fantastic beaches, surf, beautiful weather and a magical river. What else does one need?"

"Good morning everyone, and welcome aboard."

Keely was saved from answering as the flight attendant began the safety instructions. Keely gave the attendant her full attention, but the woman on her left continued to work on the crossword, and the man, Euan, leaned back in his seat and closed his eyes. Relieved that she would no longer have to make conversation, Keely watched the flight attendant closest to her, noting her nearest exit was a couple of rows in front. Had a domestic flight ever needed to use these emergency exits?

Keely shook her head to chase away the negative thoughts. She was worrying like her mother. She recalled the quiet send-off she'd just experienced. Her mum had teared up and her dad had given her an extra tight hug. They were behaving as if Keely was leaving Adelaide forever, instead of taking a three-month trip to Western Australia. "I'll be home for Christmas," she'd said. Her dad had flapped a hand and pulled her mum close while her two younger brothers had watched on with bemused looks. They'd complained when their mother insisted they come too. They'd lined up a tennis game with the girls next door and weren't keen to make the trek to the airport.

"Goodness knows when you'll see your sister again," their mother had said. "We're all going to give her a proper send-off on her big adventure."

Keely shook her head. Big adventure! What a laugh. It wasn't as if she was leaving the country. She had been saving to go overseas for a couple of years but her mum hadn't wanted her to go alone. Keely's friend Bec had agreed to go with her but when Bec had been offered a new job their plans had been put on hold till the year after. Keely had been desperate to get away for a break and opted for a West Aussie trek as an alternative until they could reschedule the overseas trip.

Broome and the Kimberley region had interested her since the time of her childhood holidays in Perth with her grandparents. Her grandfather had been an avid storyteller, keeping Keely and her younger brothers entertained with tales of his travels to the north-western areas of Australia. She'd decided on a ramble along Australia's western coast. If she put the huge expanse of the Great Australian Bight and the Nullarbor Plain between her and her nightmare, maybe she could shake it off.

The safety spiel finished, the flight attendants retreated and the plane turned onto the runway, its engines at full throttle as it surged forward, forcing Keely back into her seat. She clasped her hands tightly and took a quick look out the window. The view was partially blocked by the woman next to her, but Keely was able to catch a glimpse of Adelaide sliding beneath and the shoreline giving way to the sparkling blue of the gulf waters.

"Perth, here I come," she muttered softly and turned away to look directly into Euan's bemused smile. She blushed again – had he overheard her? She dug her book from her pack and spent the first part of the flight reading but gave up when the flight attendant offered food. It might help quell the queasiness in her stomach. It had been with her since the night before and she assumed it was because of her anxiety in the lead-up to her travels.

The woman with the crossword had packed her own food and continued to work on the huge word puzzle as she ate. Euan, on the other hand, was keen to chat.

"What were you reading?" he asked once their snacks and drinks had been delivered.

"A book written by a doctor who has worked for the Flying Doctor Service in the top of Western Australia and Northern Territory."

"Interesting?"

"Very. I'm hoping to see some of the country he's talked about."

"Are you in the medical profession, Keely?"

There was that hint of the Irish. The way he said her name reminded her of her grandfather again.

"No, I'm a secondary teacher. Art and design."

"I admire those who have the courage to teach...and you're creative as well, very clever."

His eyes held a sparkle of amusement. Keely looked down. "I do enjoy designing and making." She reached for her cup. It's the clever and the courage I lack, she thought.

"There are a few places you should visit while you're in Perth. Where are you staying?"

"In backpacker accommodation in the city."

"That's a good way to meet up with people. Used to do a lot of it myself. Where will you go after that?"

"After Perth I plan to stop where I see something I like. I haven't got a schedule." Keely found herself relaxing. Euan was easy to talk to, and she was looking forward to this holiday.

"Lucky you."

She was about to ask what he did in the south but the plane bumped and she was interrupted as the captain spoke through the speaker system, explaining they'd met some unexpected turbulence and asking everyone to remain seated and fasten their seat belts.

She gripped her hands together and tried to look as if the sudden lurch of the aircraft was something she took in her stride while inside butterflies flapped frantically. When she glanced at Euan he was leaning back with his eyes closed again. She studied his face surreptitiously for a moment. Scarecrow was a good description for him. All he needed was a straw hat. He must have spent a lot of time outside to get all those freckles and the wrinkles.

She pictured him as a series of pencil strokes, then overlaid them with subtle splashes of oranges and browns, building up an abstract image in her mind; something she loved to do when a subject really interested her. His chest rose and fell gently. Keely dug out her notebook and began to sketch.

★ ★ ★

Theo walked between the vines on the new block, inspecting the delicate green shoots. He stopped to retie a string to a wire. After three years of teasing, stretching, encouraging, the plants had grown up and along the wires, big enough now that when the first tiny bunches of grapes appeared, they would hang just under the canopy of green leaves.

This year would be the first pick from these semillon vines and he had high hopes for them; the final addition to his River Dynasty range. He had been trying for years to create a wine that reminded him of the assyrtiko wine he'd first learned to make as a young man in Greece. He hoped the lemon-zest flavours from this semillon would be as close to the real thing as he could get, until he could actually acquire the vines from Greece. That was his long-term plan.

It had been a real coup to be able to buy this parcel of land. Especially from right under the nose of his neighbour. The price had been high but it would pay off in the long term. He scribbled a note in his diary and slipped it back into his shirt pocket.

He had done well from this Margaret River property. The Ocean Dynasty property further south was expanding but this land and these vines were Theo's stronghold. This was where he produced his best wines and where he wanted to keep expanding to consolidate his family's future. His son thought they were overcommitted but Tony was a worrier. A good return from the current year's vintage would improve the cash flow.

Theo's gaze drifted over the vines and the heads of the workers, to the river and the thick bush that divided his vineyard from Levalliers' next door. He frowned. Euan Levallier was a crazy fool. His land was some of the best in the area. His vines produced liquid gold but Theo couldn't understand the man, who treated it all as a bit of a hobby.

Theo felt sorry for the son, Flynn. He'd tried to take him under his wing and give him support. It could have been a mutually agreeable opportunity: Theo could help Flynn to build up the winery and, once it was Flynn's, he would look favourably on Theo as a benefactor. Levallier Dell would be the crowning glory of the River Dynasty estate, that stretched along the river on either side. It would be the final piece in a puzzle of prime land that Theo had been accumulating for years.

Unfortunately, Flynn wasn't so easily influenced. He was his own man; a trait Theo had to admit he admired. He lifted his cap and ran his fingers through his hair. It was still thick, despite his seventy-six years. He shook his head. Young Levallier planned to expand on his own. Theo wasn't sure that he had the business knowledge or the money to do it and Flynn had the added disadvantage of Euan, who still believed he was running a cottage industry from the eighties.

A tooting car horn interrupted the still morning. Theo looked up. His face broke into a benevolent smile as he watched the red sports car sweep down the road towards the house. Katerina had arrived. He hadn't seen his precious granddaughter for over a year and that had not been here but in Melbourne. She'd been there when he'd flown over for meetings and he'd taken her out for dinner. It was good that she'd come home.

He gave one last look towards the workers, and beyond them to the Levallier winery. His smile broadened. There was more than one way to skin a cat, he thought. And he strode towards the house.

CHAPTER

2

The luggage was late appearing and after she'd checked her phone and texted her mother to let her know they'd landed safely, Keely perused the tourist information while she waited. The airport brochure stand was packed full of invitations for things to do in Perth and beyond. She reached for a pamphlet and felt a lump under her toe.

"Sorry," she said as the young man next to her yanked his foot away. She stepped back quickly and bumped into someone behind her.

"Sorry," she wailed again and clutched her bag, trying to make herself smaller.

"No harm done."

She turned to look at the smiling face of the dark-haired young man whose toes she'd squashed. He passed her the brochure she'd been reaching for.

She recognised him as one of the group who'd been seated near her on the flight.

"You planning on doing some sky diving?"

She glanced down at the pamphlet he'd given her and was stunned to see that was indeed what it was for.

"Oh no. I have enough trouble flying in a plane let alone jumping out of one. I wanted the one on river cruises."

He passed it to her. "Are you holidaying in Perth?"

"For a while."

"So are we." He waved to where his two friends waited by the luggage carousel. They were both very blonde and tanned. All three wore faded t-shirts and shorts. "I'm Marty and that's Steve and Mike." He grinned at her and Keely found herself grinning back.

"I'm Keely."

"Are you heading to the city? We could share a taxi."

"Oh…I…"

A loud whistle shrilled across the space. Marty spun around.

"The bags are coming," called one of his mates.

He turned back to her and smiled again. Keely noticed a dimple on his left cheek. "Come on, why pay full price for a taxi?"

She looked from Marty to his mates, who were engaged in an animated conversation. Why not? This was the beginning of her adventure and she hadn't come all this way to be on her own.

"Thanks," she said, and followed him back to the luggage carousel.

* * *

Euan lugged his surfboard in its bag away from the oversized luggage area. He was glad he'd decided to spend a few days in Perth before returning home. Even though he'd slept on the plane he still felt tired. He wanted to get to his sister's place and have a good night's sleep in one of Maggie's comfortable spare beds. He'd become used to Eastern Standard Time and now his body clock was out of kilter.

I must be getting old, he thought wryly. Deep down the idea scared him. He couldn't imagine himself as old, but he had to admit that at sixty-five he couldn't keep up the pace he used to without some extra sleep.

He'd enjoyed his break away from Levallier Dell. A couple of times a year he made the trek to the east, usually to meet distributors in Victoria and New South Wales, and he always managed to catch up with old friends and surf. The surfing had been excellent. Even though his patch of WA offered some of the best surf beaches he enjoyed the change. That had been his saviour, pretending for a couple of weeks that he was twenty again with nothing but the search for the perfect wave to worry about. The total indulgence of it was hard to shake. And now there was another reason to make the long flight to the east.

He dragged his feet at the thought of returning to home and work. The deals he had to make to ensure a market for Levallier Dell wines were getting harder. He didn't like that side of the business but he still insisted on doing it. That was his excuse to go east.

Raucous laughter erupted across the room. He looked over to where a group of young men were collecting their bags. Keely stood among them looking a little out of place. He hadn't realised she knew them.

She was a tall young woman with a solid but curvy figure. Not painfully thin like so many young women these days – at least there was some meat on her bones. She had long black hair that flowed down her back, but she tended to let it fall forward to hide her face.

Euan tended to collect interesting people on his travels and he suspected Keely was one. He'd seen a glimpse of an inner sparkle but she was very self-conscious. She also had artistic talent. He'd managed to sneak a look at her sketch when she thought he was asleep. He'd easily recognised his own portrait.

He envied her youth and the freedom to travel with no definite plans other than a destination. There was a time when he'd lived like that, and now he wondered if he'd ever get the chance to be that carefree again. Did he even want to be?

By the time he had collected his bag most of the other passengers had moved away. He headed to the doors where Keely now stood alone. Perhaps she was on her own after all.

"Would you like a ride?" he asked as he drew level with her.

She glanced at him with a startled expression.

"Oh…no, thanks. I'm sharing with some others." She nodded towards the group of young men already outside with their gear.

"That's good, you've got friends to go with," he said.

"They're not friends…at least I've only just met them. We're staying at the same place so we're sharing a taxi," she blurted. She lowered her face and the veil of hair fell forward again.

Euan was reluctant to leave it at that. He suddenly felt paternal. If she were his daughter he wouldn't want her going off with strangers.

"Here." He stepped to one side so he could put his surfboard down then dug in his pack and pulled out a pen and the newspaper he'd bought to read on the flight. He scribbled on a corner, tore it off and pressed it into her hand. "If you ever decide to come south give me a call. There's plenty of room at my place. That's my number and my sister's. I'm staying in Perth for a few days at her place." He patted his pocket. "My phone's not always on. Maggie can always find me."

"Thanks." She looked towards the doors. "I'd better go."

She shoved the slip of paper into her pocket and hurried away. He turned to pick up his things. What had prompted him to do that? He was just as much a stranger to her as the other men were, but something about her had brought out the fatherly figure in him.

He stood for a moment with his arm around his board and watched the laughing group pile into a taxi. With a deep sigh and a slight shake of his head, he moved off. Time to get back to reality.

He'd been away longer than he'd intended. No doubt his sister would give him a lecture about his lack of communication. He could put up with that if it meant a few more days respite before he returned home. Times had changed, there were issues he could no longer avoid, and then there was his son. Euan loved the tranquillity of his winery on the river and he knew the mounting business pressures could be faced, but it was Flynn's disapproval that he dreaded most.

* * *

Kat pulled the cap from her head, shook out her thick brown hair and fluffed up her fringe. She took a long, deep breath and drew in the fresh scent of a perfect river morning. Thank goodness she had insisted on staying the night in Perth before making the three-hour drive. Pappou had wanted to meet her at the airport but she had remained firm on driving herself. She'd had a good night's sleep in their Perth townhouse. Refreshed and looking forward to visiting her grandparents and Margaret River again, she had relished the freedom of the wind in her face and the joy of the little car all to herself. Pappou would have wanted the roof closed and would have driven at a much slower pace.

She opened the door and stepped out onto the new concrete drive. She'd already taken in the huge additions to the old house used for cellar-door sales and noted the sign describing the meals now available. River Dynasty had certainly gone more upmarket since her last visit as a teenager.

"Katerina!"

She whirled around. The old man emerged from the rows of vines behind her, his arms flung wide.

"Hello, Pappou." She surrendered to his big squeezy hug and kisses.

"You look wonderful. Maybe a bit thin though, hey?" He grabbed her arms and she noticed the deepening wrinkles on his face and the streaks of silver through his hair. When had that happened? It was hard to imagine he was getting older. Not her Pappou; he was always so vibrant and strong.

"It's good to see you, Pappou. I'm so glad I could come."

He touched her cheek with one hand while still holding her arm with his other and she noticed tears welling in his eyes.

"Thanks for lending me the car," she said quickly.

He pinched her cheek. "I hope you didn't take that machine too fast. I really shouldn't let you drive it." The serious moment was replaced by his hearty chuckle.

She felt a warm surge of love mixed with a liberating relief. It was good that she'd come. Pappou's love was open and without conditions. She was desperately in need of some of that unqualified attention at the moment. She had a big decision to make and she would appreciate his advice.

Keely looked out over the beautiful parklands to the dark water of the Swan River and let out a long slow breath. She was here, Perth, the place of happy childhood memories. She wanted to find that feeling again, that perfect happiness, and this was the starting point.

From the age of seven she had come nearly every year, either alone or with the rest of her family, to spend holidays with her grandparents. Her grandfather would take her on expeditions along the Swan in his little wooden boat. They would fish and swim and picnic, and he would tell her tales of his travels to the northern areas of Australia. She could hear him now, his Irish brogue strengthening as his stories stretched a wee bit beyond the truth. In her mind, she pictured his twinkling green eyes and his cheeky grin. Gran had always called him her little Irish leprechaun.

Keely wished they were here now as she looked out across the river. Perhaps she would have been able to tell them the things she couldn't discuss with her parents. Grandpa would have known the words to help her and Gran would have cooked an impossible amount of food to cheer her up. But that wasn't going to happen. Her grandfather had died when she was eighteen and Gran had become more and more frail and eventually moved back to South Australia, and into a residential home close to the family. Keely had visited the home before she left but these days her grandmother hardly remembered who she was let alone anything about her life in the west.

The vista in front of Keely didn't allow for sadness. The memorial to those who'd died in war was laid out before her. She didn't know anyone who had been killed in a war, but she appreciated the careful design that allowed people to sit peacefully and reflect like several were doing now. The perpetual flame rose out of a calm pool of water with the words *Let silent contemplation be your offering* engraved underneath.

She said the words quietly, then looked again over the beautifully manicured gardens, past the monument and flags, to the Swan River, with Perth spread along its banks and up to the distant hills. She snapped a few photos to send home then wandered a bit further, intrigued by the different coloured kangaroo-paw flowers. She snapped several photos from different angles. She didn't use Facebook but liked to post quirky images on Instagram. Then she took a selfie with her arm around a statue and texted her friend Bec, 'Wish you were here' with a crazy-face emoji.

A group of teenage boys slouched past. Their hands were in their pockets and they were glancing around but they weren't taking in the view. Keely watched as they walked defiantly into the path of an older couple then, at the last minute, stepped around them. One of the boys yelled "Watch it," and startled the couple, who had been looking at the memorial.

Keely dropped her gaze. The familiar feeling of helplessness returned and washed over her in a flash with the ease of an enemy knowing it could win. Black spots danced before her eyes and she gasped in some air. She'd been holding her breath.

Her fingernails dug into her palms. She forced the door shut on the dark corners of her mind, spun around and stepped straight into a toddler. The small child was knocked flat by the impact and began to wail loudly.

"I'm sorry, I didn't see you." Keely reached to help him up.

The boy wailed even louder. His mother arrived and brushed him off. "He'll be alright," she said.

"Sorry," Keely mumbled again.

"I told him not to run, didn't I, Mathew." The mother took the screaming child in her arms and smiled. "If he's making this much noise he can't be too badly hurt."

Keely apologised again before she turned and hurried away. She rushed along under the massive gum trees that lined the road leading out of the park. The child's wails followed her on the breeze and the familiar feeling of nausea squirmed in her stomach.

* * *

"Here you are, Keely."

Marty greeted her as she stepped through the door of the hostel. He was dressed only in board shorts and she took in his smooth, bronzed torso.

"We're making plans for tonight," he said. "Do you want to join us?"

The walk back from King's Park had been mainly downhill, but Keely felt breathless. She had a sharp pain in her side and she was tired. "I don't know," she replied vaguely. "What are you thinking of doing?"

"Mike's found a club that gives us free entry and some half-price drinks. They've got a live band tonight and it's not too far from here."

"I don't know," she repeated. She'd never been one for the club scene at home. She and her girlfriends would go to pubs and parties but after trying out a few different clubs she'd not bothered to go again. The noise and the hot press of bodies, the vomit in the toilet, the dark corners where you had to shout to be heard; none of it appealed to her.

Suddenly, Marty grabbed her hands and swung her round. His hair was wet from the pool, his eyes sparkled and the dimple on his cheek deepened as he grinned. "Come on, Keely, you only live once. We're on holidays, first night in Perth. It'll be wild."

His laugh was infectious and she found herself grinning as he whirled her around. This was what her holiday was meant to be about, wasn't it? Having fun. She had to stop the spinning around though, that made her already upset stomach churn.

"Alright," she gasped, and tried to pull her hands out of his. She caught him off balance and he fell against her, knocking them both into the wall. Keely was acutely conscious of his naked chest pressed against her with his arms either side.

He pushed away from the wall. "Are you okay?"

"I'm fine." Her hair flopped across her face and she brushed at an imaginary mark on her shirt to hide her embarrassment.

"Nothing like sweeping a guy off his feet." Marty's laugh was easy and infectious.

She snuck a look at him through the curtain of her hair. "When are you leaving?" she asked, to change the subject.

He was silent for a moment. His gaze was intense and she felt the heat from her cheeks burn down to her neck.

"We're going to wander down to Northbridge and get something to eat," he said. "Check out the night life, then head for the club. Let's say we meet you out the front in an hour?"

"Sure." She risked another glance at him.

He grinned then thundered off down the passage towards the dormitory he was sharing with his friends.

She sighed and made her way up the stairs to the single accommodation she had chosen for herself. It was her first night and she'd decided she didn't want to share with strangers. Maybe once she'd got used to the backpacker lifestyle she would try the dorm lodging. It was certainly cheaper and she didn't have a bottomless supply of money.

Back in her room, she peeked into the en suite she shared with the room next door. It was empty so she stripped off, piled her thick hair on top of her head and let the warm water wash over her achy body. She felt strange, a little queasy, not quite right; probably just the shock of actually being here after all of the planning. It was hard to believe she'd really done it. Her travels had begun. Excitement fluttered in her belly along with the occasional jab of pain.

After the shower she lay on her bed, breathing slowly and willing herself to calm down. She wished now that she hadn't agreed to go with Marty and his mates. It would have been better to veg out in her room and acclimatise to this newly found freedom.

Keely had always lived at home. After she'd left school she'd gone straight to university. Living at home had been the only choice. She had a part-time job but it would have been a real struggle to maintain a flat. Once she went teaching, the jobs were always contracts. She never knew from one year to the next where she'd be, so her mother had encouraged her to stay at home. Here she was, twenty-seven years old, and, apart from one term's contract at a country school, she'd never lived away from home.

She pushed herself off the bed, put on jeans and a fresh top and pulled a quirky face at her reflection in the mirror. "You need some excitement in your life, Keely."

The niggling pain grabbed her again. She grimaced into the mirror, applied some lipstick, brushed out the hair that her mother always wanted her to wear up and strapped on the neat little over-shoulder purse that her mother had said wouldn't be big enough. It held her wallet and phone, which was all she'd need tonight.

Once more she glanced at her reflection, drew back her shoulders and stepped out the door to meet Marty and his mates.

★ ★ ★

"It's nice to know you are still with us, Euan. Let's drink to that, shall we?"

Euan watched his sister raise her glass, her piercing gaze not leaving his as she took a sip of the late-harvest riesling. Not one of his own wines, of course, but this one came from an old friend's long-established Margaret River winery.

"Mmmm." He let the flavours roll around his palette. "Rich and tropical with a hint of honeysuckle. Just perfect for you, Maggie."

"Yes, some sweetness with a touch of the blarney," his sister replied. Her smile creased the skin around her eyes like a concertina. "Your wine and smooth talk might work on me but I've always been too soft on you. I think Flynn will take more winning over." She put down her glass and spoke softly. "You've been gone a month this time, Euan, and nothing but a few text messages. You don't answer our calls. Would it be that hard to keep in regular contact?"

"You always call when I'm not available."

Her eyebrows raised. "You could ring back."

He dug his phone from his pocket and glared at it. "The battery doesn't seem to hold charge for long these days."

"That phone's archaic. Time to get a new one." She sat back and took another sip of wine.

Sometimes he wished she would get angry with him. The gentleness of her words always made him feel far worse than if she'd yelled at him. She took after their French father; never loud, always calm, immaculately presented. Euan flicked his gaze around her South Perth apartment. It was exquisitely furnished with things from her world travels, but the pervading influence was definitely Parisienne. Heavy drapes, gilt edges, statues and mirrors dominated, but here and there were touches of bright Australian colours, just to remind you that the apartment was in Perth and not Paris.

"If anything was wrong you would have heard in a wink of an eye," he said.

"Euan Levallier, you are a rascal." She laughed. It was a warm sound. Maggie may have taken after their French father but they both had their Irish mother's easy sense of humour.

"But you love me." He chuckled too, and tossed the phone aside. "Now, are you going to feed me, I'm wondering? My stomach's still back on Byron Bay time and it thinks it's ten o'clock."

"Ah, *pauvre petit*." She put down her glass and glanced at her watch. "It is getting late. The food is all prepared. It won't take long to cook."

Half an hour later they were enjoying a delicious Dijon chicken and Maggie was telling Euan about her latest gala event; a fundraiser for one of the major hospitals. It promised to be a grand affair with the 'who's who' of Perth in attendance. Maggie was in her element. She was a wonderful organiser and a natural at getting people to part with their money by the bucketload.

"It's only a week away. Why don't you come back and be my beau for the night?" she said. "Several people have asked after you recently. It would be a good chance to be seen."

"No thanks, Maggie. I'd better stay put for a while once I get home. Besides, you know I hate those black-tie affairs."

"But it's good for business and I like to have an arm to lean on."
Maggie's charity events had often been a good platform for keeping
his wine on the sought-after list.

"I know, but not this time. Surely you've got a pair of arms who'd
happily take up your offer. What was that I read about a senator?"

"Absolutely nothing but gossip, *mon cher frère.*" She gathered up
their plates. "I'll make us some coffee."

Euan couldn't help but grin as she swept out the door. He'd
heard a whisper before he went away that she had been seeing a
federal politician of some sort. Maggie had never married but there
had been several special men in her life over the years. The last one
had actually moved in but he'd died quite suddenly a year later.
Maggie had been quiet for a long time after that. Euan hoped she
had found someone to share her life with. She was only a year older
than he, and was still a very attractive woman. He particularly liked
the way she kept her hair long and always wore it up in a graceful
style. He couldn't imagine her without long hair.

He took the last of his wine out onto the balcony. It was a balmy
night. The lights of the city sparkled across the water in front of
him and, higher up, he could see the blinking lights of a plane,
disappearing north.

It made him think of the young woman he'd met on the flight
from Adelaide. He wondered how she was getting on.

"What about you?" Maggie interrupted his thoughts, bringing
out her freshly made coffee and placing it on the table. "Did you
find someone nice to entertain you while you were away?"

"It's not as easy as it used to be."

"Don't tell me you're admitting to ageing."

"Perhaps I'm getting wiser."

Maggie's laugh tinkled in the warm air. "That would be something to behold." She raised her coffee cup to his. "Here's to love.

We've had our moments. May there be something more left in the pot for both of us."

Euan raised his cup. His head filled with memories of the smiling, auburn-haired woman he'd left behind in Sydney. He hadn't told anyone about Dianna yet. He avoided his sister's searching look and drank.

★　★　★

"Keely. I've been texting you." Marty's voice sounded a long way off through the press of bodies on the balcony overlooking the street.

Keely turned around but the crowd seemed to sway and the pain that had niggled at her stomach all night jabbed harder. She was hot. That's why she'd come out onto the balcony, searching for some cooling air – but it hadn't helped. The *thump, thump* from the band boomed out around them.

"What are you doing out here?" Marty yelled in her ear. "Don't you want to dance?" He had been on the dance floor half the night, obviously at home among the gyrating bodies, keeping time and moving fluidly with the beat. Keely had ventured out onto the floor with him a few times, but she'd felt cumbersome and often lost sight of him as he danced through the crowd.

She swayed again and gripped the rail for support. Nausea pushed up into her chest and little beads of sweat formed on her brow and around her lips. When the others had eaten their meals she'd only picked at a plate of wedges and she'd only had two drinks all night, neither of which she'd finished.

"Are you okay?" Marty leaned closer, a concerned look on his face.

"Hey, you two, what are you drinking?" Steve elbowed his way onto the balcony. "It's my shout."

Keely peered at him over Marty's shoulder. She gagged, pushed away from the rail and past the two men, and made for the toilets.

"Someone's had a bit much already." She heard Steve's chuckle behind her as she forced her way back into the heat of the club. She didn't care what he thought; she just had to get to the toilets.

In the relative quiet of the ladies', she leaned back against the bench and gripped it with both hands, praying for the pain to ease and for a cubicle to be empty soon.

Two girls followed her in. They wore short skirts with skimpy tops over flat chests and their faces were heavy with too much make-up; unsuccessful attempts to make them look older. They both eyed her up and down with interest.

"You don't look too good," the taller one said.

"Have you got someone with you?" the other asked. She had brilliant red lips and bright eyes that darted quickly around the room.

Keely didn't answer. She feared if she opened her mouth she'd vomit right there. They pressed in on either side of her. Why hadn't she stayed back at the hostel?

A toilet flushed and the door opened. Keely pushed past the startled woman trying to get out and just made it inside the cubicle as the vomit rose in her throat. She wasn't sure how long she half lay, half sat by the toilet as the nausea and pain continued to sweep over her. She hadn't even locked the door but she didn't care. She was vaguely aware of flushing toilets, banging doors and chatting voices, before her surroundings began to recede as her vision went dark.

On the edge of the blackness voices asked if she was okay. Rough hands tugged the strap of her purse over her head. Keely groaned as her insides cramped up and she collapsed on the floor.

Her next impression was of firm arms lifting her, concerned voices, someone asking what she'd been drinking, had she taken anything, the thump of the band receding, the cool outside air and Marty's worried voice saying her name. She was aware, in vague snatches, of the inside of the ambulance and arriving at a hospital. Someone poked and prodded and asked her questions she could only answer in gasps. Finally, gratefully, she was disappearing down a long tunnel and she slipped willingly into the pain-free void.

CHAPTER
4

"I don't need a party, Pappou." Kat swung her head and smiled pleadingly.

"Nonsense. You haven't been to the River for years. Not since you were a teenager. Now you have returned, a fine young woman. We need to celebrate." Theo rubbed his hands together. "Anyway it's not a party, just dinner with a few friends and family."

Kat shook her head. With Pappou and Yia-yia there was no such thing as 'just dinner'. There would be at least thirty people with the family alone. Theo's three sons and their families all lived nearby or further south at the Ocean Dynasty property. Everyone was involved in the family business, from tending the vines to making the wines to selling them.

Only Kat's immediate family lived interstate. Her mother, Theo's only daughter, had married a winemaker. Kat had been born and raised in the Yarra Valley in Victoria. Whether you liked it or not there was no escaping the family business whether in eastern Australia or the West. That was her big problem.

"Okay." There was no point wasting her breath trying to stop him. "I'll go see what I can do to help Yia-yia. She's not as young as she used to be you know. You mustn't work her too hard." Kat chided him with a smile on her face. She knew Yia-yia would not slow down. The house was her domain and she ran it like clockwork.

"Humph!" he snorted. "That woman is the slave driver. If ever I sit down it's out of her sight otherwise it's *Theo we need this*, or *Theo you should do that*. I tell you, Katerina, a man is not boss of his own day."

She smiled. He sounded so henpecked but there wasn't a word of truth in it. He was a shrewd taskmaster who kept his sons and their families dancing to his tune. He allowed Yia-yia some authority in the house but otherwise his word was law and it was always wise to remember that.

"Best to keep out of her way." He threw his arm around Kat's shoulders and drew her close in a conspiratorial embrace. "Now come on. You haven't seen the extensions to the cellar door. We've been so busy since we finished them we haven't had an official opening. It's very fitting we should have the dinner there. Then Yia-yia can put her feet up. Your cousin Michael is in charge of the kitchen in the restaurant." He guided her away from the house, up the path through the garden towards the newly refurbished cellar-door building.

Kat pictured her dynamic grandmother whose biggest joy was serving meals to her family. If Michael was in charge, Yia-yia would not be pleased. Pappou didn't understand that in her eyes the cellar-door dining room would be an extension of the house, and she wouldn't be happy if she was not allowed to serve dinner for her family. As much as Kat loved him, she was sad he didn't see his plans might not always make others as happy as they made him.

Now was probably not the time to discuss her future with him. It could wait a little longer till the novelty of her arrival wore off.

She would be here a couple of weeks; plenty of time to talk things over with Pappou.

* * *

"Keely, come on Keely, open your eyes now."

Keely heard the voice but she didn't want to leave the safety of the warm cocoon.

"Keely, do you remember what happened?" The male voice persisted. "Open your eyes."

There was a slight pressure on her shoulder and she opened her eyes in a panic, reaching for the strap of her bag. Her arm stung and a hand gripped it firmly.

"Steady on. We don't want you pulling your drip out."

A tall man in a white shirt was bending over her. Keely pulled away in alarm.

"It's okay," he soothed. "You're in hospital. You've had an operation. My name's Ben and I'm looking after you today."

Keely licked her dry lips and tried to take in her surroundings. She did recall dreaming she was in some kind of recovery room. Now she was awake and definitely not dreaming. She was in a hospital ward.

"What time is it?" she croaked.

"It's nearly midday. Do you remember them bringing you in last night? You've had your appendix out."

Keely recalled the pain. Nothing hurt now but she still felt nauseous. Midday? Her last memory was going into the toilets at the pub. That had been about midnight. Where had twelve hours gone? She licked her lips again.

"Would you like some ice?"

Keely nodded and accepted the cooling chips gratefully.

"Is my purse here?" she whispered.

"All your gear is in this cupboard." Ben bent down beside her, opened the door and poked inside. "No bag. Only the clothes you came in, I'm afraid. Did you leave the purse with someone?"

Snatches of events came back to her. She saw the two girls and felt the strap being pulled away. "No," she said. "I think it must have been stolen. And my phone."

"Can we call the police for you or is there someone else we can contact?"

Keely's thoughts flitted erratically. She knew no one in Perth except for Marty, Mike and Steve.

"A friend, relative…?"

"Hello, our mystery woman is awake at last." Another nurse bustled up. "You've been out to it for a while. Are you up to a few questions? My name is Pam. Your admittance details are very sketchy. Someone left this backpack and bag at the front desk for you. There's a note."

Keely answered Pam's million questions, endured more checks from Ben then lay back exhausted, the note Pam had brought still clutched in her hand. She opened the scrappy bit of paper. It was from Marty.

> Packed up your bag and checked you out so you don't have to pay another day. Manager says you can come back if you want. They won't let me up to see you and Steve has got a free ride for us so can't hang around. We're off south. Steve is going to teach Mike and me to surf. Hope you're better soon and your holiday goes well. We might catch up again somewhere.
>
> Marty.

The backpack was still beside her on the bed. She ran her fingers over the comforting shape of her jewellery making kit, squeezed her eyes shut to hold back the tears and let the dark cocoon of sleep wrap around her again.

The next time she opened her eyes a golden light was filtering through the windows and a different nurse was checking her over. This time her head didn't feel so thick and she didn't have to fight so hard to register her surroundings.

"How are you feeling?" the nurse asked.

"Okay." Keely was glad the nausea that had plagued her for days was gone.

"Can you drink some more? We'd like to be able to get rid of this drip for you."

She offered Keely a spare pillow with instructions to press it against her stomach then helped her ease into a sitting position. She passed Keely a glass of cordial and watched her drink it.

"Well done. Once you can tolerate some food we'll be sending you home." The woman smiled and moved off to her next patient.

Home, Keely thought. She had a sudden idea that her parents would be worried about her but then she remembered ringing them on her mobile when she'd arrived at the hostel. If she rang them now she'd be teary, they'd get upset and they'd want to get on a plane and come over and her holiday would be ended before it had begun.

Perhaps she could go back to the hostel but it conjured a lonely picture. There was no one who knew she existed now that Marty was gone. She didn't even have her wallet or her phone.

She took another sip of her drink then gripped the glass tightly, angry at the position she found herself in. She'd lost everything on the first night of her holiday. Then she heard her mother's words – 'put your card and some money in your backpack'. Keely looked around. The backpack was no longer on her bed. She tried to sit up and reach the cupboard but a jolt of pain made her gasp. She eased back against the pillows.

"Take it easy." The nurse was by her side again, lifting the sheet and checking her stomach. "I know a laparoscopic surgery doesn't look much from the outside but you have had your appendix removed. Use the spare pillow to press against your stomach when you move or cough. The pain relief from the op will be wearing off but you're due for some oral meds. You're going to be tender for a while yet."

The woman finished her observations then watched Keely swallow two white tablets.

"Can you pass me my backpack, please?" Keely croaked.

"You're not going anywhere just yet."

"No, I want to get something."

The nurse handed it over. Someone had put her clothes inside. She pulled out her jeans and shoved her hand inside the pack. Her fingers searched for the tiny hidden pocket and the reassuring lump inside. The money and credit card were still there. Keely had an image of her mother's smug face then she relaxed and slept again.

When she woke next, it was early evening. The drip had gone from her arm and amazingly she felt a touch of hunger. She'd hardly eaten a thing since she'd left home.

The backpack was propped against the cupboard with her jeans neatly folded on top. She looked at them for a few moments while her brain struggled from the fudge of sleep. She needed a plan. Her bag was gone. It had contained her phone and her wallet, which meant everything she needed from bank cards to driver's licence was gone, but she wasn't destitute. She had a physical bank card and a hundred dollars in her backpack. She needed a place to stay while she recuperated and organised replacements.

Keely stared hard at the jeans again. Something nudged at the edge of her memory; a scarecrow face, a slip of paper and a voice saying 'there's plenty of room at my place'. Sitting up carefully this time, she asked the nurse if she could make some calls.

CHAPTER
5

"Tell me if you need anything, won't you?"

Keely looked across at Euan's profile as he concentrated on the road ahead.

"I'm fine, thanks Euan. And thanks again for picking me up and giving me a place to stay."

"Glad I could help. I don't understand hospitals these days. Discharging people the day after an operation." He glanced across at her, his faded hair tousled by the breeze coming in the open window. "You relax and enjoy the drive. I know I'm biased but I'm taking you to one of the best spots in Australia."

Keely eased back in her seat again, the pillow he had bought her at a supermarket lying across her lap. The pain could still take her breath away and she was grateful for the security the pillow offered when she had to sit up, or take a deep breath or cough. It was amazing how many times you did those things when you were trying not to. She took in the scenery whizzing past. Open stretches of land gave way to housing estates and large signs boasting the best real estate south of the city.

What a different turn her trip had taken. The previous day, when the doctor had said she could be discharged in twenty-four hours, she'd dug out the scrappy piece of paper from her jeans pocket and rung Euan. His phone had been turned off so, in desperation, she'd tried his sister.

Keely had felt a little intimidated by the refined voice with the hint of a French accent, declaring herself clearly as Maggie Levallier. Maggie had sounded amused at the request to speak with Euan and Keely had wondered if she was doing the right thing, but he'd come to the phone immediately. As soon as she'd explained her predicament he'd insisted she take up his offer to stay at his place.

"There's only my son Flynn and I, but you'll have good food and wine, fresh air and the beautiful river itself to heal you." He'd promised to call to pick her up the next day.

Then she'd rung the police and reported her wallet and phone stolen and the bank to put a temporary hold on her accounts.

True to his word, that morning Euan had collected her and, with great care, sat her on the cracked leather seat of a rather old Volvo. He'd offered to take her to his sister's apartment while he did a few jobs before the journey home. Keely had preferred to stay in the car than meet the eloquent Maggie.

Now, a couple of hours later, they were zooming south on a sunny afternoon, with the wind blowing in their faces, the radio playing hits of the sixties and Euan's surfboard strapped to the roof. Keely smiled and shut her eyes. This really was a new beginning. She was going to a place where no one knew her, and anyone who did know her wouldn't know where she was. She could just disappear.

Her eyes flicked open and she stole a quick look at Euan. Was she mad? He could be a serial killer and she hadn't told a soul she was going with him. Apart from his mention of Margaret River, she didn't even know where he was taking her. Then she remembered his sister. Maggie knew about Keely's existence and even if she was in cahoots with Euan the hospital had kept records when they'd discharged her. And not sure about the reliability of Euan's phone, she'd given the police Maggie's number when she'd filled out the report. Keely bit her lip. She wasn't usually given to such wild flights of imagination.

"Are you okay?"

She took in Euan's worried expression and felt a flush spread across her cheeks. "I'm fine. I just remembered I haven't contacted my parents…"

"You can use my mobile if you like." He frowned. "Although it might be flat. We have a landline at home."

"Thanks. They won't be expecting to hear from me for another day or so. I'll call them later."

His face relaxed.

She reassured herself that Euan was as he seemed, a good Samaritan and nothing more. Gradually the motion of the car and the comfortable seat rocked her to sleep.

"Keely, are you hungry?"

His gentle question brought her back to life. She looked out the window at a sign drawing visitors' attention to Busselton Jetty.

"A little," she replied, trying to shake the fog of sleep so she could make sense of her surroundings.

"I'm not a very good host. I promised to look after you and I haven't even fed you."

Keely gripped the pillow and sat up cautiously. Her stomach grumbled but she wasn't sure if it was from hunger. She had eaten a small breakfast at the hospital but had sipped only liquids since then.

"What about a bowl of homemade vegie soup?" Euan asked. "I know a place that makes all kinds of things to tempt a wayward stomach."

"Sounds good." She would have preferred to keep going and not worry about food but she didn't want to rebuff his hospitality.

They drove through Busselton and Euan pulled up opposite a brightly painted cafe. Keely waited while he went in. It was a beautiful afternoon and the sun was warm on her arms through the window as she nestled against the seat and gazed drowsily at her surroundings.

Euan returned with a box and they drove on down the long street, to the beach. He dragged a tattered blanket from the back of the car, then helped Keely out, lowering her to the blanket, with her back resting against a large pine tree.

She sat regaining her breath and took in the picturesque scene before her. A jetty stretched way, way out into the water and curved off into the distance. Closer to the shore there was a bright red train, toy-like in appearance, in front of a row of beach hut–type buildings with the Australian flag fluttering gently in the sea breeze. Euan sat the box of food on the blanket beside her. He lifted the lids from foam cups to reveal steaming soup and then unpacked crusty bread rolls, slices of quiche, bottled water, chunks of chocolate cake and firm bananas.

"I hope there's something here you to tempt you," he said. "Normally I don't think a picnic is complete without a good bottle of wine but this water will have to do."

He smiled and his face creased into the countless wrinkles that had fascinated Keely on the plane. As soon as he stopped smiling his skin smoothed over with hardly any visible lines. Like a calm sea after a storm. "Thanks." She picked up one of the cups of steaming soup. It smelled delicious. Perhaps she did feel hungry after all.

"So, what do you think of Busselton?" he asked.

Keely looked along the foreshore to the jetty again. "It's pretty."

"The history here always gets to me. It's one of the earliest settlements in WA. It was a whaling station and quite lawless in its beginnings. Maggie always says she wants to write a book about the frontier time, as she calls it."

Keely took a tentative sip of the hot soup. It was pumpkin, just what she felt like. She blew to cool it and slowly sipped more as Euan told her some of the history of the town.

* * *

Euan was glad to see Keely had eaten most of the soup and some bread. She'd looked so tentative when he'd first settled her on the rug that there was no doubt she was still in pain. While they ate he'd told her about the history of the area and then he'd related some of the funny stories he knew about the town and she'd laughed, albeit gingerly, and appeared more relaxed.

Her face was pale and there were dark rings under her eyes. She looked gaunt, so different from when he'd met her on the plane. It must have been an awful experience to have a medical emergency so far from home.

"It's bad luck your holiday started with a stay in hospital."

"It wasn't quite the way I'd imagined it."

"Your parents will be worried, being so far away and no way to contact you. I should have taken you to Maggie's to ring them."

"What they don't know won't hurt them." She looked away from him towards the sea. "I'll ring them tomorrow."

"Will you go home once you're feeling better?"

"Oh, no. I couldn't bear...I don't want to miss this opportunity. I'll be fine in a few days. The doctor said a week to ten days and I'd be almost back to normal."

They both watched in silence as the little tourist train began its journey out along the jetty and Euan wondered what it was that Keely was running away from. Not that he could criticise. Avoidance was his middle name. Stretching out his return home by showing her the sights was enjoyable but Keely was starting to look uncomfortable again and he couldn't stall forever. He should have rung Flynn and warned him they would have a guest but Euan was putting off the inevitable battle that was to come. Perhaps Keely's presence would distract Flynn and give them a chance to settle back to normal, before they tackled the issues that needed to be discussed.

Euan glanced at his guest. Was that why he'd been so glad to bring her home? With someone else in the house Flynn would have to be polite. Maybe Keely's path had crossed Euan's for a reason. The strengthening sea breeze flicked her hair back from her face and she shivered.

He looked at his watch. "We should get going. There's still a beautiful drive ahead."

* * *

They took so many twists and turns that Keely no longer had any sense of direction. Magnificent trees lined the roads, thick shrubs linked branches underneath and patches of colour from the clumps of wildflowers spread below them. Every now and then a gap would allow her a view of vines or open fields where cattle grazed, only to be quickly replaced by the thick walls of trees.

"Spring is the best time to visit the south-west. Everything is fresh and flowering," Euan said. "I avoid the highway when I can.

It only adds a few extra minutes to the journey to take the alternate route and you see more of the country."

Keely took in the excitement in his face. He was enthusiastic about his part of Australia.

He slowed down as they meandered through a tuart forest.

"Oh, the lilies are beautiful." Keely gazed at the thick spread of white flowers below the ancient trees. She half expected to see a princess emerge from the bush, dressed in a flowing white gown on the back of a glossy black horse.

"A beautiful pest," Euan said, bursting her dream. "Tourists love them but they're a nuisance and spread everywhere."

They drove on but Keely couldn't resist one last quick look as they left the lilies behind. She was a tourist after all and she did think they were beautiful.

The sun was low in the sky when they finally turned onto a narrow road lined with the inevitable trees. The roadside forest was so large and thick that in some places the foliage met like a cathedral arch above their heads. Keely was exhausted now. Her stomach was aching and she longed to lie down.

"Here we are," Euan announced as he slowed the car. "Welcome to Levallier Dell…bloody hell!"

In spite of her tiredness Keely couldn't hold back the nervous giggle. "Do you welcome all your guests with rhyming poetry?"

Euan didn't answer. He was leaning forward, peering up at the gleaming sign with *Levallier Dell Wines* written in gold. The letters were outlined in black, which made them pop out from the green sign in the fading light.

"Now what?" he muttered and let the car roll forward onto a neat crushed-rock drive that swept down from the road in a curve, towards a distant group of buildings. All around them vines stretched away in lines.

The house stood apart from the assortment of sheds. The front was hidden by a tangle of shrubs and roses but Keely barely got a look as they whizzed past and pulled up with a lurch under a vine-covered carport at the back entrance. She gripped the pillow and gritted her teeth.

Euan looked at her as if he'd just remembered she was there. "You must be worn out. Wait here while I take in the bags. I won't be long."

He disappeared around a lattice wall, which was smothered in a rambling rose. Keely took a deep breath and let it out slowly. Now that she was here she was a little nervous. Euan had been very kind to her but she still didn't feel as if she knew him well and here she was about to stay the night in his house. Too uncomfortable to sit a minute longer in the car, she carefully eased herself out.

"Take it easy." Euan appeared back by her side and offered his arm.

Reluctantly, she leaned on him. "Thanks," she murmured. Her stomach ached and her legs were behaving like wobbly bowls of jelly but his support was reassuring.

He helped her into the house and onto a large comfy couch piled with cushions. Keely glanced around the room. It was a big family room with high raked ceilings and an open kitchen. Euan was busy rattling around in the cupboards. It was getting dark but he had turned on some lamps and the glow gave a cosy effect to the large space. There was no sign of anyone else.

"Did you say your son lived here?" she asked.

"Yes, but he wasn't expecting me home tonight. Would you like tea or coffee?" He waved a cup at her.

"No, thanks."

"What about food? Are you feeling hungry?"

"No, just some water, please."

He peered at her. "You're looking a bit pale again."

A throbbing ache radiated through her. The nurse had said to take the pain relief regularly but she'd forgotten. "I'm a bit sore. I should take some tablets."

He rushed away and came back with a glass, keeping a close eye on her as she swallowed the pills.

Keely stifled a yawn. "I really think I should probably just go to bed."

"Of course. You can have my bed."

"Oh, no..." Keely blushed.

"I always give it up for visitors. I've got a spare bed in the den. Maggie sleeps in there when she visits. It's got clean sheets and there's an en suite and in the morning you'll have a beautiful view of the river."

Keely was too tired to argue. After all, it was only for a night or two. Then she'd be on her way again. "Thanks," she mumbled and Euan helped her up.

CHAPTER
6

Keely struggled to open her eyes. It was dark. She fought to banish the dream where hands had clutched at her and young faces sneered at her. She tried to sit up, and the sudden pain reminded her she'd had her appendix out. But this wasn't the hospital.

Then she remembered Euan, realised where she was and relaxed, letting the tension flow away. He had been so concerned for her and she had been grateful for his kindness. She smiled and stretched again, carefully this time.

Her eyes adjusted to the gloom and she noticed light edging in around the thick curtains. It must be morning; she felt as if she'd been asleep for a long time. The distant calls of cattle reached her then, and closer, she could hear the raucous laughter of kookaburras.

There was also a glow coming from under the door that led to the family room. It was the last thing she remembered seeing as sleep had swallowed her the night before. It had been reassuring to look at that little strip of light. After she'd crawled into bed and waited for the painkillers to work, she'd had a sudden pang of homesickness. The light from under the door and the sounds of Euan moving around beyond it had been her comfort. Now, after a good sleep, she felt her determination to explore and enjoy her holiday return.

She fumbled with the bedside lamp and squinted at the dainty little clock on the table. It was only six o'clock. She lay still, listening. The house was silent. She pulled back the covers and climbed gingerly out of bed. Walking was easier this morning. In the en suite, she washed her hands and splashed water on her face then peered at her sallow reflection in the mirror and shivered. The cold air encouraged her to shuffle quickly back to bed and snuggle into the comfortable warmth.

There was a noise outside her door, a gentle knock, and then Euan stuck his head around. He was silhouetted by the light from behind.

"Hello. Did you sleep well?"

"Fine, thank you."

"Are you ready for breakfast?"

She eased herself up. She did feel hungry. "Yes, thanks." The pain was a dull throb but she'd take some tablets again to be sure to keep it at bay.

"Stay there." Euan disappeared then the door swung open and he entered carrying a tray. "Here we are, mademoiselle, your breakfast."

"I could have come out."

"No, no. I insist. You are still recuperating. We need to put some colour back into those cheeks. Rest a little longer. Later I will take you out for some fresh air but it's a bit cold outside right now." He put the tray down and pulled back the curtains. "There's a magnificent view from this window. As you eat, the river will appear." He waved his hand majestically then picked up the tray.

Keely watched him approach. He was a fit-looking man, and this morning he was dressed in mismatched shorts and a crumpled shirt as if he'd put on whatever he'd laid his hands on first. He placed the breakfast tray across her lap, then backed away, still examining her.

Her heart raced under his scrutiny. She'd put a lot of trust in a man she hardly knew.

"I really think you should call your parents once you've—"

"Euan?" They were both startled by a male voice calling from the kitchen. "So, you're home at last." The statement had an accusing tone and a tall, sandy-haired man strode through the door. He stopped when he caught sight of them.

"Flynn." Euan turned abruptly towards the door.

Keely clutched awkwardly at the sheet. This must be Euan's son. He was taller than his father but there was no mistaking the profile of his face and the sharpness of his gaze.

"Oh...I didn't realise," Flynn stammered, his look grim.

"This is..."

"I'd rather not be introduced, thanks Euan," Flynn snapped. "I would've appreciated some warning that you were home and that you'd brought a guest." He spat the last word out as if it was poison.

"You weren't home last night or I would have."

"I was out with some mates." He gave Keely then his father one last scathing look and strode from the room as quickly as he had entered.

"I'm sorry about that, Keely," Euan said. "Flynn's manners are usually impeccable."

Her cheeks burned. She glanced at Euan, not knowing what to say. Right now she wanted to be as small as a mouse and disappear under the covers.

"You stay and eat your breakfast," Euan said. "I've been away from home for a while. Flynn and I have some catching up to do."

His lips turned up in a smile that didn't dispel the sadness in his eyes or the rigid set of his jaw. He left, closing the door behind him. She released the sheet from her grasp and looked at the beautifully set tray on her lap. Euan had gone to a lot of trouble. There was a proper pot of tea – she lifted the lid – with real tea leaves; poached eggs, toast and an assortment of condiments. A dainty pink rose lay along the napkin at the side.

She heard movement in the next room.

"Where are you going?" Euan's sharp question from beyond the door startled her.

"I'm moving down to the studio." Keely could hear the tightness in Flynn's reply.

"Why?"

"I've had enough, Euan." Flynn's voice rose higher. "I've put up with your disappearances and your women but you've gone too far this time, you stupid old bugger. If you're moving one of your ladies into the house, I'm moving out."

Keely clamped her hand to her mouth.

"Flynn!" Euan barked. "Lower your voice. Keely is a guest—"

"Call her whatever you like to justify it, I don't want to be a part of your cosy little love nest."

The burning sensation spread across Keely's face to her ears and down her neck. *He thinks I'm Euan's lover.* She pushed away the tray and tumbled out of bed, pressing her hand to her stomach as she went. Outside, she heard doors thudding and raised voices retreating into the distance. The house returned to silence but there was a rushing sound in her ears.

She went into the bathroom and turned on the shower. Standing under the steaming water, she kept hearing Flynn's words over and over again. She was mortified to think he could assume she was his father's lover.

A momentary image of Euan delivering her breakfast and his slightly dishevelled appearance popped into her mind. Keely bit her lip. Damn it, she could imagine her mother's reproving words. "You've put yourself in a compromising situation, Keely. Appearances are what count."

She pressed the cool face washer to her cheeks.

Flynn had certainly assumed plenty. Damn it! How dare he? Her embarrassment was replaced by anger and she dried herself vigorously with the towel, flinching as she forgot to go easy over her stomach and then dabbing carefully over the dressings. She'd been told they'd fall off after a few days. The thought of exposing the cuts underneath made her squirm.

Back in the bedroom she pulled up the bedcovers and pushed her things back into her bag. Physically, she was feeling much stronger despite the pain reminding her if she moved too quickly. She was glad of the trackpants she'd packed. It was too soon to squeeze into her jeans.

She hoped Euan could drop her into the town and she could stay there for a day or so then catch a bus back to Perth. She certainly wasn't going to stay at Levallier Dell if there was any chance she would run into the arrogant Flynn again.

She looked around, unsure about what to do next. The phone began to ring but no one answered it. She would love to make a fresh cup of tea. Euan's lovely breakfast sat cold and untouched on the tray.

The sound of birds attracted her to the window. The view was certainly pretty. Just outside, a wooden framework supported a rambling bush rose. It was covered in pink blooms like the one on the tray. The rose created a living frame to the garden, which was edged by a wire fence signalling the start of the curving rows of vines, bursting with bright green leaves and sloping away to a screen of trees. As she studied the vista before her, Keely noticed something glinting among the trees. She peered, trying to work out what it was. The sun's rays reached the trees and she realised the glinting patches were water. This must be the river Euan had spoken about.

A movement on the lawn made her look down again to a group of hen-like birds pecking their way across the yard. They had black-and-white feathers, which gave them a speckled appearance. She counted six in the group.

In the distance she heard a motorbike, and closer she saw the top of Euan's head moving between the vines, coming back towards the house. She turned to collect her things then stopped at the spectacle before her. The large expanse of wall above the bed, stretching high up to the raked ceiling, was covered with a magnificent wall hanging. Keely was immediately taken by its beauty. She'd been so tired and in so much pain the night before she'd not taken in her surroundings.

The hanging was predominantly green, every shade of green, but there were many tiny touches of other colours. Pretty pinks peeped out close to the edges, then further in, she saw hints of mauve and purple and splashes of yellow and orange. It was a beautifully crafted patchwork. She thought about taking a picture of it then remembered she didn't have her phone. She'd definitely have to do something about getting a new one today.

She went closer to the hanging and examined the fine detail that made up the bigger picture. Among the strips of fabric there were beautiful threads and delicate beads. Hours of work must have gone into making it. She looked back towards the window. Whoever had created the hanging had cherished the view from this room and cleverly reproduced it.

* * *

Flynn revved the throttle on his bike and roared up the drive. His father's explanation, that the woman in his bed was a guest recuperating from an operation, only infuriated him more. It wasn't that he didn't believe the story, but now he'd behaved like an idiot in front of a stranger. He berated himself for it. He was usually so calm, in control; he hated the fact that his temper had got the better of him.

Flynn slowed at the gate and stopped to look again at the freshly painted sign. Euan hadn't been happy about that, or the newly gravelled driveway, and there were several other things he didn't know about yet. Flynn revved the bike again and pulled out onto the road. Too bad, someone had to face the future and make decisions. While Euan had been off finding himself, Flynn had been left behind to deal with reality, again.

Of course, the ever-reliable Hugh was always there. His skills with the vines were indispensable, and Maggie tried to help. Flynn respected her opinion and she did own a small share but, ultimately, the business belonged to him and his father. They should be planning together for the future.

Euan wanted to hold on to the past and keep Levallier Dell as a quaint little winery with a select clientele. Flynn knew it wasn't enough anymore. Margaret River had any number of wineries now. The competition was stiff and Levallier Dell needed to make changes to survive. He had his own ideas on that but Euan wasn't interested.

He eased back on the throttle as he approached the bitumen road ahead. He was tired. Sick of spending his nights alone at the house. The night before he'd gone out with some mates and camped overnight at their place. They'd drunk a fair bit and it had hardly seemed any time between crawling into bed and getting up to come home and check on things this morning. Why had he bothered? He could still be at his mates' place, asleep.

He hesitated at the crossroads. The rest of the blokes would still be sleeping. Somehow the thought of the messy bachelor flat didn't appeal but Anna McPherson would have the coffee made and her first batch of scones out of the oven. He'd go into Margaret River and have breakfast with the McPhersons; they were always good company.

He set off towards town, passing a police car going in the other direction. He wondered briefly where they were heading. Born and raised here, he knew most people in the district. In a rural community nothing much went on that wasn't soon common knowledge. His stomach gurgled, reminding him of where he was heading. He turned his concentration to the road and images of Anna's scones.

★　★　★

Keely looked up from her cup of tea at the sound of the sliding door. She had disposed of the cold breakfast, poured herself a fresh cup of tea and made up her mind to ask Euan to drop her into town. She was feeling much better, if still a bit sore, but she could manage on her own.

Euan stepped inside and the phone began to ring before either of them could speak. He picked up the handpiece from its cradle on the wall over the breakfast bench.

"Hello."

Keely could hear the babble of a woman's voice.

"Hang on, Maggie," Euan said. "Say that again."

He listened, then glanced at Keely with a bemused smile. She looked down at her cup. There was something about that smile that always unsettled her.

"Are you sure you haven't misunderstood?" he asked.

Keely could hear the voice of his sister raise an octave as she replied.

"Okay, okay." Euan patted the air as if it were his sister's shoulders. "We'll sort it out. It's all some kind of misunderstanding."

He listened again.

"Yes, alright," he said. "I promise I'll ring back later and let you know. Bye." He replaced the phone and turned to Keely. "Looks like we might have some sorting out to do."

"What do you mean?" she asked.

Euan poured himself a cup of tea. "It seems you've been reported as a missing person."

"What?" Keely watched him carefully, expecting a teasing smile to collapse his face into wrinkles, but it didn't come.

"The police have been to Maggie's and she's told them where you are and that I haven't abducted you but…" The sound of a vehicle pulling up outside made them both look up. Euan walked to the window and peered out. "You'll be able to explain it yourself. That's the local police arriving now."

CHAPTER

7

"So, what do you think of my muffins?"

Flynn had been oblivious to his surroundings. The early-morning confrontation with his father was still playing over in his mind. Sean's question and the gentle thump on his shoulder that went with it brought him back to the bustle of the McPhersons' kitchen. He picked up the half-eaten apple and cinnamon muffin from the plate and took another bite.

"Pretty darn good." He acknowledged the young man watching him closely across the table, before taking another sip of his coffee. "With the choice of your mother's scones or your muffins, no wonder you've been busy." Flynn nodded towards the doorway where they could hear the sounds of Anna McPherson and her daughter, Megan, serving customers in the little cafe. It was only nine o'clock but they opened at eight and already they'd had a constant stream of clientele, drawn in by the enticing smells from Anna's Kitchen.

"We've been flat out." Sean beamed. "The tourists have come in their droves these holidays."

"You'll be glad to get back to school for a rest."

"He's nearly finished, then it's me who will be getting the rest." Anna buzzed through the door from the shop and turned her quick eyes to the huge oven. "Are you watching those pies, Sean?"

"They're fine, Mum. Sit down and drink your tea with Flynn. I'm off to the supermarket for the supplies and Megan can mind the shop."

"Yes, sir." Anna gave a mock salute but she sat down all the same and watched her youngest brush himself off and head out the back door.

"He's a good cook, Anna," Flynn said, picking up the last piece of muffin.

"I don't know what I'd do without him, especially these last few years. And he wants to continue with it. All of my children have been capable in the kitchen but Sean has his heart set on training as a chef."

Flynn noted the glowing look on Anna's face. She was proud of all five of her offspring. Sean, the youngest, had been a baby when her husband had died in a car accident. Anna was a good cook and had used her talents to make enough money to raise her children. Eventually, she'd turned the front of her cottage into a cafe located just off the main drag, and it was popular with the tourists as well as the locals.

"Will that mean going to Perth?"

"Probably."

"You'll miss him."

"That I will but he'll be back regularly. He has grand plans for our little cafe." Anna arched her back and rubbed her strong hands across her neck. "I'd be glad if one of my children wanted to take over."

Flynn watched her swallow some of her tea. His mother, Lucy, and Anna had been good friends and the McPherson children had been like Flynn's brothers and sisters. They'd all gone to school together, played together, got into mischief together. Flynn had spent a lot of time in this kitchen. Over the years it had been modified to make it into a working cafe kitchen but the big wooden table of his childhood still remained the focal point. There had been many meals and cuppas and chats around this table.

The McPhersons had remained the constant for Flynn after the devastation of his mother's death. Euan had withdrawn from the world and it had been Anna McPherson who had made sure that the teenage Flynn had what he needed for school, provided their food and even cleaned the house for a while.

The older McPherson children had all moved away for uni and work, around the same time as Flynn. Megan, who was a bit older than him, had returned and married a local dairy farmer but the only one of Anna's offspring living at home now was Sean, who was still at school.

Anna put down her cup. "What's happening your way? You mentioned Euan's home and he's brought a guest. You should all come over for a meal."

"I don't know about...I don't know how long she's staying." Flynn studied the dregs in his coffee cup.

"She! Don't tell me your father has found himself a decent woman at last—"

"She's not that kind of woman," Flynn cut in.

Anna raised her eyebrows.

"I've only met her once." He frowned as he recalled the sight of the young woman in his father's bed. "I think she's a tourist."

"That'd be Euan. He often collects strays."

"He said she's been sick or something. Just staying to recuperate. I'm not sure..."

Anna studied him closely. "Oh, well. It doesn't matter. Any excuse for a get-together. How about Sunday night? We'll have a roast. You and Euan come and if his lady friend is still there she's welcome." The bell rang from the shop. Anna groaned and rose to her feet. "Megan must be busy again. Tourists get about earlier and earlier these days and they're always hungry for good home cooking." She washed her hands and pointed to the plate on the table. "You help yourself to another cuppa and some muffins."

"I'd better get back to work. I can't avoid it forever."

Once more Anna's look was intense. She patted Flynn's shoulder. "You and Euan will have lots to talk about. He's probably done lots of thinking while he's been away. He might need time to settle back in. You bring him over for Sunday-night roast and we'll have a good catch-up."

★ ★ ★

Keely sat on the couch forlornly studying her hands while Euan slid the door shut behind the departing police. What an idiot she'd been. If only she'd rung her parents from the hospital. The missing phone and wallet, minus its contents, had been found somewhere along the highway between Perth and Bunbury. The finder had rung the home number they'd found in her wallet, hoping for a reward. Evidently, her panic-stricken parents had been frantic and reported her as a missing person.

The two local police, a man and a woman, had been slightly amused. They obviously knew Euan and didn't have him pegged as an abductor but, all the same, they had asked her to explain what had happened from the time of her arrival in Perth. She'd gone back over everything. They'd wanted to know Marty and his mates' names and whereabouts but she knew only their first names and that they'd said they were heading south.

When she'd got to the part about having her bag stolen she'd told the policeman, who was the one making the notes, that she'd reported it. She'd explained that her parents weren't expecting to hear from her again for a few days and she hadn't wanted to worry them. Euan had remained sitting at the table silently, only speaking if the police asked him a direct question, but she had noticed him looking at her quizzically when she'd mentioned not wanting to worry her parents.

The policeman had checked his notes and said it had taken a while to connect her report of the stolen items to that of her parents' missing-person report. There'd been an outage in the system and a backlog of entries.

The woman had looked at her sagely. "It would have been much easier all round if you'd let your parents know what was happening from the hospital," she'd said.

Keely had mumbled an apology. She felt like a seven-year-old instead of a twenty-seven-year-old. Would she ever be able to stand on her own two feet? She hadn't rung her parents so she didn't have to deal with their reaction to the theft and her operation and now it had caused a huge chain reaction, making everything worse.

The policewoman gave her a sympathetic look. "We're just doing our job," she said. "Glad to see you're okay but you need to ring your parents, which I suggest you do straight away. And you'll need to attend Bunbury Police Station with photo ID to collect your property."

"Why Bunbury?" Euan had asked.

"The person who found it took it on to their home town."

"My photo ID's in the wallet and on the phone," Keely had said.

"Just take yourself in then." The policeman had shut his notebook. "We'll leave you in Euan's care and report back to the Perth office."

Now Keely forced herself to look up as Euan turned away from the door. She went to speak but he cut her off.

"You use the phone here to ring your parents. I'll be back in a minute." He crossed the room and went through the door that led to the rest of the house, shutting it firmly behind him.

Keely sat staring at the phone on the wall. She wasn't looking forward to making the call. Perhaps her father would answer. He was much easier to explain things to than her mother.

Ten minutes later Euan returned and Keely was still sitting on the couch.

"Couldn't you contact them?" he asked.

"Yes, I got through." She kept her head lowered, not wanting him to see the tears in her eyes. Her mother had fired frantic questions at her and protested at Keely's lack of concern for them in not ringing. They were all so worried about her, she'd said. Keely had barely had a chance to get a word in until her mother had suggested she wanted to jump on the next plane. Then Keely had protested, reiterating that she was safe, and made an excuse she was due to take her pain relief.

"Mum's going to ring me back tonight. I hope you don't mind. I've given her your number so I'll be staying one more night."

Euan stopped in front of her. "I thought you'd stay for several days...in fact, as long as you like."

The tears rolled down Keely's cheeks and she bit her lip, annoyed at her weakness.

"You poor thing." He sat on the couch beside her. "You've had a rough time. You probably need your mother right now."

His kindness only made Keely feel worse. A loud sob escaped from her lips.

Euan put his arm around her and hugged her tight. "I'm not very good at being a mother but you're most welcome here." He patted her arm. "If you can put up with a strange old boy like me," he said.

Keely looked up at his wrinkly smile and forced a smile onto her own face.

"Thanks, Euan," she said. "You've already been a big help."

Over his shoulder, she was surprised to see Flynn watching them through the glass. She went to speak but he walked away.

CHAPTER
8

"These vines are our backbone. We've had some excellent results from all our varieties but these are our chardonnay grapes, from which we produce our finest wine."

Keely followed the direction of Euan's outstretched arm, looking across the rows of vines extending over the gentle slope before them. They'd been on a short walking tour to various vantage points on the property with Euan naming the different grapes they grew and the wine they made from them. Rows of trellised vines stretched away to distant trees and once again she glimpsed patches glinting in the sun that revealed the river edging its way along the bottom of the slope.

She turned back to study him. This morning he had a battered broad-brimmed hat on his head shadowing the freckles and creases of his face as he stared off into the distance. Once again she was reminded of her first impression of him as scarecrow-like. Watching him survey the vines in front of him, she knew his statement about his chardonnay wasn't a boast, more a satisfied acknowledgement of the facts.

She wasn't much of a wine drinker, preferring cocktails and the odd glass of prosecco. There had been a few winery tours with friends at McLaren Vale near her home and once to the Adelaide Hills but she'd never thought much about what it took to produce the actual wine. Here she was, standing in the middle of a living, working vineyard with Euan, who was obviously passionate about his work.

"Do you sell it here?" Keely wondered if they had cellar-door sales in one of the several big sheds.

Euan frowned. "No, most of our wine is sold through our distributors. We don't run a cellar door."

Keely noted the finality in his last words. "Oh. I thought that's how wineries sold their wine."

He smiled at her. "It's one way to make sales but we don't need it. We have relied on our distributors and our wines have always sold well, both in Australia and overseas. We were dabbling with cellar-door sales a few years ago. You may have noticed the undercover area alongside the carport."

That must have been the big enclosed space she'd seen when she'd walked gingerly around the perimeter of the house the day before. After deciding to stay on at Levallier Dell, she'd gone back to bed and dozed and read. Euan had gone off and she'd seen no sign of Flynn. In the late afternoon she'd needed to stretch her legs and clear her brain in readiness for her mother's phone call. She'd peered under the large paved verandah along the side of the house but it was overgrown with plants and clogged with accumulated leaves, dirt and cobwebs. It didn't look as if anyone had been in there for a long time.

"Lucy, my wife, was the keen one but after she died and Flynn went interstate to study, it wasn't a priority."

Keely wondered what had happened to Mrs Levallier.

"We do fine without all those tourists swarming over the place," he muttered.

"It's very peaceful here." Keely sucked in another breath of the fresh morning air. All around her, young leaves reflected the light in brilliant greens fluttering above the subdued browns of their trunks.

"It is at the moment. I like this time of year. Lucy used to say the vines were holding their breath, preparing themselves for the birth of their grapes." He smiled. "She was the creative one. You'll see pieces of her work around the house."

"The wall hanging in the bedroom?"

"Yes, 'Margaret River Magic' she called it. It won several awards and she had many offers from people wanting to buy it but she always said she'd made it for us." His voice softened. "I'm glad we kept it."

"It's an amazing creation. She had a lot of talent."

"Yes..." A distant buzzing sound took his attention.

Keely followed his gaze to someone sitting on a machine moving between the rows down near the river.

"Looks like Flynn has shattered our peace."

"What is he doing?"

"Slashing the mid-rows. The weeds love the sunshine just like the vines." He sighed. "No time for peaceful pauses when Flynn's around. He's always doing something."

The group of birds she'd seen outside her window on the first morning rushed up the space between the vines beside them.

"What are they?" Keely asked.

"Guinea fowl. We have them to keep the garden weevils out of the vines but they spend most of their time in the house garden. Here they are actually among the vines and he's probably scared them off for a week."

Keely watched the last of the perfectly groomed birds bolt back towards the house.

"I'd better get back to it," Euan said. "Will you be okay by yourself?"

"I'll be fine, thanks for showing me around." Although not ready to run a marathon, she was feeling much better. She wasn't going to spend the day lying around. The trackpants were beginning to get grotty, there was the bag of things she'd brought from the hospital and she was running low on underwear. "Would it be okay to use your laundry? I need to do some washing."

"Of course. You have the run of the place. Make yourself at home. I'll be back later in the day."

★ ★ ★

"Thanks for holding the fort, Hugh." Euan shook the hand of his long-time friend. Like Euan's, Hugh's face had weathered since they'd first met. He'd joined Levallier Dell back in the days when Flynn was young and the expanding business had become too much for Euan and Lucy to manage alone. His knowledge of local conditions and his vine management skills had made him an invaluable part of Levallier Dell.

"The vines are never a problem, Euan." Hugh's deep voice rumbled slowly. "Winemaking's not my thing though, you know that. Flynn had a few concerns about the cabernet franc while you were gone. You like things done a bit different to his way of thinking."

Euan smiled ruefully. There weren't many wineries that made a straight cabernet franc and Euan's consistently ranked highly. He and Flynn did approach the winemaking from different ends of the spectrum sometimes. Especially when it came to the cab franc. In his own way, Hugh was reminding him that he'd been absent too long. "It's all fine. Flynn worries too much. If I can't take a break at this time in my life, what's it all been for?"

"You're right about taking a break. Some things are best enjoyed away from home."

Euan tried to read the expression in Hugh's eyes. He was an old-fashioned bloke, a loyal and true friend. Family, home and community were very important to Hugh. He had remained at Levallier Dell through Euan's 'rough patch' after Lucy's death. He'd said very little about Euan's lifestyle choices but from time to time Euan had been given a few unsolicited words of country-style wisdom.

"I know I can leave the place in your safe hands," Euan said. "That helps."

"Not just mine. Flynn knows what he's doing." Hugh laid a large hand on Euan's shoulder. "I hope you don't mind but I need to take a few days off. Felicity's wedding is getting closer and the wife wants a trip to Perth. Evidently there are things we can only organise from there in spite of mobile phones and the internet."

"Of course, Hugh. You head off. I'm not going anywhere for a while."

"Guess your visitor will keep you busy." The word *visitor* had a deeper note to it, as if Hugh was underlining the word. "I'll call in as soon as we're back."

"Things will be fine here. Give my love to the family."

Euan watched as Hugh turned his dual cab around and drove away. A small cloud of dust hung in the air for a minute before it dispersed on the breeze. Hugh had been giving him a message in his own conservative way. It was just that Euan wasn't sure what the message was.

★ ★ ★

Keely was tired but she didn't want to sleep. Her body was recovering well from the operation but now she wasn't doing enough to tire herself out during the day, making it difficult for sleep to consume her at night. The washing was out and drying in the perfect conditions, the bed was made and she had tidied the kitchen after sharing a light lunch with Euan. He'd gone off to work again, leaving her to occupy the long afternoon by herself.

Tempted by the sunshine warming the back verandah, she took her backpack and settled into a chair near a small table. The tangle of roses and bougainvillea protected her from the breeze but allowed her a partial view across the yard to the vines beyond. Nearby, the group of guinea fowl carefully pecked their way over the lawn. She could hear the occasional sound of a vehicle and movement at the distant sheds. From the activity she assumed there were others besides Euan and Flynn working at Levallier Dell.

A man passed close by along the outside perimeter of the house fence. He was tall and wore a khaki work shirt and a broad-brimmed hat. He stopped and glanced in her direction. The dark glasses he wore made it hard for her to tell if he was looking at her. Keely had been about to say hello but he made no acknowledgement that he had seen her and moved on.

She watched him head through the vines towards the sheds until he disappeared from her line of sight. Perhaps he hadn't noticed her under the verandah but she had the distinct feeling he had.

For a while she worked on her sketch of Euan, adding the hat he had worn that morning and more detail to the face, but eventually she put the pad away. The silent man from over the fence had left her feeling unsettled and, anyway, she preferred to have her subject in view or at least to work from a photo. Not that she could take one. It was frustrating not having her phone. Euan had said the day before that one of them would run her to Bunbury. It was only an hour away but nothing more had come of it.

Keen to keep busy, she got out her jewellery-making kit. She never went far without it and was always on the lookout for bits she could use in her creations. First she unwrapped the soft fabric from around the tools and spread it across the table, then she took out the wire and the container of beads she had gathered from various sources over the years. This was her release; the one thing that gave free rein to her creative talent and allowed her to forget everything but the thrill of piecing together semi-precious stones, beads and wire to create bracelets, necklaces and earrings.

Her current creation was a bracelet that she had begun before she left home. It needed something special to add a final dimension and she had hoped to have the chance to find something in Perth. She wanted to make jewellery with beads or stones or adornments collected on her travels. She held the bracelet up to the light then draped it across her arm.

Underneath the table she'd noticed a couple of empty wine bottles. She picked one up, brushed the dust off with a tissue and stood it in the middle of the table where she hooked the bracelet around it. The label on the bottle had faded but she could still read the words *Levallier Dell Chardonnay*.

She fiddled with the unfinished bracelet for a while. There was nothing more she could do to it for now and she didn't want to start another piece until she had found a new source of beads. The sun glinted off the gems and gave a glimpse of a cobweb effect around the neck of the bottle.

Keely looked at the bottle with new interest. She twisted the bracelet and pressed it flat then lifted it off and put it aside. The cloth was soon covered in wire and beads as her new project took shape. She became so absorbed in it that she didn't realise the afternoon was slipping away until she felt a chill in the air. The sun had moved over the house, leaving her tucked away in her verandah arbour.

She sat back, stretched carefully and smiled at the beads draped around the neck of the bottle. She was relaxed and feeling good. Perhaps Euan had been right, the river was a good place for healing.

A soft scuffling noise caught her attention. She looked up through the curtain of foliage expecting to see Euan, but instead it was Flynn stepping quietly along the verandah. He was peering cautiously in through the glass doors. She remained still. He was obviously trying to avoid someone. Perhaps his father or, she thought, shifting silently on her seat, more likely me. Perhaps he'd only taken to peeping through doors since she'd arrived.

She watched him step inside then turned to her beads and packed them away.

"Damn him."

She snapped the lid shut on the beads. It really had been comfortable staying here but Flynn had ruined her sense of peace. Euan had been very kind but his son was a different personality altogether and he was obviously avoiding her. There was tension between the two men and she was sure she had been the catalyst to make Flynn move out. Since that first morning when he'd burst into the bedroom, he'd kept away from the house and she'd only seen him in the distance.

She stood up and stuffed her things back into her pack. Flynn would just have to see that this pussyfooting around, as her mother would say, was all ridiculous. Anyway, Keely wouldn't be staying for much longer.

She stepped through the sliding door and staggered back as she bumped right into him. Her pack was knocked from her hands and some of the contents slid out onto the floor.

"Sorry." He dropped his own bag to bend down to pick up her things. His other hand still held a couple of shirts on hangers draped over his shoulder.

Keely's pad lay on the floor, open at the sketch of Euan. She bent quickly to push it back into her bag and gasped as the pain tugged in her stomach. They both raised their heads quickly and Keely's ear connected with Flynn's forehead. The bump caught him off balance and he toppled to the floor, squashing his bag and his shirts.

"Sorry." This time Keely felt it was her turn to offer an apology. She watched as he stood up and picked up his things. She had expected to come in and find him making himself at home in the house, not preparing to leave it. Keely's plan had been to chat with him, casually mentioning that she would be on her way by Monday. Now she blocked the path of his escape.

They both hesitated in the doorway.

"I didn't realise you were here," Flynn said.

Obviously, thought Keely.

"I've left Euan a note." He nodded towards the phone. "I'll be out most of the weekend. We've been invited to the River Dynasty restaurant tomorrow night and dinner at the McPhersons' on Sunday night."

Keely glanced up through a curtain of hair, which had fallen across her face. Flynn was a good bit taller than Euan but she could clearly see the physical resemblance. The ice-blue eyes and pointy nose, the hint of ginger in his fair hair, but there were no freckles like Euan's. Flynn's skin was smooth and more olive in complexion.

"I'm not sure I'll be here…" she mumbled.

"The invitations were for Euan and me but I'm sure one extra won't matter if you want to come."

He brushed past her and Keely lowered her gaze again as she felt the heat rise up her neck. Euan had said Flynn usually had good manners but she'd not seen a sign of them in her two encounters with him.

"Goodbye," he said and the door slid shut behind her.

She turned but he was already striding away and he didn't look back.

CHAPTER
9

Flynn looked around the room and nodded as several faces acknowledged his arrival. He had hoped his father might have arrived before him but he wasn't among the group of winemakers already seated. He might turn up. Euan often ran late for appointments but Flynn wasn't holding his breath.

It had taken Euan longer than most to accept the change from cork to screw-cap technology and he still insisted on cork for his precious cabernet franc. The percentage of their wine lost to bad corks had increased in the last season and Flynn was keen to look at alternatives. He thought the idea of glass stoppers might enthuse his father. Hugh was definitely interested but, as always, their head man deferred to Euan and kept out of arguments between father and son. He always said his job was the vines and it was up to Euan and Flynn to come up with the finished product.

Today they were looking at some of the different styles of glass stoppers available as well as options for screw caps. The idea of a cap with Levallier Dell embossed in gold on it appealed to Flynn. They were also going to discuss some of the different varieties of wine other winemakers were experimenting with in Australia now and what might grow well in their region. He'd reminded his father about the presentation but he wasn't really expecting him to come. Euan was locked in his ways and wasn't ever in a hurry to change.

Flynn glanced again at the men and women gathered in the room. Some of them represented wineries that had formed a co-operative to produce bulk wines. It had been another major change for the area and had caused quite a stir at the time. The Margaret River region had always produced bottled wines and there were those, including Euan, who believed cask wines would spoil the region's wine image. It hadn't, and both bottled and bulk wine had survived. There were a few here from other long-established wineries and all of them had changed from cork.

Flynn and Euan had held several lively discussions about changing the cabernet franc to screw caps or glass stoppers before Euan had gone away. Flynn had brought it up again just the day before. He'd hoped Euan would be back from the east in time to meet the visiting promotion team. His father had shut off as usual, refusing to listen to Flynn's research and getting angry when he'd suggested they both attend this presentation in town.

There was also the final decision to be made about what they were going to plant on the remaining free hectares at the Haystack Block. Flynn wanted to plant something new, Euan didn't. There'd been no chance to discuss that since he'd returned home either.

Euan had been more concerned with the woman he'd brought to Levallier Dell, Keely someone. Flynn frowned. He didn't know everything about Euan's exploits, he was sure, but she'd been a surprise. Usually Euan kept his more intimate life out of the local area and, to Flynn's knowledge, he'd never brought anyone to the house before, certainly not since Flynn had returned home to live. But it didn't stop the gossip and that was what Flynn hated.

Euan had explained again that Keely was recuperating from an operation but Flynn wasn't convinced that was all there was to it. They had looked fairly intimate sitting on the couch together when he'd returned to the house to apologise to Keely and make peace. His father's arm had been around Keely with the same tenderness he had used to nurse Lucy in those final days.

Flynn clenched his fingers into tight fists. Keely looked to be about his age. The father of one of his uni mates had left home and taken up with a much younger woman. It had been bad enough for the family but the son hadn't been able to deal with his stepmother being the same age as his sister. Flynn could understand how he felt. Perhaps Euan had really lost the plot this time.

"Hello, Flynn." A loud voice and firm hand on his shoulder startled Flynn back to the present. He gritted his teeth as he recognised Theo's voice. Flynn hadn't responded to the invitation he'd received from the neighbours to their party that night. He'd planned to not turn up and just make an excuse the next time he saw Theo.

He turned and the smile he'd assumed changed to a look of genuine surprise as his eyes met the dark brown eyes of the smiling young woman standing beside Theo.

"You remember my granddaughter, Katerina? She is visiting us from her parents' winery in the Yarra Valley." Theo beamed. "This is Flynn Levallier from next door."

Flynn held out his hand. "Welcome to Margaret River."

"Thanks." Her soft hand was pleasantly warm. "It's like coming home for me. I spent a lot of time here as a child when Pappou first bought the place."

Flynn let go of her hand and looked again at the attractive face framed by the thick dark hair that sat neatly on her shoulders. There was something about her. He glanced at Theo, then a distant memory made him look quickly back at her.

"You're the little girl who fell off the pony," he said.

She smiled. "Not that little. I was ten."

Theo let out a bellowing laugh.

"I've never forgotten scaring that pony with my bike," Flynn said. "I thought I'd killed you."

"Katerina was always falling off something. Such a tomboy." Theo chuckled.

Flynn remembered her now. She was about seven years younger than him. A little scrawny kid she'd been. He'd seen her on her visits to her grandparents' home. Theo had kept a pony for her to ride and she'd been in the drive one day when Flynn had roared past on his bike and frightened the pony. She certainly wasn't a scrawny little kid anymore.

"I loved that pony and climbing trees with the boys." Her smile lit up her face and Flynn liked the way she held her head proudly. "They were the best holidays."

"Kat, that's it. They used to call you Kat," he said.

"They still do," she said.

"Ladies and gentlemen." One of the presenters called their attention to the front of the room. "We'd like to begin. Please take a seat."

Flynn glanced once more towards the door before allowing Theo to usher him to a seat beside Kat. It would be much more enjoyable sitting next to her than Euan anyway.

* * *

"Euan, you were right. It's so beautiful." Keely stood on the little footbridge over the river, taking in the scene. Trees grew on the banks and bent their branches to meet the gently flowing water, small ducks slid along the surface and butterflies flitted in and out

of the shadows. "There's every shade of green and it looks so tranquil." She turned to him in excitement. He was watching her, that
quizzical smile twitching at the corners of his mouth.

"I'm sorry you had to have your appendix out to get here. Just
goes to show every cloud has a silver lining. It would have been bad
luck if you missed this on your Western Australian travels."

Keely turned back to the vista in front of her, breathed in deeply
and held the breath. There was hardly a twinge from her abdomen
and she felt relaxed and yet a little excited. She really was on holiday: no timetables, no students, no problems. Slowly she exhaled.
It was as if someone had given her permission to let go and at last
she was doing it.

The evening before when Euan had come home he had been
preoccupied. She'd pointed out the note Flynn had left and he'd
scrunched it up and gone off into the other end of the house for a
while. There were tomatoes, eggs and various cheeses in the fridge
and she'd made omelettes. Euan had prepared her meals up till
then. She'd hoped he liked omelette. It was a small way of saying
thank you.

When he'd returned he was showered and there was no sign of
his earlier anger. He was delighted with the omelette and opened a
bottle of his wine to go with it. The conversation had turned to her
day and she'd quietly mentioned her jewellery. Euan had insisted on
seeing it and had become animated when she'd told him of her idea
to find new beads and adornments wherever she travelled.

"There's a place in the village," he'd explained. "I'll take you
there tomorrow. River Rainbow it's called, run by Mary. She's
the most amazing woman. Set up here over thirty years ago. Lucy
bought most of her fabrics and bits and pieces there. She and Mary
worked on several projects together. I've got an idea Mary has one
of the rooms in her shop dedicated to beads."

So here they were, bright and early, stopped on the edge of Margaret River, or 'the village' as Euan called it. The river itself wandered through one end of the town named after it.

"I have a couple of people to see," Euan said as they continued on into the town. "Tell Mary you're with me and she'll look after you."

Even though it was early there were quite a few people in the main street, which was lined on either side with shops, offices and eateries. There were chairs around tables under umbrellas, signs on sandwich boards and fluttering sails; spread among them groups of people strolled in the sunshine.

"Tourists," Euan said. "Love them or hate them, they're our bread and butter these days."

He pointed out River Rainbow and managed to find a park down a side street nearby. "How long will you need? I know what Lucy was like once she got into that place. Time just disappeared at Mary's," he said. "I'll probably be an hour and then we can go on to Bunbury and collect your things."

Keely's face lit up. He hadn't mentioned that when they'd left the house.

"Great, and an hour's plenty of time for me. I only want a few things."

Euan chuckled and got out of the car. "That's what Lucy used to say."

Keely made her way back towards the main street with a spring in her step at the thought of retrieving her phone and wallet. She only hoped the phone wasn't broken.

She passed a weatherboard cottage set back from the road. The front garden had several square wooden tables sheltered by dark green market umbrellas. An old-fashioned sign hung over the fence proclaiming *Anna's Kitchen*. There were several people sitting at the tables already.

It looked inviting but Keely was on a mission. She moved on around the corner to the stone cottage, dwarfed on either side by newer glass and brick buildings. The little verandah was right on the street and strips of fabric in every colour fluttered from the eaves. Fabric on rolls stood on stands either side of the door and two big wicker baskets overflowed with hats and scarves with a sign declaring *Hand knits at bargain prices*. This was River Rainbow.

The doorway was low and Keely felt the need to duck her head. A soft chiming sound came from somewhere in the back as she entered. The main room was jammed with more material on bolts and rolls, and old shop mannequins draped in fabric, and the walls were lined with zips, threads, feathers and all sorts of haberdashery items. She stopped to take it all in, captivated by the selection available. Now she understood what Euan had been referring to.

She moved to the back of the room, dominated by a wide wooden counter surrounded by baskets and boxes overflowing with every kind of sewing accessory. The long wall behind the counter was decorated with handmade cards, scrapbook pages, cross-stitch samplers, patchwork cushions and smocked baby gowns. Here the air was filled with the delicate scent of roses.

"Won't be long," a woman's voice called from somewhere further back. Keely looked around. There was a door to the right, with a sign beside it declaring *Patchwork*. The door leading to the back of the shop had a sign that said *Paper crafts, buttons, beads and workroom*. She stepped through into a room stacked with shelves of coloured card, papers and stickers and came face to face with a large, ruddy-faced woman.

"Mary?" Keely asked.

"Good heavens no, love. I'm Peg. I'd make two of Mary. She's not here this morning. I'm minding the shop. Have you come for the card-making? We're out in the back room." The woman jerked a finger over her broad shoulder.

"No, I'm just looking for beads," Keely said.

"Right beside you, love. Do you need any help?"

Keely turned to see a door to another side room, with a sign announcing *Buttons and beads*. "No, thanks, I'll be fine."

"Righto, love. You just give me a yell when you're ready." Peg turned her large body in the small space and sailed back the way she'd come.

Keely stepped through the door and stopped. It was as if she had crossed the threshold into another world. The walls were lined with rows of shelves and each shelf held containers of beads or buttons. Every colour was represented, in all shades and patterns. In the centre of the room was a glass cabinet displaying several pieces of jewellery in various stages of construction. The items were draped over driftwood or sat among shells. Some of the finished pieces were for sale.

A low whistle escaped Keely's lips and she smiled. Now she understood Euan's comment about time disappearing. River Rainbow was a jewellery-maker's paradise. If the other crafts were as well represented, Mary must have a constant stream of customers beating a path to her door.

Keely picked up a small wooden bowl and began to work her way along the shelves. In her mind she was already creating a whole new range of jewellery inspired by her temporary home.

CHAPTER
10

The dark specks bobbed in the water like corks. Occasionally, two or three would peel off as the sea rose in a giant swell and disgorged a promising wave. Then the specks elongated and turned into surfers, slicing along the waves and riding them in close to the shore.

Keely watched from the old Volvo, parked on the cliff top. She had no idea which one was Euan. On the way back from Bunbury he'd wanted to show her the beach and promised they'd end the afternoon with a picnic tea. When they'd arrived there on the cliff top he'd deemed the conditions perfect for a quick surf.

She'd toyed with the idea of following him as he carried his board down the long series of steps. Her phone looked okay but it was flat and her charger was back at the house. Not that it would have done her any good. There was no modern technology in Euan's car and no way for her to have charged it. A walk along the beach would have been wonderful but the distance, and the thought of the long climb back up, deterred her.

The earlier outing to town and then the trip to the police station had been enough to remind Keely that she was still not fully recovered. Much to her surprise she'd dozed on the way back from Bunbury, only waking up as they'd pulled in at the cliff top. She smiled now, as she recalled the beautiful assortment of things she'd brought home from the town. Peg had been most helpful. She liked to chat and when she found out Keely had left her paints at home, she had showed off River Rainbow's range with a flourish.

Keely had been forced to economise when planning to travel backpacker style. The jewellery kit and sketchbook had fitted. She had planned to add the colour to her travel sketches when she returned home, but now she could complete the sketch of Euan. It just needed the touches of brown, the hints of yellow and the blue of his eyes, so she had succumbed to the lure of the little paint selection. Euan had been right again; every cloud had a silver lining and she'd found some. She was enjoying herself despite her bouts of discomfort.

Here on the cliff top, the wind off the sea was cold and she was quite happy to sit in the warm car and watch the ever-moving view as the Indian Ocean rolled in from the west. Her sketchpad lay open beside her with the rough outline of the panoramic scene sprawled across the page.

A thud from behind startled her and she turned to see Euan stripping off his wetsuit, his board perched against the back of the Volvo. Keely packed up her things. She didn't show her sketches to many people. She'd done a few for family and close friends and they had praised her talent but she knew they were just being kind. These days she kept her pictures to herself. They gave her a private escape and she preferred to keep it that way.

"That was good." Euan climbed into the seat beside her, bringing the fresh smell of the sea with him.

"I've never tried surfing."

His expression was bright as he turned the car around. "I can give you some lessons."

She glanced back over the expanse of water. "Wasn't a surfer attacked by a shark near here not so long ago?"

"More chance of being hit by a truck. Have you seen how some people drive?"

"I'm not very brave. The deep water and big waves scare me."

"It's not like that out there, safe as houses. Watching is much scarier than doing it. Riding a wave is a wonderful feeling."

Keely glanced back towards the sea as they drove away. A man appeared at the top of the steps carrying a board under one arm and a crash helmet under the other. She wasn't totally convinced by Euan's 'safe as houses'.

They drove back through thick bush and took several twists and turns along dirt tracks before Euan stopped the car in a small clearing surrounded by scrubby bush.

"Wait here while I get your gourmet picnic ready." He grinned and then ducked away.

It was cosy in the old car and she was happy to stay nestled in her seat as she watched him come and go, taking things from the back and carrying them to a spot through the bush just out of her vision.

"Okay, time to get out." Euan opened her door. "You might want your jacket till the fire gets going."

Keely took her coat with her and pulled it on as she followed Euan around a stand of thick bush to a smaller clearing. There was a fire glowing softly in a metal pod on legs. Nearby, he had spread the old blanket beside an esky and a wine cooler with an open bottle nestled inside.

"Your picnic, *mademoiselle*." He bowed low and flung out an arm as she passed.

Keely laughed. She sat on the blanket and watched as he poured two glasses of wine. Over his shoulder there was a break in the bush and she could see the glow of the setting sun.

"Here you are." He passed her a glass. "This is a Levallier Dell Sauvignon Blanc. Our *pièce de résistance*," he said with a perfect French accent. "Margaret River is famous for its chardonnay but we also produce a very drinkable sauvignon blanc."

She looked from him to the glass in her hand. The wine looked much paler than any other she'd tried. She couldn't recall ever tasting a sauvignon blanc. What if she didn't like it?

"Swirl the wine a couple of times." He demonstrated. "Then put your nose in the glass while the wine is still swirling and sniff. You can smell the tropical fruits and freshly cut grass."

Keely watched him then tried to follow his example but she was a bit too forceful. The liquid swished around and as she moved the glass forward, a splosh of wine went up her nose just as she sniffed. She snorted and coughed all at once, spilling the wine down her hand. Her other hand flew to her mouth and she stared in horror at the remains of the wine in the glass that she had somehow managed to keep upright.

A low clucking sound broke the silence. Keely looked up. Euan's face was contorted into a myriad of lines as he tried to hold back the laugh that was escaping in short bursts.

"I'm sorry…" she stammered.

"Don't worry." He laughed openly now.

"My mother always says I'm like a bull in a china shop."

"*Au contraire.*"

She glanced at Euan. A small frown creased his brow. "With apologies to your mother but I think she's wrong. You are elegant and graceful and very creative. You should focus on the positives, Keely. You're a very talented young woman."

He smiled and his wise eyes twinkled in the firelight. Once again his kindness reminded her of her grandfather. He'd always encouraged her talents. Not that her parents hadn't but for them her artistic side equalled a skill she could use as a teacher. A respectable position that would one day offer job security, they'd said. Just thinking about it stirred the anxiety inside her. She looked down and dabbed at the spilled wine with the end of her sleeve.

"Don't worry about the wine. I get carried away. Just drink and enjoy." He raised his glass. "Here's to holidays."

Keely echoed his words, watched as he took a sip of his wine then carefully took a sip of what remained of hers. At first there was a tart taste but then a softer fruitier flavour took over. She studied it again then took a bigger sip. It really was very light. She enjoyed the taste.

Euan was regarding her with interest.

"It's…" She hesitated. "Is it okay to describe a wine as delicious?"

"Of course, *mademoiselle*, you are the customer and the customer is always right."

She took another small sip. She would have to take it easy. She hadn't eaten much today and her head was buzzing. "It's most certainly delicious then."

"I hope you like fish." The fire was low now and he got up to tend the alfoil packages on the wire rack he'd placed over it.

"I love fish. My dad is a dedicated weekend fisherman. It's not very often we don't eat fish of some sort."

"I got these from a friend. I prefer to swim with the fishes rather than catch them but I enjoy eating them all the same."

"I learned to fish on the Swan with my grandpa."

"The childhood holidays?"

"Yes." Keely took another sip of her wine and told him about her trips to Perth as a child and about her wonderful grandparents.

Euan poured more wine and before long he was setting the alfoil parcels on the blanket. They unwrapped them and the fish steamed, releasing a sweet, mouth-watering aroma. He produced crusty bread rolls with butter, wedges of lemon and a fork each.

The fish was as delicious as the wine. They ate in silence with the soft crackle of the fire as their background. Euan had added more wood to it after he took off the fish and they sat in the glow of the flames. It was a simple meal but tasty and filling.

Once the fish was all gone, they moved closer to the fire with their wine. He found a log for her – sitting low to the ground was becoming uncomfortable – and then he settled back on the blanket.

Euan was easy company and Keely told him about her desire to visit the regions of Western Australia that her grandfather had described.

"I have to admit I haven't seen much of the country north of Perth. There are some great surfing beaches up there. I've visited a few of those," Euan said. "I came to Australia in the early seventies."

"You weren't born here?" Keely had the impression he'd always lived at Margaret River.

"No. I spent most of my childhood in my father's home region of Bordeaux in France. My Irish mother made sure Maggie and I knew her homeland as well and I spent some time in other wine-growing districts of Europe. I came to Australia as a young man. My father wanted me to check out the wine regions in eastern Australia and I was keen to try the surf. Lucy taught me all about it."

"Your wife was an Australian?" Keely was sipping the last of her wine more carefully now. Euan drained the bottle into his own glass.

"She was a breath of Antipodean fresh air to me and I fell in love with her at once. Like you, she was keen to visit Western Australia. I followed her to Perth. The rest is history. We married and found paradise here at Margaret River. Lucy was a talented artist, as well as my partner in the vineyard. We began it not long after the first wineries were established. In the days before people associated this area with serious wine. We planted everything, tended it ourselves and there was always the surf nearby. Flynn was our only child and he made our life complete." Euan stopped. Keely could see the tight set of his jaw as he stared into the fire. He tipped the last of his wine into his mouth and swallowed. "Strange how things change. The three of us did everything together but it was Lucy who made us a family, her magic that wove us together. It's more than sixteen years since her weak heart stopped. I still miss her, no matter how hard I try, but life goes on."

The wind had dropped right away while they'd been eating. The fire crackled in the silence. It was a perfect night with the stars shining above. Keely didn't speak. It was as if Euan had been telling the last part of his story to the fire and she had been eavesdropping. He obviously loved and missed his wife and yet something wasn't right. She recalled Flynn's outburst the morning after her arrival. He had assumed Keely was Euan's lover and had intimated there had been others. The memory was enough to make her squirm all over again but somehow Flynn's version didn't make sense with the gentle tale Euan had just poured out.

"Lucy would have loved those decorations."

Keely was startled from her thoughts. In the glow from the fire she could see the twinkle was back in Euan's eyes but she had no idea what decorations he was talking about.

"Those bead covers for the wine bottles," he said.

"Oh, they're nothing special. My mother and her friends have got several sets."

"But yours are made with Margaret River beads and your own creative flair. Have faith in yourself, Keely." Once again, he said her name with the hint of Irish that reminded her of her grandfather. She shivered.

"I'd better get you home," he said. "Don't want you catching cold while I'm looking after you. The days are beautiful at this time of the year but the nights can still be very chilly."

Keely was reluctant to move but the fire had burned low again and the night air was cold. She helped him pack up their things. Back in the old Volvo, Euan turned up the radio and they wound their way back to Levallier Dell accompanied by the comfortingly familiar sounds of the Beatles, Elvis and the Delltones. Keely hummed along happily. Euan and her dad shared the same tastes in music.

* * *

The lights from the huge windows of the River Dynasty restaurant shone brightly, like a beacon on the hill. Flynn stopped in the parking area by the front door. He could have walked but he was running late. He'd been working on some trellising all afternoon and had driven the tray-top ute back to the studio. There'd only been time for a quick shower and change and he'd jumped back in the ute to drive next door for Theo's dinner.

He'd noticed no lights had shone from his own house as he'd driven out. Flynn did wonder briefly what his father was doing. Probably taken Keely for a meal in town. He had no fear Euan would have accepted Theo's invitation. The two men had never been friends and Theo's involvement in the cask wine co-op had set them firmly on opposite sides. Then he'd purchased land from Euan's friend Connor in a manner Euan believed was underhanded and that had been the final nail in the coffin. Euan usually avoided anything to do with River Dynasty and its family of workers.

It had all started years ago. The two men had had a falling out over a small dingle in the main street when Theo first arrived in the district. Euan had backed into Theo's new car with his old one. Euan had accepted the blame and, to be fair to his dad, Flynn was fairly sure he would have apologised, paid up and been done with it but Theo had made a huge fuss in front of everyone in the street. Euan had got his back up and said the insurance companies could sort it out and they'd found more reasons to dislike each other ever since.

Flynn got on okay with Theo but his own intention had been to avoid the dinner. Often events at River Dynasty were a bit over the top for Flynn's liking. It was meeting with Kat that morning that made him curious. She was easy to talk to and had shared his interest in the various screw caps and glass stoppers they'd been shown. He also discovered that she had studied business management at university in Sydney and gone on to study winemaking in New South Wales.

He smiled as he got out of the ute. It wasn't as if he had anything else to do tonight. It was worth attending one of Theo's parties to have the chance to get to know Kat better.

Flynn walked along the path to the front door. There were topiary shrubs in ceramic pots covered in fairy lights lining his way. He could see people standing around inside the glass doors and, as he approached, the doors opened before him. Two of Theo's younger grandsons held them back for him to walk through.

"Flynn!" Theo threw his arms out wide then stepped towards him and kissed him on both cheeks. "Welcome to River Dynasty restaurant."

"Thanks, Theo." Flynn looked around and bent low to be welcomed by Theo's wife in the same way.

"What would you like to drink? Besides our fine wines we have many things to choose from. Would you prefer a beer perhaps?"

"Thanks."

Flynn looked around as Theo called out for a beer to be brought. There were individual tables in the front part of the room all set for service; a large bar took up one corner at the left and back walls, and along from that were doors through to what was once the original old house. Partway down the wall to his right was a huge open fire with several comfy chairs scattered in front of it. Kat stood near the fire, talking to some of her aunts. Theo was distracted as more guests arrived and Flynn took the beer he was offered and made his way towards the fire.

"I'm not sure how long I can stay, at least two weeks, I hope. It just depends," Kat was saying to the two women beside her. One of them welcomed Flynn. He recalled she was married to Theo's son who ran their other winery, closer to Augusta. Kat smiled a hello and the three women continued their conversation. The older women spoke partly in Greek and Flynn had difficulty following their words.

He took the chance to study Kat. The pale pink of her top complemented her olive complexion. It was fell loosely over her jeans, which stopped just short of white ankle boots. She was perfectly proportioned.

The aunts moved away and Flynn lifted his gaze to find Kat looking at him, a small smile twitching at the corners of her mouth. "I try to tell them I don't understand much when they speak Greek."

"Your grandfather has done a lot of work here," he said quickly, aware she had caught him out.

"It's changed from when I was here last. Pappou has grand plans for River Dynasty."

"Are you part of those plans?"

"Oh no. Pappou has so many family members here he employs already. Besides, my parents think I'm going to take over the running of their winery one day."

Flynn thought there was a sharp edge to her words. "And you've got other ideas?"

"I'm an only child." The smile left her face and she glanced at the people talking and laughing around them.

"I can relate to that," Flynn said. "Accused by many of being spoiled and fancy-free but forever burdened with keeping the parents' dream alive."

"Yes," she replied softly. Then her smile was back. "I'm glad you came tonight, Flynn. I think we have a lot in common."

They were both startled by a loud clapping of hands and then Theo's voice booming.

"Come, everyone. Michael has prepared a magnificent meal. It is being served in the banquet room. Please go through and take a seat."

Flynn hung back as the large group of people moved towards the door behind him but Kat grabbed his hand and took him along with her. The banquet room was part of the original house. It was set up with long tables covered with white cloths, decorated with trails of small olive branches and dotted with bottles of wine. Along the far wall, Michael and his team waited behind another table laden with food.

"Let's find a seat and wait for the rush to die down," Kat murmured in his ear and led him to a table where some of her cousins were sitting. She introduced him to those closest. He knew most of the faces. Next to him was Chris, who came from Ocean Dynasty further south, and across the table sat Peter and his new wife, Angela. They were all involved in the wine industry so, naturally, that was the main topic of conversation.

Flynn was particularly interested to hear about the managerial role Chris had as cellar maintenance supervisor. It was an area where Levallier Dell badly needed an extra person. Euan, Flynn and Hugh did it between them and delegated to the casual cellar hands they employed, but it was too haphazard these days, with the size of their vineyards and Euan's periodic absences.

Kat kept filling their glasses and talking about the different wines that were being served. He was impressed with her knowledge. She not only knew the Dynasty range, other Margaret River wines and those of the Yarra Valley but she could compare varieties from many wine regions in Australia.

He smirked as she informed Peter, with a challenge in her look, that his chardonnay was still not packed with the character of some of those available from the Adelaide Hills in South Australia or the Yarra Valley in Victoria.

"Come, Katerina," Peter complained. "You know it has taken me years to convince Pappou to let Dad and me try an unwooded chardonnay."

She looked contrite. "I'm only teasing. It's still got great fruit and nice acid." She picked up the bottle in question and considered the label carefully. "You've also packaged it well. The label is very distinctive."

Flynn looked at the white lines curved across the vivid blue label. It was certainly different to the plain white label used for all other River Dynasty wines.

"Angela organised that." Peter threw his arm around his new wife's shoulders and kissed her. "She's great at graphic design."

"Is that your training, Angela?" Flynn asked. He would love to make some changes to the Levallier Dell labels but Euan wouldn't have a bar of it and neither of them had the time anyway.

"No, I studied marketing at uni and I've had a variety of jobs since then. Mostly in the restaurant and wine trade."

"You'll be put to work here, then," Kat said. "Pappou has every family member earmarked for a job. What has he got you doing?"

"It's not been long since the wedding, there's been lots to do set-ting up house," Angela said.

"She helps out here in the restaurant and at the cellar door." Peter gave his wife a gentle squeeze.

"And there'll be lots more work now that the extensions are finished," Angela said.

"Pappou will realise your full potential eventually," Peter said gently. His arm was still around his wife's shoulders and he pulled her in close and kissed her cheek.

Flynn was just wondering what Peter meant when the music that had been playing in the background was suddenly turned up. One of the younger boys was fiddling with the sound system at the edge of the dance floor and all around people were getting up to make their way to him.

"Time to dance." Peter stood up, pulling Angela with him.

Flynn watched as the group on the dance floor joined arms and the familiar sounds of 'Zorba's Dance' from *Zorba the Greek* began.

"Do you like to dance?" He was startled by Kat's voice close to his ear.

"I can but I'm not good at it and I certainly don't know how to do that." He nodded towards the circle of people stepping slowly to the music.

"It's easy." She reached for his hand and stood up. "Come on, I'll teach you."

Flynn had had enough wine to think that maybe she could and he smiled as her soft hand gripped his and led him to the floor.

Half an hour later, he pulled himself from the circle and sank into a nearby chair. Laughing, Kat followed and fell into a chair beside him.

"Not fit enough." She leaned in close so he could hear her above the music. "You did very well for a beginner."

He could smell the sweat from his own body but her closeness brought the scent of her perfume to him. She looked wonderful. He would like to have kissed her deep pink lips.

She sat back suddenly. "I'm glad you came. It's been a lot of fun."

"It has." Somehow the sparkle of the moment had disappeared. "I'd better get going."

A hand clasped his shoulder and he turned to see Theo beaming at him then back to Kat. "Are you two having a good time?"

"It's been great, thanks, Theo." He stood up. "I was just telling Kat it was time I left, though. Another big day tomorrow."

Theo grasped his hand. "You are a hard worker, Flynn. I like that. But you must also remember to play. I'm glad you enjoyed our little party. Come, Katerina, walk our guest to the door."

"No, you stay please," Flynn said. "I can find my way out."

He felt Theo's eyes on him as he said goodnight to Kat and turned to thank her grandmother. He had enjoyed the evening but there was no doubt that it was Kat who had made it fun. He had come close to spoiling it. Thank goodness he hadn't kissed her. That would have been a big mistake.

He hurried out into the cold night and shook his head. His life was here in Margaret River but he already had a sense that Kat was destined for something else.

CHAPTER
11

The door slid back with a thud and Flynn strode into the room. "The pump's broken down again."

Keely looked up, startled by his abrupt intrusion. She and Euan had eaten a late breakfast and were sitting at either end of the table, he with the newspaper and she flicking through magazines.

"Good morning to you too, Flynn," Euan said. "Would you like some breakfast?"

Flynn stopped and looked from Euan to Keely then to the table as if he had just realised where he was. He took off his cap. The fair wavy hair it had been taming fluffed out around his head. His face was tanned and he looked like a sun-bleached surfie. Keely wondered if he shared that interest with his father.

"No...thank you. I've eaten." He glanced at Keely and softened his voice. "I would like some help with the pump. I told you before you went away it needed seeing to. There's no water at the studio and we won't be able to water the vines."

Keely moved away to the couch to give the two men some space. She took her phone from her pocket. Thankfully it hadn't been any the worse for wear and as soon as it had charged she'd sent a text to her mum to let her know she had it back and then had a long conversation with Bec.

"It's Sunday morning," Euan said. "You can shower here and the vines won't need water for weeks. The pump can wait till tomorrow."

"There's the spraying to do while the weather's clear." Flynn gripped the back of the chair and his voice began to rise again. "I've noticed a few spots of mildew on the chardonnay vines closer to the river, so I don't want to put that off. There're the barrels to move before the new ones arrive, which could be any day, and there's blending to be done."

Euan sighed. "Okay, Flynn. I'll come down in a minute." He stood up. "Why don't you have a coffee while I get changed?"

Euan left and Flynn hesitated just inside the door.

Keely looked up from her phone. "I can make you one if you like." There was a simple pod machine in the kitchen, easy to use like the one at home.

Flynn turned and she felt the full force of his gaze across the room. "That's okay. I'll do it." He went round the breakfast bar. "Can I make you one?"

Keely looked down. She had only ever seen him angry before. She didn't know how to deal with this polite Flynn.

"Thanks," she murmured.

*　*　*

Kat took slow deep breaths to steady the rising anticipation she felt deep in her chest. Gradually, her breathing fell into step with the rhythmic flow of the priest's voice, chanting the morning prayers, and she relaxed. This trip had been intended to give her space and time to plan her future. Her parents wanted her to be part of their expanding business and originally that's where she'd intended her university studies would lead her. That had been her goal. That was until the previous November. She'd gone to Sydney to promote Australian wine at an international medical conference and met a wine exporter called Mal Wilson. Ever since then, she had been living an exhausting double life.

This trip had been an excuse to distance herself and make some decisions. Now, her grandfather wanted to talk with her. A quiet morning tea after church, he'd said, just the two of them to talk things over before the cellar door got too busy. He had plenty of workers but he still liked to be there, talking to the customers, keeping an eye on things.

From their previous conversations, he had obviously sensed her waning commitment to her parents' winery. Unburdening her duplicity to Pappou would be a welcome release. He would understand her and help her to explain it to her parents.

They stood to sing the final hymn and she looked across and caught his eye. He winked at her and she couldn't help but smile. An ally was just what she needed.

After church, he insisted on introducing her to everyone and it took some time to get away. Finally, they sat under the front verandah of the house, with its view up the hill and across the vines to the cellar-door building standing grandly at the top.

She watched while he finished writing in his diary. She smiled to herself. How many times had the cry gone up 'Pappou has lost his diary'? Then there would be a frantic search until it was found. She remembered sneaking a peek inside one day when she'd been the one to find it on the bathroom shelf – and her disappointment in discovering he wrote nothing more than vineyard facts and figures instead of the secrets her twelve-year-old self had hoped for.

He closed the diary and slipped it into his pocket. "I'm glad you've come, Katerina. It's wonderful to have you here. This is as much your home as the Yarra Valley, you know." He looked proudly out over the vines spread before them and she couldn't help but follow his gaze. "It's your mother's inheritance and so it is right that you should have a part of it."

Kat's gaze jerked from the scenery to her grandfather. "What do you mean, Pappou?"

"I started River Dynasty for my family. As the family grew, the business grew and we began Ocean Dynasty. Your parents' holdings are only small in comparison." He stood and cast his arm towards the vines. "This is where the future of the family lies."

Kat frowned. She was momentarily distracted by Pappou's steadying grasp of the back of the chair. "Lucky you've got a big family to take it on, Pappou." She kept her tone bright. This was not the conversation she'd imagined they would have. "You should be taking life a bit easier these days."

"Exactly my point, Katerina." He turned his piercing gaze on her. "I have sons who manage the vines, make the wine and sell it. I have grandsons who follow in their fathers' footsteps and one who has become a talented chef and produces fine food for our restaurant, to complement our superior wines. It has become very popular and the new expansion will allow us to cater for big functions. What I don't have is someone to manage, market and grow our brand." He bent down and took her hands in his old, weathered grip. "You are that someone, Katerina. There is a huge opportunity here and I need someone young and clever, with bright ideas, to manage it for me."

She gaped at him. His grasp was firm and there wasn't any sign of his earlier shakiness but he may as well have been speaking in his native Greek tongue. She couldn't make sense of what he was saying.

"I know it is a big thing I am asking of you," he hurried on. "Your parents wish you to stay with them and I understand that, but I am an old man. I need you more."

"Pappou...I..."

"No. Don't say anything now." He let go of her hands and moved away.

She looked at the redness on her skin where he'd held her firmly.

"You need time to think it over. You will have lots of questions but there is time."

A door banged and they could hear the soft shuffle of Yia-yia's feet on the path.

He tapped his finger on the side of his nose. "I haven't discussed this with anyone else yet."

Yia-yia appeared around the corner carrying a loaded tray. "I have *kourabiedes*." Her cheeks glowed and her eyes sparkled as she paused to look from one to the other.

Kat took one of the biscuits coated in icing sugar and smiled weakly at her grandparents. She may well have jumped from the frying pan into the fire.

★ ★ ★

The door opened to Euan's knock and a short stocky woman stood framed in the light from the room behind her. She wore a dark green apron with *Anna's Kitchen* scrawled across the bib and had a brightly coloured tea towel draped over her shoulder.

"Hello, Euan. Welcome home." She opened her arms to wrap his wiry frame in an effusive hug.

"Thanks, Anna. It's good to be back," he said.

Keely hovered behind him. Euan had insisted she come with him to the McPhersons' for the evening meal but she felt uncomfortable about it.

"And you must be the mystery guest." Anna had stepped aside to let Euan in.

Keely saw the look of surprise flash across the other woman's face and noticed a slight hesitation before she held out a welcoming hand.

"Nothing mysterious about Keely," Euan said. "She's one of the family already. Flynn had her working for us today. That was after he gave me one of his lectures on the backlog that needed doing."

"Welcome, Keely." Anna's firm hand clasped Keely's. "I hope these Levallier men haven't been giving you a hard time. They're both passionate about that winery of theirs, but sometimes they forget they're working towards the same thing."

"Now don't you start, Anna," Euan growled but there was no malice in it. "Let Keely in. It's chilly out there and she's still recovering from her operation."

Anna guided Keely inside with the hand she still clasped tightly. "You poor love. Flynn said something about you being unwell."

"It was my appendix but I'm fine now..." Keely faltered under Anna's scrutiny and withdrew her hand. "It's kind of you to include me."

"No trouble at all. The more the merrier around our table. It can get a bit quiet with just Sean and me these days. Besides, I should imagine you'd be needing a decent feed. Euan and Flynn are lovely men but their cooking skills are fairly basic." Anna looked at her closely. "You'd better come in and sit down. It's not that long ago I had my appendix out. I know you say you're better but you've had an operation and you look a bit pale. You've probably lost condition."

Keely stepped further into the warm house. Her body ached in a pleasant kind of way from the more active day she'd had. She had been pleased to repay Euan's hospitality by making lunch and organising the house. The two men had worked all day on the various jobs Flynn had listed. She had pitched in with errands and making lunch. Now she felt tired but not unwell.

Anna was right about losing condition. Keely had worn her trackpants or drawstring shorts since her operation. Tonight, after her shower, she'd put on her jeans and they were loose. She'd looked in the mirror in amazement.

For as long as she could remember she'd struggled with her weight. Both of her younger brothers were beanpoles and her father referred to her as his 'cuddly kid'. Her mother was always telling her to be careful about what she ate, but Keely's downfall was the sweet stuff. When things got tough she reached for the chocolate and the cakes. They made life bearable.

Whatever the reason for her trimmer appearance, she felt better as well. It was almost as if she'd given herself a makeover to go with her new life.

She smiled and gave Anna the parcel she'd brought with her. "This is a small thank-you gift."

"You didn't need to bring anything—"

"Open it, Anna," Euan interrupted. "Keely made it for you."

Anna stopped her protest and opened the tissue paper to reveal one of Keely's wine-bottle decorations.

"Oh, it's very pretty," she said. The beads sparkled in the light as she spread it over her fingers and jiggled her hand.

"Here's the wine to go with it." Euan handed over a bottle. "Now come on, don't keep us hanging about out here in the cold, I can smell something good."

"Thank you, Keely," Anna said, "but you didn't need to bother." She dispatched the beads into her apron pocket. "Come and meet the others."

Keely followed Anna through the house to the big kitchen. Cheery voices spilled out into the passage and, Euan was right, there was also the delicious aroma of roasting meat. A large table dominated the room and several people were already seated around it.

"Everyone." Anna clapped her hands. "This is Euan's mystery guest, Keely, who's staying at Levallier Dell for a while."

The conversation stopped and Anna dragged her further into the room.

"This is my son, Sean." Anna indicated a young man standing at the stove stirring something in a large pot, then she waved towards the table. "There's my daughter, Megan, her husband, Terry and their boys, Sam and Tom. Next are my wonderful neighbours, Mary and David."

Keely's face radiated heat as all eyes looked her way expectantly.

"Hello, everyone," she murmured.

"There will be a test on all those names later." Mary laughed. "Come and sit by me, Keely. I hear you've got a talent with beads and you've already been into my shop."

"Yes, and look at this dear little decoration she's made with them." Anna handed over the bottle and jumble of beads from her pocket before turning her attention to the food.

Keely sat, relieved that the conversation around the table had resumed and all the eyes in the room were no longer focused on her. She glanced at Mary, who was untangling the bottle cover.

Mary's dark hair was held back from her face by a beaded head band and she wore a maroon cheesecloth top that was gathered under her bust line by some kind of stitching. The opening at the neck revealed a black turtleneck sweater. Delicate earrings made of deep red and green gems and beads dangled from her ears. She looked like someone from the seventies.

"I like jewellery making," Keely said. "This is just something I've dabbled with while I've been staying at Levallier Dell."

"Jewellery is my love too." Mary studied Keely's project with enthusiasm. "But I don't get as much time as I'd like. The shop keeps me busy. The winter months used to be the time I got on with my own projects but we seem to have extras in the town all year round now."

"Margaret River's a pretty place. I'm almost glad I had the appendix op or I might not have come this way. I was heading north."

"A lot of South Aussies end up here for one reason or another. David came from Broken Hill, which is nearly South Australian. He's a truckie. These days he directs their movements and isn't on the road quite so much."

Mary put a gentle hand on her husband's broad back.

"That's because you've got him on too short a rein," Euan teased from further down the table.

"Some people need a short rein." Anna reached over and placed bowls of steaming soup in front of them. "Flynn's had a time of it while you've been away."

"He worries too much." Euan shook his head.

"Where is he, anyway?" Sean asked. He was the one ladling the soup into the bowls. "Keely and I are the only young ones here."

"Watch it, little brother," Megan threatened. "Terry and I aren't exactly in our dotage and there are your nephews."

"Flynn called," Anna said. "He'll be a bit late so we'll start without him."

Keely smiled down at her soup. She had been vaguely disappointed there was no Flynn at the table when she'd come in. It had been good working with both the Levallier men today. She had seen a different side to them. Levallier Dell was special to both but Flynn was a very organised person and his father took life much more casually. She imagined that would be frustrating for Flynn.

There was a noise from the back of the house.

"Speak of the devil." Anna beamed as Flynn stepped through the door.

His face was flushed and his eyes shone. "Hello, everyone. Sorry I'm late." He stopped and reached behind him. "I hope you don't mind, Anna. I've brought a friend."

A tall, dark-haired woman stepped out from behind him.

"This is Katerina. She's Theo's granddaughter, back for a holiday."

Keely glanced around at the smiling faces, as the chorus of voices that had welcomed her only a little while earlier now welcomed Katerina. She noticed Euan wasn't smiling. He turned his attention back to his food. Anna shuffled chairs to make another space and fussed over Flynn while Sean jumped up to ladle more soup.

Keely concentrated on her food. She recalled her meeting with Flynn the day before, when he'd made it clear the invitation to the meal that night was for the Levallier men only. Now here he was casually bringing an extra guest himself.

"Where is home, Katerina?" Megan asked.

"Please call me Kat." Everyone listened as Kat told them about the Yarra Valley and her links with Margaret River. She was a very attractive woman. Beyond pretty, vivacious was a better word. Like Flynn's, her eyes were bright and her skin glowed. Flynn joked about knocking her off her pony when she was a little girl and put his arm casually around her shoulders. Kat smiled back at him. They looked perfectly at ease with each other.

Keely sat quietly in her chair but Kat, who was sitting across from her, was keen to include her in the conversation.

"What kind of work do you do, Keely?" she asked.

"I'm a teacher."

"So am I," Megan said. "Secondary or primary?"

"Secondary but—"

"We're often short on relief teachers here." Megan lurched forward in her chair, her eyes bright. "If you stick around there'd be work if you ever wanted it."

Keely shifted in her chair. She wished she hadn't mentioned it. "I'd prefer to have a complete break from teaching...it can be so... demanding."

"There are other avenues for creative people besides teaching." Euan's quiet words surprised her. She looked along the table and met his reassuring gaze.

"We also need to be practical." Anna tutted. "There's a teacher shortage. Last term Megan went back to school when she was still getting over a nasty wog because there was no one to take her class."

"I won't be here for much longer..." Keely stumbled over the words and was relieved when Terry asked Kat about her family winery and turned the attention of the table elsewhere.

Keely noticed Kat hesitate before she spoke. She hadn't appeared to be the shy type, just the opposite really. Self-assured and confident was how Keely would describe her. Keely felt like a faded flower in comparison to the vibrant Katerina.

Anna's beautiful roast congealed on Keely's plate. She could only pick at it. Her hunger had waned, as had the shine on the evening. The talk of teaching had brought all the old demons out to haunt her again. Just the thought of walking into a classroom made her tender stomach churn.

"So Flynn, do you need any help with the Divine Wine and Dine weekend?" Sean asked later as the teas and coffees were passed around.

Flynn lowered his gaze. Keely thought he looked uncomfortable and wondered why.

"I haven't thought about it much yet," he mumbled.

"Well, you'd better," Sean said. "It's only two weeks away. I think we've got everything organised here. I'll be into exams but I could give you a hand if you like."

"You'll have your work cut out in the cafe," Megan said and turned to Flynn. "There are a couple of kids in my home economics class who would love the experience."

"Margs will be bursting at the seams again and we haven't recovered from the school holidays yet." Anna groaned.

Mary leaned into Keely's ear. "I love it, though," she said. "It's full on but it's fun."

"Where is Margs?" Keely asked.

Mary chuckled. "It's what some of us locals call the town, a kind of affectionate name for a friendly place. We literally overflow when we hold special weekends like the Divine Wine and Dine."

"Margaret River is such a big region these days," David said. "There's a huge gourmet weekend later in the year but we've been running this smaller homegrown event for twelve years. It's a fundraiser for local charities. It's a good way to pull the community together and the money goes to a good cause."

"David's on the organising committee so he's in the thick of it." Mary patted her husband's hand. "The phone has been running hot at our place."

"Pappou has had everyone working around the clock so that the cellar-door extensions would be finished in time and Michael is preparing a gourmet menu," Kat said. "It will be a big weekend."

"It's good to have Levallier Dell on the list this time, Euan," David said.

"I didn't know it was."

Euan's reply was quiet and Keely noticed the firm set of his jaw. There was a momentary silence around the table.

"Well, that will teach you for staying away so long," Anna rebuked.

"Will you still be here, Keely?" Sean asked.

"I don't know. What happens?"

"It's a great weekend," he said. "People come from all over."

"They can just wander the region and take in the sights, the wineries and entertainment," Megan said.

"Or they can purchase a Divine Wine and Dine passport and a special map," David said. "That gives them four meals over the course of the weekend and access to some wineries, like Levallier Dell, that aren't normally open to the public."

Keely glanced past David to Euan. He was holding his coffee cup in both hands and staring into it.

"What kind of food will you have, Flynn?" Kat asked.

"I've been waiting for Euan to get back to discuss it with him."

"You're running out of time," David said. "The programs have to be printed soon. I need to know the details of what's on offer at Levallier Dell."

"Fancy leaving you two in charge of food," Anna teased.

"Perhaps we could organise something in conjunction with River Dynasty. Pappou has plenty of..." Kat was cut off by the scraping of Euan's chair on the floor as he shoved it back and stood up.

"I think Flynn and I need to discuss this privately," he said quietly. A small muscle in his cheek twitched. "Thank you for the meal, Anna. It was delicious, as always, but I think I should take Keely home. She's had a busy day, for someone who's still recuperating from an operation."

Keely felt the full force of everyone's attention as she rose from her seat. She shuffled backwards just as David pulled at her chair, which caused her to lose her balance. She flopped back down and, as if in slow motion, the chair tipped backwards and crashed into the cupboard behind her. A jolt of pain slashed across her stomach and she gasped.

"Are you hurt?" Anna rushed around the table. Everyone stood up and Euan was quickly at her side.

"David, you bully," Mary chided.

"I'm sorry...I was only..." David looked positively mortified.

"I'm alright," Keely mumbled. The spasms of pain eased a little and allowed her to breathe again.

"Can you stand?" Euan asked.

"For goodness sake, Euan, let the poor girl get her breath back," Anna said. "She's lost all her colour again. Take your time, Keely. I'll make you a fresh cup of tea."

"I should take her home," Euan said.

"Nonsense, she needs to sit for a minute. Sean, put that kettle on."

Keely felt like a rag doll being tossed about. Euan stepped back and the others started to leave.

"I'm sorry, Keely," David said again and helped her to her feet.

"Please don't worry." She managed a weak smile. "I'm the clumsy one. I'll be fine."

The room emptied quickly. Keely's tumble had finished off the evening, which had begun to deteriorate with the mention of Levallier Dell's involvement in the Divine Wine and Dine weekend. Flynn and Katerina had been the first to leave. Then Sean helped his sister and her husband bustle his young nephews out to the car. Keely looked around and realised that Euan had disappeared as well.

"There you are." Anna put a cup of tea in front of her. "I've put in an extra spoon of sugar. You could do with the energy. Now I think you should also take some pain relief."

Keely went to protest but Anna cut her off. "You will probably be sore for a while now. I've had the very same op and tried to do too much too soon. Didn't do any damage but I had a restless night with pain. A couple of tablets will give you a good night's sleep."

She left the room and shut the door behind her. Keely looked around the empty table. Behind her she heard the fridge begin to hum. She took a sip of the tea and wrinkled her nose. It was very sweet.

* * *

Euan walked back into the house. His hands were shoved deep in his pockets and his head was lowered so that he nearly walked straight into Anna, who was standing just inside the door, her hands planted firmly on her hips.

"I wondered where you'd got to," she said.

"Just getting some fresh air. Keely had enough people fussing around her."

"You seem to have taken her under your wing, nonetheless."

"What's that supposed to mean?" Euan clenched his jaw. Anna was a good mate but sometimes she overstepped the mark.

"What about your own child? When are you going to pay him some attention?"

"Flynn's doing okay. And he's not a child." Euan stepped around Anna, moving on up the passage. He didn't want to be reminded of his inadequacies as a parent. He knew them well enough.

She followed him. "He's hurting, Euan."

"He has to suck it up. He's not a little boy anymore."

"You're right. He'll be thirty-three next week or have you forgotten his birthday again? He hasn't been a little boy since Lucy died. He turned into an adult overnight. Who do you think runs the place when you're not here? He has to manage, then you come home and take over again as if you've never been away."

Euan stopped just short of the kitchen door and turned slowly back to face her. "That's enough," he growled. "We'll sort it out ourselves."

"Will you, Euan? When? It might be too late if he heads off and works somewhere else. Flynn has been trying to prove to his one surviving parent how good he is and you take it all for granted. And not only that but he has to live with small-town gossip. Stories of your exploits fly around every time you go off, even if it's only for a weekend."

"You know as well as I do it's more fiction than fact."

"Well, now you've presented the rumour-mongers with reality on a plate." She waved a hand towards the kitchen door. "Peg that works for Mary has told the whole district about the young woman you've moved into the house. Hugh's gone off to Perth and your workers have added their bit, including the part about Flynn moving out."

"Hugh's taken his family to Perth for wedding shopping. Nothing to do with us, and Flynn's been on his high horse over nothing again." Euan felt no need to explain but he knew Anna was right. The more he'd tried to keep his life private the more interesting he'd made it for the busybodies of the district. Maybe that's what Hugh had been hinting at before he left the other day. Flynn could look after himself, he always had, but Euan didn't like the idea of Keely being tainted by gossip.

There was a bang from the back of the house and Sean's heavy steps echoed up the passage.

"Whatever possessed you to bring such a young woman home?" Anna lowered her voice.

"She had nowhere else to go. She's a guest." Euan paused and looked directly into Anna's dark eyes. "That's all."

Sean reached them just as they opened the kitchen door. Anna bustled into the room ahead of the men.

"Sorry I've been so long, Keely," she said. "Oh, you've finished your tea."

Euan followed her into the kitchen. Keely was propped at the sink. She had the water running fast, rinsing her cup. She glanced back at them.

"Yes, thanks. It was just what I needed. I'm feeling much better now."

Even though her hair formed a veil over her face, Euan noticed the red flush on her neck that he'd observed several times before. Damn it, he thought. Perhaps she'd heard some of his conversation with Anna. When he'd first met Keely he'd thought she was troubled by something. He was hoping she'd find some peace at the River, not add to her worries.

"Ready to go then?" he asked.

"Yes."

Anna and Sean fussed over Keely all the way to the car. She thanked them again for their hospitality, rejected their offers of help and climbed inside. There was a pained expression on her face as she sank back into the old leather seat. The sheet of tablets Anna had pressed upon her were clutched tightly in her hand.

Euan turned on the radio, not sure what to say. Keely tipped her head back and closed her eyes, saving him the trouble of conversation.

CHAPTER

12

The sun was just a hint of light in the eastern sky as Flynn made his way up the track towards the house. He hummed softly as he walked but at the same time his mind raced over the plans for the week ahead.

The blending they had done the day before had gone well. Euan had declared the sauvignon blanc semillon was ready to bottle. Flynn was relieved. Their ideas differed. Euan still liked to store the wine in oak once the fermentation was complete and it was a process Flynn didn't feel confident with. Euan's protracted time away had Flynn worried the wine had been left too long but everything appeared to be going to plan.

Flynn almost bounced as he walked. This was the best part of winemaking. After the nurturing, the harvest, the maturing, each stage fraught with possible problems, the bottling was, for him, the crowning glory, the moment when man and nature had done their best to create the perfect wine. He and Euan had, amazingly, come to the same conclusion. The wine should be bottled.

He dug his hands deeper into his pockets and stopped to look back towards the river. Normally he loved this time of day but it was a particularly cold morning.

The chardonnay from last season was ageing well. The last summer had been a cool one and the wine in the oak barrels had developed great texture and weight and was getting ready to come out of barrel. He was hopeful they would be able to reproduce it again with this coming vintage but there were no guarantees.

He stamped his feet and exhaled. His breath formed a small white cloud in the nippy air. Thankfully, they didn't get frosts in their region but there was nothing as unpredictable as the weather. Anything was possible. He'd seen the damage the freezing conditions could do, during his time in South Australia. Frost was not good during bud burst.

Light shone from the kitchen as he approached the house. He hoped his father would be alone. There were several things they needed to sort out before Hugh and the rest of the workers arrived.

Euan was standing behind the breakfast bar, a coffee cup in his hand. He waved it at Flynn. "Want one?"

"Thanks."

Flynn glanced around before he sat down. The door to the bedroom across the room was still shut. He hoped that meant Keely wasn't up yet.

★ ★ ★

Keely lay cocooned under the covers as the murmur of male voices rose and fell beyond the door. She wished she could stay in bed all day. She felt tired and groggy after a restless night trying to get comfortable. The spasms of pain across her stomach had kept her awake for a long time. Her pain-relief tablets were all gone and if it hadn't been for Anna's she may not have slept at all. Anna had been right. Keely should have taken the tablets straight away. When she'd finally dragged herself up to swallow them, the clock had shown two am. She'd tried to distract herself with her phone until she'd drifted off to sleep but now that she was awake again she felt washed out, like she had when she'd just left hospital.

There were other things that had kept her awake. The snatches of words she had overheard the night before replayed in her mind. It was mortifying to think she was the centre of local gossip. She'd hardly seen anyone before the meal at Anna's and yet there were stories circulating about her, embarrassing stories. She blushed and eased herself gingerly off the bed. She had to move on before she caused the Levallier family any more grief.

It was a chilly morning again. She carefully pulled a windcheater on over her pyjamas and opened the door to the family room.

Euan and Flynn were sitting at the table. She could tell by their surprised looks neither of them had been expecting to see her.

"Good morning." Keely took a deep breath and slowly straightened her shoulders.

"How are you?" Euan rose quickly. "Can I get you some breakfast?"

"I'm fine." Keely gritted her teeth as another spasm tugged at her. "I don't need anything, thanks. I just wanted to thank you for your kindness. It's been great to have such a lovely place to recuperate but I should get on with my travels. I wondered if anyone was going into town. I'd like a lift to the bus." She stopped, pressed her lips together and breathed in through her nose.

Both men stared at her for a minute then Flynn spoke. "I could run you—"

"You don't have to go yet." Euan's words cut him off. "You don't look too good."

"I'll be fine, I just…" The pain surged across her stomach and Keely reached for the back of a chair to steady herself.

"This is nonsense." Euan strode across the room and helped her to sit. "Flynn, make Keely a cup of tea. We need to talk."

"Please don't fuss. I'll be fine."

"No, you're not." Euan dragged another chair close. Heat burned her cheeks and she looked down. Her unbrushed hair fell across her face and through the strands she could see a dirty mark down the front of her windcheater. I must look a wreck, she thought and bit her lip.

"Here." Flynn put a cup beside her and began to move away.

"Stay, Flynn. You're a part of this," Euan said.

"It's nothing to do with me."

"Yes it is. Sit down."

Flynn hesitated then slowly lowered himself to a chair.

Euan turned to her. "First, I must apologise for last night," he said. "I think you inadvertently overheard a conversation between Anna and myself that would have upset you."

Keely wanted to protest but, as always, she could feel the heat spreading down her neck. She rubbed at the mark on her windcheater.

"I don't know how much you heard but I am guessing the part involving the rumours about you. Flynn and I have to take responsibility for that."

"What!" Flynn jumped to his feet.

Keely took a quick look from Euan to Flynn. Euan's face was calm but Flynn's was taut with anger.

"Don't drag me into this." He gripped the back of his chair.

"We're both responsible for the rumours about Keely."

"That's ridiculous. I haven't spoken to anyone about her, except to tell Anna you had someone staying."

"It's not what we've said. You know what this place is like. It's what we haven't said. I brought Keely here and didn't introduce her to Hugh or any of the workers. Not that she was well enough but they'd have seen her about the place. Add to that you moving into the studio and I guess it's made for a good story."

"It doesn't matter," Keely mumbled.

"Yes, it does. I don't care what they say about me but it's not fair on you." Euan waved a hand at Flynn. "Sit down again."

Keely could see the rigid outline of Flynn's jaw. He was so like Euan.

"Please," Euan said softly this time.

Flynn walked slowly around the chair and sat down on the edge of it.

"Hear me out, both of you." He turned to Keely again. "I think you should stay until you're fully recovered."

"I'm—"

He put up a hand. "I know you say you are but I don't believe you. The fall you had last night was a bit of a setback. Better that you rest a few more days, perhaps see the local doctor and get the all clear, then you can leave. One of us will drive you back to Perth if that's where you want to go."

Keely wavered. She should move on but he was right, she didn't feel that well. How had she got herself into this mess? What had happened to her finding a fresh start in WA? She'd wanted a new direction, to take more control of her life, but her plans kept changing. In spite of all that, she liked Levallier Dell. Her thoughts strayed to the warm bed she'd just left.

"Flynn, you need to move back into the house," Euan said.

"That's not going to change things." Flynn shook his head.

"Maybe not, but it's ridiculous you living in that old studio when you've got a perfectly good room here in your own house."

"Please do, Flynn. I feel bad that you moved out because of me." Keely met his eyes before he looked away. Was he embarrassed? Anyway, whatever the aloof Flynn thought, it was time to make a stand and do what she wanted.

"Okay," he said, "but I'll have to do it later. We've got a full day planned."

Keely clasped her hands tightly together. "You've both been caused some inconvenience because of me."

"You don't want to take any notice of gossip."

"Euan, you've been very kind," she said. "I would like to stay but only if I can do my share. I don't know anything about vineyards but I can manage meals and cleaning. If I stay, I insist on helping where I can."

Euan's clear blue eyes watched her intently. What was it about him? It was almost as if he could tell what she was thinking. She dropped her gaze as her resolve wavered.

"So it's settled then," he said. "No more talk of leaving until you feel one hundred per cent." He patted her hand, then picked up his cup and carried it to the sink.

"We've still got things that need to be decided." Flynn followed Euan back to the kitchen.

"Later, Flynn. You said yourself we have lots to do today. We can talk again tonight."

The two men paused for a moment. Like two roosters, they eye-balled each other with their chests pushed forward and their hands on their hips. Flynn was slightly taller than Euan and he had more hair but their build was very similar, tall and lean and with obvious strength of body. Then, suddenly, Flynn turned away, grabbed his beanie from the table and pulled it down hard on his head.

"I'll see you in the cellar," he said.

In his haste to escape, he hit the edge of the glass door with his knee. It thumped loudly and made the whole door vibrate. Keely smiled, a welcome release to the tension. At least she didn't have the monopoly on clumsiness.

CHAPTER
13

Keely stepped through the front door of Anna's Kitchen. It was buzzing with people lined up at the counter and Anna was busy serving them. Keely waited to one side and looked at the sweets on display behind the glass counter nearest her. Anna had all sorts, from scones and muffins to little glazed fruit tarts and cakes filled with cream. They looked tempting but Keely didn't feel hungry. She was still a little tender from the doctor's prodding fingers.

Euan had dropped her in town earlier for her check-up. She'd had to sit quite a while in the busy surgery before someone could see her. The doctor had been thorough. A woman only a little older than Keely, she'd been chatty, wanting to know all about the op and how she'd ended up in Margaret River. The doctor had pronounced progress was good, the dressings had come off and the wounds were healing well, but she suggested Keely should continue to take things easy for a few more days.

Her next stop had been at River Rainbow. She'd spent a bit there again. Thank goodness she'd been able to unblock her card once her phone was returned.

She smiled at the memory of the delightful half-hour she'd just frittered away with Mary. Finding someone with a knowledge of jewellery-making was a pleasure for both of them. Mary had started telling her about a jewellery group that met at River Rainbow but when Keely had realised the time she'd apologised and hurried off to Anna's. Euan had arranged for Flynn to collect her from the cafe when he came into town in the late afternoon. She knew he hadn't been happy about it and she didn't want to give him cause to be annoyed if she wasn't there when he arrived.

She looked around. More customers came into the shop but there was no sign of Flynn. A yelp erupted from behind the counter.

"Sam, you're in Gran's way," Anna snapped.

"Tom hit me," a small voice wailed.

Keely leaned over the counter. "Can I help, Anna?"

Anna's harried look changed to relief. "Oh, Keely dear, that would be wonderful."

"What would you like me to do?" Keely walked around the counter, uncomfortable with the scrutiny from customers caused by Anna's gushing response.

"I wouldn't expect you to understand the workings of the cof-fee machine, dear." Anna patted Keely's hand. "Do you think you could keep the boys amused out the back? Tom's meant to be doing homework. I'm on my own here till Sean gets in and it's suddenly got busy."

Keely clenched her teeth at Anna's tone. She could manage a cof-fee machine quite well. She'd worked at a cafe in her uni days but she wasn't about to explain that to Anna, in front of all these people.

Sam was standing beside his grandmother, his feet planted firmly on the floor. He glared up at Keely.

"Go out the back with Keely, Sam. There's a good lad." Anna turned back to face her busy counter.

Keely smiled at him and held out her hand but Sam continued to stand, stony-faced, dangerously near his busy grandmother. In the kitchen, she could see his older brother, Tom, running around the table. She went through the door. Behind her, there was a yelp and a shout from Anna. Sam shot into the kitchen.

Tom stopped running and looked at her. "Hello."

"Hello, Tom. What's this your gran said about homework?"

"I had to draw a diagram but Sam scribbled on it." His jaw stuck out and he glared past Keely to his little brother.

"I did not," Sam yelled.

"You did." Tom took a step towards Sam, who quickly moved behind Keely.

"Did you draw this?" Keely picked up a large piece of paper from the table. It was an intricate plan of some kind of machinery. "Can you explain to me what it is?"

"It's the milking machine," Tom said.

"From our farm," Sam said. "But he didn't put in any cows."

"It's a diagram. It's not meant to have cows on it."

"You need cows to get the milk." Sam put his chubby little hands on his hips and underlined his words with a nod of his head.

"That's right, Sam," Keely said. "But Tom is right too," she added, as Tom's jaw jutted out again. "He is doing a technical drawing of a piece of equipment. Perhaps you could draw the picture of the cows to go with it."

When Megan rushed into the kitchen fifteen minutes later, both boys were working on their respective pages. Tom was adding more detail to his diagram and Sam was colouring cows that Keely had helped him to draw. They both burst into excited descriptions of their work.

"Wow. Thanks, Keely." Megan looked lovingly at her sons as they bent their heads to their work again. She flicked on the kettle. "Mum always has the boys on Tuesday afternoons while I'm at our staff meeting. She's not usually that busy but some days I think they run riot. You've done a wonderful job."

"They're both very talented at drawing," Keely said.

"Do you think so?" Megan made them both a cup of tea and sat down next to Keely, glancing at the boys again. "Tom is always drawing machines. Sometimes they're the real thing, like the layout of the milking machine, but quite often they are fanciful creations from his head. Sam is more into animals. He likes being out with his dad, helping with the cows, but when he sits still long enough he draws too."

"He's got a good eye for drawing. I didn't help him much. He did those cows almost by himself." Keely sipped her tea and smiled. She'd actually enjoyed her time with Sam and Tom. They reminded her of her brothers when they were younger.

"You've obviously got the knack," Megan said. "Which reminds me, I mentioned to my boss, Ken, that you would possibly be here for a while. He was most interested to know. Relief teachers are hard to find at the moment."

"I'm not sure." The brightness of the afternoon dimmed. "I don't really…"

"Hi, Megan." Flynn came through from the shop. "Are you ready, Keely?"

"Can't you stay for a cuppa?" Anna came in behind him. "I've gone from knee deep in customers to no one. I could use a cup of tea."

Flynn ruffled both boys' heads. "No, sorry, still lots to do."

"Now don't forget about the teaching, Keely," Megan said. "Ken said he'd need your South Australian registration details and info to run a police check."

"A police check!" Flynn frowned. "What's to know except Keely's been listed as a missing person?"

"Nothing to do with that, brainless." Megan chuckled and gave Flynn a playful tap on the head. "Anyone who works with children has them."

"I'd have to get Mum to post my stuff from home." Keely ducked her head, acutely aware of Anna's sharp eyes on her.

"Why don't you give her the school address, Megan," Anna said. "Then it can go direct to Ken and he can get the paperwork started."

Keely watched helplessly as Megan wrote on a piece of paper.

"I've got to get going," Flynn said.

"I hope you're not taking Keely on that bike of yours," Anna said.

Keely faltered as she got up from the table. The thought of teaching was bad enough but she hadn't imagined she'd be clutching onto Flynn on the back of his bike.

"Not this time." Flynn jingled a set of keys in front of Anna.

"Well, I suppose one of those utes of yours is a slightly better option."

Keely followed Flynn outside. The afternoon sun still held some warmth. She closed her eyes, turned her face to it and took a deep breath. Despite the underlying tension at Levallier Dell, she had been happy there but the mention of teaching had brought her back to reality. The truth was, Levallier Dell was not her home, no matter how hard she imagined otherwise. And, even if she avoided it here, one day she would have to earn an income again and that meant a return to the only job she knew, teaching.

"Are you okay?"

She opened her eyes. Flynn's look was hesitant.

"Yes."

"The car is up the street a bit. I couldn't get a park nearby."

"I'm alright. It was a bit stuffy in the kitchen, that's all."

He glanced at her again then set off. She had trouble keeping up with his long strides until he stopped abruptly beside a deep green LandCruiser with Levallier Dell Wines emblazoned on the side in gold and black.

Keely looked from the gleaming car to Flynn's smiling face.

"Do you like it?" he asked.

"It's very nice." She knew little about cars. She was simply thankful it wasn't the bike. He looked relieved. She couldn't imagine why Flynn would be the slightest bit interested in what she thought about his car. "I didn't realise you had a car."

"It's new." He opened the door for her. "I've only had it a month. It's been in having the signage painted. Euan's car is old, we've got work utes and I prefer my bike but we don't have anything decent for guests and customers to travel in."

Keely sank into the comfy seat. The new-car smell enveloped her then she recalled her first arrival at the gates of Levallier Dell and the gleaming sign, along with Euan's reaction to it. This was a very nice car but if Flynn had only had it for a month, Euan probably didn't know about it. From the way Flynn was acting, she suspected it was going to cause more angst between the two Levallier men.

Keely fastened her seat belt. She might be wrong but somehow she thought the road ahead was looking bumpy again, in more ways than one.

★　★　★

"Pappou, I'm not sure that I'm the right person for the job." Kat and her grandfather were in his office. Papers and plans were spread across the desk in front of them.

"What do you mean, Katerina? You have a university degree, your mother has told me what you have been doing for her little winery and besides, you are my granddaughter. So, you see, you are exactly the right person for the job."

"But one of the boys could…"

"Bah!" He clicked his fingers. "None of them have the flair for it. Besides, they are already busy with other jobs. A business this size does not work without people managing many things. It is not like that little place in the Yarra Valley your parents call a winery. There is work at River and Ocean Dynasty for everyone." He opened his arms wide and beamed at her.

"Pappou, I'd love to…"

He threw his arms around her and hugged her tightly. "I knew you'd do it."

She struggled out of his embrace. The time had come to confess. WA was not her future, in fact her future was probably not anywhere in Australia. "I'm not accepting. It's a wonderful opportunity…" She faltered under his expectant gaze.

"Ah, but I'm rushing you, aren't I? You are on holiday. How are you getting along with Flynn Levallier? He's a hard-working young man."

Kat was surprised by his change in conversation. "He seems like a nice guy…"

He put up his hand as his mobile rang. "You need time to think things over. Take a few more days and we'll talk again." He pulled the phone to his ear. "Yes, Tony." His face creased into a frown. "No, don't do anything. I'll be right there." He shoved the phone back in his pocket. "There's a problem in the tasting room. You have a look at things here. Take your time. We'll talk again later. I have to go."

She sank into a chair and looked at the desk in front of her. Over it, she could see through the window to the vines, which she knew spread in every direction all around her. Poor Uncle Tony. Pappou might say that everyone had a bit of the business to manage but he still controlled everything.

Things weren't turning out as she'd planned. The main reason for her holiday had been to unburden herself to her grandfather. Tell him of her plans and enlist his help to convince her parents. Now she was ensnared in an even bigger trap. Pappou wanted her to be part of his business. She stood up and paced the room. She loved it here but it was not where her future lay. She stopped and gazed out through the window again. The trouble was, when Pappou wanted something, he nearly always got it.

★　★　★

"So, you went ahead and bought it?"

"We don't have a decent vehicle between us, Euan."

The two men were standing just outside the kitchen window. Keely could hear every word.

"The Volvo is fine."

"It's falling apart and not suitable if we're trying to impress customers."

"I didn't know we were."

Euan had met them under the carport when they'd driven up in the new car. The tension between Euan and Flynn had been palpable. Keely had gathered her things from the offending vehicle and hurried inside. Now she stood at the bench quietly preparing the meal. She didn't want to eavesdrop but before she could get out of the kitchen, the door slid open and Euan strode inside.

"Margaret River has changed." Flynn followed him through the door. Neither of the men noticed Keely. "Bloody hell, the whole Australian wine industry has changed. If we don't change with it, we'll go under."

"Things aren't that bad. We can still manage as we have been."

"We're too big now to be boutique and the big players are looking at us. You know there are companies who would buy us out now, if we'd let them. They're just waiting for us to go under. Theo next door would be the first to wave money at us."

Keely could see the profiled outline of Euan's taut jaw. Flynn had his back to her. She didn't move. She didn't want to be part of this scene but she had nowhere to go.

Euan lowered his voice. "Don't mention that man's name in my house."

Flynn slapped the table. "That's just it, isn't it? Your house, your vineyards. We're supposed to be partners but I have no say."

"What is it you want, Flynn?" Euan slid onto a chair at the table and Flynn pulled one up beside him. They both had their backs to her now but they were between Keely and the bedroom, and there was no way for her to move without them seeing her.

"We've got to compete. We need a long-term business plan instead of the hand-to-mouth way we've been doing things. Our range needs expanding. We need a better online presence and we've got to open our doors and let the customers see and taste what we do here, first hand."

"A cellar door," murmured Euan. "That won't sell all our wine."

"It gets people in and then we can sign them up to online sales. That cuts out the middle man and increases the profit margin."

"It's not always about the money, Flynn."

"No, but we have to make a profit or there won't be a winery for us to fight over."

Euan's shoulders slumped. From behind, he suddenly looked small in comparison to Flynn.

"You said the trip to Sydney didn't go as well as you'd hoped," Flynn said. "Perhaps it's time you shared all the details."

Keely reached for the bench to change her position and knocked a glass. It went crashing to the floor. Both men turned, startled. She bobbed down quickly to pick up the pieces and hide her embarrassment. Chairs scraped on the slate floor.

"Careful." Euan bent down beside her and helped her pick up the shards of glass. "I know I keep apologising to you for our boorish behaviour but I am sorry."

They both stood up. Flynn was just behind Euan. He was watching her carefully and a tiny grin hovered at the corners of his mouth.

"Please don't worry." Keely put the glass on some paper and turned to go.

"Please, Keely," Euan entreated. "I do mean it. Flynn and I have become so used to living alone..."

"It's fine, Euan. This is your house." She stepped around both men. "I've just got to go to the bathroom...I'll be back to finish the meal in a minute."

She closed the bedroom door behind her, leaned against it and let out a long breath. What was it about the Levallier men that unnerved her? Since she'd met them, it was as if she was back to her teenage days of blundering and blushing every five minutes. There was a low murmur of voices from the other room, then silence. Keely went into the bathroom and splashed water on her face.

* * *

By the time Keely had set the table and cooked the stir fry, both Euan and Flynn had showered. Flynn stoked up the pot belly's fire and Euan opened a bottle of wine.

They ate their meal and kept the conversation clear of vineyard issues. Euan asked Keely about the doctor's visit and how she'd filled in her day. Keely was keen to keep the mood light and as they settled back in their chairs after the meal she enthused over her second visit to River Rainbow.

"I knew you'd like it. Mary has a goldmine there. I think she has a magic spell on the place." Euan chuckled. "Once you go in you have to keep going back."

"How much does it cost to make one of these?" Flynn was running his fingers under the bead decoration draped over the wine bottle they'd just emptied.

"Not a lot, it's more the time factor."

"They're different. Tourists are always looking for some little thing to take home. It's hard to find things that are unique."

"These aren't unique. You can buy them in homeware shops."

"But not like these, made by you with Margaret River beads."

"You think I should make more?"

"Yes, and I've got just the outlet for you."

"Be careful, Keely." Euan stood up to clear the table. "I sense a plan forming in that busy mind of Flynn's. He's always up to something."

"Someone has to plan ahead." Flynn's tone was light but Keely tensed. She didn't want their relaxed evening to be spoiled.

"It must be the French grandparents' genes." Euan winked at her. "Flynn certainly didn't inherit this need for organising from his mother or me." He carried the dishes to the sink.

"Lucky you've got me, then." Flynn turned the full gaze of his blue eyes from the beads to Keely. "Now, how many of these could you make in two weeks?"

"Flynn," Euan warned from the kitchen.

"I'm not sure but..."

"We've got the Divine Wine and Dine weekend you see. We could sell them at our cellar door."

"Flynn, that's less than two weeks away and Keely is a guest."

Flynn flung an arm over the back of his chair. "I'm sorry, Euan's right, I shouldn't be asking you to do anything extra." He smiled at Keely. "But I hope you'll stay and enjoy the fun."

She smiled back and they both ignored the snort that came from the kitchen. There was something about the enthusiasm she had seen on Flynn's face that intrigued her. His normally wild hair had been tamed a little by a brush and sat neatly around his tanned, unblemished face. Despite his often-serious appearance, she could see the crinkles around his eyes and mouth that creased easily into a smile. She had enjoyed having a conversation with him where neither of them tripped over their words, and when he smiled…Keely picked up the beaded wine cover. What was she thinking? Flynn had been a moody pain in the butt since she'd arrived. Just because he was being nice to her now didn't mean he wouldn't be grumpy again the next day.

"I'd like to stay…"

A gentle knock on the door startled them all.

Flynn stood up and they could see Kat beyond the glass. He slid open the door.

"Kat, come in."

"I'm sorry. I hope I'm not interrupting. I was out walking and…"

"Walking?" Flynn took her hand. "You're freezing, come over by the fire."

"Thanks."

"What are you doing out walking at this hour?"

Flynn led her to the fire then stood behind her and rubbed her arms with his hands.

"Sorry, I hadn't intended on coming this far."

"Are you alright?" Flynn put his arm around her shoulders.

The landline rang and Euan answered it. His look went straight to Keely. She could hear her mother's sharp tones from across the room. He held out the phone. "It's your mother."

Keely looked around for her mobile. She must have left it in the bedroom.

She put the phone to her ear. "Hello, Mum."

"Why aren't you answering your mobile? I've tried several times to call you."

"Sorry, I left it in the other room." Keely knew it was going to take a while for her mum to stop panicking every time she couldn't reach her.

"Don't forget to ask her to send the papers you need," Flynn said.

"Who was that talking about paperwork? Is something wrong?"

Keely could hear the decibels rise in her mother's voice. "No, Mum. I've been asked to do some relief teaching but I need my registration and some other things."

"Oh, I didn't realise you were staying for that long."

Keely was conscious of the others in the room. "I don't know how long I'll be here," she replied vaguely. "Besides, once I'm registered I guess I could work anywhere in WA and it would help cover the bills…" She tried to sound reassuring. She hadn't intended on actually asking her mother to send the paperwork. If Megan had mentioned it again, Keely had decided to say she'd forgotten.

"That's a good idea."

Keely lowered her voice. "I'll let you know the address."

"It's in your pocket," Flynn said. "You put it there when we left Anna's."

"Who is that?" her mother asked.

Keely dug in her pocket, ignoring her mother's question. "Have you got a pen? Here is the address."

"I've put the kettle on," Euan said. "You're in charge of making the women tea or coffee, Flynn. If you'll all excuse me, I'm off to bed."

Euan's words startled Keely into action. She put a hand over the phone. "Not for me, thanks. I'll finish this call in the bedroom."

She went to her room and closed the door on the sight of Flynn standing close to Kat.

Keely had momentarily forgotten about the young woman Flynn was obviously attached to. It had been a lovely evening and Keely had enjoyed the company of both Levallier men but the last part of the conversation at the table with Flynn had been more than enjoyable. For a moment, she'd felt a real lift of her spirits, the tingle of anticipation as Flynn had talked to her about the beads and given her his full attention.

"Are you there, Keely?"

She sighed. "Yes, Mum." She tried to concentrate on what her mother was saying but she couldn't help being aware of the rise and fall of voices murmuring gently in the next room.

CHAPTER
14

A loud crack startled Keely from her sketch. She was sitting under the verandah, at the little table that had become her daytime haven. From this secluded vantage point, she could see some of the daily comings and goings from the distant sheds but she also used the table as her work area. She'd made several wine-bottle covers and some bracelets and now she was working on a sketch of the scene in front of her.

The crack came again and a dog barked. She stood up and crossed the yard to the fence. Further away to her right between the rows of vines stood a small man in a battered hat. Beyond him, stretching away over a more exposed ridge, were the vines that, since Euan's tour, Keely knew were part of the cabernet franc plantation. She watched as the man lifted his arm in the air and flicked his wrist. The whip made another sharp crack and the sound ricocheted around them.

The man looked towards the river. It was a beautiful morning and a whisper of mist still hung over the water. He gave one more flick with the whip then turned and walked directly towards her, a brown kelpie trotting beside him.

Keely wanted to step back to her verandah hideaway but he'd seen her. He studied her as he stopped, just a few feet away, and pushed back his hat. It was an old Akubra style, quite grey. She couldn't tell if that was its original shade or if it had coloured that way from years of grime. His face had the weathered complexion of a man who'd spent many years outside. He looked to be at least eighty. The rest of his clothes were clean but well worn, from the checked shirt to the grey trousers and the heavy boots. She wondered about the twine tied around each trouser leg just below his knees. He didn't look the type to be making a fashion statement.

"Jack Telford." He smiled warmly and held out his hand over the fence. Keely took it and received a firm shake. "It's a good day when I get an echo. I'm the whip cracker around these parts." His arm did a wide sweep, giving her the impression he meant more than Levallier Dell.

"I'm Keely Mitchell." She grinned and nodded towards the house. "I guess I'm the kitchen hand about these parts."

"I'd heard the Levallier boys had a lady in the house."

The smile dropped from Keely's face.

"It's about time they had the good sense to get themselves a housekeeper. I sometimes get a cuppa here but they're not the most reliable hosts."

Despite the reminder that she was the source of local gossip, there was something about Jack's kind face that made her warm to him. He'd make a good subject for a sketch. And apart from the Levallier boys, as Jack called them, she'd seen no one else for days. It would be nice to meet someone new.

"Would you like me to make you one? I've got some fresh cake."

"Thanks, Keely. A cup of tea would hit the spot right now." He reached down and patted the dog sitting patiently beside him. "Bob and I have been loading sheep."

Keely nodded. She'd seen sheep grazing between the rows of vines and assumed they belonged there.

"Drop, Bob." At Jack's command the dog sunk to his stomach. "Stay."

Jack let himself in through the gate. Keely headed towards the sliding door but Jack went in through the laundry door, came into the kitchen minus his boots, whip and hat, and sat at the table. He'd obviously been inside before.

She'd discovered there were doors in all kinds of places in this house. At the end of the laundry, there was a small passage that passed another toilet and led into an office and store room. From there, a door led outside to the cellar-door area or back into the front of the house to a formal lounge, another bathroom and, Keely assumed, other bedrooms. She hadn't liked to open the doors to see what was beyond them.

"Have you always lived around here, Jack?"

"I was born down Pemberton way. My father was a bullock driver and taught me the same. That's where I learned to crack a whip. By the time I was a young man there wasn't much call for bullock drivers so I've done all sorts. Nowdays I run a small farm not far from here. Never lost my touch with the bullocks or the knack of whip cracking, though." He smiled as Keely put the tea in front of him.

"Do you have bullocks?" Keely asked.

"Not these days. Only sheep. I run a few at Levallier Dell to help keep the weeds down but it's time to take them back to my place."

Keely studied him as he took a large bite of the cake.

"This is delicious, Keely."

"Thanks." She picked up her cup.

"My sheep respond to the crack of the whip but Bob could round them up without it or me. I like to keep my hand in with it. Back in the day I used to crack my whip for the birds."

Keely watched Jack take another mouthful of cake, puzzled by his reference to birds.

He swallowed. "The crack of the whip frightens the silvereyes. They can do a lot of damage to a crop of grapes. Levalliers didn't ever have much bother with them. Euan's always made sure there are plenty of trees to provide blossom. These days everything gets covered with nets but I like to remind those pesky little birds that Jack the Whip Cracker's still about."

He chuckled and Keely relaxed. Jack was a man who enjoyed life.

"So, Keely. What do you like to do when you're not housekeeping?"

"Bits and pieces." She smoothed the bright floral tablecloth with her hands. She'd discovered it jammed in the back of the placemat drawer. It livened up the space.

"We all do bits and pieces," Jack said. "But everyone's got something that makes them happy."

She looked out at the view through the glass. The vines shimmered green into the distance under a cloudless blue sky. She liked to cook, she enjoyed her sketching, but the thing that she got lost in was making the jewellery. If she was honest it was the only time she was truly happy and the rest of the world didn't matter.

"I like to draw and make jewellery," she said softly.

"Well, there's a fine thing. I don't know much about jewellery but there's plenty of material for your pencil around here."

"Yes." Keely sighed and stood up. It was a long time since she'd admitted to anyone that she drew. "Would you like another cup of tea?"

"No thanks, I must be on my way, though I wouldn't mind a piece of that cake to take with me."

Keely wrapped a large piece of the lemon cake and met him on the verandah where he was doing up his laces. She watched as he adjusted the twine tied below his knees.

He looked up. "Bowyangs."

"Pardon?"

"Stops my trousers dragging on the ground." He grinned. "Bit of protection as well. Snakes start to get active this time of year. Wouldn't want one sliding up my trouser leg. Could get nasty."

Keely glanced around the yard. She'd never given snakes much thought. Surely she wasn't in any danger of meeting one here.

Jack held out his hand. "Goodbye, Keely. I hope we'll meet again."

She looked at his wise old face. She felt sure it masked a myriad of stories. Just like she'd experienced when she first met Euan, there was something about Jack that made her want to capture him in a sketch. She shook his hand and took a deep breath.

"Would you mind if I took your picture and sketched you, Jack?"

His eyes lit up and he lifted the hat he'd just put on his head and made a sweeping bow. "I'd be honoured, Miss Mitchell. I hope you're not one of those real-life artistes who likes to draw the naked figure."

"Oh…no…I prefer clothes on…I'll just get my phone." Keely rattled the glass door in her haste to get through it and behind her Jack's chuckle reverberated in the morning air.

* * *

"I'm amazed at how much busier the whole area is since I was here last." Kat sat in her cousin Michael's office while he went over his menu. "I've been looking at the tourist map with all the wineries and this week Pappou wants me to visit as many as I can."

Michael put down his pen. "Spying, hey?"

"I like to think of it more as getting to know the opposition. Surely you check out the other restaurants?"

"I don't get a lot of time."

Kat pressed her fingertips together and raised her eyebrows.

"Well, maybe sometimes," he said. "Don't look like that. You are the image of Pappou."

"Thanks." She grimaced.

"You're going to do the job then."

She studied her cousin. He was a few years older than she was. He had been an apprentice chef at one of the large hotels in Perth, then had spent several years developing his culinary skills in Greece and Europe. Now, here he was, running the restaurant at River Dynasty.

"You know about that?"

"Pappou has been pestering me to take it on." Michael dropped his pen on the desk. "He has no idea of the work involved in running this restaurant. Anyway, he hasn't mentioned it for a while. Then you turn up, the prodigal granddaughter, and he kills the fatted calf. I put two and two together."

"You've travelled overseas, Michael. Are you happy stuck here, working for the family?"

Michael contemplated the question, his deep brown eyes pools of thought. His hair was closely cut over a perfect olive complexion and when he wasn't frowning, like he was now, he was quite handsome. This was the first time they'd had a chance to talk alone and she wondered if he had a girlfriend. His brothers and most of his cousins were married.

"I don't feel like I'm stuck here, as you put it," he said. "I could have kept wandering Europe or even other parts of Australia but I was ready to come home. This business is a good opportunity. People come from all over the world to sample our wines and now we can also provide them with world-class food."

"Now you're sounding like Pappou. Did you get a choice? Don't you feel trapped?"

Michael frowned again. "No. This is a family business. We all work together. I guess you don't feel quite a part of it yet because you're tied to your mother's business. Is there work for you there?"

"Oh, yes. Pappou thinks it's only a small estate and I guess, compared to what he has here, it is, but I could have plenty to do there if I wanted." Her last words trailed away.

"But maybe there are other things. You're young, Kat. Perhaps you need time to decide what you want. Travel like I did, see the world before you settle down."

"My parents have a path mapped out at home for me and now Pappou has one here."

"I'm sure your parents could manage, and Peter's wife, Angela, would take on the marketing here. She's a bit shy of Pappou but I know she'd do a good job."

Kat let out a long sigh. "They all expect me to do what they want."

Michael snorted. "The little cousin I remember never let anyone boss her about. How many times did we have to rescue you from scrapes? You would always do what you wanted and we had to keep an eye on you. Mumma! Look out if a hair on your head was harmed. Remember that time you wanted to go to explore the caves? You set off on your own when the adults wouldn't take you. Peter and I followed you to make sure you didn't get into trouble and we got the blame for taking you."

"I was a little girl then."

"The same Katerina lives within." He reached across and put a hand on her shoulder. "Follow your heart."

* * *

Keely kept to the path through the vines that led to the little tin roof she could see from the back verandah. While Flynn had occupied the studio, as he and Euan called it, she had avoided coming this way on her walks around the property. Now that Flynn had moved back to the house she was keen to get a closer look at the studio and the river. This path was well worn and the obvious choice.

She'd given up on her sketching. The portrait of Jack was coming along but the bright promise of the morning had turned to a murky, dull afternoon. There was no wind but an almost ominous gloom hung in the warm air and large, dark clouds clung to the horizon. It had made her feel restless and she'd decided to explore.

The vines suddenly gave way to an open space and she was standing at the back of the studio. There was a door in the middle of the ramshackle wall but the newly cut grass grew right up to it and Keely had the impression it hadn't been opened for a long time.

She followed the path around the building. In front of her the river meandered away to a distant bend. In the poor light of the late afternoon, the water was a deep green, a reflection of the trees that bent over it, some caressing the water with wispy branches. It was a restful sight. The path continued on down to the edge of the water, then split and followed the bank in both directions. The studio had been built above a slight bend in the river so that the front door faced a long stretch of water..

Keely dragged her gaze from the river and turned to look back at the old structure. The tin roof was speckled brown with rust. There was a wobbly verandah right across the front. The building was made of wooden slats and at one end a chimney reached above the roofline in a tower of solid brick. From the front, it looked old but not neglected. The remains of a garden still grew around an old birdbath and someone had mown the grass and cut it away from the flagstone steps that were an alternate route to the front door.

She looked around. The interest she had in the building overcame her fear that she was snooping. It was dark under the verandah and she was keen to get a closer look. She stepped up the flagstones. The front was paved with an assortment of old bricks, and two cane chairs sat either side of the door and an old bunch of dried lavender hung on the wall.

She cupped her hand to the window in the chimney end of the building and looked in. The room beyond appeared quite large. She could see a big wooden table, chairs and a couch. Glancing around once more, she moved to the door and tried the handle. It opened easily to her touch and she stepped quickly into the room.

The floor was polished wood. She walked past the big table to the end of the room where an old wood stove and kitchen bench took up most of the wall. An even more archaic-looking rounded cream fridge and little low sink were the only other kitchen facilities. She turned back to the room. A couple of small patchwork pieces hung on the walls. It was furnished with an assortment of chairs and throw rugs and there was a cosy feel to it.

The door leading to the back was shut but opposite her the door to the bedroom was open and through it she could see an old wrought-iron bed. It was stripped, and the patchwork quilt draped over the bed end reached the floor. Another large patchwork wall hanging covered the wall above the bed.

This had to be Lucy's studio. The place she had come to work on her patchwork. Suddenly, Keely felt guilty at her intrusion and went back to the verandah, closing the door behind her. The river caught her attention again and she sat for a moment, letting the tranquillity of the scene wash over her.

A rustling noise came from the side of the studio. Someone was coming. She stayed where she was, frozen to her seat, afraid to be caught snooping. A man came into view, dragging a large roll of poly pipe behind him. She recognised his tall frame and broad hat. It was the same bloke who had walked past the house a few days earlier.

Keely huddled into the chair. He continued down the dirt track to the river then turned and followed the path to his left, which took him past the studio. He was intent on his job and seemed unaware of Keely's intrusion. Just as he was about to step out of her line of sight he stopped, bent down, fiddled with his boot then glanced in her direction.

Keely held her breath, silently cursing herself for being nosey.

He turned back to the pipe and walked on, dragging the bundle behind him. He mustn't have seen her or, surely, he would have spoken.

She pushed away the thought of being an intruder and gazed along the length of the river stretched out in front of her. She could sit here if she wanted. Euan had told her to go where she liked. It was such a tranquil setting with a creative feel. It was easy to imagine Lucy would have liked it here. Maybe, if it was okay with Euan, she could spend some time at the studio. It would be the perfect place to sketch on a day with better light and she could leave her beads spread out on the table in the kitchen.

Keely pulled herself up. What was she thinking? She couldn't expect Euan to extend his hospitality for much longer, although both Euan and Flynn had seemed happy for her to stay, at least until the Divine Wine and Dine weekend. She stood and made her way back to the house. The other night her mother had grilled her for several minutes on the Levallier men. It was when she'd started questioning their motives that Keely had become annoyed and made an excuse to end the call. She understood why her mother was worried but she wasn't going to have the comfortable comradery she felt with Euan spoiled. She wasn't ready to include Flynn in that statement but at least he was being civil most of the time.

She glanced up. The weather was looking as if a shower was imminent so she put her head down and quickened her steps.

Flynn appeared from between the rows just in front of her. He was looking the other way, inspecting one of the rose bushes that grew at the start of alternate rows of vines. She briefly toyed with the idea of ducking into another row to avoid him then decided she needed to be more confident where Flynn was concerned. She straightened her shoulders and strode on.

The rose bush was covered in young blooms and, as she came up behind him, Flynn stooped to sniff one.

"They're beautiful, aren't they," she said.

He jerked back as if he'd been pricked by a thorn. "A beautiful nuisance."

"Oh…" Keely's resolve flooded away and she felt awkward with him again.

"Lucy planted them."

"Out here?"

"The roses supposedly foretell what is going to happen to the vines," he said.

Keely looked from Flynn to the rose bush, totally lost for words now.

"Euan says they are the first to show water loss and bug infestation."

"Are they?"

"I'd rather rely on checking the vines themselves," he said. "The roses just get in the way."

Keely looked down at her feet. Perhaps that's what he was thinking about her. He'd only accepted her presence because Euan had asked him to.

"I'd better get going. Hugh needs some help replacing a pipe."

He strode past her down the track. Keely resisted the urge to turn and watch him. She didn't know how to take Flynn. He was as prickly as the roses. She glanced at the threatening sky. Strange, it looked as if it might rain but the air was so warm. Another conundrum like Flynn.

By the time she reached the back door, she was walking briskly and replaying their brief conversation in her head, wondering if there was a hidden message in his words. She slid back the door with some force, only to be met by the startled faces of Euan and two guests seated at the table.

"Oh...I'm sorry." She lowered her head to let the protective veil of hair fall across her face. "I'll come back later."

"Keely, wait." Euan stood up and beckoned her in. "This is Pam and Connor, good friends of mine."

Keely glanced at the newcomers, who both studied her with interest. They looked to be in their forties and both were dressed in jeans and plain shirts.

"Hello, Keely." Connor reached out to shake her hand. "I'm glad he can still call us friends."

"We're not letting that mug next door come between us," Euan said grimly.

Keely let her hand be clamped in Connor's firm shake. His expression was unreadable.

"Come on you two, you'll be scaring Keely." Pam's smile was warm. "It's nice to meet you. Euan's been telling us about the rough start to your holiday. I hope you're on the mend."

"I'm much better now. Thanks to Euan's hospitality."

"So you can add healer to your repertoire of talents," Pam said.

"It's the peace and the river that have done the trick," Euan said.

"It's certainly a beautiful spot just here." Pam's look was wistful as she glanced towards the window.

"Pam and Connor used to own the land next door," Euan said.

"Oh, it must have been hard to move away," Keely said.

"We didn't actually live on the property. Just planted the vines there." Pam gave a rueful glance in Euan's direction. "We live in town."

"Has Euan got you out on that surfboard yet?" Conner changed the subject.

"No…"

"If he tries to convince you it's safe as houses, don't listen to him. He nearly killed me and I've got the scars to prove it."

Connor started to pull up his shirt and Pam put a restraining hand on him. "I think it's a bit early to be showing Keely your war wounds, darling."

Keely looked at their empty cups and made a move to the kitchen. "Can I make anyone another coffee?"

"I'll do it," Euan said.

"We really have to go." Pam stood up.

Connor draped a casual arm over his wife's shoulder. "We wanted to call in and say hello, once we heard on the grapevine that you were back."

He chuckled, and Pam shook her head. They were a friendly couple. Keely already felt relaxed with them in the short time she'd known them.

"We thought we might have a barbecue this weekend. Can you come?" Pam asked. "All of you, of course." She nodded at Keely.

"That's a great idea," Euan said. "But why don't we have it here? Keely hasn't met many of the locals yet and it's Flynn's birthday. I'd better organise something to mark his thirty-three years. How about Sunday night?"

Keely walked with Euan to see them off. Perhaps when she spoke to her mum next she could tell her about Jack and Pam and Connor. It would give them something else to focus on and make a change from questions about the Levalliers and possible work as a relief teacher. The latter only made her feel anxious.

Connor tooted the horn. Keely smiled and waved. She was determined to stay and enjoy the carefree days at Levallier Dell, just a little longer.

CHAPTER
15

The phone rang in the kitchen. Keely pushed back the covers, shivered and pulled on the jacket she had been using as a dressing gown. She was getting used to the early mornings. In South Australia, they would have changed the clocks to daylight saving hours by now, but Western Australians still kept the same hours regardless of how early the sun rose. Here it was seven o'clock, and she was still in bed. Euan and Flynn got up at six, so she didn't join them for breakfast. The early mornings were still cool but this morning was particularly chilly and not as light as usual. Maybe the murkiness of the day before was still about.

The phone stopped ringing and she heard the murmur of a voice. Euan or Flynn must still be inside. She pulled back the curtain and looked down the slope to the river. The day was very grey and she could barely see the trees. She closed her eyes, breathed deeply then turned and looked at the wall hanging. There was certainly something therapeutic about this place. She could almost feel herself healing. She hummed as she crossed the room to the bathroom. She wasn't going to let the grey spoil her day. It was full of promise.

When she finally stepped out into the family room, she was surprised to see Flynn sitting at the table. Lined up in front of him were three bottles of wine and his head was bent over a pad of paper. Outside, she could see the roses blowing in the wind and a light shower of rain dampened the path.

"Good morning," Keely said.

Flynn glanced up, a momentary look of surprise on his face. "Oh, hello," he said, and then looked back at his paper.

Nice to see you too, Keely thought. He really could be the rudest man. She was determined not to let the weather or Flynn spoil her good mood. "Have you had breakfast? Would you like me to get you something?"

He was silent for a moment, staring at the page. He looked up just as she gave up and moved towards the kitchen.

"What? Oh, no…thanks. I've eaten."

Keely boiled the kettle and put some bread in the toaster. Flynn continued to worry over his paper and she took her breakfast to the other end of the table. Just as she sat down he leaned back and threw down his pen.

"Bugger it," he muttered. He looked like a man who'd had little sleep, his eyes were red and the wispy ends of his hair fluffed out around his head.

"Is there a problem?"

"Only for me." Flynn grimaced and stood up. "I have good ideas but sometimes I bite off more than I can chew. I need to clone myself." He went to the kitchen and made himself a coffee.

"Can I help?"

"Not really." He came back to the table. "Oh, that was Mary on the phone earlier. She said to ask you if you'd like to join her jewellery group tomorrow night. Evidently there are a few keen women who get together and share their talents. You're welcome to use one of our vehicles or I could run you in if you're not up to driving."

Keely stared at Flynn. He was looking back at his paper again, coffee cup in hand. She really couldn't make him out. He was almost rude when she first came in and now he was bending over backwards to be helpful.

"Thanks, I'm not sure. I'll see..." Her voice trailed away. She liked Mary but she wasn't certain she'd enjoy the jewellery group.

Flynn chewed on his pen and looked at her. "What's an easy food to prepare and serve in large numbers?"

Keely was taken aback by his question.

He stood up and paced the room. "Sorry. It's not your problem. I'm just thinking out loud really. Mary was also ringing to remind me that I have to organise the menu for the Divine Wine and Dine program. Euan gets angry every time I mention it but I've committed us to it and it will be good for business. We have to go ahead now."

"If I understood what you were trying to do, I might be able to help."

Flynn stopped pacing and looked at her as if he was seeing her for the first time. "You're good with food, aren't you? The meals you've cooked have been great."

I'll take that as a compliment, she thought. "What is it you are trying to do, Flynn?"

"I need to come up with a menu that matches our wines." He tapped each of the bottles in front of him.

"Why?"

"OK, so, to take part in the Divine Wine and Dine weekend people have to buy a passport. That entitles them to visit a number of wineries including Levallier Dell. They may call in just to taste the wines but I've also put us down for lunches on Saturday and Sunday."

"How many people would you expect?"

"I don't know. Could be hundreds."

"Really?" Keely grimaced. No wonder Euan wasn't happy about it.

"We'll have a bit of an idea closer to the weekend. People tend to book once they've decided on their route for the day, some will just come for the tastings but we could get others making last-minute decisions to eat."

Keely could understand he was under pressure. Who could possibly manage such a thing?

"Kat says they're running their full restaurant menu at River Dynasty. That will give us some opposition."

"Where were you planning to feed these people?" Keely thought perhaps they must have had some kind of kitchen facility at the sheds.

"Out the side in the old cellar-door area. When the house was built my mother insisted on including a bar and undercover area that could be used as a place for tastings and sales. We haven't used it much."

He paused, the muscle in his jaw twitched. She'd noticed Euan did the same when he was tense.

"Anyway, it needs a good clean-up but it should be fine."

"What did you think you would feed them?"

Flynn turned and she looked down quickly. His look was intense – when he studied her it was as if he could see right inside her. A chair scraped and she peeked up. Flynn was sitting at the table again, his head in his hands.

"We need something with fish or chicken for the chardonnay, maybe a red meat for the cab sauv and finish with something sweet for the semillon."

There was silence for a moment, as they both digested what he was saying.

Finally Keely spoke. "Let me see if I understand this. You want to supply a possible hundred or more people with a lunch, under that pergola area, without any kitchen facilities but a sink."

Flynn's face was full of anguish. He pushed back his chair. "I'll ring Mary and tell her we can't do lunch. I don't know why I ever thought it could be done." He strode towards the phone. Keely felt an urge to help. He certainly didn't do things by halves but his passion was infectious.

"Wait, Flynn. Can you give me the morning to get my head around this, before you cancel?"

He spun around. "Have you got an idea?" There was that spark back in his eyes and, once again, Keely had to look away.

"Maybe. I need a while to think it through."

"Take all day." Flynn grabbed her hands. "Keely, I'd be forever in your debt if you came up with a good idea."

She pulled from his grip as the familiar warmth spread over her cheeks and down her neck. "I'm not making any promises. Anyway, you might not like what I come up with."

He picked up his beanie and smiled. "I'll be back about lunchtime." He pushed the sliding door open, then turned back. "Thanks, Keely."

"Don't thank me yet," she said as he closed the door. Well, Keely Mitchell. What have you got yourself in for now? Keely shook herself. It was as if her mother was right there. She must remember to ring her later, before the police got called out again, although, with the task in front of her, perhaps she did need to be carted away. Not by the police but by those who cared for the mentally unstable.

She sat down and picked up the wine bottles, one at a time. They each had the distinctive green label with Levallier Dell emblazoned in gold and black lettering. She read the description of the different types of wine and sat back.

On the far wall was a huge bookcase and during her stay she'd spent some time looking at the titles there. Among them were quite a few books on winemaking and tasting and an assortment of magazines. She smiled. It might be cold and wet outside but no longer did she have the niggling pain where her appendix wound was healing; it had been replaced by a general tingle of anticipation.

* * *

"Thanks, Anna." Kat accepted the take-away coffee.

"What are you up to today?" Anna walked around the counter and followed her to the door.

"I was being a tourist, but it's not much fun on your own in this weather." They both looked out at the grey day. The rain had gone but the wind still flapped the umbrellas in Anna's front yard.

"Where's Flynn? He should be showing you the sights."

"I guess he's working. I haven't seen him for a few days."

"He's been running the place alone while Euan's been away. He should take a break."

Kat nodded. She liked Flynn. He was an easy companion, no strings, and at least he understood her dilemma. She wouldn't pressure him to go with her on her exploration mission. Anyway, it had probably been better she went alone. No one knew who she was, so they treated her like any other tourist, which suited her purpose.

"We've had a bit of time together." She stepped off the verandah as a bike roared down the street. The shape of the rider was familiar and she couldn't help but smile. "He does take time out every now and then."

The bike slowed and stopped beside them.

"Hello, Flynn," Anna called.

He pulled off his helmet and raised a hand in a wave.

"What are you up to?" he asked Kat.

"Being a tourist."

"Do you want to come for a ride? You can have my helmet."

"She will not, Flynn Levallier. Apart from the danger, you've already been fined for riding without a helmet once. Kat can borrow Sean's."

Anna bustled inside before Flynn could argue. Kat took the lid from her coffee and blew gently over its surface.

"Where are you taking me?" she asked.

"I have a special project on the go. I think you'll be interested." He grinned and put his finger to his lips.

Kat only managed a few sips of her coffee before Anna was back with the helmet. She gave Anna the cup. "Sorry. Can you get rid of this?"

"Of course."

Kat strapped on the helmet and straddled the bike behind Flynn. She put her arms around him. He was deliciously warm. She closed her eyes and imagined he was Mal.

They both waved as Flynn pulled away from the curb. He was focused ahead but Kat felt a pang of guilt as she noticed the smug look on Anna's face.

* * *

It was Euan who came back later in the day to discover Keely with books and magazines spread across the table. He looked windswept and bleary eyed, a bit like Flynn had that morning. She glanced up at the clock. It was after two. She'd become totally absorbed in the book she was reading. It was all about growing and making Australian wines.

"I've made some sandwiches if you're hungry."

"Thanks, Keely. I've got a couple of phone calls to make and I'll be back."

"Is Flynn coming in?" Keely was keen to talk over her menu suggestions and see what he thought.

"He went off to the Haystack Block earlier. Chasing another of his wild ideas. We could have done with his help. Hugh and I have been moving barrels on our own." Euan frowned. "I don't like the look of this weather."

Keely glanced out at the clearing sky. There had been several heavy showers during the morning but the rain had passed and the leaves had stopped flapping on the vines outside. She wasn't sure what it was he didn't like the look of.

He disappeared into the front of the house. She assumed Hugh must be one of the workers. Perhaps he was the man who had passed her the day before, down at the studio. Something was bothering Euan. She looked at the spread of papers and books on the table. It was probably best if he didn't see all this, in his current frame of mind. She packed up, her thoughts drifting to Flynn. She wondered where the Haystack Block was. She hadn't heard it mentioned before.

Flynn's bike thrummed outside as she placed some lunch on the table. She switched on the kettle just as Flynn's shadow went past the window and the sliding door flew open.

Keely smile faded as she took in the dark look on Flynn's face.

"Where's Euan?" The glass rattled as he shut the door with a clunk behind him.

Keely was speechless. Was this the same man who had been here this morning, eagerly discussing food and wine ideas?

"I'm here." Euan came back into the room.

"What have you done?"

"Obviously something to upset you. What is it this time?"

"When were you going to get around to telling me your plans for the Haystack Block?"

Euan crossed the room and stood calmly at the end of the table. "I assume Benny Bensen and his team have started planting the new sauv blanc vines."

"He's nearly finished."

Keely felt as if she was at a tennis match. Her eyes flicked from the angry Flynn to the sad-faced Euan. Why did they argue so much? Once again, she was trapped in the kitchen. It was like deja vu.

"The sauv blanc has sold well. We need more." Euan leaned on the back of a dining chair.

"You know I wanted to plant something new there." Flynn gripped the back of the chair at his end of the table.

"Replicating a wine that's selling well is good business."

"How could you make that kind of commitment without talking to me?"

"I've always done the marketing. I can sell a lot more of the sauv blanc."

"And what happened to consultation?"

"You weren't there."

"You could have phoned."

At that moment, the phone rang. Both men glared at each other down the table and it was Keely who picked up the receiver, relieved to be able to do something.

"Levallier Dell," she said.

"Hello, is that Keely?"

Even though she'd only spoken to her once before, Keely recognised the perfect tones of the voice in her ear. "Yes."

"It's Maggie Levallier here. Is my brother at home?"

"Yes." Keely held out the phone to Euan. "It's your sister."

He took it from her and disappeared into the other end of the house again.

Flynn thumped the back of the chair, then winced. "Ouch." He shook his fingers, dragged the chair out and sat down. "Damn him. It's like trying to talk to the wind."

"Would you like a coffee or tea?"

Flynn turned, the look on his face suggesting he'd forgotten she was there again. She held her breath as his eyes searched hers.

"A coffee would be great. Thanks, Keely."

He was silent while she made two coffees. She brought them to the table and placed one in front of Flynn, who was studying the wine bottle he held in his hands. He looked so dejected. She resisted the urge to reach out and put her hand on his.

"Have you ever wondered if you're doing the right thing?" He looked up quickly and caught her studying him.

"Pardon?" She reached for her coffee, then had to steady the cup with two hands, as the hot liquid threatened to slop over the rim.

"You're a teacher. You must love working with kids. For me, it's growing the grapes to make wine and then reaching that moment when everything is just right. When the best fruit and the best technique bring it all together. That's my passion. Then to share the finished product with people and get their reaction...at least that's what I've always believed. Sometimes though, I wonder if I should have chosen another path altogether...or maybe I just need to be somewhere else." He took a sip of his coffee.

Keely watched him over her cup. She could tell he wasn't expecting a response. Just as well. She didn't know what she should say. She'd never really thought about why she'd chosen teaching. It'd just happened, a natural progression. Both her parents were teachers and it was expected that she would follow in their footsteps. She loved art but did she love teaching it? Somehow, it all got lost in yard duties, meetings, professional development, reports and…She thought of her last class and her stomach lurched.

"Sorry."

Flynn's voice startled her.

She looked up to find him grinning at her. They'd both been lost in their own thoughts.

"Didn't mean to scare you with a deep and meaningful," he said. "I always believed Euan and I wanted the same things but I'm not so sure anymore." He took some of the sandwiches and put them on his plate. "How did you get on with the menu?"

Keely jumped up to retrieve the pad she'd shoved out of sight. She was keen to change the subject but also to hear his response to her ideas for the food.

"I took into account our facilities and also what our nearest neighbour offers."

"River Dynasty?"

"Yes, I walked up to the road and along to their gate. An old guy drove up while I was there. Asked me where I'd come from and invited me in for a meal. He said he owned the place."

"That would've been Theo."

"He was full of questions. Anyway, they've got a menu board at their gate. It's different food and restaurant prices."

"We can't compete with Theo's facility." Flynn looked glum again.

"But why try? There must be all kinds of people attending the Divine Wine and Dine weekend. You believe your wines are outstanding; the food is just an extra on the day. Keep it basic and let the wine do the talking. There must be people who would appreciate that."

Flynn sat up straighter in his chair. Keely had to look away from those searching blue eyes. She fiddled with the pad in front of her.

"I've gone for three courses. Like you suggested, something for each of your wines. I don't know anything about wine so I've had to use your books to do some research. I've come up with things that are easy to prepare and serve. We won't need cutlery or plates."

Flynn came to stand beside her and look over her shoulder. She tensed, imagining the touch of his hand.

He leaned close and picked up the pad. "May I?"

There was a fresh earthy smell about him. "Of course. Take a look. You might not like my ideas." Keely's words tumbled over each other. "I know you suggested chicken or fish to accompany the chardonnay but from my research I thought we could pair it with a Margaret River charcuterie board. You said your chardonnay is full-bodied with bigger texture and flavour so I was thinking we could use a selection of local cured meats, cheeses, olives, hummus, and pickled vegetables, that type of thing. That's easier to prepare and is one course that also caters for vegetarians and people who need to be gluten free. We could follow it with a pulled pork and slaw roll to accompany a glass of your cabernet sauvignon. I got stuck on the dessert. In the end I thought a bite-sized pavlova swirl with unsweetened cream and berries might be okay for the glass of late-harvest semillon and once again that's suitable for quite a few dietary requirements."

She stopped. Flynn continued to stare at the paper he held. She rushed on to fill the silence. "It might not be what you wanted but I thought, seeing that Levallier Dell was a mixture of French and Australian, the charcuterie board and the pavlova were a good combination." Suddenly she wanted him to approve her ideas. She'd enjoyed planning the menu and looked forward to helping with the Divine Wine and Dine weekend.

The silence continued for a moment longer then Flynn spoke. "This looks great." This time, he did put his hand on her shoulder and leaned in closer. "With some helpers, I think it's actually feasible."

Keely relaxed and allowed herself to smile.

"Perhaps you could throw in some boiled potatoes for the Irish touch."

Euan's voice startled them. Flynn's hand fell from her shoulder and they both spun around. Euan stood in the room behind them. How long had he been there? He gave her a speculative look. What was he thinking? She dropped her gaze. Once again, she felt torn between her allegiance to Euan for his kindness and her interest in Flynn because…because of what? She wasn't sure.

"I'm only joking about the potatoes. *C'est bien.*" Euan crossed the room and replaced the phone in its cradle then moved to the outer door. "Flynn, you'll have another slave for the weekend. Maggie is coming to stay. There's work to be done, you know. I don't like the look of this weather."

Keely looked again at the sky, which was now a brilliant blue with big white clouds. It was warmer now than it had been all day.

"We might be in for a storm," Euan said before he shut the door and walked away.

Flynn glanced through the glass behind him and straightened up. His look was serious for a moment, then he turned to Keely and broke into a smile again. "Euan's losing the plot. Those clouds are like big white cauliflowers."

He had the most gorgeous smile but Keely could only manage a forced grin in return. She wasn't so sure she was looking forward to meeting Maggie Levallier.

"I can't believe it." Flynn shoved his hands deeper into the pockets of his jacket. In the moonlight, he could see the white sparkle of ice over the ground. "That storm came from nowhere."

"October weather can be beautiful but it can also be treacherous. We're lucky we've only suffered bad hail damage at Levallier Dell once before." Euan's hat was stuck firmly on his head and his bony fingers gleamed from the ends of his fingerless gloves.

Flynn looked towards the easterly skyline, where a faint smudge of light signalled the arrival of dawn. He wanted to be able to see the sky. Not that seeing it the day before had given him an indication of the wild storm they'd had in the night. They were insured against hail loss but that didn't put their wine in the bottle shops.

He arched his shoulders, rubbed his face then pushed his hands back into the warmth of his pockets. He had been up since four am, when the pounding of hail on the roof had drowned the sound of the wind.

Now the wind had gone but it was so cold the ice was still lying in clumps on the ground. He peered at the vines in front of him as the sky lightened. It was the early budding chardonnay vines that were most vulnerable at this time.

"It's small consolation," Flynn said, "but if we lose them, we've got insurance."

"What?" Euan turned a weary, puzzled face to Flynn.

"I've included it in our insurance for the last few years."

"Why?" Euan's voice rose a little. "It's a freak occurrence."

"I'm sure we discussed it when I changed the policy. You said yourself it happens here sometimes and now it has. When I was updating the policies, it was one of the options we decided to leave in."

"I don't remember any mention of it."

"Perhaps you were away at the time."

Euan slapped his leg. "Damn it Flynn, you worry too much. It's an extra expense we don't need."

Flynn drew his hands from his pockets and gestured towards the chardonnay vines. "Look around you. We might need it."

"Might!" Euan shoved his hands in his pockets and strode away along the edge of the vines.

Flynn watched his silhouette move into the distance for as far as the early light allowed. "Bugger you, Euan. Every time there's an important conversation you walk away."

★　★　★

Keely heard the sliding door open and close and decided to get up. It was only six o'clock but she had been awake for a while. The sounds of the storm had disturbed her several times in the night and, after it passed, the sudden quiet had left her sleepless.

When she opened the bedroom door, it was Flynn who was stoking up the fire in the pot belly. "Good morning."

He glanced briefly in her direction. "Morning."

Obviously not a good one though. Keely crossed to the kitchen. "Have you had breakfast?" she asked.

"No, I'll get something later." He shut the door on the fire and carefully hung the poker back on its hook. "I have to go back outside for a while."

"Is something wrong? I heard someone moving about in the night."

"Sorry, that was Euan and me coming and going. There was a bad storm and lots of hail. It's still so cold out there and the ground looks like we've had a visit from Jack Frost." He stretched his arms high in the air above his head, yawned and leaned back. Keely glimpsed a strip of firm flesh across his stomach as his t-shirt pulled away from his jeans. He let his arms drop, his gaze locked on hers.

She turned away quickly, saying the first thing that came into her head. "I met him the other day. He seemed a very interesting character."

There was silence for a moment before Flynn asked, "Who?"

"Jack Frost. He was out cracking his whip…"

Keely was cut off by a strange sound. She looked around to see Flynn laughing. She put her hands to her cheeks as the warm glow spread down to her neck. "Oh. It's the wrong person isn't it? His name was Jack Telford. Who is Jack Frost?"

Flynn struggled to contain his laughter. "You haven't heard the expression 'Jack Frost'?"

"Expression?"

"Jack Frost. It means frost, as in the weather." His face became serious again. "There's ice everywhere this morning, from the hail. It reminded me of the frosts I'd seen in South Australia."

"Oh." Keely stuck her head in the fridge to look for some eggs and to cool her cheeks. "You must be freezing. I'd be happy to cook some breakfast for when you come back."

He didn't answer. She shut the fridge up and realised he'd moved across the room and was standing right behind her on the other side of the breakfast bar. He looked as if he was going to say something, then he picked up his jacket and went to the door.

Before he closed it he looked at her again. "Thanks, I'll be about ten minutes."

Keely stared after him and put a hand to her chest where she could feel the thumping of her heart. What was going on? In spite of Flynn's changeable moods there was something about him that she found very attractive.

She stifled a giggle. Jack Frost. Now that she thought about it, she did have a childhood memory of someone using that name. Flynn must think she was silly but, all the same, she couldn't help humming to herself while she prepared the scrambled eggs.

He returned, true to his word, ten minutes later. Keely had the table set, the juice poured and coffee ready to go.

When they sat down to eat the scrambled eggs, Flynn explained about the storm and their concern that the hail may have damaged the young buds.

"You must both be tired," Keely said. "Is Euan coming in for breakfast?"

"He's still doing something outside."

No sooner had he said it when Euan came in the door. He removed his hat and ran his fingers through his hair. He looked exhausted.

"I don't think we need to worry too much," he said. "We've been lucky."

"We can check it out in the full light after breakfast," Flynn said.

Keely got up to serve some eggs for Euan.

He intercepted her. "Don't worry about me, Keely. Thanks, but I need to clear the cobwebs. I'm going for a surf."

"What about the chardonnay vines?" Flynn snapped.

"Give Hugh a call and ask him to come over later. The vines aren't going anywhere."

"But…"

Euan cut him off. "Nothing's going to change in the next few hours. You can look at them if you like but I'm taking a break."

He went through to the laundry where he kept his wetsuit and they heard the outer door shut. Keely sat down again. She couldn't imagine wanting to go out into the ocean on such a cold morning. In the silence, she heard the old Volvo come to life and drive away.

Flynn's cutlery clattered on his plate and Keely jumped.

"Bloody hell, he infuriates me so much." He stood up and looked out of the glass, his hands on his hips. "It's like trying to pin down the wind."

Keely got the impression his last sentence was said more to himself. She had become invisible again.

★　★　★

"It's a disaster."

Kat stood with her back to the window as Pappou paced the room.

Her uncle Tony sat in one of the big leather chairs. "I said we should have insured." His voice was little more than a murmur.

"We are insured," Pappou snapped.

"But not against hail damage, Baba. We've talked about it but you said it never happened here and you wanted every cent that River Dynasty brought in used to set up Ocean Dynasty."

"Don't tell me what I want." Pappou stopped pacing and thumped the desk with his fist. "What I want is for the chardonnay vines to be blossoming with new shoots instead of tattered shreds, shrivelling and dying."

"It might not be so bad. It might only be a setback," Tony said.

"A setback! While you were warm in your bed, I was watching our wine harvest being destroyed. It was like a white Christmas out there." Pappou jabbed his finger towards the window. Kat could see the veins on his forehead standing out. He was so wound up, he didn't even notice her. She was worried he'd burst.

"Theo, stop that shouting in my house." Yia-yia came through the door carrying a tray piled with cups and the coffee pot. Kat made a space for her on the large wooden desk. "No one can help the weather. Not Tony and certainly not you. Calm down and have a coffee."

"This is my office and I didn't say we wanted coffee."

"Well, if you don't want it I'm sure Katerina and Tony would like a cup."

Yia-yia began to pour and Kat held her breath as she watched Pappou struggle to control his temper. She took a cup from Yia-yia and passed it to Tony.

"Please, Pappou. Sit down and have a coffee." She smiled at him.

"Bah! I am getting too old for this." He took the coffee Kat offered and sat behind his desk. "Four million dollars just like that."

"Surely not that much, Theo," Yia-yia said.

"You do the cooking, I grow the grapes." He swivelled his chair towards the window. "I know how much they are worth."

Yia-yia gave Kat a little smile and patted Tony on the shoulder as she left. Kat picked up the tray and followed. She knew there was nothing she could say that would make a difference, either. Poor Uncle Tony would have to stay and bear the brunt of Pappou's disappointment.

★ ★ ★

Keely pegged the last sheet on the line and turned at the sound of a vehicle coming down the drive. Cars came and went all day but this one was coming to the house. She hoped it was Euan return-ing. She'd been pondering her future at Levallier Dell ever since he had announced that Maggie was coming to stay. Now she'd come up with an idea and she wanted to test it on Euan.

She reached the laundry door just as he came around the corner from the carport. His hair was still damp from the sea and it stuck out in tufts from his head.

"Hello, Keely. I feel as if I can face the day now. Do you fancy joining me for a coffee?"

"Of course." She was pleased to see he was in a better mood.

While he showered, she made him an open toasted sandwich with ham, tomato and some of the locally produced cheese she'd come to love. He only protested mildly that she didn't need to cook for him, before he sat down and tucked into the food.

Keely cleaned up the few things she'd used and wiped down the already gleaming sink. After Euan had gone surfing, Flynn had left for the sheds and she had spent her time cleaning. She'd stripped her bed, aired the bedroom and cleaned the bathroom. She didn't know when Euan's sister was arriving but she wanted to make sure everything was ready. It was during her cleaning frenzy that she'd had her idea.

She brought her coffee and sat at the table with Euan. He looked at ease. From across the table, she could barely see the fine lines she knew crisscrossed his face.

"Thanks for this, Keely."

"You've both had a long night."

"I'll be alright. The surfing is my way of letting go. Flynn doesn't have that. Unless you count riding that blasted bike of his too damn fast. He worries too much. He used to surf with me when he was kid. He hasn't been surfing since Lucy died. She had the knack of lightening him up."

Keely tried to imagine how tough it would have been for Flynn to lose his mother. She couldn't picture her teenage years without both of her parents being there. She also had two younger brothers, so there was always something happening at the Mitchell house. It was strange how she didn't really miss them here though.

"I love the vines but surfing is my total release."

Euan had his elbows on the table, his coffee cup clasped in both hands and his face turned to the glass door. Keely suspected that in his mind he was still on the water.

"When I'm on the board nothing else exists. There's just peace and solitude." He turned back and caught her studying him. Creases lined his face as he smiled. "When I'm out there, nothing bothers me."

"I'm like that with my beads. Once I get going on a piece of jewellery, I forget about everything else. Time just disappears."

"Everyone needs some kind of release. It's healthy." He picked up his plate. "Maggie will brighten Flynn up. When she's here he drops some of that tough shell of his."

The mention of Maggie reminded Keely of her idea.

"I've cleaned the bedroom for her."

"She won't be here for another week and you don't have to move out. We'll work something out in the front rooms."

"Maggie won't want the studio?"

"No. She doesn't like it at all. Lucy and I lived there when we first bought this place. Maggie hated it then and she's never changed her mind." He chuckled. "Too rustic for her."

Keely followed him into the kitchen. "Would it be okay for me to move in there?"

"You don't have to." Euan turned and the full force of his ice-blue eyes searched her face. "This is your home for as long as you want to stay."

"You've been very kind and I would like to stay and help with the Divine Wine and Dine weekend. If I moved into the studio, it would give us all some space."

Euan opened his mouth but Keely rushed on.

"I'd be happy to still help with meals but I could use the studio for my beads. It would be lovely to be able to spread out for a while and not have to pack up my work in progress. It's so beautiful down there."

"If that's what you want, you're most welcome but you don't have to cook and fuss over us. Flynn and I have managed between us in the past."

"If I don't cook, I have to pay rent." Keely stood her ground. She felt sure Euan wouldn't want her to pay for her accommodation. "Anyway, I enjoy cooking. I didn't get free rein at home much. My mother likes things done her way, even when she isn't there."

"Very well, *mademoiselle*, it's a deal. Accommodation in return for cooking some meals." Euan took her hand and bowed his head as if to kiss it, but instead he gave her one of his charming smiles.

Keely withdrew her hand, grateful there was no heat flooding her cheeks. She was getting used to Euan's theatrics. "Flynn said to tell you Hugh would be over just before lunch."

"Good. Now, I am going to shut my eyes for a few minutes, before we go and see if there's any major damage."

Keely watched him leave. He'd been very kind to her, cared about her, showed an interest in what she did and said. Already she thought of him as a reliable friend.

So many times he reminded her of her grandfather. A different generation of course, but it was his manner that made her realise why she was drawn to him. With Euan, she had the same secure feeling she'd had as a young child with her grandfather. She smiled; coming to Levallier Dell had been the right thing to do in many ways.

CHAPTER
17

Kat watched Pappou from the verandah. Her cousin Peter and her uncle Tony were with him. The mid-afternoon sunshine was warm on her face. It was hard to believe that it had been so cold this morning. The men were inspecting the chardonnay vines and from the way Pappou was shaking his head and waving his hands, she didn't think it looked good.

The local radio had reported hail damage in several places in the region. The severity of the storm certainly hadn't been forecast and it had taken everyone by surprise.

It wouldn't be good for their business if the damage was as bad as Pappou predicted. Kat had been given free rein to find out all she could about River Dynasty and how it worked. He wanted her to come up with a package to attract people to their cellar door for all kinds of functions, from conferences and weddings to birthdays and christenings. From what she had seen, a lot of the profits from River Dynasty had been used to set up the newer Ocean

Dynasty property further south, and Pappou still had a large loan for the piece of land adjacent to Levallier Dell. His resources were stretched. If he lost the chardonnay, it would be a major blow.

Not only that, Kat knew she had to tell him the truth about her visit to Margaret River. There never seemed to be a right moment but her time was running out. Mal had rung. It had been so good to talk with him and, understandably, he wanted her answer. Never before in her life had she agonised so much over a decision. Michael had been right; she was usually tenacious when it came to making choices. It was just that this time there was a lot at stake.

She smiled as she recalled her ride with Flynn the day before, to visit his special project, as he called it. There was a man who knew what he wanted and went for it. He had bottled his first sauvignon blanc semillon blend and he was so excited about it. From what she'd tasted, he was doing a good job of it as well. He was like an adoring father who had asked her opinion on his baby. They had both agreed that the semillon gave great texture and intensity to the wine and the sauvignon blanc added tropical aromatics. It was a great blend and she'd said so.

Flynn had whirled her around the makeshift tasting room. It would have been easy to stay in his arms and kiss him, if her heart wasn't somewhere else. Flynn was a very attractive guy. But she could tell at that moment it was thoughts of his wine that put the sparkle in his eyes. He was passionate about his winemaking.

Of course, such people had surrounded her all her life. That's how she'd developed a finely tuned palate and knowledge of wine herself but she wasn't so interested in the making. Her passion was in matching the right wine to the right food or person or occasion. That's why Mal's offer was such a good one. A combination of her knowledge of wine and her marketing skills was required. Not only that, she'd fallen in love with him and he with her. Their few days and nights together before she'd left for Perth had sealed the deal for both of them as far as their feelings for each other were concerned. She closed her eyes and breathed in deeply. Taking up Mal's offer would mean saying goodbye to all this.

Pappou's raised voice carried on the breeze. Her eyes flew open and she clicked her tongue. She knew what she wanted but family ties were very strong and she didn't want to upset Pappou or her parents.

★   ★   ★

"Thanks for your help, Flynn." Keely smiled as he put her bag down inside the studio door.

"No problem."

She turned away from his piercing gaze and put her backpack on the kitchen table. In her haste, it fell sideways and several things slipped out, including a packet of loose beads.

"Ohhh, damn!" She reached out as they bounced every which way over the wooden floor.

Flynn crouched down and helped her collect her things. She managed to retrieve several of the beads but decided she'd do better with a broom later.

"This drawing is great, Keely."

She looked up from the beads, to see him holding her open sketchpad. It must have slipped out of her pack with the other things. She busied herself pouring the beads back into their packet.

"I like to sketch people and places I see. It's kind of like a journal of my travels." She reached for the pad. "I don't usually show people."

"That's Euan, isn't it? It's a very good likeness." He handed it back. "You've captured something more than a face. It's almost as if you can read what he's thinking. I like the name you've given it."

Keely glanced at the sketch she had named 'Scarecrow'. "He's got the kind of face that asks to be drawn."

"Perhaps one day, you'll show me the rest."

"Perhaps." She closed the sketchpad and placed it on the table. "Thanks again for giving me a hand, Flynn, but I don't want to hold you up any longer."

"Ouch. I've been dismissed."

"I didn't mean—"

"It's not a problem." He grinned. "I had to check the water was working alright again. We've fixed the pump so everything should run okay."

Keely watched as he turned the taps on over the old sink.

"There's an overhead tank for hot water but that's still got plenty in it from when I was here. Come through to the bathroom and I'll show you the tap system. It's a bit archaic but it works."

Keely followed him through the door leading from the kitchen to the back of the studio. One end was partitioned off with an old shower curtain. The other end was stacked with odds and ends of furniture and bric-a-brac in boxes. Flynn pulled back the curtain to reveal an old claw-foot bath, stained with rust, and drooping over it was a huge showerhead. Opposite was an equally rust-stained handbasin and beyond that there was a small door in the wall.

"That's the toilet and this is the trick with the taps." He gave instructions about moving a middle tap one way or the other, depending on whether you were bathing or showering. It didn't look that tricky. Keely was sure she could work it out.

"The back door doesn't open anymore. You can only use the front door for coming and going."

He headed back to the kitchen with Keely trailing behind, when he stopped suddenly and turned.

"Do you need a car to go to Mary's tonight? You could borrow the LandCruiser."

"Oh, I don't know. I'm not sure about the roads yet. There seem to be a lot of twists and turns between here and Margaret River. I'd probably get lost in the dark."

"I can drive you. I might go in for a drink with a few mates tonight."

"Thanks, Flynn. I'll let you know."

He went on through the front door then turned back again.

"If you want to move back to the house at any time, you can. It doesn't matter to me."

"Thanks," she said. Then she added, "I think," under her breath as he walked away along the river path in the direction of the sheds. She never quite knew what to make of him. Today he'd been helpful and shown a more affable manner.

She sighed and turned back to the room behind her. Excitement took over and she forgot about Flynn. This place was hers until she moved on.

She carried her bag into the bedroom and ran her hand over the beautiful patchwork bedspread. It was nearly all white with little touches of deep burgundy and green and was quilted with an intricate pattern of stitches.

She'd brought the sheets down earlier and made the bed. Now she opened her bag, pulled out her clothes and put them in the little cupboard. She had her own room at home but it was small and the house was never empty of people with five of them living there and friends and family calling in.

"Damn." After all her good intentions she'd forgotten to call home the night before. She retrieved her mobile from her bag and saw there'd been a text from her mother. She dashed off a quick reply saying she'd ring tonight.

Not now. She wanted to settle in to her new surroundings. There was still some time before she needed to go back to the house to organise the evening meal. She took out her bead container and began to play with different combinations. She had several ideas but craved some new inspiration. Perhaps she would go with Flynn into town and attend Mary's gathering of jewellery makers.

★ ★ ★

"Flynn, I really need someone to talk to." Kat's voice wavered.

Flynn pressed his phone to his ear. "How about we go in to the pub? I've offered to drive Keely in to Margs to a meeting at Mary's. We can go for a drink while she's there."

"Thanks, I have something important to ask you." There was a hint of desperation in her voice.

"Sounds mysterious. I'm always up for a bit of intrigue."

There was silence for a moment then Kat was back. "Sorry. I thought I heard Pappou calling. What did you say?"

"Nothing. I'll pick you up at seven."

"No, don't come here. I'll come and get you. Seven you said. See you then."

She was gone. Flynn looked at his mobile then shoved it back in his pocket. Kat was usually so self-assured. He wondered what was bothering her.

"Are you going out?"

He turned to face Euan.

"Yes. I'm taking Keely into that jewellery thing at Mary's. We ate earlier. Your meal's in the microwave."

"We could get used to this kind of treatment." Euan opened the door and peered at the chicken in mango sauce.

"Perhaps we should consider getting a housekeeper."

"You're full of ideas to spend money, aren't you?"

"I was joking."

"About the housekeeper, maybe, but you have spent a lot of money in the last month or so. New signs, gravel driveway, new car…"

"It's not wasted money, it's investing in the future of our business."

"We've always managed fine with what we've got."

Euan sat at the table with his meal and Flynn pulled up a chair. They needed to have this conversation. Now that Keely was out of the house, maybe they'd get the chance. He took a calming breath.

"I know we have, Euan, but times have changed and we have to change if we want to remain competitive."

"Our wines speak for themselves, you know that. The distributor only said the other day it's hard to find an Australian wine that has such good persistence with food as ours, and our sauvignon blanc is sought after."

"And that's why you had trouble selling it?"

Euan put down his cutlery. He'd hardly touched his meal. "I didn't have trouble selling it, Flynn. They wanted me to commit to more than we've got."

"You said yourself it's better to run out and keep demand high."

"If I want this guy to keep buying I have to supply him with more."

"We could try another market. You know I'd like to try a different variety and you've filled our last remaining hectares with more sauv blanc vines."

"They do so well at the Haystack Block."

Flynn put his elbows on the table and clenched his hands together. They'd bought the second piece of land several years earlier after he'd returned from Europe and come home to stay. He'd pressured his father then to expand. It had been a good opportunity and Euan had given in when he'd lost the property between Levallier Dell and River Dynasty to Theo. The Haystack Block was the other side of Margs but complemented the land they had at Levallier Dell. They had more sauv blanc and semillon vines there, which Flynn was using to make a blend. SBS was very popular in their region, and they'd planted merlot, which they'd never had before. Getting those vines in the ground had been one of the few wins Flynn had had with his father. It was new for them but not groundbreaking for the region. He'd hoped to have more control over what happened on the Haystack Block but Euan's back-door tactics had blown that idea away.

"You know I've been looking at planting something different. Something that would be totally new for us and for Margaret River."

"Why change what we're good at, if it's what the market wants?"

"The market wants all kinds of wines." Flynn gripped his hands tighter. Now that he'd managed to get Euan to talk, he didn't want to spoil the moment by losing his cool. Neither of them were good at talking without emotion taking over.

"Of course it does." Euan smiled and began eating again. "But we can't supply everything."

"If we don't try something new every so often, we won't keep up."

"There's nothing wrong with being steady and reliable, Flynn. When people buy Levallier Dell wines they know the quality they've come to expect will be there. A lot of value is placed on that and we get a good price for that value."

"I know. But the soil and topography at the Haystack Block are totally different. The grapes produce a different flavour." Flynn looked at his hands. His knuckles were going white. He took another deep breath and relaxed his fingers a little. "Wine drinkers are trying all kinds of varieties these days. We need something new to show we're moving with the times."

"You've got your red blend. It should be ready to bottle soon. It's promising to be very full bodied and ageable. It will be totally different to any of our other wines."

"And what about the dry white blend?"

Euan put a piece of chicken in his mouth. He didn't look up.

"All it needs is a label. I've got a few ideas—"

Euan put down his cutlery again and met Flynn's look. "We usually make that decision together."

"You said it was my baby." Anger niggled in his chest. "You didn't want to have anything to do with a blend."

"If it's got the Levallier Dell label on it, I want to know."

"It doesn't have any label yet." Flynn wanted to shout: because I want to come up with something different and not keep the plain old label we use on everything else, but he pressed his lips firmly shut.

"You could sell it as a cleanskin. It seems to be back in fashion at the moment."

"I don't want to do that, Euan. It's a good wine. The semillon has added the weight and flavour. It has sauv blanc aromatics but it's got backbone. It's ready to drink now."

"We need next year's vintage for the single varietal labels. The merchants want as much as we can supply. That's why I've planted more sauv blanc. We can't afford to dabble with other things."

Flynn studied his father across the table. The lines were deeper on his face, his hair wispier. He looked thinner, older. They were both good winemakers. Surely Flynn had developed his passion at Euan's knee. Flynn had been so excited when Euan had finally given in and let him create two blends but, as the months passed, he was disappointed when Euan showed little interest in their progress. Now he was wiping away Flynn's dream. They had a dry white blend, the SBS, which showed great promise and Euan was telling him he couldn't do it next year.

"Damn it, Euan." He thumped the table and pushed back his chair. "You haven't even tasted it. It's a bloody good wine. There's interest in these blends in the market and you're dismissing it without a chance."

Euan stood opposite him. His voice was low. "You've had your little experiment. Anyway, you've still got the red blend. I've let you have full control of that."

"But the SBS is good, too."

They glared at each other across the table. The silence was broken by a knock at the door. Kat waved from the other side of the glass. Flynn lifted his hand in acknowledgement.

"I thought you were taking Keely to town," Euan growled.

"Kat is coming along for the ride."

"You're spending a lot of time with that girl."

"That's one part of my life you have no control over." Flynn grabbed his jacket from the back of the chair and let himself out.

"That looked a bit intense." Kat nodded back towards the house as he followed her to her car.

"Euan and I don't see eye to eye on everything."

She stopped, stepped closer, peered at him. "You look upset, what is it?"

"Nothing I can't sort out. Don't worry about me. You sound like the one with the problem. What's up?"

"Let's not talk about it yet. I'm looking forward to that drink."

They got into the little red sports car.

"We need to go via the studio to pick up Keely," Flynn said as Kat started the motor. "Turn right after the house."

* * *

Keely heard the vehicle and was already shutting the front door of the studio when Flynn stepped under the verandah.

"Ready to go?"

"Yes." She bent to pick up her backpack. She was looking forward to going to Mary's gathering. She'd had a satisfying afternoon sorting through her jewellery kit and she'd finished another bottle decoration. Now, as she followed Flynn around to the car, she was also looking forward to the drive with him.

She paused as she came to the back of the studio and saw the red sports car parked at the end of the track.

"Hello, Keely." Kat waved. Her thick brown hair was swept up onto her head and covered with a scarf, and gold earrings gleamed from her ears, matching the bracelet that jiggled on the arm she rested along the back of the seat. She looked the picture of elegance.

"Hi, I didn't realise you were…" Keely stopped as Flynn opened the door and indicated the front seat for her. "No, I'll sit in the back."

"That's my spot." He grinned. "I'm the thorn behind the two roses."

"I don't want to be a bother. I don't have to go."

"It's no bother," he said, clambering into the cramped space.

"Not all." Kat patted the seat. "Hop in."

Keely stepped into the little car but the seat was lower than she anticipated and she lost her balance. She fell the last distance to the seat with a thud.

"Careful," Flynn said. "That caught me out earlier."

"I'm the impromptu add-on, I'm afraid," Kat said. "Flynn has kindly offered to give me an ear to confide in."

"Is that what I'm doing? I thought you were buying me a drink."

"That too." Kat chuckled, put the car into gear and sped up the track.

"That's if you get us there in one piece," Flynn yelled.

Keely grabbed at her hair, which was flying in all directions and whipping around her face. So much for a leisurely drive!

★　★　★

Anna waved to them from the front gate as Kat cruised past. She did a quick U-turn and pulled up in front of Anna. Keely felt her hair slowly settle around her like leaves after a whirlwind. A quick glance in the side mirror gave her a glimpse of the wild tangle on her head.

"Hello, you three. What are you up to?"

Flynn jumped out and opened Keely's door. "Keely's off to creative business at Mary's and Kat and I are going to the pub."

"That sounds like a good evening for everyone," Anna said.

Keely was trying to push her hair back into some order and reach for her backpack at the same time.

Flynn offered his hand to help her out. She struggled up onto the footpath and stood next to Anna, clutching her pack to her chest with one hand and trying to tidy her hair with the other.

"You need to tie your hair up when you travel in an open car." Anna smiled at Kat, who was now removing her scarf.

Keely grimaced through her hair and adjusted her hold on her pack. She would have worn one if she'd known.

"How long will you be at Mary's?" Flynn asked.

"I'm not sure."

"The pub's just down the road from Mary's. Do you want to come down for a drink when you've finished?"

Keely didn't want to play gooseberry but she did think a drink with Flynn would be nice.

"No, Keely can come here," Anna said before Keely could speak. "You'd be better to leave the car here too. I'll look after them both till you get back." She made a shooing motion at Flynn and Kat. "You two go off and enjoy yourselves. Don't worry about Keely."

Keely resisted the urge to shrug Anna's hand away as she was patted on the back, gritting her teeth instead.

"Megan left the relief teaching forms for you. She said your paperwork had arrived from SA. You can fill them out here if you have to wait for Flynn," Anna said.

Keely felt trapped. Flynn waited, Kat's arm slung through his.

"Thanks." She forced a smile onto her face. "I'll wait for you here."

"I nearly forgot." Flynn dug his hand in his pocket and pulled out a folded sheet of paper. "Would you give this to Mary, please. It's the hard copy of our Divine Wine and Dine menu. Tell her I've emailed the original too."

Keely took the paper and he set off down the street with Kat.

"Do you want to come in and tidy up?" Anna asked.

"No thanks," Keely said. "I'll be fine. See you later."

She hurried off down the street and turned the opposite way to the other two, towards River Rainbow, where a cheery light was shining into the darkening street. Anna was the Levalliers' friend but Keely didn't like the way the older woman tried to organise everyone. She presumed far too much for Keely's liking.

CHAPTER
18

"So here we are. You've got your drink and I've brought my listening ear." Flynn tugged at his ear and Kat couldn't help but smile. He really was a nice guy. If she hadn't met Mal she may easily have fallen for Flynn, taken up Pappou's offer and settled in Margaret River.

She sighed. "Are you happy living here, Flynn?"

"That's your big question?"

"Not really. I just don't know where to start."

"How about the beginning?" He reached over and squeezed her hand.

Kat felt the warmth of his touch but there was no more to it than that. No tingle up her arm or butterflies in the stomach, like she had when she was with Mal. Flynn was a friend. She relaxed a little. A friend with a listening ear. She grinned.

"Well, I was born during a particularly good vintage, much to my father's delight..." She paused as Flynn stood up. "Where are you going?"

"If you're going back that far we'll need more drinks."

"Sit down." She grabbed his arm and they both laughed as he tumbled back into his chair.

"Now come on, Kat," he said. "Enough procrastinating, spill your guts."

She took a sip of her drink and put the glass down carefully in front of her. "I've been offered a job. I need to start in a month... in Singapore."

★ ★ ★

There were three other women sitting around the table when Mary ushered Keely through to her back workroom. They were chatting over the top of the classical music playing from a sound system and the table was spread with cloths and tools, wires, beads and gems.

"Girls, this is Keely."

They all looked up and under their scrutiny she wished she'd accepted Anna's offer to tidy up. These women all looked so fresh.

"Bella is on the end, Claire next to her and Letitia."

Each woman waved in turn.

"I'll go and shut up the front of the shop now," Mary said. "The girls will look after you."

"Come and sit here, Keely." Bella patted the empty chair beside her. "We've saved you a bit of space. We tend to spread out."

Letitia reached across to pull in some of her things. She was younger than the others and her wrist sparkled with an intricate aqua-blue bracelet.

"That's gorgeous," Keely said. "Did you make it?"

Letitia held her arm closer for Keely to see. "Yes, I like working with fine detail and gems."

"Her eyes are better than mine." Claire peered at Keely over the top of her glasses.

Keely bent to get a closer look at the bracelet. It was made up of tiny bead flowers and the centre of each flower was a gem.

"Are they aquamarines?" she asked.

"Yes." Letitia looked at Keely appreciatively. "You know your stones."

"I use them from time to time but I've never made anything like that."

"I prefer the beads," Claire said. In front of her was a partly made necklace. It had a large, flat green bead in the centre and assorted smaller green beads either side, some with just a hint of mauve in them.

"And Bella is the nature lover." Mary stepped back into the room. "Most of her pieces have shell or feathers or bark in them."

"I was into weaving before I got into the jewellery phase." Bella held up a plaited bracelet with small pieces of shell and tiny sea-green beads.

"Between us, I don't think there's a form of art or craft we haven't tried at some stage." Mary chuckled and the others all nodded in agreement.

"Now come on, Keely," Bella said. "Your turn. Show us your wares."

Keely hesitated. These women were obviously very talented. Her bracelets were no match for their work. She fumbled with the ribbon that tied her bundle of cloth together.

"Talk about pressure," Mary said. "Don't mind us Keely, just tip it all out."

The ribbon came free and Keely unrolled the cloth and pulled out one of her finished bracelets.

The other women all leaned in for a closer look.

"That's gorgeous," Letitia said.

"It's three dimensional. I love the way there's no symmetry to it," Claire said.

"That style lends itself to using shells and stones," Bella added.

Mary spread a necklace in front of her. "You and I have similar taste, I think Keely."

They admired Mary's work and very soon they were all busy with their pieces, chatting and laughing. Keely relaxed and immersed herself in the happy atmosphere. She didn't know the people that the four women talked about but there couldn't have been anyone left in Margaret River they hadn't discussed by the end of the night. Keely finished her bracelet and had started another before it was time to pack up. Reluctantly she folded her things away. She would have been happy to keep going – being with these women had been motivating. Even better was being able to go and select things from Mary's shelves as she needed them. She couldn't wait to get back and add her new purchases to her collection.

They gathered at the door of Mary's shop to say their goodbyes.

"Sometimes, Letitia and I meet during the day at my place if you'd like to join us, Keely," Bella said. "I have a little cottage near the river end of town. Mary will give you directions."

"Unfortunately, some of us have to work for a living," Claire said.

"Make more jewellery, dear, and you could live off your creative earnings." Letitia's tone was pompous and they all laughed.

Keely and Mary waved as the other women headed for their cars.

"Your bracelets really are quite unique, Keely," Mary said. "The other girls sometimes put their finished pieces in my shop to sell. As you can gather, there's not a living in it but we do okay. If you ever want to do the same, I'm sure your range would be popular."

"Thanks."

"How are you getting home?" Mary asked and a large yawn escaped her. "Sorry." She patted her mouth. "I love getting together with the girls but it makes for a long day. Do you want me to drive you? My car's out the back."

"No, thanks. I'll be fine. Flynn is in town and Anna said I can wait for him at her place." She waved and took a few steps up the footpath. Mary went back into her shop and Keely could hear the sounds of the door being locked behind her.

She went as far as the corner, stopped and looked along the street towards the pub. Loud voices, laughter and music carried on the breeze. She should just walk on and join Flynn and Kat but she realised there was another pub opposite. Flynn hadn't said which pub they were going to and she didn't want to be wandering in search of them. She could send him a text. She took out her phone then realised she didn't have his number and tossed it back in her bag.

"Damn."

She gave one more wistful look in the direction of the pubs then turned off along the side street. Anna's shop was in darkness but the outside light was on for her to find her way to the back door. She sighed. The jewellery group at Rainbow River had been such a lot of fun and she'd forgotten about the teaching paperwork for a while.

"What are you standing out here in the dark for?"

Keely jumped and spun around. Sean was standing on the path, his hands on his hips.

"Oh." She breathed out. "I've just finished at Mary's. Your mum said I could wait for Flynn at your place."

"You'd better come in then," Sean said. "Flynn could be a while. He and that bird from River Dynasty have got their heads locked together in a corner of the pub. They're so engrossed they've hardly noticed anyone else. I've been down having a final drink before exams with some mates. Flynn barely knew who I was." Sean grinned. "He's only got eyes for her."

He pushed open the gate and led the way down the side of the house. Keely followed with heavy steps. The shine was quickly evaporating from her night.

It was more than an hour later when Flynn burst through Anna's door. "Are you ready, Keely? Sorry we're so late. Kat has the engine running."

"If we'd have known, Keely could have slept the night here, Flynn," Anna said.

Keely stood up from the table where she'd spent the time sipping a cup of tea and dithering over the forms while Anna and Sean prepared pastries for the next morning's baking. Sean was on a high. School days were nearly finished forever for him. What a wonderful feeling that must be. Every stroke of the pen on the papers Megan had left stripped one more layer from the barricade Keely had built between her and her teaching. She should just say no but faced with their determination, and in Megan's case desperation, she couldn't summon the courage.

To make things worse, she'd had to listen all over again as Sean had told his mother about Flynn and Kat's close encounter in the pub and then sit through Anna's pronouncement that Kat was the best thing that could happen to Flynn. Now, here was Flynn bouncing through the door as if he'd won a million dollars.

"Sorry, Keely," he said again.

She pulled a smile. "I've been well looked after." She thanked Anna for the cuppa and handed over the papers she'd picked up.

"I'll be seeing Megan tomorrow. I'll give them to her," Anna said.

Keely followed Flynn out into the yard with heavy steps. Just when she was enjoying a total change, the threat of having to teach again had come back into her life. She should turn straight around and snatch the papers back but she knew she wouldn't. It had been easier to go along with Anna's meddling than have to face a barrage of questions from the interfering woman.

Once they were away from the house, Flynn stopped and waited for her to catch up. "I am sorry we've been so long. I hope you're not too tired."

"I'm fine."

In the dull glow of the outside light, Keely could see the sparkle in his eyes. He looked at her earnestly and she wondered briefly how much he'd had to drink.

"If you can stand it, there's something I'd like to discuss when we get home."

"Well...it's late." Keely glanced down. The pleading look in his eyes almost took her breath away.

"Please, Keely." He reached for her hand and she couldn't pull away. What was happening? Flynn obviously had feelings for Kat but when he looked at Keely like that, she could almost imagine herself in his arms. She bit her lip and removed her hand from his. She couldn't allow herself to like him too much; she might need to move on in a hurry.

CHAPTER
19

Light was filling the room when Keely opened her eyes but in the transition from deep sleep to waking she couldn't think where she was. She turned her head towards the window where the old curtains failed to block much of the light, then she remembered. She had slept her first night in the studio.

She stretched her arms out to the sides of the bed. Night was probably not the right word, more like morning. It had been after one when Flynn and Kat had left and she'd been much too excited to fall asleep easily.

She plucked her phone from the bedside cupboard and peered at it, trying to focus on the numbers. Ten o'clock! She started to sit upright then flopped down on the bed again. What did it matter? It was Saturday, she was on holidays and there was nothing she really had to do yet.

Saturday!

"Damn." She should ring her mum.

Nearly an hour had passed and her phone was almost flat by the time she put it down. Her mum hadn't sounded quite so anxious and she'd been interested in the jewellery-making group. At the end of the call her mum had put her on speaker so she could talk to her dad and brothers as well before they headed off to tennis. Then Keely had rung Bec. She was still in bed too and they'd had a good catch-up, filling each other in on all the details of their lives. Bec was enjoying her new job and had been out to a couple of bands. Keely had told her about the winery, the upcoming food and wine weekend and her latest bead projects but she'd changed the subject when Bec had wanted to know more about Flynn.

Now she thought about getting up but there was no rush. Flynn wasn't coming to collect her until after lunch. He was going to take her to the Haystack Block. If she was having a part in his new wine, he'd said she should at least taste it, so she knew what she was getting involved with.

She felt a flutter of excitement as she recalled the discussion the three of them had had around the kitchen table the night before. Flynn had been cautious to begin with and her curiosity had overcome her initial disappointment that Kat was still with them. He had taken great care to explain how he respected Keely's privacy but he was really interested in the sketch of Euan and could he please look at it again and show Kat.

Keely had been surprised by Kat's enthusiasm and then her declaration that it was perfect. Flynn had explained he was looking for a new label design. This wine would still carry the Levallier Dell name but it was a separate label and needed something catchy and distinctive. It was then that he'd asked Keely if she would mind if her picture of Euan and the Scarecrow name were used on the label. It suited his wine perfectly, he'd said.

She'd been so absorbed in what he was telling her that she hadn't even minded Kat flicking through the other pages of her sketchbook. Keely didn't have anything to drink in the studio and they'd ended up toasting the new label with water. Flynn had kissed Kat and then Keely. She touched her cheek where his lips had brushed her then rolled over and curled herself into a ball, savouring the memory.

★ ★ ★

"So, you were out late last night." Pappou studied Kat across the lunch table.

She raised her chin. "I'm not a little girl anymore."

"Of course you are not. I am glad you are enjoying life here. Am I right in assuming it was Flynn you were with?"

Yia-yia smiled at her from the other end of the table. Kat relaxed again. "Yes, we went to the pub then caught up with Keely, who is staying at Levallier Dell. We were just hanging out. It was fun." For a moment, Kat had thought Pappou was going to give her a lecture.

"Who is this Keely?" Yia-yia asked. "There have been a few different stories."

"You women and your gossip," Pappou scoffed. "She seems a respectable young woman. Very reserved."

"How do you know, Theo?"

"I met her up at the gate a few days ago. She was reading our menu." He lowered his voice. "I heard she was Euan's girlfriend."

Kat laughed. "Oh Pappou, I hope you didn't say anything. Keely is only a few years older than me. She was travelling and got sick. Euan offered her a place to recuperate, that's all."

"What does Flynn think of her?" Pappou asked.

"They seem to be friends." Kat was puzzled by all this interest in Flynn and Keely. It wasn't the conversation she'd intended to have. She wanted to get her plans out in the open. Now that she'd made her decision she was determined to explain the future she'd chosen and make it clear to her grandparents. Flynn had said she'd feel better once she did and she was sure he was right.

She smiled as she recalled the evening they'd spent at the pub, then afterwards at Keely's studio. She really had enjoyed their company.

"He would be a good catch, that young man." Pappou nodded sagely.

Kat frowned. For whom, she wondered.

Yia-yia began clearing the plates and Tony appeared in the doorway.

"Tony," Yia-yia said. "Have you had lunch? I can make you something."

"No thanks, Mama. I ate earlier."

Katerina looked at her uncle. His face was grim.

"How are things in the vineyard?" she asked.

"Most of the chardonnay shoots have shrivelled."

"You've still got time to get secondary shoots, haven't you? I know Dad managed to recoup a little last time we had damage."

"Maybe, with care." Pappou glared at Tony as if he was personally responsible for the hail that had fallen from the sky. "The yield will be greatly reduced."

"That's not the only problem," Tony said. "We've found garden weevil in a couple of rows of the shiraz vines."

Kat helped Yia-yia clear up while she listened. Garden weevil could do a lot of damage if not controlled.

"The same vines as last year?" Pappou asked.

"No, a strip further over on the northern edge."

"How bad?"

"We've trapped four or five per vine."

"Time to spray the butts."

"If that's what you want, Baba." Tony stepped from one foot to the other. "It's not too late to try something else, dacron wrap perhaps?"

"Bahh!"

Pappou stood quickly, his face an angry red. Kat took a quick step towards him as he grabbed the back of the chair for support but he righted himself. It wasn't good for him to get so upset. She glanced at Tony and Yia-yia but he was looking down and she was stacking dishes; neither had noticed Pappou's wobbly legs.

"We've got a new patch of vines to get up to scratch," Pappou said. "There's a mortgage on the last block, we've lost our chardonnay crop and now you want to spend money on expensive strips of plastic when a dose of spray will do the same job."

Tony looked up. His face was expressionless but there was a definite droop to his shoulders. Kat felt sorry for him, knowing how difficult it must be for him to get Pappou to change his mind once he dug in his heels. "Dad tries to avoid chemicals these days," she said. "He uses the sticky wrap to trap the weevils."

"He can on his little winery," Pappou snapped. "It's much too big a job here. Spraying is the best option and the cheapest."

Kat gave Tony a weak smile and was pleased to see him wink back. It was good to see he hadn't lost all his spark.

"Come, Katerina, we will leave the men to their business," Yia-yia said.

Kat picked up a stack of plates and followed her out. Any last thoughts about staying in Margaret River had been squashed. She definitely couldn't work for Pappou.

* * *

Flynn arrived to collect Keely in the new car. This time she was a little disappointed he hadn't brought his bike. She'd tied back her hair and put on her jeans just in case. At least there was no sign of Kat and the car was easier for conversation.

"Are you ready to taste the great wine that will be adorned with your artwork?" Flynn asked.

Keely smiled. "Yes."

"I hope you'll approve."

"I'm afraid I'm not a very competent wine judge." She looked over the rows of vines bathed in sunshine. It all looked so simple but she was beginning to realise there was much more to winemaking. "How do you know when it's time to bottle the wine?"

"It's a combination of things." He was looking ahead, manoeuvring the car out of the driveway and onto the road. "We do lots of blending trials, or at least in the case of this sauv blanc semillon blend, it's been me rather than 'we'. I keep careful notes. There are lots of things to take into consideration. I want to make sure I get the percentages of the blend in perfect harmony."

His eyes were on the road but Keely could hear the enthusiasm in his voice.

"How did you learn what to do?"

Flynn glanced at her then back to the road. "I think I took a lot in by osmosis. I was kind of submerged in winemaking from birth." He chuckled. "I guess that helped. I used to concoct wine brews in the kitchen. Then I studied and travelled overseas. I spent four years at uni in Adelaide."

"South Australia?"

"Yes. It's a renowned course and I wanted to…try somewhere different for a while."

"Did you see much of the state?"

"Mainly the wine-growing areas. I visited quite a few including the Clare Valley but the Adelaide Hills was closest, I have a good mate there, and I spent time in the McLaren Vale region."

"I live near McLaren Vale."

"It has a similar climate to this region. We both benefit from the sea breezes."

Keely sat back and watched the scenery. Sometimes the trees along the road were so thick you couldn't see what was beyond them, then a break would give a glimpse of rows of vines or paddocks with cows grazing in the sunshine. It was funny to think that Flynn had spent some time in her patch of Australia. She wondered if they had ever passed each other, oblivious to the fate that would one day bring them together on his home turf.

They drove through Margaret River. It was a glorious afternoon, sunny with a gentle breeze. Groups of people strolled along the footpaths on either side of the main street.

"If we had a cellar door, we could be attracting some of these people to try our wines."

Keely glanced at Flynn. She wasn't sure whether he was speaking to her or himself.

He gave her a quick grin. "You may have noticed Euan and I have opposing views on the subject."

She looked back to the people in the street. "I had assumed all wineries had a cellar door. I guess they're the only ones I know about."

"Precisely my point."

"I thought Euan said you sell all your wines through distributors."

"We do at the moment but I'd like to try something different with the Haystack range. I've only got this dry white you'll taste today and a shiraz that's nearly ready to bottle. They will be cheaper than our usual Levallier Dell wines. I'd like to have tastings and have our complete range available at the cellar door."

"I guess you've tried to discuss it with him."

Flynn strummed the steering wheel with the fingers of one hand. "Many times, but Euan doesn't like to be pinned down and he doesn't like change."

"Maybe the Divine Wine and Dine weekend will be the way to show him it can work."

"Possibly, but he's not keen on that idea either."

"I'd love to stay and be part of it. That's if I can be of any help," she added quickly.

"You've helped a lot already." He glanced her way then back at the road. "This is the Haystack Block." He turned through an open gateway and the car bounced over a pothole and onto a rough track.

No fancy signs or gravelled driveways here, thought Keely. She looked at the rows of vines they drove through. Something about them was different from those at Levallier Dell.

"The branches here don't stick out like your others," she said. "Is that because they are younger?"

"Partly." He gave her an appreciative look.

"It's probably a silly question."

"No, it's very astute of you, considering you don't know much about them."

Keely looked out at the passing rows. He was right about her lack of knowledge.

"These vines are managed by spur pruning. It's another thing Euan and I don't agree on but it allows the grapes here to be mechanically pruned. Euan has always stuck to the traditional methods he learned back in Bordeaux. He uses cane pruning methods. It's done by hand and the grapes are harvested by hand. Much more labour intensive."

"Does it make a difference to the wine?"

"It depends who you ask. Euan would say yes. I agree to a certain extent but it depends on the end use and price you want. Ask different vignerons and you'd probably get several varied responses."

They pulled up in front of an old stone shed. Before Flynn got out, he turned to Keely. "Thanks for your interest and your support. I do appreciate it."

Keely smiled and lowered her gaze. There was something about those piercing blue eyes that made her heart thump.

"You and Kat have both been great." He jumped from the car.

Keely followed him. The lightness had gone out of her step. How could she have forgotten about the gorgeous Kat?

*　★　*

Flynn unlocked the weathered wooden door and led the way into the tasting room. The walls were thick stone with only one small window and the air was cool. The bright sunshine from outside had little chance to warm the room. He flicked the switch to activate a row of modern fluorescent lights.

"Welcome to the Haystack tasting room."

He crossed to the opposite wall, drew a bottle from the floor-to-ceiling wine rack then set it down on the old wooden cupboard in the middle of the room that served as a table. From the basic sink under the window, he retrieved the glasses he'd washed last time he'd been here with Kat. He smiled at the recollection. She'd been enthusiastic about the wine but she knew what she was talking about. He hoped Keely would at least like the taste well enough to allow her artwork to go on the label.

She was a good choice as a guinea pig. It was the young and less sophisticated wine drinkers he was aiming this wine at and he was keen to see what her response would be.

He unscrewed the cap and poured wine into the two glasses, set one on the table in front of her and picked up the other. He exhaled slowly, swirled the contents in his glass, sniffed it then stopped. He was conscious of Keely's deep brown eyes watching him closely. She hadn't picked up her glass.

"Are you going to try it?" he asked.

"I…I had a bad experience the last time I tried the swirling and sniffing. I really don't know what I'm doing."

"I'm not looking for an expert. Just your honest opinion." He could see she was hesitant. "I tell you what, I'll take you through the steps of tasting wine."

He walked around the makeshift table and stood beside her. Her worried expression made him smile.

"Just relax."

She looked down quickly, leaned forward and he watched over her shoulder.

"What do you see?"

"It looks almost clear." She glanced back at him.

"Yes, but now pick up the glass, tilt it and look at it with the white cloth on the bench behind."

Her hand hovered over the glass then she picked it up. "It still looks the same to me. Maybe a tinge of green around the edges."

"Good, now put it straight to your nose and take a sniff."

Keely held the glass so gingerly. It was as if she thought it might bite her. He watched as she slowly tipped it to meet her nose.

"That's it, now swirl the wine and sniff again." He moved closer. "Close your eyes and let your sense of smell take over."

She didn't look comfortable but she did as he asked. His own sense of smell was certainly working well. He inhaled her clean soapy scent.

"It has a fresh smell like...like mowed grass." She opened her eyes and frowned. "It's kind of fruity as well."

He grinned.

She shook her head. "I told you I'm no good at this."

"You're doing okay for a beginner. Now for the taste test. Take a small sip of wine, roll it round your mouth then open your mouth a little and breathe in. Think about the flavours then swallow the wine..."

"Aren't I supposed to spit it out?" The worry had left her face and the hint of a smile played at the corners of her mouth.

"You can if you want. After you swallow…or spit it out," he conceded, "think about the feeling that lingers after the wine has gone."

She took a sip of wine, rolled it round her mouth and swallowed.

"Take your time," he said. "What did you experience when the wine was in your mouth?"

She turned to look at him. They were standing quite close and she was nearly as tall as he was so her eyes looked directly into his. He could see a sparkle of excitement.

"At first it was quite tart, almost acidic, but after I swallowed it was different, fruity…passionfruit I'd say, then there was a clean crisp finish."

She kept looking at him, those deep brown eyes watching him carefully.

"That's it." He picked up the bottle and pointed to the label. "The variety is sauvignon blanc semillon, or SBS as we call it, from the Margaret River region. The winemaker is yours truly and now it has a name." He poured more wine into her glass and picked up his own. It was all falling into place. With or without Euan, he was moving forward with this wine. When people were lining up to buy it, Euan wouldn't be able to go back to only producing single varietals. "Here's to Scarecrow. The latest creation from Levallier Dell wines in their Haystack series."

Keely touched her glass to his and they both took a sip.

"I've entered it in a wine show."

"With this?" Keely pointed to the handwritten label.

"It's only a small local show. That's all it needs. The wine has to speak for itself. Besides, I hadn't decided on the label until I saw your sketch."

"I can't believe my artwork will be on the bottles. It's so exciting." She took another sip. "I think I could get the hang of this wine tasting."

"Well, if that's the case, you can help me taste the red." He put down his glass and picked up two more from the sink. "Finish your wine then follow me. The steps are a bit rickety so wait till I've put the lights on." He was pleased Keely had liked the wine. It had been different with Kat. She understood it all from a winemaker's point of view but Keely was like a clean slate, she was keen to learn and he was enjoying the role of instructor.

★   ★   ★

Euan replaced the phone in the base and put a pod in the coffee machine. He wanted to make a few calls while Flynn wasn't about.

He'd headed off earlier saying he was taking Keely out for a drive. That was a good thing for both of them. Euan was pleased to see them together. Flynn could do with someone like Keely. It was a shame she had moved to the studio but Euan understood her reasons and at least it meant she was staying on at Levallier Dell a bit longer.

He glanced around the room and noticed the bowl of roses on the coffee table among the carefully placed magazines. He and Flynn had managed for years but there was something comforting in having a feminine touch around the place again. Maggie did her bit when she came to stay but that wasn't often. His mind flitted briefly to Dianna but there was no point in wishing for things you couldn't have.

Euan pushed away thoughts of their recent time together in Sydney and then in Byron Bay and how much he'd enjoyed being with her and went to inspect the contents of the freezer. They were going to need more meat for the barbecue. The guest list had grown once he'd started making a few calls and Pam had rung and mentioned a few more people she'd contacted. Trouble was, the weather forecast wasn't sounding good. They would have to squeeze a lot of people into this room if the predicted showers came through.

He looked out onto the verandah, which was perfect in good weather. Then he thought about the large area along the side of the house that had once been Lucy's dream for the cellar door. Flynn was hell bent on resurrecting it for the Divine Wine and Dine weekend and they were committed now. It was also the perfect place to hold a barbecue.

He took his coffee and went out to see how much work it would take to clean it up.

* * *

Keely downed the last of the wine and crossed to the door in the wall that Flynn had disappeared through. She took some deep breaths. She hadn't had that much wine but she'd only had a quick bite to eat for lunch and she felt light-headed.

That could have something to do with Flynn stepping her through the wine tasting. She was pleased he had taken the trouble to try to teach her but his proximity had been quite unnerving and when he smiled and looked at her with those piercing blue eyes her head spun, without any help from the wine. She had to admit she was attracted to him.

It wasn't as if she hadn't felt this way before but she was always so awkward with men. Past relationships had never lasted long. Either they'd wanted more than she was prepared to give or she was a stepping stone for them to get close to one of her girlfriends, usually Bec with her long blonde hair and bubbly personality. Not that Keely could blame them; Bec's bright smile and easy banter was what had made her a ready friend on their first day at high school. Whatever the reason, Keely's relationships had never lasted more than a couple of months. She had been attracted to plenty of men but it never seemed to eventuate into anything.

"Watch those steps," Flynn called as she hovered in the doorway.

There was no rail, so she stepped down the three rungs carefully then stood in the dim cellar and waited for her eyes to adjust after the brightness of the tasting room. The packed-dirt floor enveloped the room in a musty earthy smell. Along the walls were barrels, each lying on its side, with letters and numbers scrawled on their ends.

"This used to be a farm storage shed. It's built into the side of the hill with door access at the other end." Flynn waved in the direction of two ceiling-height wooden doors filling the far wall. "When we bought the Haystack Block I remodelled it as a cellar. We planted the semillon and sauvignon blanc vines and then because the previous owner had already planted the cabernet sauvignon I talked Euan into planting the merlot so we could make a red blend. The cab sauv and the merlot are in these barrels, along with a small amount of Euan's precious cabernet franc."

"But you said we were going to taste it." Keely looked around. "Surely not from a barrel?"

"That's what this is for. It's called a wine thief." He held up a curved stainless-steel tube-like instrument then took the stopper out of one of the barrels and inserted the thief. There were already red stains around the hole. "You draw up a little, hold your thumb over the end and then let it run into the glass." He demonstrated then passed her the tube and a glass. Keely watched fascinated as the wine ran from the tube into her glass. Suddenly the glass was almost full.

"Stop now," Flynn said.

"How?" Keely wailed as the red liquid flowed over the glass, ran down her arm and dripped onto her pale pink shirt.

Flynn took the thief from her hand and the wine stopped. There was silence for a moment as they both stared at Keely's trembling glass then the red stain that had splattered down her shirt and jeans.

"How about I tip some of that off?" Flynn took her glass and poured some of the contents onto the dirt floor. A smile tugged at the corners of his mouth.

"Clumsy Keely strikes again," she said.

"I should have done it. You're such a quick learner I thought you had the hang of it."

"Lucky you've got a dirt floor."

"Red stains are one of the hazards of winemaking." His face broke into a grin. "You might need to soak those clothes."

"Don't worry. I'm sure they'll be fine." She flicked her hand dismissively over the damage.

"Are you still game to try it?" Flynn offered her the glass, divested of half its contents.

Keely took it and tried to remember the tasting steps he'd taught her with the white wine. She was extra careful with her swirling and sniffing then she took a sip.

Aware of Flynn's close scrutiny, she tried to disguise the involuntary grimace that contorted her face as the wine bit into her tongue. She turned away quickly and spat the contents onto the floor. It was terrible. There was a noise behind her. She glanced back to see Flynn putting the stopper back in the wine barrel.

He looked up. To her surprise his eyes were sparkling and his face wide with a smile. "I take it you don't like my red."

Keely looked down at the glass. What could she say? He was so proud of his wine but it had tasted like a cross between sarsaparilla and kerosene. "I told you I'm not a competent wine judge," she mumbled.

"Don't worry." He put a reassuring hand on her shoulder. "Reds aren't to everyone's liking." He laughed even louder. "Besides, there's still time. It's not quite ready to bottle yet."

Keely ran her tongue around the inside of her mouth. Just as well, she thought. The only thing that stuff would be good for was cleaning paint brushes.

Euan sat up. In spite of being back in his own bed, he'd had a restless night. Pain snaked down his neck and across his shoulders. He grimaced. Surely I'm not so old that I can't recover from a hard day's work, he thought.

Most of the day before he'd spent cleaning out the cellar-door area, ready for Flynn's birthday barbecue. Keely and Flynn had returned in the late afternoon and had pitched in and helped but before that he'd been up on a ladder, chopping back plants and cleaning off rafters and walls. The bagged finish on the walls had been authentically coated with years of dust, which wasn't very tasteful for entertaining.

He reached his hand behind, massaged a shoulder blade then slowly slid his feet to the floor. The clock showed nine am. He couldn't believe he'd slept that late. He hoped a shower would spark him up. Pity he didn't have time for a surf but there was still too much to do to get ready for the barbecue.

It was hard to imagine that Flynn was thirty-three. At first, each day after Lucy died had seemed an eternity, but the last few years had flown by. He wondered what Lucy would think of Flynn now. It had added to her distress to know she would miss seeing him turn into a man. Euan couldn't pinpoint when that had happened. Flynn's last years of school were a blur, then he'd gone interstate to study and then overseas to work.

Somehow, Euan had kept the vineyards going with Hugh's help. Even in the deluge of despair that had engulfed him after Lucy died, Euan had found the winemaking had kept him sane; that and escaping to the surf whenever he could.

He gave the surf one more wistful thought then stepped under the shower, hoping the water would wash away his aches and pains. Times had changed and he had to keep his wits about him when it came to marketing their wine. Levallier Dell produced premium wines and Flynn was an important part of that. Euan tipped his face to let the water sluice over him. He understood Flynn's youthful need for change. That had been one of the reasons for Euan's own trek to Australia all those years ago. But he'd had to make a new start without the benefit of his father's help back then. Levallier Dell was doing well and Flynn didn't need to forge his own path, but Euan didn't know how to talk to him about it.

Lucy's death had changed their relationship. Anna had become a substitute mother *and* father for Flynn. Maggie had done her bit. Euan hadn't felt needed and in any case he'd been incapable of offering comfort to anyone else. It wasn't until Flynn had been gone a couple of years that Euan had begun to regret not offering more solace to his son. Slowly shedding his grief, Euan had realised he was lonely and began seeking female company. There had been several women over the years but none of them had been able to replace Lucy and so the relationships had never lasted, until now.

He grimaced at himself in the bathroom mirror. That's if you could call seeing Dianna a couple of times a year a lasting relationship. She seemed to accept their long separations, never making demands. The first time they met was at a wine dinner and he'd been attracted to her immediately. She liked wine and was knowledgeable about it as well, and they had the French connection in common – her parents were French – but there was more to it than that. They'd met again the next day and often over the following weeks and a relationship had developed. They were a good match, not just physically but intellectually.

In the last couple of years, he'd made extra trips to the east on top of his work travels and several visits up to Perth when she flew in there. This last time, they had even discussed travelling overseas together. Suddenly, there was more to this relationship than just a convenient affair. He had to admit it had been harder to leave her this time and he had stayed on an extra week, making the excuse that it was the surf he was enjoying. That wasn't a lie but he could surf here. What he didn't have here was Dianna.

He walked back to the bedroom, rubbing his wet hair with the towel, and was greeted by the sound of dishes from the kitchen and the delicious smell of fresh baking. His empty stomach rumbled. There was no point in imagining Dianna living here in domestic bliss. Her work kept her too busy.

He sighed and opened the door. Keely looked up from the book she was thumbing through as he crossed the room.

"Doing a spot of cooking?" He couldn't help but smile. Keely usually maintained a tidy kitchen but this morning things were quite different. Not only did it appear that every cooking utensil was in use, Keely herself was splotched with puffs of white, including a smudge that crossed from her cheek to the tip of her nose.

* * *

Keely jumped. "I didn't know you were still here." She straightened the books in front of her. She'd thought she had the house to herself. "Would you like some breakfast?"

"I'll just get myself some toast and coffee."

She leapt up. "I don't know if you'll be able to find it in the mess."

"What are you doing?"

She bustled around Euan, trying to clear a space on the bench so he could plug the toaster in. "I thought I'd make a cake for Flynn."

Euan raised his eyebrows. "Some cake."

Keely followed his gaze to the benches. There were things everywhere. "Well, I thought I'd make a couple of different kinds so there'd be enough for everyone. Then I decided to make some mini pavlovas. I hope you don't mind, there were plenty of eggs."

"I don't mind but you don't need to go to all this trouble. Everyone will bring something."

"The pavlovas will keep. I wanted to test them out before the Divine Wine and Dine weekend, anyway."

Euan let out a deep sigh as he sat down with his breakfast. "You don't have to be involved with that, Keely. It was Flynn's idea. He needs to organise it."

"Well he is, of course." She began to stack up the dishes. "But I'm happy to help."

"You've already helped us a lot about the place. Flynn and I need to have a serious talk about what needs doing but you don't have to wear yourself out over it."

Keely gripped the benchtop. She didn't want to interfere but she hated to see Euan and Flynn at loggerheads. Besides, she was looking forward to the coming weekend. Living here had given her the feeling she'd swapped her life for someone else's. She relished it and didn't want to let it go just yet.

"I'm not. I enjoy helping." She looked over the mess at Euan. "Levallier Dell is a special place. I can understand you not wanting lots of strangers tramping over it but it's only once. If we make a good impression, it can't harm the reputation of your wine and it's a chance to showcase Flynn's new wine. His new label should look great and I like the wine, if that's any recommendation." She gave a wry smile.

Euan's expression wiped the smile from her face. She'd said something wrong.

"Where is Flynn?" he asked.

"He's gone to get the chairs and tables for the party. He said something about them being scattered around the place, in sheds and things. I need a few bits and pieces from the shop and he said he'd drop me in town later, when he goes to the Haystack Block."

"I'd better go and help him before he's rearranged the whole property."

Keely watched Euan go and tried to think back over what she'd said that might have upset him. She'd thought he was getting used to the idea of having the cellar door open for the coming wine weekend and he surely knew about Flynn's wine. She put her hand to her head and rested an elbow on the ledge above the bench.

"Bloody hell, I'm such an idiot," she muttered. Euan knew about the wine but probably not about the label or Flynn's intention to sell it at the cellar door. "Damn those two prickly men." She put the baking trays in the sink and began to scrub.

* * *

Kat sat at a corner table, away from the remaining diners, and picked at the late lunch Michael had prepared for her. The marinated octopus salad was delicious, with just the right combination of lemon and garlic, but she didn't feel hungry. For the last three hours, she'd worked the cellar door. It was the manager's day off and they were short-staffed. She didn't mind. She loved the people contact.

Peter's wife, Angela, was the only other family member there besides Pappou. Kat liked her. She was very good with the customers and quietly managed the staff. The only time she was a little flustered was when Pappou spoke to her. Poor thing was obviously intimidated by him.

After a slow start, the visitors had kept coming thick and fast. The lunch tables had been filled and re-filled, she'd lost count of the covers they'd done, and Pappou had been in his element either behind the counter promoting his wines or moving from table to table, talking to those who stayed on to dine. Perhaps Kat had inherited some of her love of working with people from him. He certainly knew how to turn on the charm, but he was genuine and he was confident in the quality of his food and wine.

"It's nice you can take a break. You've been busy." Pappou stood beside her holding a plate. "Can I join you?"

"Of course," she said brightly. They were all but alone in this part of the room. Maybe this was her chance to talk to him. Time was running out.

"You're fitting in very well here," he said.

"It's easy to fit in. Everything runs so well. Angela does a great job."

He ignored her reference to his granddaughter-in-law. "The cellar door is a good operation. Now that we've expanded, we need to attract bigger events. Weddings, corporate conferences. We could even have music and put on shows." He waved his hands. "The sky's the limit. I'm sure you are full of good ideas. You can have an office next to Michael's out the back. We can convert a storeroom, there's plenty of space. Where do you want to start?"

"Pappou...I need to talk to you about that." Kat put down her fork and reached for the water glass, twirling it in her fingers.

"What is it?"

She took a breath. "I have to return home next week."

"I understand. You need to talk to your parents and collect your things. That's fine. I can ring your mother and explain—"

"No, Pappou. It's not that. I really appreciate your offer but...you already have someone who could do the job."

"Michael says he's got enough to do."

"Not Michael. Angela."

"She is not true family. The job is yours."

"I can't accept it." Now that she'd finally said it she felt such a relief.

"You are my granddaughter."

"I'm sorry. It's a very generous offer."

"I don't understand. Your parents' business won't be a challenge for you. I've watched you, Katerina. You are good with wine and people. You are calm and level-headed in business. Managing the cellar door at River Dynasty is the perfect opportunity for someone with your talents."

"I know it is." Her heart raced. Pappou might think her calm but when it came to dealing with him, she was a bag of nerves.

"What's the matter then? Do you need time at home?"

"No...I've been offered another job...in Singapore."

"What?" He pushed back in his chair. "When did this happen?"

Kat glanced around. The other diners were leaving and there was no one nearby. "Mal offered me the job a while ago. I came here to take a break and think things through."

"What kind of job is it and who is Mal?"

"Mal Wilson. He's an expat Australian living in Singapore. He runs a big wine-buying consortium and he wants me to be the Australian face of the company in Singapore."

"How long have you known him? How do you know he's who he says he is?"

"I've checked it all out, Pappou. We met at a wine promotion in Sydney and we've met several times since then. Besides...I've fallen in love with him."

"You've what! That's ridiculous." Pappou shouted and slammed his hand on the table. The cutlery clattered on the plates.

A few customers at the tasting bar looked with interest in their direction.

"I hoped you would support me with this," she said softly.

"Bah!"

"Please, Pappou. I came here to give myself space to think things through and I have."

"What does your mother say? Surely she doesn't agree."

"I haven't told her yet."

"There, you see." He stood up. "It just won't happen. Singapore! You can't go there when your family needs you here."

Kat looked from her barely touched plate of food to her grandfather striding down the room. He went through the glass doors without looking back. A hand rested on her shoulder. She looked up into Michael's gentle eyes.

He grimaced. "You've told him then."

★ ★ ★

Euan came back into the quiet house. He made himself another coffee and sat down. Everything was ready for the party. Keely had cleaned up the kitchen and the fridges were overflowing with food. He'd be sorry to see her go. She had brought some spark back to their family life, made the work enjoyable. Flynn had helped him stock the drinks, and he'd even cracked a few jokes. Now all that was needed was a bit more meat for the barbecue and everything should go to plan.

He had to admit the job of cleaning up and organising it hadn't been so bad. Keely and Flynn had put the final touches to the setting up and he and Hugh had acted as gofers. It had all come together so well. Flynn knew the look he wanted and Keely had the creative flair to make the dullest corner look appealing. She'd brought up some of Lucy's wall hangings from the studio and arranged pots of coloured plants and cushions around the planking Hugh had brought in for extra seating. Flynn had been busy with lights and he'd turned an old cupboard into a useful appendage to the original bar. Teamwork, that's what it had been.

The cellar-door area had cleaned up well. It was a shame it didn't get utilised more. Although with Flynn involving them in the coming wine and food weekend, it would get another use. After that, who knew?

Euan couldn't bring himself to commit to Lucy's dream of the cellar door. Earlier it was because it was too painful to be reminded of Lucy and these days it was because he couldn't be bothered. Markets had changed but Levallier Dell wine was still sought after. They didn't need the hassle of a cellar door. And it was joined to the house. Back when they first built their home he'd gone along with Lucy's idea of having it there but now he couldn't abide the lack of privacy it would mean. There'd be people everywhere, children racing around the garden, cars parked under every available tree. He'd put up with it for the special wine weekend, it was for charity after all, but that was it.

He groaned when his mobile rang and he had to get up to find it. It had been good to just sit.

"Levallier Dell, hello."

"Euan?"

He stood up straight and gripped the phone tightly. "Dianna?"

"Yes, it's me, and guess what! I'm on my way to the plane. I'm coming your way. I'll be in Margaret River tomorrow morning. Can you meet me?"

* * *

Flynn pulled up outside the supermarket. "I'll be about half an hour. Is that long enough?"

"Plenty," Keely said. "I only need a few things and the extra meat your dad wanted."

She waved him off then wrestled a trolley from the stack and joined the other weekend shoppers inside. The thought of the crowd coming for the barbecue made her a bit anxious but at least she knew a few of them.

She'd enjoyed the cooking but there wasn't enough cream for the pavlovas or fruit to put in them. The salads needed some finishing touches, and she wanted candles for the birthday cake and a few basic supplies for the studio. It took some time to find what she was looking for in a strange shop.

"Hello, Keely. Those men have got you shopping for them, have they?" Anna tut-tutted up behind her.

"Hello, Anna."

"I hope you haven't done too much work for this party. Sean and I are bringing all the sweets."

"Oh…" Keely faltered. "I just made a birthday cake and a few other things…"

"There's no need. You're a visitor. Family take care of these things. I always make Flynn a birthday cake."

Keely nudged the packet of candles underneath the assortment of goods in her trolley. "That's nice of you."

Anna chuckled sharply. "If it was up to Euan, poor Flynn would never have had a birthday after Lucy died. I'm amazed they're having this barbecue. They've hardly—"

"Keely!"

She looked over Anna's shoulder to the bushy-haired man who was hurrying towards her. Something about his faded t-shirt and ripped shorts was familiar.

"Keely, it's good to see you're okay."

He wrapped her in a warm hug and she smiled. "Marty?" Over his shoulder she noticed Anna's disapproving look.

"I'll leave you to catch up with your friend," she said.

Marty let Keely go and stepped back. "Everything went alright then? I didn't like to leave Perth without seeing you but the nurse said you couldn't have visitors for a while and Steve had organised a ride—"

"I'm fine, Marty." Keely watched Anna push her trolley slowly on up the aisle. "Thanks for packing up my things."

"So, what are you doing here? I thought you'd planned to go north after Perth."

"I did, but I needed somewhere to recuperate after the operation and Euan…a friend, offered me a place down here. Are you staying in Margaret River?"

"Not far away. Just up the coast a bit at Gracetown." He smiled and ran his fingers through his hair. "I haven't quite got the hang of surfing like Steve and Mike. I guess I'm a slow learner. They've gone to try out the Boneyard today."

"Sounds scary." Keely smiled.

"They say it's aptly named." He glanced back behind him. "Was that woman from the family you're staying with?"

Keely followed Marty's nod in time to see Anna move stiffly around the corner. "No, a friend of theirs. I'm staying at Levallier Dell Winery, it's a bit of a way out of town. Two blokes run it, a father and son, and they've let me have their little studio overlooking the river."

"Sounds good. Have you got transport? You'll have to come and spend the day with us."

"I don't think surfing's for me."

"You don't have to surf. The beaches are magnificent. Just come and have some fun." The dimple on his cheek deepened as he grinned.

"How will I find you?"

"Mobile reception can be patchy but send me a text or you can try to call me."

Keely got out her mobile. "My phone was stolen that night I ended up in hospital but I got it back." She searched her contacts and found his name. "Yep, I still have your number. The studio doesn't have a phone so I'll text you the house number in case you can't get me. I'm sure Euan or Flynn would take a message."

"There's no Mrs Levallier Dell?"

"No, but—"

"Keely!" Anna's sharp call made them both turn. "I see Flynn is parked out the front, waiting for you. Should I tell him your friend will drop you home?"

"No, thanks." Keely turned back to Marty. "I'd better go."

"Who is that old girl?" he asked.

"Everyone's favourite lady, it seems."

"Everyone, but you?" There was that dimple back again.

She gave him a hug. "It's great to see you again, Marty, but I'd better not keep Flynn waiting. Say hello to the others for me. I might come and catch up this week."

"Make sure you do." He winked and gave a wave as she turned and pushed her trolley towards the checkout.

"How's your day been so far?" the girl behind the counter asked in a sing-song voice.

"Fine, thanks," Keely replied, acutely aware of Anna's eyes watching her closely from the next lane.

CHAPTER
21

"It's a great idea to use this space." Pam put the large bowl of salad and the platter of nibbles onto the makeshift table in the cellar-door area.

Keely was amazed at the food everyone had brought. It was hard to imagine they'd need it all.

Pam did a slow scan of the room. "It has a real welcoming feel to it," she declared.

Keely agreed with her. There were fluorescent lights on the rafters but they'd left them switched off. The sconce lights along the walls gave a softer illumination and Flynn had hung strings of festoon lights in loops between the exposed beams. Clear blinds had been rolled down on the open wall, guests were entering via a side door, and Euan had borrowed some pole gas heaters in case it was cold later.

Flynn had also brought the old wooden cupboard from the Haystack Block tasting room to add on to the bar. It had a solid wood top and he had nailed flattened corrugated iron around three sides of the base. All the walls had a rough bagged finish and down the middle of both sides he had nailed pallets. Keely had helped him attach pots of plants to create sections of cascading greenery. Along with the tables made from old wine barrels, the whole room felt country chic and perfect for a cellar door.

"Great place for a party." Connor put down his esky, lifted the lid and pulled out some cans. "Anyone for a beer?"

"Put that away, Connor." Euan came up behind them. "We've got plenty."

"I'll have one." Sean arrived, loaded down with containers of food.

"What's all this?" Flynn said.

"Happy birthday," Anna and Megan chorused from behind Sean, their arms just as laden.

"I've made your favourite cake." Anna kissed Flynn on the cheek before she handed over a large plate with a beautifully decorated cake. "I know how much you love strawberry and hazelnut cream."

"Thanks, Anna." Flynn smiled and helped them take the food inside.

Keely tried not to think about the chocolate layer cake she had slaved over. Someone would eat it. She hung back as more people arrived, most of whom she didn't know. The space was filling fast. Perhaps the extra food would be necessary.

"What are you drinking, young Keely?" Connor's cheerful voice spoke close to her ear above the sound of the music and voices.

Before she could answer Euan appeared on her other side.

"I've poured you a glass of wine."

"Thanks." Keely took the glass he offered and sipped from it. She smiled. "Your chardonnay?"

The creases of his smile spread across his face and he nodded. "This young lady is a fast learner, Connor. And she has good taste. She likes the fine wines from the exclusive Levallier Dell cellars."

"You're full of the blarney as usual, I see," Connor said. "Speaking of chardonnay, I hear a few vineyards suffered a bit of damage with that storm we had. How did you get on here?"

"Only minimal shoot loss. The hail didn't last long here. We must have been on the edge of it. I don't think it will have too much impact."

"It's weird, isn't it? Evidently your neighbours didn't fare so well."

"I wouldn't know." Euan stiffened.

"The word is – a *lot* of damage. Theo will be under pressure with a loss like that. He's outlaid a lot of money for the cellar-door extensions and he still owes big on our old patch of land."

Keely could see the twitch in Euan's cheek.

"You know I don't listen to gossip, Connor," he said.

"This is not gossip, mate. I've heard it straight from Tony. Theo has his back to the wall at the moment."

Keely took a sip from her glass, frantically trying to think of something she could say to change the subject.

"I am not interested in anything to do with Theo or any of his family," Euan said.

Over his shoulder, Keely could see the door and at that moment Kat appeared through it. Keely saw her glance around, probably looking for Flynn, who was nowhere to be seen.

"Come on, Euan. This is me you're talking to," Connor said. "A breakdown of communication meant you missed out on that land of ours once before. There might be a chance to get it back."

Kat saw Keely, gave her a little wave and walked towards her. Keely glanced from Euan's serious face to Kat's smiling approach. "Excuse me, I'll leave you two to the business talk," she said and stepped around him.

"Sorry, I didn't mean to..."

She heard the start of Connor's apology as she greeted Kat. "Hello. Are you looking for Flynn? I think he must be inside." She decided to steer the new arrival away from Euan. Kat was a good person but Euan didn't appear to be in the mood to recognise that. All he would see was Theo's granddaughter.

The party was in full swing by the time Keely spied Mary and David.

"Hello, Keely."

"Oh, Mary, you made it. Hello, David." Keely had to shout above the music and the loud voices of the large crowd now packed into the cellar-door space.

"We thought we'd pop out and say a quick hello. David is still madly organising things for next weekend."

"How's it all going?" Keely asked.

"Shaping up well," David said.

"What about here?" Mary raised her eyebrows. "Has Euan come to terms with Levallier Dell's involvement yet?"

"I think so." Keely sidestepped as one of Flynn's friends lurched her way past from a boisterous group nearby.

"Looks like everyone's enjoying themselves." Mary laughed. "Where's the birthday boy?"

Keely glanced around. "I'm not sure." She'd hardly seen Flynn since Kat had arrived. He had introduced Keely to some of his friends but, with so many people arriving, he had been swallowed up in the crowd. She'd kept herself busy putting out the meat Euan and Connor had cooked, setting out the salads and cleaning up.

At one stage, she'd been in the kitchen doing some dishes and had seen Flynn and Kat on the back verandah. They were talking earnestly together, their heads close, and Keely saw Flynn rest a hand on Kat's shoulder before someone came into the kitchen and interrupted her. When she had looked back, they were gone.

"I can see Flynn." David's call brought her back to the party. He set off through the crowd. Mary mouthed *see you later* and followed behind, saying hello to other friends as they passed through the crowd.

Keely was envious of the ease with which they mingled. Flynn's friends were a friendly bunch but she felt as if she remained on the outer. From their conversations she gathered they worked hard and they obviously partied hard, too.

One guy they called Noddy kept climbing on top of the keg tables. He was tall and thin and wore an Akubra hat. He'd down a shotty, then pretend to surf. Once he'd swallowed the drink, he'd slap his bum and whoop, looking more like a cowboy than a surfie. Everyone would laugh and he'd jump down, ready for the next round.

Keely continued to keep herself busy. Eventually she turned up next to Hugh with a platter of sweets in her hand. He was the man she'd seen around the winery on several occasions. Even though she had only been officially introduced to him that morning, he was one person Keely felt as if she knew after all the work they'd put in since, preparing for the party.

"Thanks, Keely." Hugh looked around then took another piece of the slice she offered. "Don't tell the wife. She's already on about me not fitting into my wedding suit."

Keely smiled and took a piece of slice for herself. She'd been too busy to eat much. She'd been eyeing off the chocolate nut slice Anna had brought, determined not to succumb, but she was hungry. She bit into it and almost moaned it was so delicious.

"Did you make all this?" Hugh waved his large hand over the plates of assorted sweets she was handing around.

Keely brushed her lips. "Not all of it."

"You've gone to a lot of trouble. It's good for Euan to have some support."

"Well, Hugh Lansdale, as if he hasn't had support over the years." Anna appeared at his shoulder and wagged her finger at him. "You've enjoyed plenty of my cooking. And I'll still be here when Keely leaves."

Keely glanced down at the plate. In a flash, Anna had spoiled her evening, reminding her of her interloper status again.

"You're not staying on then?" Hugh turned his steady gaze back to her.

Keely took a breath and forced a smile. "No, I'm on holiday. My original plan was to travel north. If I hadn't had my appendix out I'd be somewhere well beyond Perth by now."

"Lots to see in the west. I hope it works out for you." Keely glanced at Hugh's face. He was hard to read. Was he genuinely wishing her well or hurrying her away like Anna?

She carried the platters through to the kitchen to top them up. A group of girls had gone ahead of her to the main bathroom so she decided to nip in to the en suite attached to Euan's bedroom. Leaving the door ajar, she left the bedroom light off. The light from the room behind her and the moonlight through the open curtains lit her way to the bathroom where she flicked the switch. Euan's work clothes were in a pile on the floor and his shaving gear littered the handbasin. She hoped he wouldn't mind but she'd be quick. Just in case she locked the door behind her.

It had been kind of him to take her in but he must be glad to be back in his own space now. She'd be sorry to leave Levallier Dell. The time was getting closer for her to move on and yet a part of her didn't want to. Even though there'd been a few shaky moments during her stay, she'd enjoyed it.

Her mother had pressed her again about her plans earlier, when Keely had managed to put in a quick call before the first guests arrived. She hadn't needed to be too evasive as her mother was full of news from home. Evidently, her father and brothers were away on a fishing-trip weekend and her mother had been gardening all day and was just on her way out for dinner and a movie with some friends. The doorbell had chimed in the background and the call had ended hastily.

It had been a strange conversation. So different from the earlier ones where her mother had been full of worry and she'd wanted Keely to return home. Keely felt a mixture of relief that she was no longer being pressured but it was tinged with regret that they were all busy and not missing her. How contrary is that, she thought to herself as she came back through the bedroom. She'd wanted her mother to stop fussing and pressuring her and she had. Keely should be pleased.

Anna's voice carried from the kitchen. Speaking of people interfering, her mother paled in comparison to Anna. Keely slowed and stood silently behind the door. She'd had enough of Anna for one night and decided to avoid her if she could.

"Is this what you wanted me to carry?" Hugh's voice rumbled from the other room.

There was a clatter of plates. "Thanks," Anna said. "I thought Keely might be in here washing dishes. Can't have her doing too much work."

Keely gritted her teeth. No, not when you want to claim the prize for being the Levalliers' star friend and helper, she thought. She should just step out into the room. Surely she could embarrass Anna a little by suddenly appearing.

"Perhaps she's nipped down to the studio," Hugh said.

"She's certainly making herself at home."

"What do you mean?"

Keely had been about to step around the door but she hesitated.

"Flynn said she'd moved in there and she's got it all set up for making jewellery. Perhaps she's planning on staying."

"She just told me she was moving on."

"Yes but is she just saying that?"

"Come on, Anna, she—"

"She's not paying rent, you know."

A flush warmed Keely's cheeks. She couldn't step out now.

"She does a lot around the place," Hugh said.

"Piffle!" Anna's sharp response made Keely jump. "She's recovered from her op. Why doesn't she just move on? I think she's got an ulterior motive."

"Like what?"

"Flynn would make a good catch. I've seen the way she looks at him."

A door banged.

"Oh, Anna. Have you got the cake ready?" It was Pam's friendly voice. "Euan is going to make a speech."

"I'll bring it right out."

Keely stayed behind the door, waiting for them to leave. The music boomed in the background, masking the partying voices. Her emotions surged from embarrassment to anger. She stepped into the empty room, strode across to the kitchen and picked up the paper plates she'd bought for the birthday cake to be served on. No longer the beautiful chocolate cream cake she had made but Anna's strawberry and hazelnut creation. Keely gripped the plates tightly. Right now, she'd like to push Anna's face smack into the middle of it. The meddling old bat; she knew nothing about Keely. And what did she mean about the way Keely looked at Flynn? She kept her feelings to herself.

Outside, the music stopped and she could hear Euan's voice calling the crowd to attention. She went through the office door to join the party. Damn Anna and her snooping. Keely's earlier enjoyment had evaporated.

"We won't hold you up for long." Euan's voice carried across the room. Keely edged around the group in front of her and found a spot close to where Euan stood near the food table, with Anna's cake covered in candles and Flynn beside him.

"We'll be brief. I'd just like to thank you all for coming to celebrate Flynn's thirty-third birthday…" There were a few whoops from the crowd. "He was in South Australia when he turned twenty-one and we didn't have a party."

"Make the most of this one, Flynn," called a voice. "You may not get another till you're fifty!"

There were chuckles from the crowd.

"Thanks for that, Bennie." Euan shuffled his feet then continued. "I was about Flynn's age when Lucy and I came to Margaret River and started Levallier Dell. So Flynn has been part of this place since before he was born—"

"So unlike you he's a local." It was Bennie's voice again and there was more laughter.

Euan waited for quiet and went on. "I want to say how proud I am of his achievements."

Keely watched both Levallier men closely. Neither looked comfortable at being the centre of attention. Though Flynn was taller, the facial likeness was striking. Even their lopsided stance was the same.

"He has an affinity with the vines and is a talented winemaker."

The crowd was very quiet. Euan looked straight ahead but Keely saw the quick look of surprise that flashed across Flynn's face before he shifted his weight to his other leg and looked down.

Euan went on. "It's good to see so many friends here to share the celebration with us."

"And good that we've been fed some decent food," a voice called from the back; not Bennie this time, but people laughed.

Euan's face crinkled into a grin and deep smile lines formed on Flynn's as his lips turned up. Keely held her breath. She was growing to love that smile.

"Yes, Noddy, I know we don't always provide a gourmet meal but we have damn good wine," Euan said.

There were some cheers and murmurs of agreement.

"Anyway," Euan continued, "Anna has outdone herself with another superb birthday cake, which Flynn is going to cut."

He handed Flynn a knife. There was a moment's pause as both Levallier men studied each other then Flynn stepped forward.

"Before I do, I'd like to thank Euan and Pam for organising tonight. Thanks for coming everyone and for the food you've brought, especially Anna for the cake." Flynn's eyes searched the crowd.

Keely glanced around. She couldn't see Anna but she noticed Kat standing near the food table.

"And thanks to our South Aussie visitor, Keely. She's done a lot towards preparation for tonight and I really appreciate her help."

Keely could feel the warmth spread up her neck to her cheeks and she pressed back against a wall, not wanting to be seen.

"Cut the cake," Noddy yelled from close beside her and there was soon a chorus singing 'Happy Birthday', as Flynn did the honours.

Someone shouted out a toast and three cheers. Kat offered Flynn a glass of wine and then there was the sound of clinking glasses as the group closest to him urged Flynn to give Kat a kiss. Keely watched him hesitate then Kat moved closer and kissed him.

It was a brief brush of their lips but Keely's heart sank. She knew they were good friends, an item, her mother would say, but she found herself wishing she were the one kissing Flynn. Not here in front of everyone, but somewhere away from the crowd, just the two of them.

"They make a lovely couple, don't they?" Anna murmured in her ear.

Keely shivered and spun around. Anna was standing on her other side.

"They're good friends," Keely mumbled and looked down as she recalled Anna's words about the way Keely looked at Flynn.

"More than that, I'd say…"

Raised voices from the group beside them made them both look around.

Noddy was climbing onto the keg table again.

"You want finely tuned bodies, check out this one," he called to one of the girls beside him.

He hauled his lanky frame up, downed the shot glass of liquid then undid his belt. His jeans slipped down to reveal a pair of gangly legs emerging from snug-fitting boxers.

He slapped his behind. "How's that for a fine set of chiselled buttocks," he called. Then he whooped and leaned forward in a surfing pose, but at that moment the table wobbled and he lost his balance.

There were screams and yells as he toppled forward. A couple of his mates tried to catch him but he slid across them like a crowd surfer in a mosh pit, losing his jeans as he went. Keely felt as if the world had been switched to slow motion. She saw him sliding towards her. She raised her hands to protect herself, but one of his arms went around her shoulders and she lost her balance. They crashed to the ground in a tangle of arms and legs, then everything went black.

* * *

The lights from the old Volvo reflected off the tunnel of trees as Euan drove Keely back to Levallier Dell. Luckily, Noddy had only broken a collarbone and nothing else. He was spending what was left of the night in hospital.

Keely ran her fingers self-consciously over the plaster on her forehead as she recalled Noddy landing on top of her. For a moment, the only sound had been the blare of the music, then voices had come from everywhere and Noddy had been carefully lifted, allowing her to see again. Keely had been so embarrassed she hadn't known what to say. She'd been acutely aware of Noddy sprawled across her, his lower body clad only in his boxers.

Anna had tut-tutted next to her, muttering about people drinking too much, and insisted they both get checked over. Keely blushed again as she remembered Flynn's wry smile, once they'd established no one was badly hurt.

"That's Noddy for you," he'd said. "Always sweeping the girls off their feet."

Keely had a deep cut above her eye but it hadn't needed stitches. The nurse had used some kind of glue and assured her there would hardly be a scar. Apart from a few sore spots that would probably make fine bruises in a day or so, she had been declared fit to go home.

There weren't many cars left in the yard as they pulled in under the carport but the lights in the cellar door were all on. Keely noticed the little red sports car was also still there.

Euan turned to her. "Here you are, safely home. Once again, I apologise for what happened, Keely."

"Euan, it's okay…" she started to protest. He had apologised several times already.

"Noddy's not a bad lad. He drinks a bit much but he's a talented young winemaker and he loves to surf, so he has got something going for him." Euan's smile crinkled across his face.

They got out of the car and walked through the carport to the cellar door. Euan stopped in front of her. "I forgot, you've moved to the studio. I can drive you down there, unless you'd rather stay up here tonight."

"No, I'm fine. I'll walk down in a while. I'll just see what else needs doing."

"No, you won't. We'll do it tomorrow."

Keely was wide awake and she hated dealing with messes the next day. "Euan, please, I'm fine." Acceptance settled on his face. She really needed to assert herself more often.

They walked through to the cellar door, which was packed up and tidy except for a stack of plates and leftovers on the food table.

"I'll take these through to the kitchen." Euan took up a tray loaded with dishes.

Keely stopped to pick up some cans from the garden. The floor had been swept and the chairs stacked. She looked across to the keg table that had toppled Noddy. Up until then the party had been going well. She checked her watch. It was one am.

There was a noise behind her and Flynn came through the door, an empty tray in his hands. "Euan said you're okay. I'm glad Noddy didn't cause too much damage, to you or to himself."

"I was going to clean up but it looks like most of it's done."

"Anna and Sean did a lot of dishes and Kat helped me clean up here after the last lot had left. Things kind of went quiet after Noddy's accident."

Keely couldn't help but replay the accident over in her head. What had she looked like, trapped under a half-naked man? She recalled Flynn's smile and snatched up an empty platter, turning away so he wouldn't see her colour up yet again. "I'll clean up in the kitchen before I go down to the studio."

"There's not much left to do. Just as well Noddy brought a halt to the proceedings, everyone went home early. Most of us have to work tomorrow, or I should say today." He stepped closer and took the plate from her hands. His eyes studied her closely.

She was mesmerised, unable to move.

He reached up and brushed the plaster on her head. "I'm sorry about that. I hope it's not too painful."

His touch sent a shiver through her. "No," she murmured. "I...I'd better head down to the studio."

"I'll walk with you."

Keely wanted him to but she thought of Anna's comments and—

"Oh, you're back." Kat came from the house. "How are you?"

Keely jerked back from Flynn. "I'm fine."

"I just want you to show me which bed, Flynn. Your dad has disappeared somewhere." She lowered her voice. "I don't want to end up in the wrong room."

Keely bolted for the door. Her head was spinning but not from the bump she'd received earlier. She didn't trust herself to speak.

CHAPTER
22

A persistent thumping echoed in Keely's head. She tried to ignore it then, beyond the noise, she heard her name.

"Keely." Euan's voice was raised.

She sat up, clutching the sheets to her and willing her eyes to focus. She was in her bed at the studio. What could he want? Surely it was still early. She felt as if she'd only just gone to bed.

There was a tap on the window. "Keely!" Euan called more urgently.

"Yes, I'm coming," she croaked.

Her mouth was as dry as a potato chip. She picked up her watch and peered at the little numbers that swam before her eyes. It wasn't even seven o'clock.

She stumbled to the door and tugged it open.

Euan stepped forward, a look of concern on his face. "Are you alright? You took so long to answer, I was worried."

"I'm okay." Surely he hadn't come down to wake her up just to ask how she was. "What's wrong?"

"I've had a call from Ken at the school. He's been trying your mobile."

Keely glanced around, wondering where she'd left it.

"He says he's frantic for a relief teacher and hoped you could come in."

She slumped against the doorframe and wrapped her arms around herself. The outside air was chilly and she shivered, but not just from the cold.

Euan was apologetic. "I said yes but I explained you'd had a fall. I said I'd come and check with you and ring back if you couldn't do it. I thought perhaps those bumps might be a bit sore today."

She tipped her head forward, letting her hair fall around her face. Her stomach churned. This was it. The demon had caught up with her in peaceful, idyllic Margaret River.

"I don't know…" She gulped in some air and held her breath.

Euan looked contrite. "I shouldn't have said yes. You're not feeling well enough. It's just that Ken sounded desperate. I think you were his last chance but I'll call him back and say you can't do it."

"Thanks, Euan. I really don't feel up to it today. If I went in they might end up needing a relief teacher for the relief teacher." She tried to keep her tone light."

"Sorry. Can I get you anything?"

"No. I'll be fine. I think I'll just go back to bed for a while."

"I've got to go in to the village this morning. Flynn will be around the place. You let him know if you need anything."

"Thanks."

Keely closed the door and went to the bedroom to find something warm to pull on over her pyjamas. Back in the kitchen, she put on the kettle and turned on the small heater. She took some long slow breaths. She had been so close to saying yes and returning to the classroom.

Thank goodness for the excuse of her cuts and bruises. She didn't feel that sore, just tired, but it had been a plausible excuse. Noddy had done her a favour with his surfing antics.

She sat down, let out a sigh and put her head in her hands. She would have to move on soon. It would be hard to keep coming up with excuses for not accepting the relief teaching role. If they were short, she was sure to be asked again and next time she might not have a good reason for saying no.

She wasn't in a hurry to go up to the house either, now there was the added complication of Kat sharing Flynn's bed. Keely didn't want to see them together. In some ways she wished Kat was an awful person so she could at least dislike her, but she wasn't so she didn't. Kat had been nothing but kind to Keely and in other circumstances Keely felt they could have been good friends.

Keely gripped her coffee cup, absorbing the warmth. Her time was running out. After this weekend she would have no more need to stay at Levallier Dell and she could head north, where no one would know her.

* * *

Euan had just hung up the phone when Flynn came into the family room.

"Who was that?" he asked.

"Ken rang to see if Keely could teach today but she's not up to it."

"Is she okay?"

"Just tired, she says. I have to go into the village for a few hours. I said you'd be around if she needed anything."

"You and I need to discuss the arrangements for the Divine Wine and Dine weekend."

"I know. It will have to wait till later."

"It's this weekend."

"I've got other things to do. I'll be back by lunch." Euan picked up the keys of the old Volvo then changed his mind. If he was going to meet Dianna, he wanted to do it in style. "I'll take your new car for a run if you're not using it."

"Take it whenever you like. It's a business car, not mine."

Euan decided to leave that topic alone. It could prove useful to have a good vehicle on the place, after all. "I noticed the little red car is still here."

"Kat stayed the night."

Euan watched Flynn square his shoulders as if he was preparing for a fight. The party had gone well the night before. They'd had a happy, relaxed time. Even Noddy's accident hadn't been too bad but already Flynn was taking on his defensive manner again.

"I see." Euan knew he had no say in what his son did with his personal life but he liked Keely and he had begun to hope she might be the one for Flynn. He sure as hell didn't like the idea of one of Theo's brood under his roof.

"No, you don't see," Flynn snapped. "Because there's nothing to see."

"Well, just take care. Theo's a snoop and I wouldn't put it past him to send his granddaughter to do his work for him."

"What work? You're paranoid where Theo's concerned."

"He'll be up to something. He always is." Euan knew he couldn't put his finger on it but he didn't trust Theo. There had been several incidents over the years and the land deal with Connor had been the last straw. Not that Euan blamed Connor. His back had been against the wall and Theo had made the offer via a third party so his real identity wasn't known until after the deal was done.

"You haven't spoken to Theo for three years, so how would you know?"

"He snuck around making that land deal with Connor, when he knew we wanted it."

"He's a shrewd businessman. If there's a prime piece of vine land beside your property for sale, you buy it." Flynn glared at Euan.

"We were going to buy it."

"You had a loose discussion with Connor then you went interstate and, as usual, we couldn't contact you. Connor needed to make a decision. Besides, we'd also been looking at the Haystack Block, which was a better deal in the end."

They were going over old ground. "I've got to go." It still annoyed Euan that he had missed out on the small piece of land along his boundary, even if the larger Haystack Block was proving to be good value.

"I hope you won't be gone all day. We need to go over the plan for the coming weekend."

"No doubt you'll tell me what I have to do." Euan didn't want to think about it. He was anxious to get in to the village to meet Dianna. He wondered what was bringing her to his part of the world. At the door he stopped and turned back. "Damn foxes took some guinea fowls last night. I cleaned up the blood and feathers out in the drive but you'd better have a look around. Not a good look if we're expecting customers."

Flynn's eyes blazed. "I don't know why you keep them, just to feed the foxes."

"They get rid of the garden weevil. There've been a few outbreaks but not here."

Flynn shook his head. "They're about as useful as your rose bushes that attract the bugs rather than help us to get rid of them."

Euan felt the vitriolic barb as sharply as if it had been a real knife stabbing at him. He turned from the anger in his son's eyes and walked away.

* * *

Theo shoved the diary back in his shirt pocket, rubbed his fingers back and forth over his chest and massaged the skin, trying to erase the ache. Things were not going well with the vines at River

Dynasty. First the hail, which seemed to have done the most damage on his property alone, then a large outbreak of garden weevil and now Tony had just confirmed there was downy mildew on the vines close to the Levallier Dell boundary.

Things were going from bad to worse with that patch of land between him and Euan Levallier. Perhaps it was cursed. He was beginning to wish he'd never bought it. The opportunity had seemed too good to miss at the time. Connor was desperate to sell and Euan had been away somewhere out of contact. Theo had done Connor a favour, offering a good price for the land with immediate settlement. What he'd really like to get his hands on was Levallier Dell itself. The soil was perfect, especially for Euan's cabernet franc vines, which produced high-quality wine year after year.

Theo stopped rubbing and picked up the coffee cup his wife had just brought in. She had given him a tongue lashing for making Katerina stay away. As if that was his fault. Their granddaughter was capable of making her own decisions, as she'd clearly pointed out. He still couldn't believe she had turned down his offer to work for the family business. Evidently she'd rung and said she was staying with a friend for a few days.

He gave a wry smile. Hopefully, the friend was Flynn Levallier and so maybe all was not lost. If Theo couldn't get Katerina to stay, perhaps Flynn could. Nothing like a bit of romance to make young ones change their minds.

* * *

The hire car pulled away with a toot and Dianna waved to the occupants. Euan strode forward and wrapped her in his arms. His lips found hers. Damn, how he'd missed her. He hadn't realised how much until now when he held her close. Her gentle perfume was intoxicating.

"Euan, I can't breathe."

He dropped his arms and took both of her hands in his. "Sorry." He bent forward and gave her another kiss, gently this time. "I've missed you."

Her hazel eyes were bright with humour. She squeezed his hand. "I've missed you, too."

"What brings you here? I didn't think you'd ever come this far south."

"The features editor was suddenly taken ill. We had a whole section planned for next month's edition on Augusta and the whales. I got told to get on the plane. I've managed to get the crew to stop over here for a night, instead of Perth. So…" She spun around and flung out an arm. "I want to see more than a car park. Show me this wonderful Margaret River you rave about."

Euan's thoughts raced. Where would she stay, what would they eat, how could he make the most of the time? "I want you all to myself." He certainly didn't want to spoil the day by introducing her to his grumpy son but he'd have to take her home eventually.

"You've got me." She smiled and nodded over his shoulder. "I like your car."

He turned to look at the gleaming LandCruiser with the Levallier Dell name adorning its side. "It's new…"

"Come on, then." She pulled at his arm. "Take me on tour."

"Alright, but we'll save Levallier Dell till the end."

"Saving the best till last." Dianna linked her arm through his.

"*Mais certainement, mademoiselle.*" And he kissed her again.

CHAPTER
23

Keely followed the path from the front of the studio down along the edge of the river. The day was sunny and warm and the well-worn track led her to a small wooden landing jutting precariously from the bank. Up higher was an old seat in the shade of some large trees and beyond that an old stone shed. Opposite her, on the other bank, the trees and shrubs crowded down to the water but on this side the vegetation was cleared a little, to allow access to the crude jetty below.

She had decided on a walk before she went up to the house, delaying the reality of seeing Flynn and Kat together. She hesitated again. The seat looked very tempting; a place to sit and enjoy the solitude for a while.

She turned at a sound behind her to see Flynn heading down the path. She started towards him.

"Stop where you are." His words were urgent and his voice low. He held both hands up, palms out.

She was surprised by his gruff manner and took a half step more before a movement on the ground a few metres in front of her made her freeze. A large snake was edging its way across the path away from the river.

"Just stay there," Flynn murmured. "He'll go on his way."

Keely watched with morbid fascination as the snake meandered slowly back towards the bush. It was in no hurry and seemed oblivious to their presence. Its head searched the ground in all directions and its body rippled over the bumps and leaf litter until it blended with the dappled colours of the bush beyond the track, where finally, to her amazement, it disappeared altogether.

Flynn came towards her but she kept her eyes locked fearfully on the spot where she'd last seen the snake, in case it suddenly reappeared.

"That was a big one," he said. "Must have been down for a drink. They can get very aggro at this time of the year. It's best to leave them alone."

Keely looked from the bush to Flynn. Suddenly her knees felt like jelly.

"Are you okay?" He put a hand under her arm. "Come and sit down."

She let him direct her further along the path, to the old seat.

"I guess you don't like snakes," he said as they sat.

"I've never seen one before. At least not in the wild."

"It's not exactly the wild around here." Flynn chuckled.

"No, but it's a real place." Her words tumbled out, not making sense. "I mean…I've only ever seen them on television or in a zoo."

"We have our fair share. It's best to avoid them, if you can."

Keely shuddered and looked across the river. It was so pretty here. She hadn't anticipated sharing it with a snake but it was the country, after all.

"I came to see if you were alright," Flynn said. "Euan was worried about you."

"There's no need. I've got a few sore patches but I'll be fine."

Flynn looked out across the river. "This is a good place. I sometimes come here to think."

Keely relaxed against the old seat. "You're very lucky. Levallier Dell is a beautiful property."

"Yes, it is." He continued to gaze into the distance. "It's just that it was more fun when Lucy was alive."

"You were younger then. Everything's more fun when you're young. No responsibilities. Perhaps you're just taking it for granted now. Sometimes you need to look with fresh eyes." Keely was studying the river. This would be a wonderful scene to sketch.

"Life isn't as bright without Lucy."

"You still miss her?" Keely snuck a quick look at Flynn. He was hatless and his hair fluffed out around his head. She resisted the urge to reach out and touch it.

"Some days more than others. She's been gone a long time. After she died…life changed, Euan changed. We were both grieving of course, but instead of supporting each other Euan shut himself away. Some weeks I hardly saw him. When I eventually finished school I was glad to get away."

"But you came back?"

"Lucy loved Levallier Dell…she loved me and she made me laugh. But life goes on. Euan's a different man but at least he's functioning again and this is home."

Keely looked back at the river. "Our families are so different."

"Yours would be bigger."

"I have two younger brothers. But I mean our parents are so different. Mine are both teachers and everything runs according to a plan. We don't…" Keely hesitated, trying to find the right words.

"I don't know, we just don't talk about things like you and Euan do." She picked up a stick and twirled it in her fingers.

"What, yell at each other you mean?"

"No. You both love this place. When you're passionate about something, it's bound to lead to differences of opinion as well as joy. I'm sure you both want the best for Levallier Dell and your wines."

"I suppose…"

They were silent for a moment, both gazing at the water as it drifted past.

"Your parents are teachers." Flynn broke the silence. "Don't chalkies all talk shop when they're together?"

"I prefer not to. Besides, they're both primary teachers. They wouldn't…they don't…I just can't talk about teaching with them." Keely drew squiggles in the dirt at her feet with the stick and thought about the way her parents shared the happenings of their day. They always managed to laugh even if they'd had a tough class. They just wouldn't understand hers. "Neither of them are into art. I used to like fishing but Dad always takes one of the boys these days. We have little else in common. I love them and I live under their roof but we don't share our lives outside our home." Keely twisted in the seat a little to look at him. "You and Euan are more like brothers than father and son."

"You think so?"

"My parents are more formal. Dad would have a fit if I called him by his first name, like you do Euan."

Flynn smiled at her. "That's probably Lucy's influence. She thought names and their meanings were very important so you should use them. Flynn is of Irish Gaelic origins and means son of a redheaded man. If I had been a girl, I'd still have been Flynn. Evidently it's also a suitable female name but I'm not sure if a girl would want a name that means she was supposed to be a son."

Keely laughed. "You're so lucky."

"Why?"

"I looked up my name meaning once. It's Irish too, and means beautiful and graceful." She laughed again. "My parents didn't know that when they picked it. They really mucked up there."

She glanced at Flynn then looked down. His eyes held a look she didn't understand. He probably felt sorry for her. She'd almost begged him to say 'no, they didn't muck up, you are beautiful'. Heat crept down her neck. Just for a short time she'd felt relaxed in his company, but he had only come to find her because Euan had been worried about her. What was she doing here?

She jumped up. Flynn got up too. She half turned to him. He placed a hand on her arm and his eyes searched hers.

"Keely…"

She winced as his grip tightened on her bruised elbow.

"Sorry…" He let go as if she were a hot potato.

"I'd better get going," she said. "It must be lunchtime."

"You don't have to get the lunch."

His words drifted behind her as she hurried up the path without looking back. In her mind, she saw Flynn's face close to hers again. What was that look? Had it been surprise? Her heart thumped in her chest and her hands trembled. He would be surprised if he knew she was falling in love with him. She couldn't allow herself to be such a fool. Kat was the one who had his heart.

★ ★ ★

Euan had taken Dianna for lunch at a new winery further north. He liked their wine and he'd heard the food was good and that had proved correct. They'd consumed some delicious seafood over a bottle of SBS and he had to admit it was a fresh, vivacious drop. Not bad for a blended wine. They sat in the corner of the balcony, which gave them a view over a neatly manicured lawn to a small lake.

Euan poured the last of the wine into their glasses and tilted his towards Dianna's. "Officially, welcome to Margaret River."

"I am beginning to understand why you like this corner of Australia." She stretched her arms luxuriously towards him, like a cat. "The scenery is beautiful, the wines are magnificent and the food is to die for. Who wouldn't want to live here?"

Euan raised an eyebrow. "Who indeed, *ma chère*."

"Are you implying I wouldn't?" She rested her elbows on the table, put her chin on her clasped hands and tilted her head sideways.

Euan held her gaze as he took a sip of his wine. "We come from different worlds, you and I."

"We do. However, when you left this time I had hoped you'd miss me enough to come back."

He put down his glass and reached forward. Taking her hands in his, he gently pulled them towards him and brushed them with his lips before he met her eyes again. "I did miss you. But you are tied to your world and I to mine."

"Love overcomes many obstacles."

Euan looked down at her soft hands, still clasped in his weathered grip. He had believed he'd never know the feeling again but he had realised, during his last visit to the east, that what he felt for Dianna was more than a convenient friendship. It was love. He just wasn't sure whether she felt the same. The logistics of combining their two lifestyles permanently were huge.

"You have your magazine and I have my vines."

"I do admit it would be hard for you to move them." Her pretty hazel eyes had a playful glint and her lips curved up in a smile. "And, if I'm to believe what you tell me, they are some of the best in the west. So…I've decided to make some changes with my work."

Euan studied her carefully. He felt too vulnerable to declare his feelings straight out. It was not like her to play games and yet…he managed a small smile and raised an eyebrow again, desperately trying to quell the rising hope he felt. "Are you saying you love me, *ma chère*?"

"Is this your French charm?" she mocked. "You wine me and dine me then expect me to do the proposing."

Euan needed no more encouragement; he pushed his chair back and took her in his arms.

★ ★ ★

"I think we've got everything under control." Flynn looked from Kat to Keely. "Let's open a bottle from Levallier Dell's new Haystack label…Scarecrow Dry White."

He said the name with such flourish that Keely expected him to pull a bottle from his sleeve. "Have you got them labelled already?" she asked.

"No." He made his way to the fridge. "But the labels should be here in the next day or so. We'll have to stick them on with the manual labeller to have some ready for the weekend."

"Uh oh, Keely." Kat laughed. "I don't like the sound of that 'we'."

Keely looked from Flynn, who had his head in the fridge, to Kat, who was getting out glasses, and grinned back. They'd worked well together, and she hadn't felt like the odd one out as she'd feared. Flynn and Kat hadn't been all over each other, as had happened with Bec when she had a new guy. Keely smiled as she recalled the text she'd received that morning from her friend declaring she'd met the love of her life…again. The last guy she'd met, at a New Year's party, had only lasted till May.

Flynn poured the wine and they raised their glasses.

"To teamwork," he said.

Keely took a sip of her wine. He was right. The three of them had certainly made a good team today.

Once Flynn had given up waiting for Euan to return, they'd set about making sure the coming weekend was planned to the last detail. Kat had said she'd have to go back to River Dynasty to help on the weekend but she was happy to do what she could to assist the preparations at Levallier Dell.

They'd gone over the menu and decided Euan could cook the meat for the pork rolls the day before. The mention of his father's name had made Flynn restless again until Kat had distracted him with her light banter and they'd got back to planning the food production.

Flynn had contacts for the local produce they needed and Megan's suggestion of a couple of teenagers to help with food prep and serving had been followed up. Keely had contacted a local couple who made gourmet crackers and were happy for their products to be used on the platters. Her job was to organise the food service over the weekend. It was a big task and Kat had given Flynn a pointed look that suggested she thought he was asking too much but Keely wasn't daunted. She'd been looking forward to it before Flynn remembered his aunt was coming to help. That had dampened her enthusiasm. Maggie was probably one of those people who, like Anna, would come in and take over.

Hugh had called Flynn away to look at something in the vineyard and Kat and Keely had baked another big batch of meringues for mini pavlovas. They'd got the production down to a fine art and were just cleaning up when Flynn returned.

"Euan's still not back?" he'd asked.

Keely shook her head in unison with Kat.

"It doesn't matter," Kat said. "You and Keely have everything running like clockwork."

"There are plenty of other things to be done."

Keely had seen the disappointment on his face. It wasn't her he wanted to be organising events with, it was Euan. Flynn badly wanted the coming weekend to be a success for Levallier Dell and he wanted Euan to share his interest.

Now as they drank their wine she could tell Flynn was still watching for Euan to appear. He turned away from the window and opened the fridge door. "I'm getting hungry. Is there anything in here we can use to rustle up a meal?"

"Uh oh. There's that 'we' again, Keely." Kat laughed.

Flynn pulled back his shoulders. "In spite of what some say, I am actually quite a good cook, you know."

"If you say so. Keely and I have been in the kitchen all afternoon. We're happy for you to prove it, aren't we, Keely?"

She nodded.

"Right!" Flynn rubbed his hands together and chuckled as he began to dig around in the fridge again.

Keely was pleased to see his good humour return. Kat had the knack of making him laugh. He put cheese and olives and salami on the bench while Keely finished the dishes. She was tired and there were still a few tender spots from her fall but she was happy. Flynn's laugh was infectious. How she loved to hear that laugh.

A shadow passed the window and she glanced up in time to see Euan approaching the door with a woman at his side. Damn, was this Maggie here already? Keely had hoped for a few more days without her.

The door slid back and Euan gently propelled the woman into the room. Kat and Flynn looked up from their preparations in the kitchen. There was no greeting from Flynn and the woman looked younger than Keely imagined Maggie would be.

"Hello, everyone," Euan said. "I'd like you to meet Dianna…a friend of mine from the east."

Keely noticed the pause in Euan's introduction. She glanced from him to the attractive woman beside him. Dressed in designer jeans and a black leather jacket nipped in at her waist, Dianna had a petite frame and the animal-print scarf at her neck highlighted her auburn hair. She looked smart and was regarding them all with interest.

Keely looked back to Euan. There was an air about the pair of them, a sparkle. Of course, he could put on the charm. He liked to act that way with women but there was something more to this.

"Dianna, this is my son Flynn."

"Pleased to meet you, Flynn." The newcomer stepped forward and reached out a well-manicured hand in a confident movement. She was a very attractive woman, younger than Euan, perhaps in her mid-fifties. "I've heard so much about you and this wonderful place. Now I know why your father doesn't want to leave."

Flynn shook her hand. He did it slowly, a puzzled expression flitting across his face before it was replaced with that steel he used to hide his feelings.

"Hello, Dianna." He straightened up. "I can't say that I've heard anything about you."

"This is Flynn's friend, Kat." Euan moved on quickly. "And our South Aussie visitor, Keely."

"Hello." Keely smiled at Dianna across the room.

"Dianna has work in Augusta tomorrow so she'll be staying the night," Euan said.

There was silence for a moment then Keely's mobile rang. She took it from her pocket, relieved to see the name on the screen.

"Hi, Marty," she said.

With the silence broken, the others were all suddenly moving and talking at once behind her.

She moved away to the corner of the room.

"How about coming to the beach tomorrow?" Marty said. "I'll be in Margaret River early so I could pick you up on the way back."

Dianna and Kat chatted happily behind her. There were still things to do for the coming weekend but the place was getting crowded. Maybe some time away would be good.

"That sounds great."

By the time they'd finished making arrangements, Flynn and Kat were working on meal prep together in the kitchen and Euan was pouring wine for everyone. Keely was the only one who noticed another well-dressed woman walk gracefully to the door and slide it open. Her long hair was swept up onto her head, her face was elegantly made up and, although it was plumper than Euan's, there was no mistaking the family resemblance.

"This party is in my honour, I hope," she said as she entered.

The babble of voices ceased for a brief moment before Flynn and Euan called out in unison, "Maggie!"

Flynn rushed across the room and squeezed his aunt in a bear hug.

"Hello, darling." She kissed him on the cheek then rubbed at it with her thumb before she put her arm through his and looked back at Euan. "No wonder I haven't heard from you two. You've been entertaining." She raised one elegant eyebrow and her lips turned up in a mischievous smile.

"Maggie, you should have let us know you were coming," Euan said.

"I did, brother dear. I'm just a few days early. Aren't you going to introduce me to this bevy of beautiful women?"

Keely thought Euan almost blushed. His face looked a little rosy as he introduced Dianna to his sister. Once again, he used the words 'friend from the east'. The two women shook hands then Maggie looked at Kat.

"And you must be the young woman Euan rescued from the hospital." Maggie held out her hand.

"No, Maggie. This is Katerina," Flynn said. "She's Theo's granddaughter."

"I see." Maggie shook Kat's hand. "Hello."

Keely steeled herself as Euan nodded in her direction and everyone looked her way. The other three women in the room were all beautifully groomed. Even though Kat had been cooking with Keely all afternoon she was still so tidy. Keely knew her hair needed brushing and she looked down at the pale pink shirt that had patchy wine stains and now extra splodges from her efforts in the kitchen.

"This is our traveller, Keely," Euan said.

"Hello Keely." Maggie clasped Keely's hand in her soft grip. "You must be much better. You look beautiful. My Levallier men have been looking after you properly, I hope." Her eyes were ice blue like Euan's and they held an almost mischievous gleam. Keely could see the fine lines in her skin and noted the hint of colouring in her elegantly groomed French roll and the soft fragrance of her perfume.

"Yes...I am...thanks..." she stammered, wondering if Maggie's eyesight was impaired. "It's nice to meet you."

"So, what have I interrupted?" Maggie turned back to her brother. "Were you having a party?"

"No, Maggie." Euan jumped in quickly. "Dianna has turned up unexpectedly."

"I hope there's a bed for me then," Maggie said. "You know I don't like that old hut you grandly call a studio."

Keely saw the glances flying between Euan and Dianna and from Flynn to Euan. This was all getting very complicated.

Euan ran his fingers through his hair. "We might need to do some rearranging—"

"I can go back to River Dynasty," Kat cut in.

"There's plenty of room," Flynn said.

"I'll leave you to it." Keely headed for the door. "I'm going to the beach tomorrow with a friend, so I think I'll get an early night. Last night's party is catching up with me."

"You'll eat first, won't you?" Euan said.

"I'm not that hungry and I can make a snack at the studio if I need." Keely turned back to the others. "Nice to meet you both, Dianna and Maggie."

Dianna gave a wave from the other side of the room where she had been examining the artwork on the wall. Maggie smiled and turned her steady gaze on her brother. Euan made a show of opening the door for Keely. Her last sight was of Kat, who was giving her a pleading look from the kitchen where she stood next to the stony-faced Flynn.

Keely stepped out into the fresh air and let out a long sigh. She was looking forward to escaping to the peace of her little studio.

CHAPTER
24

Theo rattled around, looking for the right container. There were plenty of others who could see to the spraying but he wanted it done now and everyone else was busy. He peered at the writing on the plastic drum and cursed again. A globe had blown and it was quite dull in the shed.

His eyesight was not as sharp as it used to be. His wife had been nagging him for ages to get glasses but he managed without them. Everyone he knew who had glasses for reading spent their whole time looking for the damn things. He had enough trouble with his diary.

Thankfully the downy mildew outbreak was small but he wanted it seen to now. He was determined to eradicate it before any further damage was done. The burst of hot weather could be enough to expose the vines to secondary infection. He'd seen the ruin downy mildew could cause and he knew he couldn't face any more losses.

He didn't want Euan blaming him if it spread to Levallier Dell either. The outbreak was close to their boundary. Who was to say it hadn't come from Levallier Dell in the first place? The pestilence had to come from somewhere.

While he mixed the spray his thoughts drifted to Katerina. She hadn't come home again the night before. She was a headstrong girl. Always had been but he liked that. As a young girl she had her cousins dancing to her tune. Surely Flynn Levallier would be an easy target for her charms.

Everything was ready and he sat down on a drum to write in his diary. He had just slipped the battered little book back into his pocket when Tony arrived. Theo stood up quickly and teetered as the world spun.

"What are you doing, Baba?" Tony clutched him by the arms. "You're not as young as you used to be. You don't have to do this, I said I'd…"

Theo pushed his son away. "I'm alright. I just stood up too quickly. It will pass. Don't fuss." He stood still for a moment, aware of Tony hovering close beside him.

"How often does this happen?" Tony asked.

"Every now and then. I'm alright," Theo said again.

"Perhaps you should see the doctor."

"I have. He gave me tablets."

"Do you take them?"

"Sometimes. Look Tony, I'm fine. Let's get on with the spraying."

"I told you I'd get to it. I'm ready now. I'll do it."

Theo looked into the concerned face of his son. "Alright, but no more wasting time. Get the spraying done."

★ ★ ★

Keely approached the house cautiously. It was an overcast morning and the lights were still on inside. She could see Maggie sitting at the table. Keely hoped Flynn or Euan would be about. She didn't want to be left alone with Maggie.

"Good morning," Maggie said as Keely tapped on the door and stepped inside. "Did you sleep well? Flynn and Euan told me all about the party and your misfortune. I can't believe Euan allowed such crass behaviour."

"It was an accident. No real harm done." Keely gave a wry smile. "At least not to me."

"Would you like a coffee?"

"Oh, no…thank you."

"Would you prefer tea? Please have something."

"Tea would be fine." Keely had intended to collect some of the party leftovers to take with her, then make a speedy exit. Marty should arrive soon.

"I'm the only one here, I'm afraid." Maggie boiled the kettle in the kitchen. "Euan has taken his surprise visitor into the village to join her crew, whatever that is. I don't imagine there's a ship in the main street of Margaret River." Her chuckle was warm and gentle. "I can't believe I didn't know anything about Dianna till now. I can't wait until he comes back. I have lots of questions."

"She seemed a nice person."

"You hadn't met her before?"

"Only about five minutes before you did." Keely glanced around. The family room was neat and tidy. Everything in its place. She wondered where Flynn and Kat were.

"Here you are." Maggie placed a cup of tea in front of her. "What a shame you're going off as well. I was looking forward to hearing about your travels."

"I haven't made it very far yet."

"You haven't had the best of starts for a holiday." She pinned Keely with her look. "Still, I believe things happen for a purpose, don't you? I'm sure everything will work out."

Her piercing gaze was like Euan's. Keely felt as if Maggie could see right through her. She lowered her eyes, letting her hair fall forward.

Maggie's gentle touch brushed Keely's hair to one side. "You've got such healthy hair. I couldn't help but think how striking you looked when I entered the house last night. By far the most beautiful woman present."

Keely looked around the room, anxious to steer the conversation in a different direction. "It's quiet here this morning."

"Flynn and Kat have gone to Perth. They left quite early. Flynn had to pick up some labels he's been expecting. Evidently, they missed the post. I can't believe everyone has deserted me when I've just arrived. If only we'd known earlier, I could have brought them. He tells me the label has a sketch of Euan on it and that you are the artist."

"It was just a rough sketch. Flynn took a fancy to it."

"You like to draw and paint?"

Keely lowered her gaze to her cup. "Yes."

"It's a fine talent to have. Flynn has a good eye for art. I look forward to seeing the labels. His young lady friend, Kat, raved over your work as well. She suggested another of your caricatures for Flynn's red once it's bottled."

Keely looked up from her tea. She hadn't shown anyone her other pictures. Then she remembered the night the three of them had been in the studio. Kat had flicked through her sketchbook. It had to be Jack Maggie was referring to. "The whip cracker?"

"That's it. I think Flynn likes the sound of the whip cracker for his cab merlot blend." Maggie's obvious affection for her nephew brought a glow to her face. "He has wonderful ideas, don't you think?" Once again, those piercing blue eyes pinned her from across the table.

"Yes." Keely stood up. She wanted to shout across the room just how much she loved his wonderful ideas and being a part of them but instead she took a breath, picked up her cup and moved to the kitchen. "I'd better get organised. Marty will be here soon. I thought I'd take some of the leftover cake I made for the party. It won't keep much longer with cream in it."

"You take whatever you like," Maggie said. "I know Euan and Flynn won't mind. They've appreciated having you here. Sounds like you've been helpful in many ways."

Keely got out the chocolate cake she had made for Flynn. There was only one piece missing; they'd had so many sweets the night of the party. Oh, well, she thought, Marty and his mates would probably enjoy it.

Maggie walked her to the door. "Will we expect you home for the evening meal?"

"I'm not sure. It depends on my ride. I'll ring." Keely's words tumbled out over each other.

"No need, my dear, there will be plenty. I'm cooking a grand feast tonight. I think we need a special meal." Maggie's face glowed with vitality. "It appears there is much to celebrate."

★ ★ ★

"That's it, Keely, bend your knees," Steve called from beside her.

She glanced across, lost her footing on the board and crumpled. Luckily, the sand was soft and she rolled over laughing. Steve and Marty extended a helping hand each and pulled her to her feet.

"You're getting the hang of it," Steve said. "Are you sure you don't want to try a wave? The beginners' set is perfect today."

Keely looked along the beach to the area of ocean he indicated. A number of bodies bobbed in the water and one teetered on a board, riding a wave in.

"I don't think so," she said. "But thanks for trying to teach me the basics."

"You're nearly as good as Marty." Steve nudged his mate's arm.

"That's being unkind to Keely," Mike said. "She's much better at it than Marty already." He grinned and Steve chuckled beside him.

"What about it, Marty?" Steve asked. "We thought we'd try the Gallows this afternoon. You can show off your talent to Keely."

"I'd like to but someone has to keep her company while you two risk your necks," Marty said. "Besides, surfing is dangerous. Keely's got the scar to prove it."

He was referring to the cut above her eye. It was healing but had a deep purple bruise around it. Keely wished it wasn't in such an obvious place so that he wouldn't have asked what happened.

"Don't stay on my account," she said. "I can entertain myself."

Steve smirked and dug Mike in the ribs. "I'm sure Marty has better plans."

"Yeah, we'd better clear out and leave you to it," Mike said.

"Fair go, you blokes." Marty gave Mike a playful shove then grinned at Keely.

She turned her face to the breeze so it cooled her cheeks. She'd had a great day with the three of them. They were good fun. Even though they hadn't got to know each other that well before her operation, she thought of them as her friends now; fellow South Aussies on holiday together.

Her initial meeting with Marty at the airport seemed so long ago. She had thought he was quite cute back then. She snuck a glance at him as he helped Steve and Mike collect up their gear. He was a good-looking guy and she had been attracted to him initially. He'd been very kind but her thoughts strayed to a different face with a gorgeous smile, ice-blue eyes and a crown of fluffy fair hair. She sighed. It was wasted energy thinking about Flynn but she couldn't help it.

"What would you like to do, Keely?" Marty's question startled her. "We can stay here and wander the local area or go with the Steve and Mike and check out the beaches there."

"I don't mind."

"Let's go with them for the ride then. We only get to use the car when Steve's mate doesn't need it." Marty was referring to the old green station wagon that he had driven to pick her up in. The bodywork was battered and the engine burbled but it had four good wheels with a rack for surfboards and that was all they needed.

"If we had a decent kitchen we could have left Keely there to knock up some more food." Steve patted his stomach. "That cake was delicious."

"Idiots!" Marty threw a towel at their retreating backs.

Keely followed them up the road to the little shack they were sharing with Steve's mate. Most of the places around it were modern holiday homes but this was an old place. It was basic accommodation, not too far from the beach, perfect for the group of surfers. The little fridge held beer and a few basic food items. It looked like they lived on cereal for breakfast, barbecues for tea and fruit in between. They had devoured the cake she'd brought in record time. At least someone had got to enjoy her efforts.

★　★　★

"That was magnificent, Maggie. Thank you for a fine meal." Euan stood and collected the plates they'd just emptied of the generous servings of one of Maggie's famous light lemon puddings and put them in the kitchen.

"I think I'll turn in," Flynn said.

Euan came back to the table. "Before you do, there's something I'd like to say…" He paused and looked from his sister to his son. Flynn was smiling, at least for the moment, and Maggie had that stare as if she already knew what he was going to say. Euan was pleased it was just the three of them. "To both of you."

It had been quite late before Flynn had arrived back from Perth and Theo's granddaughter hadn't been with him, thank goodness. Evidently, Flynn had dropped her next door on the way home and Maggie had received a call from Keely, saying she was eating with her friends. Now was the perfect time to tell them his news.

Euan took another sip of Flynn's wine. It had the intensity of semillon but he could detect the tropical fruit notes of the sauvignon blanc. Flynn had every right to be proud of his wine. It was very crisp with a smooth finish and fine to drink on its own without food. Perhaps Euan had been too hasty in committing all of the next year's vintage to their traditional wines.

"Oh, do come on," Maggie said. "Spit it out."

"I'd rather not, sister dear. I was just thinking what a good job our young winemaker has done with this wine." He tilted the glass towards Flynn in salute.

Flynn opened his mouth to speak but Maggie jumped in before him.

"I don't mean the wine and you know it full well. Who is this Dianna and why haven't we heard about her before? I've been waiting all day to talk to you and you've been carrying out your usual avoidance tactics."

"Yes, Euan, you sly old bugger. First you trick me, thinking Keely was one of your lady friends, and then you turn up with Dianna, who I assume did share your bed last night…unless she slept on the floor."

"There is no need to be crass, Flynn," Maggie said. "I think it's wonderful your father has found someone at last."

"At last!" Flynn snorted. "She's just the one he's brought home. At least she seems an appropriate age."

"Flynn, dear, you know I love you but I really will not have this kind of talk at the meal table." Maggie gave him a disapproving look.

Euan ignored Flynn's barbs. He probably deserved them, although he was surprised he was being so openly crude with Maggie present.

"I've been seeing Dianna for quite a while now, a couple of years on and off—"

"Years!" Maggie's eyebrows shot up.

Flynn remained silent

"This is the first time she's come here. I haven't said anything because I didn't dare hope we'd be able to make a life together."

"A life together!" Now Flynn reacted, his face creased in a frown. "What do you mean?"

"They're going to be married," Maggie announced.

"Now hang on, Maggie." Euan was still trying to come to terms with his and Dianna's plans for the future himself and he could see from the look on Flynn's face that he needed time to digest the information. "Our lives are very different. Dianna has always been based in the east but she has rearranged her work commitments so she can spend more time here and…well…we'll see how things work out."

"That's wonderful." Maggie clapped her hands. "Come on, Flynn. Open another bottle of this delightful wine. What a pity Keely isn't here to celebrate with us. The birth of a new label and true love flourishing."

"Who is this Marty she's with?" Euan asked. "Have you met him, Flynn?"

"No. Why should I have met him?" Flynn stood up and went to the fridge. "There's still half of that bottle left, Maggie. I'm tired and I'm going to bed. Goodnight." He brought her the wine and bent to kiss her on the cheek.

"Goodnight, darling," Maggie said. "Tomorrow we must have a celebration with Keely. Those labels are stunning."

"They will adorn a very good wine," Euan said.

A hesitant smile lifted Flynn's lips. "That's high praise." He left them without another word.

"He's very tired, poor love." Maggie turned her piercing gaze on Euan. "Now, brother dear. There's just the two of us. Pass me your glass and tell me all about Dianna."

CHAPTER
25

"It can't be the downy mildew, Baba." Tony dragged his fingers backwards through his hair. "It's got to be something else."

Theo stood with his son among the semillon vines staring at the rows and rows of yellowing leaves. He shook his head slowly from side to side, then stopped as he felt the giddiness begin. He'd forgotten to take those tablets again.

Tony had come before breakfast to tell him something was wrong with the vines. He had thought the downy mildew had taken hold but there were no patches of white down on these leaves. They were yellow and had turned that way virtually overnight. He pulled off a leaf and inspected it closely. "It looks as if they've been poisoned," he said.

"That's what I thought, but how?"

Theo looked across the last row of yellowing vines beside him to a gap in the trees following the fenceline that marked the boundary between River Dynasty and Levallier Dell and he clenched his teeth. "Euan Levallier," he muttered.

"What?"

"Everything has gone wrong with this piece of land."

"You surely can't blame Euan for that?"

"Maybe not the weather but the beetle outbreaks…"

"What do you think, that he keeps a supply in a jar and releases them here?"

"These vines have been poisoned, Tony," Theo snapped. "None of us would do such a thing. It has to be our rivals."

"That's ridiculous."

Tony walked around the row of vines and over to the fence.

Theo followed him. "What are you looking at?"

"I wondered if there was any sign of whatever it is on Levallier's vines. Maybe they've been affected, too."

Both men climbed the fence and inspected the first row of sauvignon blanc vines. There was no evidence of the yellow leaves that covered the vines behind them.

"He's not going to poison his own vines." Theo cast a searching look over the Levallier Dell vines. The vines all appeared to be very healthy. He pursed his lips. His own vines had looked like this, before Tony found the downy mildew.

Theo trudged back behind his son to their land and the sick plants.

"It might just be killing the new growth. Perhaps we can save the vines," Tony said.

Theo tugged off a hand full of leaves and dropped them to the ground. "I don't think so. Whatever this is, it's killing the whole plant." He looked across the decaying rows to where the green vines began again. "Every vine is affected. We're going to lose four full rows of semillon."

"I don't understand it," Tony said. "These are the vines I sprayed yesterday." He walked beside Theo as they stepped up and down the rows, until they reached a row of perfectly healthy vines. "This is where I stopped. Maybe they had something else wrong with them."

Theo looked from the first healthy row to the yellowing vines beside it. It didn't make sense. If it were poison, why would the saboteur stop here?

"There couldn't have been something in the tank," Tony said. "We're always meticulous with our cleaning."

"Of course it's not us. Someone has done this." Theo stamped his foot and looked back to his neighbour's healthy vines. "And Euan Levallier is high on my list of suspects."

* * *

Keely came back along the river path, placing her feet carefully with each cautious step; even though it was early and still cool, she couldn't help but glance nervously at the spot where she'd last seen the snake. She recalled Jack and the bits of string around his trouser legs. She'd thought he'd been joking about keeping out snakes.

"There you are."

Flynn's statement startled her. She'd been so intent on watching the path, she hadn't seen him standing up ahead.

"I've just been for a walk," she said.

"We didn't see you last night."

Was that an accusing tone? Keely glanced at Flynn but there was nothing to indicate his mood. "I came in late. There were no lights on at the house."

"Did you have a good time with your friends?"

He was watching her closely. What did it matter to him what she did? "Yes, thanks. Did you and Kat enjoy Perth?" She forced herself to be polite. If only Kat was an awful person, Keely could at least dislike her.

"We had lots to do. It was a flying visit." He gave her a weak smile as she drew level with him. "I've got the labels. I thought you might like to see them and… if you're not too busy. I wondered if…" Now his look was pleading. "You might help me put them on the bottles?"

She relaxed. "I'd love to see them and I'm happy to help. It's not as if I'm doing anything else for the next few days."

"Oh, that reminds me, Ken's been on the phone again. He wants you to call in and see him about some work for next week. We could drop in at the school on the way to the Haystack Block, if you like."

Keely's stomach lurched and she hurried ahead of Flynn so he wouldn't see the dread she knew was written all over her face. "I've got something to do in the studio. I'll come up to the house in a minute."

Keely didn't look behind to see if he'd gone. She rushed into the studio and shut the door behind her. She could just say no but there was no need; next week, she would make sure she was heading north, away from Margaret River.

* * *

Maggie was washing the breakfast dishes when Flynn returned.

"Isn't Keely coming?" she asked.

"In a moment. She had something to do in the studio first."

"I hope she likes the labels," Maggie said. "Sometimes artists can be temperamental about their work."

"Keely's never temperamental." Flynn thought back over the conversation he'd just had with her. She'd looked surprised to see him and then she'd been flippant about her whereabouts. As if he had no right to ask, which he supposed he didn't, but…

"Is something wrong?" Maggie asked.

"No. Why?"

"You're frowning." She reached across the breakfast bar and ran a wet gloved finger along his forehead. "You look so serious. Do you know how much more handsome you are when you smile?"

He rubbed his damp skin and grinned at her.

"That's better." Maggie turned back to her dishes. "I bet Keely can't resist that smile."

"Maggie, don't cause trouble. Euan brought Keely here, not me."

She made a soft *humph*. "Euan was just being kind. She's much too young for him and besides, he's got his hands full elsewhere."

"Don't you go matchmaking for me again," Flynn warned. "Anyway, Keely's got other friends. I don't really think she likes me that much."

"What gives you that idea?" Maggie looked over her shoulder with an odd smile, her eyebrows arching delicately.

"Just a hunch." Flynn headed for the office. He could tell Maggie was in a meddlesome mood. "I've had a bit of experience with women over the years, Maggie, at least enough to know whether they like me or not."

This time it was a loud snort that came from behind him.

He didn't look back. If he was honest, he'd been disappointed when Keely had said she was spending the day with her friends. He would've asked her to go to Perth. Kat had gone her own way once they reached the city with several errands of her own. Keely could've come with him to collect the labels. It would have been great to have her there for the first look, gauge her reaction and spend time with her while he waited for Kat.

Instead she'd been with this Marty and his mates. Flynn rolled his shoulders and sat at the desk. Why should he care where she'd been? She was always polite to him but he thought she would be that way with everyone. There'd been no indication she thought of him as any more than a friend.

He looked at the paperwork in front of him but it was her shy smile that played on his mind. There was something about it that brightened his day. He'd got used to her being here, looked forward to seeing her each day, appreciated her opinion. She'd said she'd planned to leave after the weekend but maybe she'd stay longer if the teaching job worked out. He hoped so; he would be sorry to see her go.

His thoughts drifted to Euan and his surprise lady friend, Dianna. By the sound of it, she was going to be around a lot more. Flynn loved Levallier Dell but perhaps the time had come for him to move on as well, give his father some space and find something that didn't set them at loggerheads. He thought of his recent conversation with his mate, Tim, who was part of a family winery in the Adelaide Hills. They were expanding and needed a business manager who understood winemaking. His discussions with Kat about her new job and making a move away from her family had stirred a restlessness in him. Tim's suggestion he look at the job specs was tempting.

★ ★ ★

Kat was sipping the cup of coffee Yia-yia had made her when Pappou burst through the door with a face like thunder.

"You're back. I'll have one of those." He stabbed a finger in the air towards the coffee pot.

Yia-yia simply got up and went to make it. Kat marvelled at her calm compliance. What was wrong with Pappou? She hadn't remembered him as such an old grump, but perhaps he'd always been that way and she hadn't realised.

"Is something wrong, Pappou?" she asked.

"Someone has poisoned my vines." He lowered himself into his chair.

"Poisoned?" Yia-yia's voice echoed a split second behind Kat's. "Are you sure, Theo?" Yia-yia asked.

"Of course I'm sure. Four rows of semillon vines have been wiped out. They are dying as we speak."

Kat clutched her coffee cup in her hands. This was terrible news and perhaps explained his gruffness. "What makes you think they've been poisoned, Pappou?"

"How else would four rows of vines suddenly die?" Pappou glared at her. "It's sabotage and I know who did it."

"You do?"

"Yes." His eyes blazed and deep lines furrowed his brow. "Some-one who has never been able to accept River Dynasty."

"Here you are, Theo." Yia-yia put a cup in front of him and resumed her seat.

"Who do you mean?" Kat asked.

"Euan Levallier." Pappou thumped the table with his fist and all their coffee cups vibrated.

"Surely not," Kat said.

"Surely yes. Four rows of semillon vines on the Levallier Dell boundary have been poisoned. Who else besides Euan Levallier would want to harm my vines?" He gave a sharp nod.

"But why…" Kat was stuck for words. She couldn't associate Euan, the man she'd got to know, with such a terrible act. It was true he had kept her at arm's length but she had put that down to there being no love lost between Euan and Pappou. There was no way Euan would purposely poison his neighbour's vines.

"He has never liked the way we do things at River Dynasty. He thinks no one can make wine like he can. And…" Pappou stabbed a finger in the air at her, "he has never forgiven me for buying that piece of land right out from under his lazy nose."

"Theo, are you sure?" Yia-yia asked. "Euan is an honest man."

"Who else would poison my vines? It has to be that Levallier fool."

Keely sat in the front of the tray-top ute beside Flynn, watching the scenery whiz by as he drove them in to town. She was going with him to collect boxes of his wine to bring back to Levallier Dell, so they could stick on the labels ready for the weekend cellar-door sales.

Her first glimpse of the labels had sent a surge of excitement through her. Not that she had said too much. Maggie had been enthusiastic but Flynn had remained aloof when he handed over a label for her to look at. She hadn't known how to react. Perhaps he was disappointed with the finished label but she thought her sketch of Euan had come up really well.

The paper colour was Tuscan Tan, an off-white, and the printer had deepened the hues of her sketch, so that the Euan on the label had a much darker brown hat and quite ginger hair. They had used gold to depict the straw stuck in his hat and gold for the lettering.

She had been relieved to see that Flynn at least gave a small smile when she said she was pleased with the result.

She gripped her bag tighter as they neared the outskirts of town. Flynn had offered to go via the school. She'd told him not to worry, but he'd said it was no trouble. She'd run out of excuses and any strength to say no had deserted her. She could talk to the principal but she would be gone from Margaret River before he called her to do any relief teaching.

She looked away from Flynn, out the window, to the school buildings as he pulled into the carpark. Her stomach churned. Suddenly, she was back at her previous school feeling trapped and alone. Faces leered at her, smirking and taunting. The panic rose up inside her and she gasped in some air.

"Are you feeling okay?" Flynn's concerned voice startled her.

"I'm fine," she mumbled.

"I'll drop in our food orders for the weekend then come back to collect you," he said.

Keely's excitement over the coming weekend was gone, replaced with dread at the sight of the school buildings in front of her. She fumbled with the door handle. She couldn't open it.

Flynn reached across. "That's always getting stuck." He pressed into her as he wrestled with the handle. She breathed in his masculine scent and wished he was wrapping his arms around her. She knew she would feel safe in those arms.

"There you are."

The door flew open and she stumbled out onto the path.

Flynn continued to lean across the seat looking up at her. "You sure you're okay?" he asked.

Keely nodded and turned her back on him to search for some inner strength. Flynn couldn't save her, no one could do that but herself and she wasn't sure she was up to the challenge.

She took the path to the door marked *School Office*. She faltered in the doorway as the sound of young voices met her. A group of girls in uniform were talking excitedly to someone behind the desk. Keely stayed near the door. Once Flynn was out of sight she could leave, tell him the principal was busy.

"Okay girls, you'd better go or you'll be late." The woman spoke in a firm but amicable manner and sounded vaguely familiar. "You can come back and tell me all about it, after school." She looked past them and smiled at Keely. "Can I help you?"

Keely waited while the girls left, still talking ten to the dozen. They hardly even glanced in her direction; they were so involved in their discussion.

"The principal is expecting me." She hadn't moved from her place by the door. If he was busy, she was going to dash straight back outside. "I'm Keely Mitchell."

"Oh, for goodness sake." The woman got to her feet. "My eyes really are failing me. Of course it is. Hello, Keely."

She came around the counter and Keely relaxed, just a little, as she recalled the jewellery night at Mary's. "Claire?"

"Yes, that's right. Welcome to our school. How's your jewellery making coming along? I haven't had a chance to touch mine since we were at Mary's last."

"I've made a few more bracelets," Keely said. Words whirled around in her head and disappeared. She couldn't even remember what she'd done. "I've been making...wine bottle decorations. They're for...Flynn wants to sell them at the cellar door this weekend." Her words tumbled over each other.

"You have been busy." Claire smiled. "I didn't realised you were a teacher. I can usually pick them a mile off and Megan tells us your artistic talent extends to sketches and painting. Ken has been keen to speak with you. I'm sure he's in his office, I'll just buzz through." She picked up the phone. "Would you like a coffee?"

"No, thanks." Keely's stomach was doing gymnastics and she felt a lump in her throat. She knew she wouldn't be able to swallow a thing. She clutched her hands together and turned to look through the glass doors. Behind her, Claire spoke on the phone.

Keely looked out into a well-manicured garden courtyard and, beyond that, to an expanse of paving and covered walkways leading to other buildings. There was not a child in sight. If only schools were childless, they wouldn't bother her at all. Anyway, it didn't matter. She'd made up her mind to put off any work offers from Ken and then she'd be gone.

"Hello, Keely."

She spun round and almost lost her balance. She looked down at the portly man with a broad smile who was stepping towards her with his arm extended.

"I'm Ken Retallick." He shook her hand vigorously. "It's great to meet you at last. Are you feeling better?"

"Oh…yes…thanks," she mumbled.

"Come into the office. Would you like a drink? I'm sure Claire would make you something?"

"No, thanks. She did offer." Keely gave Claire a feeble smile, before she followed Ken.

"Catch you later, Keely," Claire said.

With feet of lead, Keely followed Ken into his office. He seemed friendly enough but so had the principal at her previous school, at first. Outwardly pleasant and open with staff, but if you didn't see eye to eye things were very different. Ken exuded that same relaxed and self-assured air. She played with the words in her head, ready to tell him she was leaving soon so she wouldn't be able to work at the school.

"Have a seat, Keely. I'm so glad you've come. I was hoping you might be able to help us out next week."

"I'm not sure that…"

He leaned forward across the desk, his hands clasped in front of him. "I know you're on holidays and it's a bit presumptuous of me. You see, we're running an electives program and we want it to be relevant for the kids. But we've got a few gaps and one of them is in the art area. Megan told me what a good job you did with her two young fellas."

"I didn't do much." Keely rubbed at her fingers.

"They're much younger than our students, of course," Ken said. "But you are a secondary teacher aren't you?"

"Yes, but…"

"You'd only have kids who wanted to be there, so it would be a dream class."

"I'm not sure…" Keely faltered, yet again, frustrated at her inability to simply say no and annoyed by her fear that made the words spin in her head and not come out of her mouth.

"We've got some artistic students here. I want someone to work with them who can foster that spark. I was hoping that someone might be you."

"I'm planning to leave next week." Finally, she managed to get a whole sentence out.

"The pay's not bad." He went on as if she hadn't spoken at all. "I don't know if money is a consideration for you but most people on holidays could do with a bit more." He sat back and smiled at her again with a look that was almost pleading. "It's only for four days."

Keely hesitated. All the words she'd tossed around in her head about leaving deserted her.

"You could do whatever you like," Ken said. "There's only about twelve or fifteen in each group. You can stay in the classroom or head off and explore the local scenery. Get them drawing and sketching. You can paint a mural if you want. We've got a few walls that need brightening up."

"I might not be the right person." She frantically tried to think of ways to say no politely.

"I'll be honest with you, Keely." Ken clasped his hands on the desk in front of him again and the smile left his face for the first time since she'd met him. "I'm short-staffed, I've exhausted all other avenues and I'm desperate. You're a teacher and you enjoy art. My hope is that you can foster some of that enjoyment in this group of kids."

He looked at her expectantly and she glanced down at her fingers. They were red from being twisted and rubbed. She had come in planning to say no, but his frankness had overwhelmed her. One more week in Margaret River wouldn't be terrible and it would help her bank balance. If these students had elected to do art they shouldn't give her too much trouble. Eventually, there would come a time when she had to face a class again. At least none of these students knew her.

"I guess I don't have a set schedule…"

"You'd be doing us a big favour."

Keely sighed. "Perhaps I could stay one more week…"

"Thanks, Keely." Ken beamed at her from across the desk. "I'll get Claire on to the paperwork straight away so we don't have any hiccups and you get paid promptly. Now, how about you come and check our facilities and see what you'd like to do."

★ ★ ★

"Flynn has taken Keely to help put the labels on his bottles." Maggie stood behind Euan in the office doorway. "She's settled in well."

Euan was rummaging through the papers on the desk. Flynn must have been tidying up again. He couldn't find the order that he was looking for. They'd just had a pile of extra cartons delivered from their usual supplier and there were way too many.

"Yes." He didn't look up.

"There's something about her, though, isn't there?"

"What do you mean?" Euan rifled through the 'pending' file.

"She's a lovely girl, a bit on the shy side, and she appears to be happy but…"

Damn! He still couldn't find the order he was looking for. Then he realised Maggie had stopped talking. He looked up. She had that enquiring expression that past experience told him could mean trouble.

"But what?"

"Something's not quite right."

"Now, Maggie, Keely's a great girl. You said so yourself. Don't go stirring things up."

"You've noticed it too, haven't you?"

Euan pulled open the filing cabinet. The packaging order had to be there somewhere. Where would Flynn have filed it? He would have done it online. Perhaps he'd forgotten to print a copy.

"Euan?"

"What?" He gave up looking, pushed the drawer shut and glanced at the computer. Flynn was all about saving files there, said they didn't need paper copies, but Euan still liked to be able to hold a piece of paper in his hand.

"Keely has been living here for nearly two weeks. Surely you've had a chance to discover what it is that's troubling her."

He looked at his sister. "Probably people interfering in her life." She cocked her head to one side and raised her eyebrows.

"Oh, alright. I'm not really sure but I think it might have something to do with her teaching."

"What exactly? Has she said something about it?"

"Not in so many words. It's the way she tries to avoid the topic when anyone asks her about her work and she plays down her ability. She's had offers of work since she's been here but she's said no." He shrugged his shoulders. "There could be more to it or it could simply be that she's on holidays and she wants to relax. It is her life." He emphasised the 'her'.

"I thought she looked absolutely terrified when Flynn offered to drive her in to the school today."

"Damn Flynn. Why would he take her there?"

"Something about the principal wanting to talk to her about a job. Why?"

"Flynn doesn't notice what's right in front of him."

"He must have learned that from somewhere."

Euan glared at his sister but her face was the picture of innocence. He gave a cursory glance at the computer. No point in even attempting that. He gave up the search and walked past Maggie on his way back to the family room. "We should just respect her wishes," he said, over his shoulder. "I told Ken she wasn't available."

"The poor girl. Something's troubling her, I can tell."

"You mean, besides the fact that she's smitten with Flynn, and that's another thing he can't see."

"So you've noticed it, too." Maggie followed along behind him. "I thought you were too caught up in your own love life to be aware of anyone else. What are we going to do about it?"

"Nothing."

"Flynn needs a good woman in his life."

"He's been too busy chasing after the smooth-talking Katerina."

"She's a lovely young woman but she's not for Flynn."

"Maggie…" Euan's warning growl was interrupted by a tap on the glass and Hugh slid open the door.

"Hello, Hugh," Euan said. "What good timing."

"Hello, Hugh." Maggie went forward and greeted him with a hug.

"Nice to see you here again, Maggie. It's time you came back to the River for some quiet, away from the city highlife."

"Oh, it's far more entertaining here than in the city." Maggie chuckled. "I think I'll go for a walk and see if Flynn and Keely are back."

"Now, Maggie…" Euan growled.

She smiled and waved.

Euan frowned at his sister's departing back. He knew he was wasting his breath. Maggie would do what Maggie would do. Perhaps she'd have some luck in getting Flynn to see what was right before his eyes.

"It's nice to see Maggie here again," Hugh said. "Did you find out about the extra cartons?"

Euan dragged his thoughts back to the job in hand. "I can't find the paperwork. I'm sure I didn't order any extras but Flynn may have. I'll ask him later."

"We've stacked the boxes in the packing shed for now." Hugh continued to stand by the door, a concerned look on his face.

"Is there something else?" Euan asked.

"I've just heard there's been a bit of trouble over at River Dynasty."

"Oh?" Euan studied his long-time head man. It wasn't like Hugh to listen to gossip.

"Someone has poisoned four rows of their semillon vines."

"Poisoned! Are you sure?"

"I went and had a look for myself. It's right on our boundary."

Euan scraped his fingers through his hair. "Theo has upset a few people in his time but who would do something like that?"

"Evidently they think they may have had downy mildew there as well."

"Downy mildew! The news just gets better. You mean there's an outbreak right on my boundary?"

"Not any more. The vines are definitely dead."

Euan snatched up his hat. "I think we'd better go and check this out." His precious sauvignon blanc vines edged that boundary. If Theo had done anything to jeopardise them, he would damn well pay.

★　★　★

"You've got the idea." Flynn stood next to Keely as she turned the handle and rolled another label onto a bottle.

"It's not that difficult."

"Just repetitious." He put down the box of bottles he'd been carrying at her feet.

She glanced at the boxes he had stacked behind her. They had brought a ute load from the Haystack Block. She'd thrown herself into helping him pack the boxes, anything to avoid discussing school. When they got back to Levallier Dell, Flynn had shown her how to put on the labels and then he'd left her to it while he brought in the rest of the boxes.

"Do you think we'll need more?" he asked.

"There's no time to label more than what you've brought over. There's a lot of food prep to be done and the final touches to the cellar door."

"You're right." Flynn picked up some of the bottles she'd already labelled and slid them back in their box. "It's hard to know how many of these we'll sell over the weekend. It's a new wine for us. People won't be expecting it."

"If you bring some more from the Haystack Block, we can always dash out and label them as we sell them." Keely smiled at the lunacy of it. They were going to be flat out keeping the food and wine up to the customers.

"You're right." He counted the boxes again. "If you're happy to continue on for a while, I'll go and get another ute load."

Perhaps it was her surprise that he would even contemplate bringing more or perhaps it was disappointment that he was leaving her, either way, when he looked at her face, he stopped and broke into a grin.

"I'm sorry, Keely. I'm getting carried away again, aren't I?"

When he gave her his undivided attention, it took her breath away. "You could say that." She turned the handle so quickly the bottle thumped through the roller.

"I'll keep going with that if you want to take a break, and Maggie's a good stick. She'd do some for us."

A good stick, thought Keely. Was that how he saw her as well?

★   ★   ★

Euan inspected the vines closest to the River Dynasty boundary.

"They all look fine to me," Hugh said. "No sign of mildew or wilt."

"We'll have to watch them carefully." Euan straightened up and looked at the trees marking the fence line between his vineyard and Theo's. He walked along a little way until there was a gap to look through, then stopped and let out a slow whistle. Before him stretched rows of yellowing vines. "Bloody hell."

"Not a pretty sight, is it?"

"Are you sure it's not mildew?"

"They went from green to yellow overnight."

Euan turned his back on the dying vines and surveyed his own beautiful green canopy. If anything happened to them…he couldn't bear to think about it. He and Lucy had planted these vines thirty years ago.

Something in the grass at his feet caught his eye. He poked at the blue object with his toe. It was a small notebook. He bent down, picked it up and opened the front cover.

"Bloody hell," he said again and strode towards his vines, inspecting them more closely.

"What's the matter?"

"Theo's been on my land." Euan waved the little book at Hugh. "This is his diary. He must have climbed through the fence here and dropped it. What would he have been up to?"

"Maybe he was just checking to see if we had been poisoned as well."

"He could have seen that from the fence, and why would he care about my vines anyway?" Euan tapped the diary on his palm and cast another wary eye over his vines. "We'd better keep a close eye on things. Theo's up to something and it had better not be harming my vines."

CHAPTER
27

"I've made my decision." Kat felt relaxed under Yia-yia's comforting gaze. They were enjoying some peace and quiet after the uproar of Pappou's accusations earlier in the morning. "Pappou will just have to live with it."

"He will come round. He's got a lot on his mind at the moment." Yia-yia took her hands and gave them a squeeze. "But what about your parents, Katerina? They are the ones who will be upset."

"Not as much as I thought. I rang them when I booked my flights. I spoke to Dad first. Once I'd explained my job, he thought it was a great opportunity. Mum was shocked at the short timeline. They want me to come home so we can spend some time together before I leave, but they took it well. It's only Pappou who's not happy."

"He had hoped you would work here. I would have liked that too but you must follow your heart, Katerina." Yia-yia squeezed her hands again and went back to her baking. "Your Pappou only wants what's best for all his family but sometimes he tries too hard to make things happen. He's put a lot of time and money into the new cellar door and restaurant. He's been very focused." She nodded slowly. "With you out of the picture, he might be free to notice Peter's Angela."

"Michael said something about that. Hasn't anyone mentioned to Pappou that she might do the job?"

"You are his favourite, Katerina. He would love to have you here but he will come round and he will understand this job in Singapore will make you happy."

"He seems so grumpy."

"He is getting older and he can't do everything he used to. He doesn't like the thought of losing control. Sometimes he is like a big lion, roaring and raging, but underneath he is really just a little pussycat."

Footsteps thumped along the verandah and the back door banged, followed by a thud and then another, as boots dropped to the floor. Kat frowned. She wasn't so sure if Yia-yia's metaphor was quite the right one for Pappou. Yet in some ways she was correct. He would never dare wear his boots into Yia-yia's kitchen.

Pappou burst through the door. "Have you seen my diary?"

Yia-yia tsked. "Theo, you and that diary. Have you lost it again? I tell you to button it into your top pocket."

"I would if I had a button." He flicked the flap of the pocket up and down.

Kat could see a little tear where a button had been.

"You've got plenty of shirts." Yia-yia tugged at the shoulder of his shirt. "Take this one off and I will mend it."

"Not now." He shrugged her hand away. "I need to go into town."

"I was going to get some groceries for Yia-yia," Kat said. "Can I get a ride with you?" She wasn't sure she should ask. In the mood he was in, she'd rather avoid him but she would be leaving soon and she didn't want to go without making peace with her beloved Pappou.

"If you want." He strode across the kitchen in his slippered feet. "I have some things to do in the office first. And I want to find my diary. It must be here somewhere." He gave Yia-yia a final glare before he left.

She sighed. "That diary of his, sometimes I would like to have it permanently attached to his body. When he misplaces it, he's that raging lion again." She smiled and patted Kat on the arm. "I will make you a shopping list."

* * *

Flynn looked up from his phone and stared out the window, across the yard and beyond to the vines, which were brilliant green in the light of the morning sun. His mate, Tim, had emailed him the details of the management job coming up at his family's Adelaide Hills property. They wanted a 'hands on' winemaker to join the management team and develop an emerging label. If he couldn't do it at Levallier Dell, maybe he could do it somewhere else. He had some serious thinking to do once this weekend was over.

A movement off to the right caught his eye. Keely was coming towards the house from the direction of the studio. He glanced back at the job description he'd printed. Working in South Australia might have more than one advantage although he wasn't sure what she thought about him.

He still felt bad about his behaviour when she'd first arrived. He thought he'd made it up to her but just when she seemed to relax in his company, she would suddenly act like a startled rabbit. He wondered if there was still something he was doing that upset her. She had thrown herself into helping with preparations for the weekend but Flynn never felt as if he could get beyond polite conversation. Not that she was obliged to do more than that, especially if she had a boyfriend. He frowned. It was something they'd never discussed but perhaps she was keen on the Marty guy she'd spent the day with.

She slid the door open. "Hello." Her smile lit up her face. Not for the first time, he noticed how beautiful that smile was. A smile that he thought was brighter when it was just the two of them, or was he imagining it?

He closed the email with the job description he'd been reading and shoved his phone in his pocket. "Hope you slept well."

She paused in the doorway, her smile changing to a cute kind of puzzled look.

"We're working you hard." He grinned. "The least we can do is provide a good night's rest."

"Oh, yes...thanks." Keely made her way to the kitchen. "I hope it's okay to be here now. I wanted to check the pavlovas again and work out how to serve the taste plates. I'm not keen on using paper plates for that."

"Do whatever you like. I'll get out of your way."

"That's okay. I'm just double checking. I've never done any catering on such a large scale as this before."

Keely had thrown herself into the preparations for the weekend with enthusiasm and Flynn found himself wishing it was more than those preparations that kept her here. He'd been pleased to hear she was staying another week so she could help out at the school. Not that she'd mentioned it to him. She'd remained tight-lipped about her visit to see Ken until after they'd eaten the night before, when Flynn had heard her quietly ask Euan if it would be okay to stay on a bit longer.

"Lucky Maggie's here to help. I'm sure the food will all be fine." He picked up his cap, disappointed that Keely was busy looking in containers, and didn't say any more. He hovered for a minute. Her long dark hair fell like a silky veil down her back and he had the urge to caress it with his fingers. Instead he shoved his hands firmly in his pockets. "She's out in the cellar door. I'd better see if she approves of my arrangements."

"I'm here." Maggie came through from the front of the house. "And of course I approve of what you've done…both of you."

She gave Flynn a look and nudged him as she went past.

"Isn't it wonderful of Keely to take on the food side of things? She's done such a good job of the menu," Maggie said. "You just tell me when you need help, Keely. I am at your service. Is there anything else that you need?"

Keely gave his aunt a shy smile. Flynn felt a sudden flood of remorse. Maggie was right. It was a huge job Keely was doing for them and he kept expecting her to do more.

"We're using bamboo plates for the pork rolls and the pavlovas," Keely said. "But I'd like something sturdier…more elegant perhaps, for the Margaret River charcuterie boards."

"I'll leave you to it, then." Flynn edged towards the door.

"Flynn, you can't go." Maggie gave him that look again and started opening cupboards. "I'm sure Lucy had an assortment of suitable platters. Do you still have them?"

Euan stuck his head in the door. "Flynn, you'd better come and look at the sign I've put up at the front gate. I think it looks okay but you might have other ideas."

Before anyone could answer, Euan had gone. Flynn clenched his fingers. Why couldn't his father just make a decision, like he did for most things that went on at Levallier Dell?

"I'd better have a look at this board," Flynn said. "If it's not right, we may not get many customers anyway."

"Take Keely with you." Maggie placed a hand on Keely's shoulder and gently propelled her towards Flynn.

He looked from Keely's startled expression to Maggie's beaming smile.

"Keely's worked hard and done all the food," Maggie said. "She has an investment in this as well."

"Yes...come if you want," Flynn mumbled. It was only a board at the gate, for goodness sake. Both Euan and Maggie were turning it into a major event.

★ ★ ★

They travelled the short distance to the front gate squashed into the front of the tray-top ute. Keely was acutely aware of the brooding silence between the two men, and of Flynn's warm shoulder and hip pressing into her with every bump.

She wished she'd just left them to it. Maggie had almost pushed her out the door. Perhaps she wanted the house to herself. Keely had tried to keep away as much as she could but it wasn't possible to avoid spending time in the house, with all the organising there was to do.

Euan pulled up just inside their gate and they all got out to inspect the signs.

The new Levallier Dell sign still gleamed, as it had when she'd first arrived. In some ways it seemed so long ago and yet the two weeks had passed so quickly. She felt a pang of regret, knowing her time here was coming to an end. In spite of the two prickly men inspecting the board by the fence she had enjoyed her stay. It had been the healing experience Euan had promised. She pushed away her niggling fear of facing a class again. Once the weekend was over she would deal with that. She wasn't going to let it spoil the next few days.

Euan had created a sandwich board with *Divine Wine and Dine* and the Levallier Dell name at the top and *Come in for a light meal served with our award-winning wines* underneath.

"It should be fine." Flynn helped Euan lift it to the roadside. "If we put it here each day, it will be clearly visible."

A vehicle came along the road and pulled up sharply, its wheels sliding to a halt in the gravel.

It's attracting customers already, Keely thought, smiling to herself, then spun in surprise as a voice shouted, "Euan Levallier!"

Theo was striding towards them. "Euan Levallier," he shouted again.

Kat was scrambling out of the passenger door. "Pappou!"

Theo ignored his granddaughter and came to a stop barely a metre in front of Euan. "What did you do to my vines?"

Keely could see the muscle twitching in Euan's rigid jaw. Flynn stood up straight beside his silent father.

"They're dying. What did you do?" Theo's finger stabbed the air in front of Euan, who maintained his silence.

"Theo?" Flynn's voice was calm. "What's going on?"

"Ask your father! I have four rows of vines poisoned. Four rows that edge the Levallier Dell boundary. He's jealous I got that land before he did and he's poisoned them."

Keely drew in a breath. Theo was wrong. There was no way the Euan she knew would do something like that.

"He wouldn't hurt your vines, Theo." Flynn's tone was calm. His words echoed Keely's thoughts. "Would you, Euan?"

Keely was watching the confrontation from the side. And she saw the cold look Euan gave Flynn, before he turned back to Theo.

"You're a fool," Euan murmured.

Theo shifted from foot to foot. His fists were clenched and his eyes blazed.

"A fool, am I? At least I stay and run my business properly, not like some hobby."

"I don't have to listen to this rubbish." Euan turned his back on Theo and began to walk away.

"It's the truth. Everyone knows Flynn does all the hard work." Theo raised his voice another notch. "You can walk away but this is not the end of it." Theo stabbed the air with his finger again.

Euan stopped, put his hand in his trouser pocket and turned back. "Be careful what you do, Theo." His voice was low. "And don't set foot on my land again. I was going to send this back later but you might as well have it now." He pulled his hand from his pocket and tossed a small notebook at Theo's feet then strode through the gate to his ute.

"My diary," Theo spluttered. "He stole my diary."

Kat put a hand on his arm. "I don't think Euan would have—"

"Bah!" Theo flung off her arm, bent to pick up the little book, then toppled as he tried to straighten up.

"Pappou!" Kat grabbed his arm. Flynn and Keely both rushed forward but Flynn was closer and managed to help keep him on his feet.

"What's wrong, Pappou?" Kat asked.

"Nothing. I'll be alright."

"I think you'd better sit down." Flynn directed Theo towards his car.

Keely heard Euan's ute start up. She watched as he turned the vehicle and drove back down the drive. Flynn was beside Theo's car talking earnestly to Kat, and Theo sat inside looking at something, probably the diary.

Keely wondered how Euan had ended up with that. She glanced once more at the welcoming sign and then walked slowly back down the drive. What a strange lot they were. She'd spent two weeks here and felt no closer to understanding them at all.

CHAPTER
28

It was mid-afternoon when Keely heard a sharp crack resonate through the air. She looked up from the table in the studio, where she had all her beadwork laid out. There was quite a bit to take up to the cellar door and they still hadn't worked out how they were going to display it. The last two days had been a frenzy of finishing off pieces in readiness for the weekend.

Another crack split the air and she went outside to investigate. Over on the ridge among the cab sauv vines, she could see Jack giving his whip a workout. She watched him until he looked in her direction and she waved. He folded his whip and came to meet her.

"Hello, Keely. I've come to collect the last of the temporary fencing I put up for the sheep. Couldn't resist giving the whip a workout."

She smiled at the old man and noticed the string around his trouser legs again. She couldn't help flicking her gaze around the grass at her feet. It was a warm afternoon.

"You've moved house since I was here last," he said. "It's good for the old place to be used again."

"I've done some work on your sketch. Would you like to see it?" She didn't usually show people her sketches but if Flynn did want to use Jack's portrait for his red label, it was important to her that Jack liked it.

"I would."

He followed her to the door and bent to undo his laces.

"Don't worry, Jack. The floor in here is very basic."

He hesitated, then took off his hat and stepped inside. Keely turned from her sketchbook as he let out a long low whistle. He was standing by the table. "You have been busy. These look very pretty. I'm not an expert on ladies' things but I reckon there's a few who'd like these."

"We're going to have them for sale at the cellar door over the weekend. I was just trying to work out how I could display them." She opened her sketchbook and held it up for Jack to see. "Here you are."

He turned from the table and looked at the sketch. She held her breath, waiting for his response. His old weathered face studied the portrait for a moment, then he let out another low whistle.

"You've made me look quite distinguished. Not bad for an old man. Thank you, Keely. You've even got the whip just right."

She looked down at her sketch. It was of Jack's head and shoulders and she had deliberated over how to include the whip. In the end, she had drawn it clutched in one hand and draped over his shoulder.

"Flynn used my portrait of Euan on his dry white label. He might want this one for his red blend, if it's alright with you." She tried to read his expression. "What do you think?"

Jack lifted his chin and his face twisted into a smile. "I think I'd be honoured." He gave the portrait one last glance, then moved back to the bracelets and wine-bottle covers she had laid out on the table.

"Euan's a smart bloke. He's done lots for this area. He deserves to have his face on a bottle of good wine. I've been around a bit longer. I guess that earns me a spot as well." He ran a finger over one of the bracelets, then went to the window and looked out. "I've known Euan since he started this place and the crack of my whip kept those jolly birds away. Euan had to clear out lots of trees to plant his vines. He and Lucy dug out their roots with a pick and shovel back then. But they planted far more trees than they removed, species that bloom with the grapes. Euan has always produced quality wine and Flynn follows in his footsteps. They're decent people."

He stopped talking and Keely could hear the birds outside. It was another beautiful day.

Suddenly, Jack turned around. He glanced at the table, then back to Keely, his face bright as if he'd just thought of something.

"I'd better get going." He grabbed his battered hat and moved to the door, where he paused. "I'll find you something to display your jewellery on." He gave a sharp nod towards her creations on the table. Then, with a brief smile, he was gone.

* * *

The smell of meat cooking made Keely's mouth water as she approached the house. Euan had the meat roasting in the outdoor barbecue, ready for the pork rolls the next day. Her heart did a light skip and she had a moment of cheerful anticipation, before the feeling of dread settled on her again. She was looking forward to the coming weekend. The whole concept excited her but, always in the background like a shadow, was the thought that when the weekend was over, she had to face a class again.

For the hundredth time since her meeting with Ken she toyed with the idea of ringing and cancelling, but now that she'd met him, saw how welcoming he was and knew how desperately he needed her help, she couldn't bring herself to let him down. She sighed and tried to concentrate on her mental checklist of things to be done.

As soon as she entered the Levallier house she could sense the tension. Maggie and Euan were in the kitchen and Flynn was drying a large tray of wine glasses at the table.

"Hello, Keely." Maggie's welcome was bright but Flynn and Euan simply nodded in her direction.

"Can I help with anything?" she asked.

Euan was up to his elbows in frothy water at the sink. "We've got everything ready for the hordes to come and ravish...including the fatted calf."

The glasses he'd dried clinked together as Flynn lifted the crate that held them. "If you're going to have that kind of attitude towards potential customers, perhaps you'd better stay at the sheds tomorrow."

"I think we're just about done here." Maggie smiled at Keely.

"We're done, alright," Euan muttered. "And by Sunday night we'll be done over."

Flynn put the crate back on the table with a crash. Several glasses wobbled precariously but righted themselves without falling.

"It's one weekend," he said. "It's not as if we're going to do this all the time."

"That's why you bought all those bottle bags. For one weekend?" Euan nodded sharply at a pile of deep green napkins on the table beside Flynn. "And the extra cartons and the serviettes with our name on them?"

"The cartons will get used regardless. There was a better deal per bag for the number I got and we needed serviettes anyway. I guess I was hopeful we might do it again, at some stage."

"We're certainly not. We don't want strangers hanging around our house yard, and the best way to taste wine is to sit one-on-one with the winemaker. You can't discuss wine properly when you've got people queued up." Euan turned back to his washing.

Flynn's shoulders slumped and he sighed as he bent to take up the tray again. "Don't worry, when word gets around about the grumpy old bugger running this place, no one will come anyway." He carried his tray off in the direction of the cellar door.

Keely picked up one of the serviettes. *Levallier Dell Wines* was printed inside a black frame across one corner. They looked smart. She glanced up and saw Maggie's concerned look as she watched Flynn leave.

Keely had that sinking feeling that her excitement over the coming weekend may be short-lived.

Euan wiped his hands on a towel. "I think I'll go for a surf and clear my head."

"Can I borrow a vehicle to pick up the groceries?" Keely asked.

There was a moment's silence. Euan glanced at her in surprise, as if he had forgotten she was there.

"We can take my car and I can give you a hand." Maggie gave Euan a glare and picked up her keys. "The air is far too stuffy here."

★ ★ ★

"Baba, I want you to come..." Tony's voice was drowned by the noise of the tractor and Theo didn't look back to acknowledge his son. Instead, his gaze was fixed on the tractor in front of him with his grandson at the wheel. He'd been standing in the same spot all morning watching the dead vines being pulled from the soil. Some of the yellow leaves were flicked off with the violent wrenching and drifted slowly to the ground, which now resembled an autumn landscape instead of spring.

He gazed over the land stretching away from him. With the vines removed, it looked like a huge gaping wound in the earth, bounded by the trees of the Levallier fence line on one side and the reassuring green of healthy River Dynasty vines on the other.

Theo still couldn't understand it. Fifteen years ago, they had moved to Margaret River and bought the land they named River Dynasty. It was a family affair, his three sons and their sons, and everyone had worked hard to create the wines they produced. Everyone in the family could have a job here.

He frowned at the thought of Katerina's refusal. Headstrong, just like her mother, who wouldn't come to River Dynasty either. Fifteen years earlier he had offered his daughter and her husband the opportunity to join the family business but instead of selling up and coming west they had stayed in the Yarra Valley. It would have been a comfort to have his only daughter a little closer but Theo could respect their decision.

"Baba."

Tony was right behind him but still Theo didn't turn. He knew why Tony had come. There were some tough decisions to be made. They had asked the accountant to drive out and look over the books. He'd probably arrived and was waiting at the house.

They had stretched themselves with the expansion to Ocean Dynasty but it had been a natural progression. The more southerly property was still developing and was still a drain on finances, but all the signs were good. He poked at a clod of dirt with his toe. It was just this piece of land that he stood on that had brought them bad luck. Perhaps it was cursed.

"Baba, I want you to come and look at something."

Theo dragged his eyes away from the destruction in front of him. "What is it, Tony? Isn't the accountant here?"

"Not yet." Tony started walking away. "Come to the chemicals shed."

Theo hesitated. For the first time, he heard a tone of command in his eldest son's voice. He rolled his shoulders and breathed deeply.

While he still had breath there was only one boss at River Dynasty. He strode off and overtook his son, reaching the shed in front of him.

"What's the problem?"

Tony unlocked the door and went in. He flicked the switch. Theo noticed how bright the light was now. Someone must have replaced the globes.

"What did you mix in the spray unit the other day?" Tony asked.

"Why?" Theo bristled. "Don't you trust me?" He strode to the corner where two drums sat side by side and began to lift the drum he'd used. It was very heavy. He put it down again, puzzled by the weight. It was so heavy that it could be still full. He peered at the drum beside it, then carefully, as if it was fragile, he reached down and picked it up. The drum lifted easily. He looked at the name and the words seemed to flash at him. Slowly, he put the drum down again and lowered himself to sit on it.

Tony came and stood beside him. "You used the wrong one, Baba," he said softly.

Theo put his head in his hands. He had poisoned his own vines.

* * *

There were crowds of people meandering in and out of the shops as Keely and Maggie made their way back to the car. Keely clutched a bright pink shopping bag packed with new clothes. She couldn't believe they'd shopped together and she'd let Maggie talk her into two new shirts and a pair of jeans. They'd all been on sale, thank goodness, but even so they'd made a dent in her savings.

The shopping trip hadn't happened till after they'd loaded the car with the food. Maggie had wanted something from the newsagent and they'd passed a clothes shop with a sale sign out the front. Maggie had discreetly pointed out that Keely's clothes didn't seem to fit her. Keely had said no one would see her in the kitchen anyway but Maggie had insisted they check out the shop.

Keely had to admit it was nice to try on pants that she didn't need to keep hitching up. They'd had some fun in the shop with Maggie bringing her all kinds of things to try on, some of them way too out there or extravagant for Keely but they'd laughed together all the same. So different from shopping trips with her mother when they went with a list, tried on a couple of things, made their purchases and left with little fuss. They always enjoyed a coffee together afterwards but it wasn't like the treat today's experience had been.

Shopping with Maggie was more like the times when Keely went with her girlfriends and they would try on things that they'd pick out for each other. The difference was, Maggie picked out clothes with a classic style while Keely's girlfriends would pick fashion of the moment or something with outlandish appeal. Euan's sister wasn't turning out to be quite as scary as Keely had imagined her.

"I hope some of these people will be coming our way over the weekend," Maggie said as they sidestepped another group peering in a shop window.

"Yes." Keely agreed, although she wasn't sure whether to hope they came for Flynn's sake or hope they all stayed away for Euan's.

"Hello, Keely, Maggie. It's nice to see you back in Margs. It's been a long time."

They stopped and turned back. Neither of them had noticed Anna on the footpath.

"Hello, Anna," Maggie said. "It's good to be here."

"It'll be a busy weekend ahead. I'm glad Flynn has you there to support him. I can't spare Sean, and Euan is still not coping with the idea of hordes of people at Levallier Dell."

"He's coming round," Maggie said.

"Is he? Poor Flynn was quite down in the dumps about his lack of enthusiasm."

"Flynn can be a worrier," Maggie said. "Things are sorted out now."

Keely glanced at Maggie and a picture of the glum faces of Flynn and Euan flashed through her head. Maggie's lips were turned up in a little smile and her eyes gazed steadily at Anna, almost daring her to say otherwise.

"Oh, well...that's good," Anna said.

"We've all pitched in to get things ready. Keely has been a marvellous help."

Anna turned her attention to Keely. "After the trouble of filling out the paperwork for relief teaching I heard you'd planned to move on but now Megan tells me you are working at her school next week."

"Yes, I'll be on my way after that."

Anna searched her face and Keely sucked in a breath and studied the pavement at her feet.

"I guess that lovely Katerina has been busy at River Dynasty. Have you met her yet, Maggie?" Anna asked.

"Yes, Flynn has introduced me."

Anna leaned in closer to Maggie. "She's just perfect for him, don't you think?"

Keely looked at the people strolling by, the shine fading from her shopping expedition.

"As always, Anna, you are far more well informed than I." There was a stiffness to Maggie's response.

Further down the street Keely noticed a battered green station wagon. She took a few steps towards it. There were a couple of boards tied to the racks on top. Perhaps Marty was in town. It would be nice to see a friendly face. She went closer and bent to look in the window.

"A car thief!"

Strong arms grabbed her and Keely let out a surprised yelp.

"Hello, Keely."

She turned to look into the laughing faces of Steve and Mike.

"Marty's not with us." Mike grinned. "Steve's mate is giving him a few lessons at the beginners' pool."

"We're about to head back to the shack," Steve said. "We stopped in at the tourist centre to get the details for this food and wine weekend." He waved some brochures at her.

"Are you calling in at Levallier Dell?" Keely asked.

"The breweries sound more our thing," Mike said. "But we thought we'd check out a couple of wineries. We'll make sure we mark yours on the list."

"I'll wait for you at the car." Maggie's voice startled Keely. She hadn't noticed the older woman coming up beside her.

"I'll be right there," Keely said, as Maggie moved off.

"I thought it was an all-male show where you were staying," Steve said.

"As it's turned out, there seem to be quite a few women involved in the place." Keely glanced at Maggie's retreating form.

"She looks like a bit of a battleaxe," Mike muttered.

"She's okay." Keely smiled at him. "Look, I'd better go. It would be great to see you at Levallier Dell over the weekend."

She gave them a wave and nearly bumped into Anna as she turned to walk away.

"Sorry Anna, I didn't see you there," she said.

"No, you didn't have eyes for me." Anna's eyebrows raised. She gave a quick nod and stepped briskly away.

Once again, Keely quietly seethed. She really didn't like that woman.

CHAPTER
29

Keely hummed as she walked the track through the vines to the house. It was a beautiful morning. Perhaps a little chilly but there were only scattered clouds and the forecast was for pleasant sunny days, just perfect for the Divine Wine and Dine weekend, and everything was in readiness. Even the vines looked dressed up, with their tops of green leaves bathed in the early sunshine. The roses in full bloom were a perfect adornment to the scene.

Her earlier nerves about not knowing exactly how many to cater for had been dispelled by Maggie. The menu was made up of things easy to put together at short notice, they had plenty of the basic ingredients and the two waitstaff from Megan's class would arrive mid-morning to help serve.

Flynn was in charge of stocking the cellar door and Maggie had reorganised the office and storeroom to allow ease of access from the kitchen. They would use the office as the final prep area for the food, before it was brought out.

Keely wondered how Euan would cope with the day. Flynn wanted him to help sell the wine. Maggie would move from kitchen to cellar door, wherever the greatest need was. Euan had been tense and elusive for the last couple of days. He'd helped with the preparations because Maggie asked him to but he kept disappearing at every opportunity, which, in turn, put Flynn on edge.

What a strange pair Euan and Flynn were. She had envied them their shared love of Levallier Dell and the wine business and yet now she could see it also drove them apart.

Today, she hoped they would put their differences behind them. The weekend held such promise. Keely glanced down at her long-sleeved shirt, striped with pink, brown and taupe, which she'd put on with the jeans, held up by a wide leather belt. Maggie had suggested she tuck the shirt in to the front of her jeans. It was a style Keely had avoided but when she'd looked in the mirror earlier she'd tried the French tuck and liked it. The soft green jumper she'd brought from home was draped around her shoulders but, with the bright promise of the morning, she knew she wouldn't need it for long.

She bounced with every step. It was hard to remember the last time she'd felt so happy. At the gate, she paused as a little group of guinea fowl scurried into the garden ahead of her. They were strange birds. Their bodies looked way too big for their tiny heads.

Then she faltered as the reminder that she would return to teaching the next week flicked at the edge of her mind. She took a deep breath and strode through the gate, burying the disturbing thought deep, where it wouldn't trouble her. If this was to be her last weekend at Levallier Dell, she was determined to enjoy it.

Instead of going to the back door, she walked through the carport so she could have another look at the cellar-door area. Euan's old Volvo was missing from its spot beside the gleaming new car with the Levallier Dell sign painted on the side. Flynn wouldn't be happy if his father had disappeared already. It was a pity Euan's friend Dianna couldn't have stayed for the weekend. Perhaps that's why he was so edgy. Maybe he was missing her.

Keely looked at the cartons of wine stacked along the wall between the carport and the cellar door, ready for the sales they hoped to make over the weekend. At one end, the cartons contained bottles of Levallier Dell Sauvignon Blanc. Euan hadn't been happy about that either. He'd grumbled he barely had enough for his distributors. Flynn assured him it wasn't for tasting and only available for sale by the bottle. The other wines from the Levallier Dell range sat along the wall and finished with cartons of the Scarecrow Dry White from the Haystack Block.

When she stepped through the door it was like entering another world. Flynn had transformed the cellar door to accommodate the tables and chairs they would need to serve lunch to their customers. He had left the old makeshift bar joined to the main bar, as it had been for his birthday party.

The ironwork arrangement that Jack had dropped in the night before sat on one end of the bar, adorned with her bracelets and bottle decorations. She ran her fingers under a bracelet, feeling the comforting smoothness of the beads. Maggie had helped her to decide on a price for each piece. Keely had never sold any of her jewellery before and had been sternly berated by Maggie for underestimating the value of her work.

The polished-wood top of the bar gleamed. Glasses were stacked in the shelves underneath alongside the wine fridge, and there were bundles of dark green paper carry bags, bearing the Levallier Dell label, neatly stacked on another shelf. Keely thought back to the tense scene she'd walked into the previous afternoon. Flynn must have ordered the straw-handled bags especially for the weekend and Euan hadn't been happy about that, either.

Beyond the bar, the large floor area was scattered with small tables and chairs. Taller stools were pulled up to the keg tables they'd used for the party. Keely cast her gaze sideways to the rendered wall that joined the house, then turned to face the wall full on. Hanging near the bar, with framed certificates about prize-winning wines, was her original sketch of Euan. It was in a rustic frame, and the wood looked like it had come from an old paling post. It suited the sketch perfectly.

"Good morning." Maggie entered from the house door carrying an armload of welded metal shapes. "Doesn't your picture look great? Jack made the frame up for me and brought it back when he called in to drop off these table number holders this morning." She nodded at the jumble of metal she held in her arms. "Can you give me a hand?"

Keely stepped forward to help as Maggie deposited her load on the top of the nearest table.

"Aren't they delightful?" Maggie chuckled. She had disentangled a shape from the pile and held it up for Keely to see.

The figure was formed from welded metal that had been painted black like the arrangement that held her jewellery. This one had a coiled base to allow it to stand and one outstretched arm had a gap where a cardboard square with a number on it was slotted in. Keely smiled. It looked like a small scarecrow.

"A man of many talents is Jack Telford." Maggie began to untangle the rest of the small figures. "I worry that the next generation may not be skilled in some of these old crafts."

They put one of the scarecrow figures clutching its cardboard number on each table.

"I hope it goes well today," Keely said.

"It won't be through lack of effort, if it doesn't."

They were silent for a moment as they both surveyed the room.

"How's Euan this morning?" Keely asked.

"You mean, has my brother got over his grumps?" Maggie chuckled again. "He'll be fine. I made him organise the meat for the rolls, then I sent him off for a surf. Flynn has managed to bring him kicking and screaming to this point but Euan has impeccable manners. He may not like all these people coming to Levallier Dell but he will put on a smile and entertain them. He could charm the birds from the trees if he put his mind to it."

Keely remembered the picnic Euan had prepared on her first weekend. Maggie was right. He could be very charming.

"Flynn is not so good at hiding his feelings," Maggie said.

"This weekend is very important to him." Keely thought back over the planning and preparation they'd done together. She'd enjoyed it all, but would it have been as interesting with someone different?

"The two of you have made a good team." Maggie was smiling at her.

Keely glanced down and her hair fell forward. She sensed Maggie move closer.

"Keely, tell me to mind my own business if you want but you have such beautiful bone structure. Do you ever wear your delightful hair up?"

Keely swept her hair back from her face with her fingers. "My mother is always at me to wear it tied back but—"

"No, not back. I mean up. We have a bit of time. Will you let me show you?"

Keely hesitated. She hated it when her mother went on about her hair but her mother's hair was always cut short and neat, a no-fuss style. Maggie's hair was swept up in some kind of elegant roll.

"Thank you." If she was working with food all day, she knew she would have to do something with her hair. Maybe Maggie's idea would be better than a ponytail.

★　★　★

Theo handed over the box of wine. "Enjoy!" he said brightly to the happy group he had just entertained with stories of wine production. He looked across the room where the lunchtime crowd was filling the tables and spilling out into the courtyard area. Along the bar from him, Katerina and Angela were talking to customers, explaining the style of wine they were offering. It was good to have family selling their wines. They had outside staff as well but family knew best how to promote their own product.

He studied Angela closely now. She was a good wife to Peter. A little shy perhaps, but even so she related well to customers and he'd noticed she'd upsold several times already that day. He had hoped Katerina would take up the offer of brand manager but if that wasn't to be, then maybe Angela could do the job. Perhaps he would talk to her about it later. There was certainly no money to employ someone outside the family.

He felt the tightness in his chest again as he recalled his meeting with the accountant. They needed to quit some debt quickly. With the loss of the chardonnay crop and…Theo prodded at his breastbone to try to dispel the ache. He still couldn't believe he had wiped out half of the new semillon vines. He ran his fingers through his hair. No one else was to blame but himself. It was a personal blow and a financial one.

"Pappou, are you feeling okay?" Kat touched his arm.

He smiled at her frowning face. "Of course. Do you need a break?"

"No, the next shift will be here soon and we can stop for a bite to eat. There are some customers who would like to meet you."

He looked past her to the stylish group sampling his reds at the bar. "Always happy to talk to the customers." He rolled his shoulders to ease the ache then tapped his granddaughter under the chin. "Come on, Katerina, smile. I don't want you scaring off potential buyers."

★　★　★

Flynn grinned as another group of satisfied customers walked out with bottles of his Scarecrow Dry White in the green Levallier Dell bags. It was selling very well. He glanced across at Euan, who was propped against a barrel in the corner talking earnestly to an older couple who were interested in his sauvignon blanc. It was late afternoon and the customers had been coming steadily since eleven.

Euan was in full swing, explaining the process of his wine from vine to glass. Flynn could do that, too, if the customer wanted to know – but he was just as happy to share his wine with those who weren't so knowledgeable when it came to the process. All kinds of people bought wine for all kinds of reasons. If they liked his wine and wanted to buy it, he wasn't going to bore them with the details.

He bent down to collect a tray of glasses to wash. Maggie and Keely had been kept busy with the food but they'd stopped serving a couple of hours earlier, apart from a few groups who'd asked for the Margaret River taste plate.

"I'll take those inside."

He straightened. Maggie was on the other side of the bar.

"Are you sure?" he asked. "It's gone quiet out here now. Time to shut the doors soon."

"I'll wash them, then I'm going to put my feet up for a while before dinner."

"Are you feeling okay?" Flynn had to remind himself, as he got older, that she did too. Maggie always seemed young to him.

"I'm perfectly fine. I want to rest my legs before dinner, that's all. Everything ran like clockwork in the kitchen. Keely is such a clever girl, don't you think?"

"She's great."

Maggie winked at him and picked up the tray. As he watched her walk inside, he realised Keely was more than great to do what she had done. While he and Euan had been busy at the cellar door, Maggie and Keely had done all the food. He'd lost track of how many people had eaten lunch, perhaps eighty. He knew his aunt would have worked hard but Keely was the one who'd planned the food, organised it and managed the preparation, and she'd run the kitchen without a hiccup, from what Flynn could see.

Another group of customers came inside, just as Keely stepped through the side door. She was tall, nearly matching him in height, and for the first time since he'd met her, she wore her hair swept up onto her head. It changed her face, or maybe it was that he could see her more clearly. She gave him a quick smile and headed towards Euan.

"Euan, Dianna is on the landline for you inside," Keely said. "She says she's tried to get you on your mobile several times."

Flynn raised his eyebrows but said nothing and instead began lining up some glasses for the group walking his way. Euan's phone was probably switched off or lying in the house somewhere. Maybe Dianna could convince him to pay a bit more attention to it and perhaps even invest in a new one.

"Thanks, Keely," Euan said. "Would you mind packing six bottles of our sauvignon blanc for Bob and Barb. They're all the way from California."

Keely faltered, just for a second, then she brushed at her shirt and stepped around the bar with a smile. "Of course."

She glanced at Flynn and held his gaze for a moment before she tackled Euan's request. Her bright smile lingered before him as he turned his attention to his next lot of customers. He was keenly aware of Keely working nearby as he welcomed them. He started his spiel while she packaged the wine for the Californians and then went on wiping down the surfaces, restocking the wine and generally tidying up. He'd hardly seen her all day and he enjoyed having her share the space behind the counter with him, just the two of them.

The two men and two women lined up along the bar had heard about the Levallier Dell whites and were keen to try the sauvignon blanc. He explained again about the quality and the limited number of bottles left but he didn't think they would buy. They looked more like the one- or two-bottle types. The women drifted along to Keely's beads. The two men stayed to talk.

"We South Aussies are very fussy about our wine," one of the men said and he took a sip of semillon. "Our whites still come out on top."

Flynn's patience was waning a little. It had been a long day and it was time to close up. If this guy wasn't going to buy, he may as well leave.

"I'm from South Australia and I'd say the Levallier Dell Sauvignon Blanc is the best I've tasted yet." Keely smiled confidently at the two men.

"That's a high recommendation," the other man said.

Their two female companions were exclaiming over the jewellery.

"We're just about to close up," Keely said. "Seeing you are our last customers for the day, I'm sure our jewellery maker would be happy for us to give you a bottle cover if you buy a sixpack of wine."

Flynn stood silently beside Keely, amazed to see her so assertive. The group decided to take a mixed dozen of reds and whites, including the sauvignon blanc. He smiled and took their money. Keely packaged everything up, gave both women one of her beaded bottle decorations, waved them off and shut the door behind them. She turned to look back at Flynn, a nervous smile tugging at her lips.

He wanted to jump the bar and kiss her but remained fixed to the spot, surprised at the strength of his reaction.

"I hope that was okay," she said.

"Fine by me, but perhaps you should have checked with our 'jewellery maker' before you gave away her work." He held her gaze. She looked worried now. Damn it, he'd upset her again. "What's the matter?" Euan was standing in the doorway, looking from Flynn to Keely.

"It wasn't really a lie," Keely said. "I told them your sauvignon blanc is the best I've tasted. It's just that I haven't really tasted any others."

Euan laughed. "I'm happy to take your praise."

Flynn couldn't hold in his own laughter any longer.

"Oh, Flynn," Keely said. "I thought you were going to tell me off."

He took a breath and straightened up. She was smiling now.

"Why?" he asked. "You just made an excellent sale. Besides, one should never argue with a jewellery maker. I think we'll have to keep Keely front of house, Euan. She's just sold a dozen wines to the hardest customers of the day."

"Let's open a bottle of our best then." Euan took out a bottle of the Scarecrow Dry White. "All in all, it's been a good day."

Flynn looked from the bottle of wine, his wine, to the huge smile on his father's face. Maybe the tide was turning.

CHAPTER

30

Flynn tripped and bumped against her. "Sorry Keely," he mumbled. "Here I am walking you home and it's me who can't see the way."

Keely enjoyed the steadying arm he put across her shoulders, even if it was by accident. They'd all had several celebratory wines with dinner and it wasn't until they were out in the fresh air that Keely had felt the full effects. Maybe Flynn was feeling it too.

"There's plenty of moonlight." She looked up at the night sky sprinkled with glittering stars. There were only a few clouds and a full moon. "I told everyone I'd be fine. It's not as if I don't know my way to the studio by now."

"I needed to clear my head, anyway. It's been quite a day."

She glanced at his face, which was silhouetted by the moonlight. He was looking ahead but she could see his lips were turned up in a smile. He was right. Day one of the Divine Wine and Dine weekend had gone exceptionally well and they'd just topped it off with another of Maggie's delicious meals and a couple of bottles of wine. Keely's head was buzzing.

"I like your wine but it goes to my head quickly," she said.

"It's partly yours, you know," Flynn said, as they rounded the studio and stepped onto the verandah.

"Now I know you've drunk too much." She chuckled and moved past him to open the door. "I had nothing to do with making your wine."

He took her arm and gently turned her back to face him. "You have your artwork on the label, which you helped to stick on dozens of bottles. You've cooked and cleaned and run the kitchen for our first cellar door where Scarecrow Dry White has sold very steadily. And you believe in it." He dropped her arm but continued to look into her eyes. "I'd say that showed clear involvement."

She couldn't look away. He was right. She had done all those things and it had been easy to believe in something he was so passionate about. He took a small step closer. They held each other's gaze for a moment. She saw some kind of longing there. Surely not for her but Kat wasn't here. She turned away from him to reach for the kitchen light. "I'm going to have a tea. Would you like one?" She held her breath, waiting for the reply.

"Thanks."

He followed her in and she was conscious of him moving about the room as she filled the kettle and got out the teabags and the cups. To have some time alone with Flynn was appealing but she felt guilty, as if she was betraying Kat with her thoughts.

"There's money in this, you know."

She turned to see him flicking through her sketchbook.

"They're personal. I wouldn't want to sell them."

He closed the book quickly.

"I'm sorry—"

"Oh, no," she cut in. "I don't mind you looking at them but I didn't sketch them for an audience...to sell, I mean." She realised in that moment she wanted him to look at her sketches and enjoy them. There had never been anyone else's approval she'd craved as much as she did his.

"Not these perhaps, but there is money to be made. Look at how many labels there are just in the Margaret River region alone. Someone has to design them."

"But I didn't design your label." She passed him his tea. "You saw a sketch and it matched an idea you had."

"Maybe...shall we sit outside?"

She followed him through the door.

"If I had come to you with my idea for a label with a rustic farm-hand image, you probably would have created something I liked."

They settled in the old wicker chairs. The river stretched away from them, glinting in the moonlight.

"Perhaps," she murmured. "I'm pleased your wine sold so well today. Everyone liked it."

"It was fortunate in many ways."

She glanced over at him but he was staring ahead towards the river and his face was in shadow from the kitchen light behind.

"Last week, I'd nearly made up my mind to leave Levallier Dell."

He spoke so softly she had to strain to hear him.

"Why?"

He turned to look at her with a wry smile. "You may have noticed Euan and I don't always agree."

"You're both dedicated to Levallier Dell."

"We are and most of the time it works. Euan's a traditionalist and while I like to use more modern ideas, I wouldn't want to throw the baby out with the bath water. Euan is an exceptional wine-maker and our wine has won many awards."

"You're a part of all that, aren't you?"

"I guess so. I'm just not sure how much of a part. When we bought the Haystack Block it was to give me a chance to experiment a bit more but…I don't know…these last couple of years, since I returned from overseas, Euan has become restless and yet more possessive of Levallier Dell. It's almost as if he's shutting me out. I might as well be a paid hand for all the say I get. Then, when I discovered he was planting more sauv blanc at the Haystack Block to make more traditional Levallier Dell wine I was devastated, but now…" He shrugged.

She waited for him to go on.

"I think Euan actually enjoyed himself today and he was pleased to see the Scarecrow Dry White selling so well. Maybe it was because his face was on the label." He looked back towards the river. "Perhaps things will work out here."

"Where would you have gone?"

"Maybe to South Australia. There's an opportunity there I'm interested in."

Keely watched him for a moment. "I wish I had your courage."

He snorted. "If I had courage, I'd have it out with Euan. Anyway, there's all kinds of courage. Look at you, facing those kids in the classroom. I wouldn't want to do that. I remember what I was like at school. It can't be easy to be a teacher."

Keely's stomach churned and the heavy weight settled quickly on her shoulders. She had been so busy all day that she'd successfully blocked any thoughts of the looming teaching job. Now the thought that it was only a day away hung over her like a shroud. She stared at the glinting dark water of the river. The mind was a strange thing. How can you be blissfully happy one minute, then trapped in fear the next?

"It's not," she murmured.

"But you enjoy teaching, otherwise why would you do it?"

She turned to look at him. He was only an arm's distance away. "I don't enjoy it."

Surprise flickered across his face.

"In fact, I loathe it." She slumped in her chair and looked back to the river. Just saying it out loud eased the ache in her shoulders. She hated feeling so miserable, hated teaching and even hated the students who had made her feel that way. Hate was a strong word, her mother always said. You should never say you hate someone. But hate was what she felt, and admitting it was a relief.

"Why don't you just say no?"

She looked at Flynn. "I can't."

"But why do something if you hate it?"

Keely jumped up, sending the chair skittering away behind her. Why had she said anything? She'd never admitted her hate of teaching to anyone. Why now and to Flynn of all people? It was such a jumble and confusion inside her she couldn't find the words to make proper sense of it to herself, so how could she explain it to him?

She wrapped an arm around a verandah post and leaned her head against it. "I shouldn't have said anything. I've just enjoyed being here and doing something totally different. But I have to earn a living. Teaching is what I do." The shroud settled back around her with its familiar weight. She rolled a shoulder to ease the ache. "But I feel like I'm always holding my breath, waiting for something."

Flynn came to stand beside her. "Stop waiting," he said earnestly. "Use your talents to do other things. We still owe you payment for the labels but wine labels are just a drop in the ocean. You can earn money from your art in other ways."

"I don't expect payment."

"Why not? A good label is very important and if we use the sketch of Jack as well, the remuneration will be quite substantial."

Keely gaped at him. It had never crossed her mind that she would receive payment. The Levalliers had been so good to her, letting her stay rent-free. She'd eaten their food and drunk their wine.

"I couldn't take your money."

"Why not? If you hadn't done those sketches, I would've had to pay someone else to create something."

He reached up and pulled back a tendril of hair that had fallen across her face. The updo Maggie had created that morning was still in place but a glance in the mirror back at the house had shown her that strands were beginning to escape. She needed to let it all down and brush it.

"Keely, you have to believe in yourself a little more."

He was standing very close. He took her arm from the post and held both of her hands in his. Trapped between the light from the studio and the glow of the moon, shadows fell across his face and hid his eyes but she could feel his gaze.

"I'm sorry you and I didn't get off to a very good start," he said. "I was rude and I made certain assumptions when we first met and I've never really apologised properly. I hope you…"

He didn't finish the sentence but leaned forward and kissed her. Not on the cheek but on the lips. It was a brief touch but it was like an electric shock. She gasped and every bit of her tingled.

Flynn straightened up and let go of her hands. "Euan and I are grateful for what you've done for us."

She looked down. It wasn't his gratitude she wanted but it was all she was entitled to. Just for a moment, she'd allowed herself to think that he might like her as more than a friend but she was dreaming. Kat was the one he loved.

"I have enjoyed helping." She straightened and stepped away from the post. "I'd better get some sleep, though. Maggie thinks we could be even busier tomorrow."

She reached the door and turned back. He faced her and, in the light, she thought he looked sad.

"See you in the morning." He gave a half wave and slipped off into the night.

★   ★   ★

Kat stood with her arm around her grandmother as they watched the paramedics lift the trolley into the back of the ambulance with Pappou firmly attached. He was propped up with an oxygen mask over his grey face and his right hand clutched his left arm but even so, he managed to wiggle his fingers at them.

"I'm so glad you were here, Katerina." Yia-yia shivered.

Kat pulled her grandmother close in a hug. "Come on. I'll get your jacket and we'll follow in the car."

Yia-yia had woken her in the middle of the night to ask for her help. Pappou was in pain and not feeling well. Kat took one look at him and called the ambulance. She'd never witnessed anyone have a heart attack before but her first-aid training told her Pappou had the symptoms. She'd wanted to ring her uncle Tony while they waited, but Pappou had said no more fussing and she hadn't wanted to cause him any extra distress.

They went inside as the ambulance drove away.

"I'll ring Uncle Tony now," she said. "He will want to know."

"Yes, I want him to be there." Yia-yia crumpled into a chair. "Oh, Katerina, I couldn't stand to lose my Theo." She wailed into her hands.

"You're not going to lose him, Yia-yia. It's just that he's just not as young as he used to be." Kat took her grandmother's small wizened hands in her own and squeezed them. "Come on, we'll go to the hospital and you'll see, he'll be fine."

She smiled reassuringly to hide her own fear. Pappou held the family together. The thought of him dying was terrifying.

CHAPTER
31

Keely had to stop and check she was in the right place. The mood in the Levallier house was the opposite to the happy scene she had walked out of with Flynn the night before. She could hear the anger in Euan's voice even before she opened the sliding door.

"It's crazy, Maggie, and thoughtless. You know what it's like. Today will be our busiest day. You wait and see. Flynn just dashes off to that woman and leaves us to carry out what was his idea." He waved his hand at Keely, who still hesitated in the doorway. "Keely is a visitor and she's running the kitchen. It's not fair."

"Good morning, Keely." Maggie gave her a quick smile. "Do come in if you're brave."

"Yes, good morning." Euan's face didn't look very welcoming. "If you want to leave at any time, I will completely understand."

"Is something wrong?" Keely wasn't sure how she would cope with the day ahead, after a restless night imagining Flynn's kiss over and over and turning it into something more than it was. She was terrified he would be able to read on her face what she imagined in her head. Thankfully he wasn't in the kitchen.

"Flynn's gone off to be with Kat," Euan said.

Keely stared at him. He'd almost spat the name. She couldn't understand why he disliked Kat so much but at the same time her insides were in turmoil. At first she was relieved Flynn wasn't there. She didn't know how she was going to face him after that kiss. It had obviously been a simple thing for him but Keely still tingled when she thought of it. But then to discover he was with Kat sent a stab of jealousy through her. No matter how much she told herself she liked Kat, her heart didn't feel that way when she thought of Kat and Flynn together.

"It was something urgent, Euan. The poor girl sounded quite distressed on the phone," Maggie said. "Anyway, you're exaggerating the situation. He's coming back and he's promised to pick up the fresh rolls on the way. Someone had to do that anyway."

"And this business about him going off interstate to work. Why did that suddenly pop up at the breakfast table?"

"You pushed him into a corner," Maggie said.

"So, it's my fault he wants to leave?"

"He's young. He wants to make his mark. He's weighing up his options."

"You seem to know a bit about it. I suppose he's discussed it with you already."

"Only in passing."

"Anna mentioned something a while back but I thought she was overreacting," Euan said. "He's probably even spoken to Keely about it."

Keely felt the colour flood her cheeks as she recalled the conversation she'd had with Flynn the previous night. She looked from Euan's angry face to Maggie's sympathetic smile and wished she hadn't put her hair up in the style Maggie had taught her. "He only mentioned something vaguely," she said.

"I see," Euan snapped. "Everyone knows my son's business, but me."

"Oh, Euan." Maggie's response was just as sharp. "If only you weren't so pig-headed. Sometimes you can't see the wood for the trees."

"There are plenty of people trying to tell me what to see."

"You mean bloody busybody Anna actually told you his plans, and you still didn't see how your son was feeling?"

"Anna has our best interests at heart, especially Flynn's."

"Of course she has." There was a hint of sarcasm in Maggie's voice.

Keely looked at her quickly. What a relief she wasn't alone in her dislike of Anna.

"Thank goodness Dianna is coming in a few days," Euan said. "I might have someone on my side."

"Oh dear. Should I get out my violin?" Maggie's look was smug now. "I hope she's not too soft on you. From my brief introduction to her, I think she has more sense than that. Anyway, brother dear, I'd better get myself ready for the day. It's going to be a long one."

"I'll make sure everything is ready outside." Euan snatched up his cap.

They left the kitchen in opposite directions and in the ensuing silence Keely switched on the kettle. Maggie was right about one thing, she thought. It's going to be a very long day.

★ ★ ★

"He's got to have bypass surgery." Kat's voice croaked and she looked exhausted, propped in the hospital waiting-room chair, her face nearly as pale as the white wall behind her. Flynn put an arm around her shoulders.

"When?"

"They'll move him to Perth today."

Flynn glanced up as more of Theo's family arrived and another babble of explanation took place.

"Will you close River Dynasty for today?"

Kat shook her head. "Pappou's had a heart attack but he's still giving orders. Uncle Tony will take Yia-yia to Perth and the rest of us will make sure the business goes on."

There was a loud wailing sound from one of Kat's aunts.

Flynn looked around. "Has something more happened?"

Kat sighed. "No, my aunt reacts that way to everything."

"How about we get some fresh air?"

"I'd love a decent coffee." Kat gave him a little smile.

"Anna will make us one."

Flynn stood back while Kat told her family she was leaving. The night of the River Dynasty party, he'd been envious of her big family. He thought again of the scene he'd had with his own little family that morning.

He'd already been on edge, waiting for Keely to appear at the door and wondering how she would treat him after his bungled attempt at a kiss. The night before he'd wanted to take her in his arms and kiss her properly and he'd got the sense that she wanted that too but he'd read it wrong again. As soon as he'd got close to her she'd bolted. He shook his head. He had no luck with women but his ageing father had no trouble catching them.

Euan had casually mentioned at breakfast that Dianna was coming to stay for a few weeks and something in Flynn had snapped. All the good work of the day before vanished. He was tired of trying to work out where he fitted and what Euan wanted from him. With Dianna in the house, Flynn was convinced that he wouldn't be comfortable. He'd flung in the suggestion of the job in South Australia, to try to force Euan's hand, but it didn't work. It took

Euan by surprise but, as usual, he evaded the discussion and then Kat had called.

Her tired face appeared before him, interrupting his thoughts. "I'm ready."

He led the way to the car. Even though the morning was mild, Flynn had noticed her shiver a couple of times, probably a reaction to all that had happened. He kept a protective arm around her shoulders while they waited at Anna's back door. Why did he find it so easy to be close with Kat and yet with Keely he was so awkward?

Anna opened the door. "Hello, you two. What's brought you here so early?"

Flynn gave her a quick explanation and she whisked them inside to the cosy kitchen full of warmth and delicious smells.

* * *

Maggie's prediction had been correct. The customers had come in their droves as soon as Levallier Dell was open for business. It was another beautiful day and Euan had dusted off the garden furniture he'd set up just outside the cellar door for the overflow of people to enjoy the sunshine. Keely and Maggie had been flat out in the kitchen until mid-afternoon when their supplies had all but gone, and they had decided to say the kitchen was closed.

Maggie sent the two waitstaff home, then she collapsed onto the couch and kicked off her shoes. "I'm reminded why I've become more of a facilitator than a worker," she groaned. "It's easier on my feet."

Keely finished wiping down the benches. She was tired but restless. She'd hardly seen Flynn since he'd rushed in with the rolls, then dashed back to open up the cellar door. He'd only given her a quick hello and when Maggie asked after Kat he had briefly explained Theo's emergency.

Keely imagined the people still tasting out in the cellar door. She'd enjoyed the previous afternoon and her brief introduction to 'front of house', as Flynn had called it. Whether it was that or working beside Flynn, she wasn't sure, but it had been fun.

"Why don't you go out and see what's happening, before you rub a hole in that bench," Maggie said. "There's nothing more to do in here for now."

Keely dropped the cloth and glanced at Maggie but she was stretched out on the couch with her eyes closed. There were probably glasses to wash. She picked up a tray and went outside.

"Keely!" A set of arms wrapped her in a bear hug as she stepped through the door. The tray dropped to one side.

"Hi, Marty."

The quick brush of his lips on her cheek was accompanied by the smell of alcohol. Mike appeared at his side on slightly wobbly legs and Keely disentangled herself from Marty's arms.

Marty glanced around the cellar door. "This is a great place."

"Best winery we've been in all day," Mike said.

Marty leaned in closer and chuckled with beery breath. "That's because it's the only winery we've been in all day."

"We had to check out the breweries first," Mike said.

"Where's Steve?" Keely looked towards the door. She hoped he was designated driver. Both Marty and Mike looked a little worse for wear.

"He's with the old guy over at the bar." Marty nodded over his shoulder and swayed.

"He says he knows every surf spot between here and the top of WA," Mike said.

Keely looked the other way to where Steve was in earnest conversation with Euan at the bar. He looked steady enough. There was an empty table beside her.

"Shall we sit down?" she said.

They all reached for chairs to drag up to the table.

"We're heading north next week," Mike said. "Steve's mate has to go back to work in Perth. We're going to try the surf further up the coast." He nodded in Euan's direction. "The old bloke says that's where the best action is at this time of the year."

Keely looked from Mike to Marty. They were both smiling at her, and Marty's look was almost imploring. She felt a pang of sadness. They were moving on. Their paths might never cross again. She hadn't spent a lot of time with them but it had been comforting to know they were around.

"What about you, Keely?" Marty asked, and he looked steadily into her eyes. "Are you heading north yet? Do you want to come with us?"

"I'm not sure." She looked away, fiddled with the little scarecrow stand on the table, brushed at some scattered crumbs. "I've got a few days' work here next week."

"At the winery?" Marty asked.

"No, at the school." As soon as Keely said the words, her stomach tumbled and the day seemed dull.

"Can we buy you a drink?" Marty asked.

"You don't need to do that." A glass of wine appeared in front of her and Keely looked up into Flynn's unreadable expression. He held out a hand to Marty and Mike in turn. "I'm Flynn Levallier."

"So, the guy at the bar is your old man," Mike said.

"That's right."

"I guess you know all about the surf like he does."

"Not really. Surfing's not my thing. Can I get you blokes a drink?"

"Maybe a glass of red," Mike said. "What do you reckon, Marty?"

"Sure, my shout." Marty reached for his wallet.

"No, put that away," Flynn said. "You're friends of Keely's, this one's on the house."

Keely watched him walk away. It was great to catch up with Marty and Mike but she wished it were Flynn she was sharing a drink with.

"Nice bloke," Mike said. "No wonder you're not interested in Marty."

"Mike," Marty groaned.

Keely felt the heat in her cheeks and there was no hair to hide it.

"Hello, Keely."

She looked up and felt the burn deepen. She'd never actually officially met the guy standing beside her but she knew who he was.

"Hello, Noddy," she said.

"I'm sorry to interrupt but I haven't had a chance to apologise properly."

"Please, don't worry." Keely was acutely aware of Marty and Mike watching with interest.

"No, I must," he said. "I really am very sorry. I don't usually throw myself half naked at chicks on the first date."

He grinned and Keely felt as if she was glowing like a lighthouse.

"You're the body surfer." Mike wagged his finger at Noddy.

"I'm better on the water," Noddy said.

"Have a seat." Marty dragged another chair closer. "Would you like a drink?"

"I'll get it." Keely leapt to her feet, nearly upsetting her own glass, still untouched, on the table where Flynn had placed it.

"Thanks, Keely. A glass of Levallier red would be good." He grinned. "Not as good as ours, of course, but a passable drop." He turned away back to Marty and Mike. "So, you guys do a bit of surfing?"

Keely went to the bar where Flynn had lined up three glasses of red.

"I assume Noddy is having a glass," he said.

"Yes."

"I'll take them over."

Keely didn't follow him but watched from the bar as he put down the drinks and joined in the conversation with the other three. Steve was still talking with Euan at the end of the bar. Beside him, her collection of bead jewellery was all gone but for a couple of bracelets. She allowed herself a little smile.

There was a clutter of used glasses under the counter and she realised she'd left her tray over by the door, where Marty had caught her in the hug. She bent down to look for something else to put them on.

"I've got to duck inside for a moment," Euan said quietly beside her. "Do you mind keeping an eye on things here?"

Keely straightened up. "That's fine," she said. There was no one left at the bar anyway. Steve had gone to join the others. Besides them there were only a couple of other small groups at tables, lingering over their drinks.

She busied herself cleaning up behind the bar, until a woman left one of the groups and approached her.

"I'd like to take a dozen of the Scarecrow Dry White," she said.

"Certainly." Keely went through to the carport where the boxes were stacked. She was amazed to see how much the supplies had dwindled. She picked up one of the last cartons of Scarecrow and carried it back, just as Flynn was rounding the bar.

"Oh, Keely, you're here."

"Yes. But you're just in time. This lady wants a dozen of your dry white." She put the carton on the bar.

"Are you the winemaker?" the woman asked.

"I am," Flynn said.

"We really enjoyed it and the label is a nice touch."

"That's Keely's." Flynn rested a gentle hand on her shoulder. "The original is up there on the wall."

The woman studied the painting, then turned back. "That's the other man who was behind the bar, isn't it?"

"Yes, my father," Flynn said.

"So this is a real family business. My friends and I were saying we liked the atmosphere here. Some of the other wineries we've been to this weekend have been too big, too upmarket for us. We like the feel of this place and your wine is very drinkable."

"We're glad you've enjoyed yourselves," Flynn said and they went on chatting as the woman paid for her wine. The last of the customers stood and gathered their things, ready to leave.

Marty and the others came over to say goodbye. Keely enjoyed the warmth of his farewell hug, smiled at his final pleading look and leaned against the entrance to wave them off. She let out a sigh, tired but happy. The weekend had been a success.

Behind her the house door banged open. She spun to see two young men burst into the cellar door, glancing over their shoulders as Euan stormed out after them.

"You can leave now." His face was dark and his voice held a threat Keely hadn't heard from him before.

"Settle down, Grandpa," one of the men said.

Flynn came round the bar. "What's going on?"

The other man shrugged his shoulders. "We were only making a coffee and Grandpa here came in and went off his trolley."

"Out." Euan pointed towards the carpark.

"Glad to go, old man." The bloke turned, his companion gave Euan the finger and they both strode off.

"What happened?" Flynn asked.

"I found them in the kitchen making themselves at home."

"How did they get in there?"

"Continued on through from the toilet area, I suppose." Euan rounded on Flynn. "They frightened the life out of Maggie. She'd been asleep on the couch. This is why I don't want a cellar door."

Flynn's hands went to his hips. "Because of one mistake?"

"Who knows what they might have got up to if I hadn't come through at that time? It's our home, Flynn. I won't have strangers traipsing through it."

"It's your home, you mean. I don't get a look in. I'd be better off out of it altogether."

"Are you two arguing again?"

Maggie came out and Keely took the opportunity to slip away. This was an argument she could see would have no winners.

CHAPTER
32

A shiver prickled across Keely's shoulders and she rubbed her arms. What a difference a day makes. The morning air was very cold and the sky was dull and cloudy. The vines didn't look quite as green and some of the roses that had looked so pretty over the last few days had started to drop their petals.

She approached the house with legs of lead. She was tired from the weekend and in spite of falling into bed exhausted the night before, sleep had eluded her for some time. She'd woken with the first of the sun's rays edging around the curtain and tried to keep busy by tidying the studio. Not a big job. Then she'd attempted to eat some toast and swallow a cup of tea. The knot that had formed in her stomach had made it difficult and now it threatened to force back up the small morsels she had managed to get down.

Keely sucked in a deep breath and pushed through the gate into the house yard. A little group of guinea fowl huddled together under the bougainvillea, the breeze ruffling their well-groomed feathers. Both Euan's Volvo and Flynn's LandCruiser were missing from the carport. She hoped that meant they were both out. She didn't want to face them again after their argument the day before. Then she had a jolt of panic as she wondered how she was going to get to school. Next to the carport was the ute that Flynn sometimes drove but she wasn't sure how reliable that was.

She slid back the door and stepped into the house. There were no lights on in the kitchen and no sounds came from the rest of the house. Keely had seen Maggie's car still parked under the trees beside the carport. If she was like Keely she'd be avoiding her brother and his son. Who knew, she could be still sleeping after their hectic weekend.

A note had been written on the pad at the end of the table and a set of keys lay next to it. Keely read the message from Euan. It seemed Maggie would be heading home some time that day, Flynn was driving Kat to Perth and Euan had gone surfing, so he had left the keys of the ute for her to drive herself to school. Her heart sunk lower at that. He'd wished her a good day and said he'd cook dinner for her that night.

Keely slumped into a chair and clutched the keys in her hand. She hadn't realised Euan's sister would be leaving so soon. She'd come to like Maggie, who hadn't turned out to be the formidable woman Keely had imagined.

The last few weeks were a blur and now everything was changing. She wondered if Maggie had been able to calm the waters between Euan and Flynn. Surely Flynn wouldn't leave if Kat was going to live next door. Keely stood up. There was no point in worrying over the Levalliers' problems; right now she had her own nemesis to face.

It took several tries to get the ute started but once she got going, it was easy enough to drive. She clutched the steering wheel as she bounced along the track to the road. It'd had a lot of traffic over the weekend. She worried she wouldn't remember the way to town. It always looked different when you were the driver and there were quite a few twists and turns before she reached the main highway. Even when she did she only relaxed a little; before her stretched not only the road, but also the thought of four days' teaching.

At the school, Claire welcomed her and Ken introduced her to a few staff who were chatting over early-morning cups of coffee in the staffroom. They seemed friendly enough but she wanted to get to the art room to make sure everything was set out and ready. Ken walked her there, talking all the way. It was hard to concentrate on his words and she found herself caught out a couple of times as she realised he had paused, waiting for an answer.

Once he'd left, Keely closed the door, leaned back on it and shut her eyes. She took some long slow breaths and waited till the sick feeling eased; then she opened her eyes and surveyed the room.

"You can do this, Keely." Her voice sounded loud in her ears.

She forced herself away from the door and began to set out the gear she needed for the first lesson. She'd planned a simple project – to design a pattern or scene for a wine bottle and paint it using wet on wet technique.

It seemed no time at all before the first group of students gathered outside the door and Ken was back to introduce her. Once he'd gone, Keely launched into her explanation of the task ahead. To her surprise, the students listened attentively and were keen to begin. They all liked the idea of painting the used wine bottles. Her first class ran very well and she noted some real talent but couldn't bring herself to relax. She knew at any moment the mood could change. It only took one or two to misbehave then the rest would follow, no matter how nice they first appeared.

Each new class of the day heightened her anxiety and, as she sat listening to the babble of teenage voices outside, she forced herself to put on a smile and open the door to them.

* * *

"I'm not telling you what to do, Euan." Maggie's voice was gentle. "I'm simply saying you have to make up your mind about what you want."

"You've been telling me for years to find someone to love again. Someone who makes me happy." Euan wished he was still out on his board enjoying the solitude of the ocean, instead of getting a lecture from Maggie in his own house. "Now that I've asked Dianna to be a part of my life, you're saying I have to choose between her and my son."

Maggie sighed. "That's not what I'm saying at all."

Euan thumped the table. "Well, damn it, Maggie, what are you saying? You told me Flynn is leaving because Dianna is coming to stay."

"But it's not Dianna herself that's driving him away. Can't you see that he doesn't know how he fits in? He's not sure of his place."

"This will always be his home."

"Of course it will but Levallier Dell is more than a home. It's a business. Where does he fit with that? Do you want your son to be a part of this winery or not?"

Euan glared at his sister. Flynn was already a partner in Levallier Dell. What was she talking about? "I've congratulated him on his dry white."

"He wanted to plant something different over at the Haystack Block and you didn't let him."

Euan sighed. "I know, it was probably a bit rash in hindsight."

"Does he know that? And what about the cellar door?"

"It went well enough but I don't like people having access to the house."

"There was no real harm done. And maybe there are other ways to run it. You've got several buildings on this property. Perhaps you need to think it through further. It's an aspect of the business Flynn wants to expand."

"He's got his hands full with the Haystack Block wines."

"The small section you allow him to have a say in."

Euan put his hands to his head. "We're just going round in circles."

"So now you're starting to get a taste of what Flynn is experiencing."

"He needs something else in his life." Euan looked at the scarecrow sketch that now hung on the wall by the bookshelf. "I had a small hope Keely might be the one to help him with that. I tried again last night to get him to stay. I thought with everyone gone that he and Keely might have a chance to get to know each other better. It seems Kat is the one he's interested in."

Maggie gave a snort.

"I didn't like the idea either," he went on, "but, as Anna reminded me the other day, she can't help being Theo's granddaughter and she understands a winemaker's life."

"Anna's always full of suggestions."

"She can sometimes see things with Flynn that I don't notice. Since Lucy died she's been a great support."

"There's a fine line between support and meddling."

Euan frowned at his sister. "Anna understands these things better than me," he said. "I have enough trouble sorting out my own love life.

"That's such an avoidance," Maggie snapped. "Bloody Anna! She interferes far too much."

Maggie went into the kitchen and started clattering plates in the sink. Euan followed her.

"She's a close family friend. Anyway, what's the difference? You're interfering."

Maggie stopped stacking plates and turned to look at him. "I *am* family. Besides, I'm trying to get you to make a decision so that everyone knows where they stand and you can all get on with your lives. I'm not trying to make the choice for you, Euan. Only you can decide whether you want Flynn to stay and play a full role in the family business. If you can't let him do that, then cut him loose and let him go somewhere else. He deserves a chance to make a go of things just like you did when you were his age."

Euan glared at his sister. She wasn't usually this direct. "Perhaps you're right…"

"Thank goodness you can see sense."

"I mean about me needing to make my own choices. I need some thinking time. Flynn's in Perth and who knows when he'll be back, Keely's teaching all day and Dianna's not coming till tomorrow. I could do with some solitude." He looked pointedly at Maggie.

"I'll be gone when I've finished the washing. Then you can have your wish of some peace and quiet." She brushed past him to the laundry door. "Oh, and one other thing that your precious Anna hasn't got right. Flynn and Kat are just good mates. It's as plain as the nose on your face that Keely is the one for him. They just need some time to realise it for themselves."

Maggie swept through the laundry door and shut it firmly behind her. Euan shook his head.

Keely was anxious. For two days she'd been anxious. It hovered at the edge of everything she did, robbing her of sleep and draining her ability to think clearly. She'd just finished her second day of teaching. There were still things to be cleaned up before she could go home, but she couldn't bring herself to move from behind the desk where she'd crumpled into a chair once the last group of students had left.

That afternoon her fears had been proven right. A couple of boys, who hadn't been in the class the day before, had started mucking around. She'd separated them and finally had to send one to the principal's office. The mood in the room had changed instantly. The rest of the students became stilted and stiff when she spoke to them and she knew then that her time was running out. Soon they would all get a sniff of her inability to cope and, like sharks in a feeding frenzy, they would circle and attack. Even the nicest of kids would join in.

She'd made it through to the end of the lesson and now here she was, collapsed at her desk. The room swam and she had to remind herself to breathe. She recalled Flynn's voice, "Why don't you just say no?" She grimaced. Why couldn't she do that?

The music from the radio was the only sound in the room. She wasn't sure how long she'd been sitting there, her hands clenched in front of her. Ken had invited her to the staffroom after school. Apparently they were having a short staff meeting followed by drinks and nibbles for someone's birthday but Keely thought she'd rather go home. Flynn and Maggie were gone and the night before Euan had cooked her dinner. Their conversation had been stilted and forced. He'd seemed preoccupied, she assumed, with Dianna's pending arrival. Keely would be happy to do her own thing tonight. She looked forward to the tranquillity of the studio and the gentle flow of the river past her door.

A shadow fell across the desk. She looked up, startled to see a student standing right in front of her. She hadn't heard him come in.

"Hello." He gave her an odd kind of smile as if he were summing her up.

He was a tall boy, perhaps about fifteen or sixteen but it was hard to tell. He hadn't been in any of her classes.

"Hello," she said and looked past him to the open door. There was no one else with him. She stood up. "I'm just getting ready to leave."

"You're nice," he said in a low voice.

Keely froze as she saw him reach a hand towards her.

"I like your hair."

In an instant, she was back at her last school with the leering faces, the whispered comments, the pressing hands. She gasped in a breath, grabbed her bag and made a dash for the door.

"Wait…"

She heard him call something but she didn't stop. She rushed across the yard, around the building and out to the ute, where she paused and dug frantically for the key.

Why had she come here? She should never have let Ken talk her into it. No matter where she went, her failure would follow her. At last she found the key and managed to slide it into the lock with trembling fingers. She wrenched open the door.

"Hi, Keely." Claire called cheerfully from across the carpark. "Aren't you staying for..."

Keely didn't hear the rest. She was in the vehicle, starting the engine. She pulled away from the footpath and there was a loud toot and a screech of brakes behind her. She didn't look back. Her hands gripped the steering wheel and the ute took her away, around the corner, along the road and out of town.

★ ★ ★

"Thanks for staying, Flynn," Kat said. "I would have gone mad listening to Yia-yia and the aunts all day."

Flynn had picked her up from the hospital and they were drinking coffee in the late-afternoon sunshine.

"How is Theo?"

"Doing well. It's amazing how quickly they get you going after an operation. I thought he'd be out of it for days but he says he's feeling better already."

"Probably the drugs talking."

Kat's eyes brimmed with tears. "I couldn't imagine what we'd do without Pappou."

Flynn reached across and squeezed her hand. "He's tough. This is only a blip for him. I admire what he's achieved with River Dynasty."

"He said the same thing about you."

"What, that I'm tough?" Flynn flexed his muscles in a Popeye impersonation.

"No." Kat chuckled. "He likes the way you think things through for yourself."

Flynn was speechless. He couldn't imagine Theo ever gave him much thought. Why would he?

"Pappou likes to keep his eye on things, even when they're not always his business. He likes you."

Flynn took a sip from his coffee, embarrassed at the compliment. "How much longer can you stay?" he asked, to change the subject.

"A few more days. I was able to delay my flight home and Mal has been very understanding. Everything is organised and there's still plenty of time before we leave for Singapore." She bit her lip.

"Everything will work out, Kat. This is a great opportunity. Not only is it a fantastic job but it sounds like you get the bloke as well."

He envied the longing in her eyes as she smiled a dreamy smile.

"Mal is very special. I can't believe I kept him from Mum and Dad. They've been great. It's funny how you expect the worst reaction from your parents."

"What do you mean?"

"I came to Margaret River to think things through and get support from my grandparents. It turned out Pappou was the one who didn't want me to go and my parents have been the ones to encourage me. I should have been up-front with them from the start, instead of anticipating their reaction."

"You're lucky." Flynn sat back as he recalled his parting words with Euan. They'd argued about him going, although Flynn couldn't understand why Euan wouldn't want the place to himself, with Dianna coming.

Euan had made vague comments about Keely needing company but she had her job at the school and Flynn had the impression she was going to go north with her friends, Marty and co. She'd been particularly close to Marty, and since his bungled kiss on Saturday night, Flynn had kept his distance. At least he could support Kat if he was in Perth.

"Things will work out for you too, Flynn. The Scarecrow Dry White is very good and it's only the beginning."

"That depends on Euan." Flynn had decided they all needed some space. He was thinking he'd jump on a plane and check out the job in the Adelaide Hills. If it worked out Euan could have Levallier Dell to himself with his new woman.

"It's your wine and it's good." Kat leaned in. "Don't give it up too easily."

"We'll see." Flynn smiled at her and raised his coffee cup. "Now, let's drink to a new job for you and this bloke you reckon is a bit of alright."

Kat laughed. "It feels so good to have made the decision. I'm actually going to Singapore and Mal will be waiting for me."

Her happiness was infectious. She was right; some things were worth fighting for. He knew he wanted to make good wine and the Whipcracker blend was still in the barrels. He didn't want to leave it, or Margaret River if it came to that. He'd spent enough time away. He looked again at Kat's happy face and realised something else. Levallier Dell wouldn't be as much fun without Keely to share it.

★ ★ ★

The gentle touch on her shoulder made Keely gasp. She turned to see Euan, his face creased into a myriad of lines. She'd been lost in her thoughts, mesmerised by the river, and hadn't heard him approach.

"I didn't mean to frighten you. I called you but you didn't seem to hear. Are you alright?"

Keely knew her face would be red and blotchy from crying. She turned back to the river and he came and sat beside her on the old seat. Tears welled in her eyes again and rolled down her cheeks.

"What is it?" he asked gently.

Keely had replayed the incident in the classroom over and over in her head. Nothing had happened and yet here she was, a blubbering wreck.

"Nothing, It's just…just me. I'm hopeless."

Euan shook his head and put an arm around her shoulder. "Keely, Keely, Keely," he murmured. "What are we going to do with you?"

"I don't know." She allowed her head to rest against him. His kindness overwhelmed her and a fresh sob hiccupped from her chest.

She didn't know how long they sat. Neither of them spoke and the river was the only other witness to the floods of tears she cried. Eventually her sobbing subsided and she felt empty and exhausted. She sat up and rubbed the shoulder of Euan's shirt, which she'd soaked with her tears.

"Don't worry about that," he said. "Do you feel you can talk now?"

"I don't know."

"Come back to the studio and I'll make you a cup of tea."

She followed him up the path, sat on one of the wicker chairs on the verandah and concentrated on taking slow, deep breaths. This was a world away from everything that troubled her. If only she could stay.

"Here you are." He put the cup into her hands, then sat down in the other chair.

"That's the second time you've rescued me." She managed a smile. "I owe you a life debt."

"We can talk about how you can repay me later," he said, then worry creased his face again. "I'm more concerned about what has brought this on. Ken rang, he was worried when you didn't answer your phone. That's why I came looking for you."

Keely clutched the cup unsteadily and she put it down beside her to cool off. She'd left her phone in her bag inside, not wanting to talk to anyone. "He must think I'm an idiot."

"Not at all. He was quite worried about you. Said something about wanting to explain about a special needs boy called Raff. Ken said he'd call out here later."

Keely shook her head. "No, please tell him not to bother. It doesn't matter."

"Ken seemed to think it did."

She gripped the arms of the old chair and looked at him. "Please, Euan. I can't face him."

"Ken's a good bloke."

"You don't understand. No one can."

"I can listen."

Keely sank back and watched the river again. Perhaps he was right. It wouldn't change anything but she'd bottled up her despair for so long that the thought of telling him seemed intoxicatingly simple.

"I shouldn't be a teacher." She sighed. Just saying it out loud was a wonderful release. "I did it because I knew it was what my parents expected but I've never been very good at it. I love art and I enjoyed planning things that I thought would interest kids and I did have some successes, but then I'd have to move on to another school. I've been teaching for five years and I've worked in eight different schools, always contracts, filling in for someone on leave. I know I was not always good at dealing with bad behaviour but it was bearable, until this year."

She stopped and reached for her tea. Her mouth felt dry. She was aware of Euan sitting beside her but she didn't look at him. She sipped her tea, then put it down again.

"This year I had a contract at a big high school. It was for three terms. I was pleased. That's the longest I'd been in one school. I thought it would give me a chance to actually settle in. Turns out it was the worst experience."

She stopped at the sound of footsteps. Ken came around the corner of the studio.

"Join us," Euan got up from his chair and brought another out from inside. "Keely was just explaining what happened at her previous school."

She didn't look at Ken but focused on the river again. She pretended he wasn't there. What did it matter what he heard anyway? She wasn't going back to his school. She really would have to move on now.

"At first I enjoyed it. There were only a few on the staff under about forty-five, but everyone was friendly enough to begin with. The students were much the same as anywhere. I found they responded well to my style of teaching, which was less formal than what I observed in other parts of the school. I liked to play music in my classes once the students were working on their projects. They'd often chat over the top but I called it productive noise.

"My first indication that some of the staff didn't like it was when a senior teacher walked into my class, stormed across the room and unplugged the speaker. The kids and I were stunned into silence. He said his senior class were trying to study next door and left, slamming the door behind him. I was so embarrassed and the kids all looked to me to do something about it, but what could I do? I was mortified."

She remembered the moment so well, it was as if she'd been stripped bare in front of her class. She took another sip of her tea, then leaned forward in her chair, clasping the cup in both hands.

"After that I'd put the music on softly, but the kids would want to turn it up and I was constantly on edge if their talk got any louder than a murmur. That was the start of the decline. I got so worried about the noise that I decided to leave the music off and then the students complained. They started pushing the boundaries. I'd do anything to try to keep them quiet and they knew it. They started playing up, even the normally compliant kids gave me trouble. I spoke to my senior teacher but he said I just needed to use some discipline. Other teachers avoided talking to me. I could see them looking down their noses at me."

Keely stopped again. The only sounds were the birds and the gentle rustle of the leaves in the trees. It was another perfect afternoon. Neither Euan nor Ken spoke. She could stop there and they wouldn't know any different but she'd come this far and knew she had to say the rest.

"One of the boys in my class had an older brother who was a senior boy. He was popular, good at sport and a school captain. He burst into my class one day, wanting to speak to his brother. I asked him to come back at the end of the lesson. He ignored me and, as he left, I asked him to come and see me before he went home. I didn't expect he would but he did. He came into my class after everyone was gone. He shut the door behind him, roughed up his hair and pulled the shirt out of his trousers. Then he...he came right up to me and said...he said I had the hots for him and that his mates were just outside and if I gave him any trouble he'd tell them I'd come on to him."

Euan stood up. "The little bugger, I'd..."

"Wait, Euan," Ken said. "Let her finish."

Keely kept looking at the river. She heard Euan sit back in his chair.

"Go on, Keely." Ken's tone was low and encouraging.

"I went straight to my senior teacher and told him what had happened. He virtually accused me of overreacting and misunderstanding what the student had said, but I knew I hadn't. The boy was a school captain. It was my word against his. I let it go but that wasn't the end of it. The boy started harassing me. It was subtle and never when another adult was around. He would bump into me in a corridor, whisper suggestive comments, make rude gestures…One day a group of boys jostled me and he…he squeezed my breast."

She heard Ken draw in a sharp breath. She couldn't look at him.

"The spineless little bugger," Euan snapped.

"Did you report it to anyone?" Ken asked.

"I did try but I was told that, without evidence, it would be difficult to do anything. My senior said the boy had never given a moment's grief to any other teacher and perhaps I was misunderstanding. He insinuated that as I had difficulty controlling my classes, I may be reading something more into what was probably just high spirits."

"Was there no one else on campus you could talk to?" Ken asked.

"I tried, but by then I was struggling with my classes and I didn't want anyone to know how badly I was doing. I avoided the staffroom. Some days I would lock the classroom door and eat my lunch alone. I put up with unruly classes, with senior teachers walking in and telling them off without a look or a word to me and then, wherever I went in the school, I was always watching my back…I felt powerless. Every afternoon, I would collect my things and go home and, when my parents asked me how my day had been, I would say fine, as if it all was."

"You couldn't talk to them?" Euan asked.

"They're such perfect teachers. They never have trouble with their classes. They wouldn't understand."

"Perhaps you didn't give them the chance," Euan said. "Although it sounds like the management of that school needed a kick up the bum. This wouldn't happen at your school would it, Ken?"

"I would like to think not."

"It's not the school," Keely said. "It's me. It must be something I do. That boy this afternoon...it was just the same."

"I don't know a teacher who's never had trouble with a class." Ken drew his seat up next to hers. "And today was not the same. That's what I came to talk to you about. I feel a bit responsible. We're all used to Raff. He can say the wrong thing sometimes but he's nothing like the boy at your last school. Raff has a type of autism and his parents and teachers have put a lot of effort into his development. They would hate to cause you any grief and, most of all, so would Raff. He came to me, very distressed, after you left. He knew he'd done the wrong thing but he was so upset I couldn't get a full sentence out of him. What did he say to you exactly?"

Keely dragged her gaze away from the river to look at Ken's concerned face.

"See how stupid I am? He said I was nice and he liked me or something then he reached towards me. I overreacted."

"That's understandable, given what happened at your last school," Euan said.

"Was it your hair?"

Keely looked at Ken. "My hair?"

"Was he reaching for your hair?"

She thought back. It had all happened in such a rush. She'd thought the boy was reaching to touch her body but..."He could have been," she said.

"He can get fixated on things. His mother has grown her hair longer and he loves to brush it for her. I imagine he was attracted to your hair. He wouldn't have meant you any harm. His family and teachers work very hard at trying to get him to understand the difference between appropriate behaviour with family and what's okay with friends or at school. We're a relatively small community and everyone at school knows Raff. We have several special needs students, perhaps we need to revisit our procedures for visitors."

Keely looked at him in amazement. "I really did imagine it. The poor kid must have thought I was crazy."

"Considering what you've been through, I think you're amazingly sane," Euan said.

"Keely, I can't make up for what happened to you at your last school," Ken said. "What some of the students did to you was beyond misbehaviour, it was harassment, even assault. And the fact that senior management didn't give you some support was both negligent and appalling."

Keely could feel the tears brimming in her eyes again. "You can't imagine how it feels to have someone believe me," she said.

"Not everyone is suited to be a classroom teacher but from your two days at my school, I can tell you the students are very happy you came. Those painted wine bottles are the talk of the yard at the moment. We've had lots of relief art teachers while the current teacher's been on leave and you've sparked more enthusiasm in two days than the rest of us have managed in any of our relief art lessons. I can understand that you may not want to come back tomorrow—"

"I don't think I could."

"That's fair enough. As long as you know your teaching ability is not in question and I would happily have you back as would the students. Raff wants to apologise but I told him I'd see you and pass on his message."

Keely shook her head. "It wasn't his fault that I reacted the way I did."

"He still needs to learn what's appropriate behaviour and not to cross the boundaries. There will be many people, both strangers and friends, who won't want him to touch their hair. This will be a good learning point for him. I just don't want you to stay away because of Raff."

Keely nodded.

"I'll head home now." Ken stood up, his smile caring like Euan's. "As long as you know you're welcome at our school and my door is always open if you want to talk anything over more."

Euan stood up too. "Will you be okay for a while, Keely? I'll go up with Ken and let Dianna know where I am. She's probably wondering where I've got to."

"Please don't tell anyone about this, Euan. I feel so foolish," Keely said.

"The only foolish thing you've done is harbouring all this anguish. It's not good for you. The issues from your last school aren't resolved but at least I hope you feel better having shared them."

"Yes." She smiled at him through watery eyes. "I do. Thank you."

Keely listened as the sound of their footsteps receded, then she walked to the edge of the bank and looked at the gently flowing water. She stretched her arms up into the air. Tears rolled down her cheeks again but this time they were tears of relief. It was as if a great weight had been lifted from her shoulders.

CHAPTER
34

"Are you sure you want to sell, Baba? There are other things we could do. Besides, we've got some time. It can wait till you feel better."

Kat sat on the hospital chair, silently watching the exchange between Pappou and her uncle Tony. Pappou had asked her to sit in on the discussion but she didn't know why. Several days had passed since his heart attack and she was glad to see he was looking much better. Her flight to Melbourne left the next day and she wanted to be able to reassure her mother that he was on the mend.

"I am sure, Tony," Pappou said. "I have had nothing else to do but lie here and think about things."

"We should run it past the accountant," Tony said.

"I rang him first thing this morning and he agrees with me."

He'd be a brave man to disagree, Kat thought.

"We need to quit some debt and generate some funds," Pappou said.

"I know, Baba, but you badly wanted that land when we bought it. Are you sure you don't want to look at other options?"

"That piece of land has given us nothing but grief. It will have the least effect on our plans for River and Ocean Dynasties. I do have some conditions, however."

He closed his eyes for a moment and Tony raised his eyebrows at Kat across the bed.

"Pappou, should you be discussing business?" she asked. "I don't know that your doctor would approve."

His eyes flew open. "He doesn't approve of anything, that man. He doesn't even drink red wine. What kind of man doesn't like red wine? Now, I will tell you what my conditions are."

Kat shrugged at her uncle. She had tried.

* * *

Keely got off the bus at the central busport in the city and made her way towards Elizabeth Quay. She hadn't visited the waterfront when she'd first arrived in Perth and had determined it would be her first port of call. It'd felt strange, checking in to the backpacker hostel again. She hoped this time she'd actually get to spend the night there. She smiled. It seemed ages since she'd flown in, ready to embark on her holiday, but only one month had gone by. Just as well we can't see into the future, she thought. Who could've predicted everything that had happened in that time?

After spilling her story to Euan and Ken she had ended up going back and working two more days at the school. She'd been nervous at first, but everything had gone well – even Raff's apology, where she discovered he liked to paint. After that he'd come with a mate after school each day and done some painting while she'd packed up the room. She'd been impressed by his talent with a brush and let Ken know.

Euan and Dianna had invited her for dinner each evening and Euan had said she could stay on at the studio for as long as she liked, but once her job at the school had finished she really had no more excuses to stay.

She'd accepted the connection she thought she'd had with Flynn had been nothing more than friendship. He'd gone a couple of days earlier to be with Kat, and Keely was doing her best to forget him and move on. It had been difficult enough saying goodbye to Euan. He'd been a great friend to her when she'd needed one most and she was very fond of him. She'd also enjoyed the opportunity to get to know Dianna. Keely was pleased to see their obvious happiness in being together.

Her phone pinged with a text message. She dug it out and smiled. It was from Marty. She'd let him know she was starting her journey up the coast. He and his mates were a lot further north already, in Carnarvon. He'd sent a photo of himself in front of a huge satellite dish and had said they were going to try kite surfing. She sent a reply. She didn't know if she'd get there before they moved on but she hoped she'd catch up with them again at some point.

She wandered down near the water's edge where a ferry was pulling in and then strolled on towards the bridge that spanned the mouth of the quay. There were things she had to do but it was such a beautiful day she was happy to delay her chores. She needed a few items from the supermarket before she began the next leg of her journey north, and she wanted to find something for Bec. It was her birthday next week and Keely thought she'd send her some kind of funny souvenir and perhaps even something for her brothers. Her mum had become worried again when Keely said she was heading north and she'd promised to check in daily. She'd also promised Euan she'd call from time to time.

Keely crossed the bridge and took a few photos of its structure from different angles. She needed to update her Insta account. It had been sadly neglected while she'd been in Margaret River. She gazed over the wide expanse of the river to the buildings of South Perth. Maggie had issued her with an invitation to stay with her in Perth but Keely had decided against it. She'd gathered from Euan that Flynn was still in Perth and she presumed he would stay with his aunt or with Kat. Either way, she'd decided to keep her life simple after all the trauma of the last few weeks. It was best if she didn't see Flynn.

"Keely?"

She spun, surprised at the sound of Kat's voice. She was beckoning to Keely from under an umbrella, outside the cafe beside the bridge. Kat was alone and Keely felt a pang of disappointment. She berated herself. Hadn't she resolved not to see Flynn?

"I thought it was you. How amazing to see you. I had to leave Margaret River in such a rush, I didn't think I'd get the chance to say goodbye."

"How is your grandfather?" Keely asked.

"Much better, thank goodness. It was fairly scary for a while." Kat patted the empty chair next to her. "Have you got time to sit?"

"Oh...yes, a few minutes." Keely glanced around, then sat down under the umbrella.

"Isn't it a beautiful day?" Kat stretched her long arms back over her head in a graceful movement. "I feel as if I've been cooped up for ages."

"I suppose you've been spending time in the hospital."

"Yes, you do a lot of sitting around and then feel exhausted. Thank goodness for Flynn. He kept me sane. He's inside getting me another coffee. Do you want one?"

Damn, thought Keely. She had assumed Kat was alone. "No, thanks. I can't stay long."

"Hello, Keely."

Her heartbeat quickened at the sound of his voice and she had to take a calming breath before she turned. Flynn came from behind her, carrying a coffee cup. He put it down in front of Kat but continued to keep his gaze on Keely.

"How did the job at the school go?" he asked.

"Well, thanks," she said, without flinching. "Incredibly well, actually."

The sounds of building from a nearby construction site ricocheted around them.

"So, you're getting ready to continue your holiday north now?"

"Yes." Keely looked over the water to avoid those sparkling blue eyes.

"We're all embarking on something new." Kat raised her cup in a mini-toast.

"Look, I'm sorry to rush off." Flynn put his hands on Kat's shoulders and gave them a squeeze. "Kat has just given me some great news and I've got to go and sort some things out."

"I must be off, too." Keely stood quickly. "It was great to see you both."

Kat stood too and drew her into a hug. "It was great to get to know you, Keely. Safe travels."

"Thanks, you too."

Flynn stood slightly apart from them. He stared at Keely and she had to turn away, terrified he'd draw her into a farewell hug and she'd make a fool of herself. "Maggie was hoping to catch up with you again," he said. "You should give her a call."

"Of course…that'd be great." She stumbled over her words.

"I'm going back to the flat when I've finished my coffee," Kat said.

Flynn nodded. "I'll see you there later."

He turned back to Keely and there was longing in his look. She hurried away, unable to bear seeing his open desire for Kat.

★   ★   ★

"Let's drink a toast."

Flynn looked up from the backpack he was stuffing clothes into. "Make mine lemonade, Maggie. I've got to drive."

"Tonight?" She was leaning against the bedroom doorframe, arms folded.

"I'm picking up the paperwork in Margaret River first thing in the morning and driving back here with it. By tomorrow afternoon, everything should be done."

"What about Kat?"

"I won't see her again. Her plane leaves in the morning."

"Oh. Well, you and I can have a proper celebration of our partnership when you get back."

Flynn slung his pack over his shoulder and followed her to the kitchen where she poured them both a drink.

"Euan said Keely had left Margaret River." Maggie smiled at him as she passed him his glass.

"I forgot to tell you, I saw her in the city."

"When?"

"Earlier this afternoon. She'll probably give you a call."

"How did she look?"

"Fine, I suppose. She was chatting to Kat. Why?"

They clinked glasses and both took a sip.

"Euan said she'd had a bit of a tough week but she'd come through it well," Maggie said.

Flynn frowned. "She said she'd had a good week."

"Where is she staying?"

"I don't know. I forgot to ask."

"Flynn!"

"What?"

"Sometimes I do wonder if you are your father's son. You must have inherited all of the Irish work genes and none of the romantic French."

Flynn looked at his aunt. Sometimes she talked in riddles. Where was she going with this?

"It's as plain as the nose on your face that you and Keely have feelings for each other."

Flynn gulped down the last of his lemonade. He wished that what his aunt said was true. The part about him liking Keely was – but he knew the feelings weren't reciprocated. She'd been quite cool towards him that afternoon.

"Flynn?"

He let out a heavy sigh and shook his head. "Maggie, you are my aunt and my business partner but I'm not going to discuss women with you." He leaned forward and kissed her cheek. "I'll be back here tomorrow afternoon."

CHAPTER
35

Euan heard the car and placed a cup under the spout of the coffee machine. Dianna had gone to bed but he'd stayed up to wait for Flynn. Maggie's phone call, to tell him Flynn was on his way with some interesting news, had piqued his curiosity and he also had other things he wanted to talk to Flynn about.

Euan had done a lot of reflecting in the last week. Dianna being here was one thing but hearing what Keely had been through and that she felt she had no one to turn to, not even her parents, was startling. Would Flynn feel he could turn to him in a crisis? Euan certainly hadn't been much help to him when Lucy died, but he thought they'd got past that.

Since Flynn had come back from his travels, Euan thought they'd settled into some kind of routine. They didn't always see eye to eye on making wine, but they managed. Euan respected Flynn's opinion but somehow things weren't right. He realised he was still keeping his son at arm's length. He'd made plenty of blunders but the last week had made one thing perfectly clear: Euan didn't want

Flynn to leave Levallier Dell for good. What was the point of all the work, if not to share the future with Flynn?

Maggie had been right, as always. Euan needed to be open with Flynn about the business. They had to plan the future together so they both knew where they stood.

Flynn slid back the door and stepped into the room.

"Coffee?"

He spun around. "I didn't realise you were still up."

"Maggie phoned and said you were on your way. There are some things I'd like to talk to you about."

"Can it wait?" Flynn dropped his pack by the couch. "I don't want to argue but I would like a coffee. I've got some good news."

Euan reached for another cup. It hurt to think that Flynn naturally assumed he was looking for an argument. He cleared his throat. "What is it?" He kept his tone light and interested and he made eye contact with Flynn.

"Theo's selling that piece of land we wanted."

"Why would he do that?" Euan leaned forward. Flynn had his attention.

"From what I can gather, he's overextended."

"He'll want a lot of money for it."

"Yes and no."

"What do you mean? Do you know what he's asking?"

"Yes, as a matter of fact, I do." Flynn looked over the kitchen bench. "How's that coffee coming along?"

Euan took the cup from under the machine and passed it to Flynn. "Do I have to beat it out of you?" He picked up his own cup and went round to sit at the table. "How much?" He was already mentally checking their current overheads. Things were fairly tight, the new vehicle had been an unexpected expense, but they might be able to borrow enough money, if the price was right.

"Theo's price is more than reasonable and he's given me first chance but—"

"You're kidding!" Euan slapped his hand on the table.

"There is a 'but'. Theo has two stipulations."

"What are they? He'll probably want a quick settlement if he's got cashflow problems." Euan frowned. He hoped Kat wasn't somehow one of the conditions.

"Yes, he wants to settle as soon as possible but the other thing is, if we buy, the land has to be in my name."

"Why?"

"Come off it, Euan. You and Theo aren't exactly the best of friends. It must have dented his pride to have to sell and he knew you'd want the land. I've already spoken to Maggie. Between us, we can come up with the money."

"Sounds like you've got it all organised." Euan was disappointed Flynn had gone to Maggie instead of him with the planning of this deal. He would have to work hard to repair the damage to their confidence in each other.

"We had to act fast. It's a great opportunity."

"I'm amazed that Theo offered it to you. Perhaps Kat influenced him. There are others around he could have sold it to."

"It turns out it was his idea. Evidently, he quite likes me." Flynn gave a soft snort. "I think he had plans for me to marry Kat."

"I told you he was up to something, that wily old bugger." Euan blew out a quiet breath, glad that hadn't been a condition of the sale. "Mind you, he didn't have to drag you. You fell for his plan, hook, line and sinker."

"What do you mean?"

"You and Kat."

"What about us?"

"You've been quite an item."

"No, we haven't. We're mates, nothing more. She's got a job in Singapore and a boyfriend to go with it."

Euan put down his cup and inspected Flynn's face. "But you spent all that time together."

"Friends do. She needed someone to talk things over with."

"And she stayed here a couple of nights."

"In the spare bed." Flynn stood up. "Damn it, Euan. Not everyone's like you with a woman in their bed every five minutes."

Euan flinched. "Keep your voice down. Dianna is sleeping."

Flynn's hand flew to his forehead. "Wait, did you really think me and Kat were..."

"Are you telling me you weren't?"

"Of course not. I told you we're just good friends."

Flynn glared at Euan for a moment, then he sighed. "Dianna seems nice. I hope she knows what she's letting herself in for."

Euan scratched his head. He had a lot more bridges to build than he'd realised. "Flynn, sit down. We need to talk." Euan could see the indecision in his son's face. "Please, I know it's late but I want us to sort things out. I don't want to fight with you. This is your home. More than anything, I want you to stay here. Levallier Dell is a family business...father and son."

He felt a little surge of relief as Flynn sat back in the chair and picked up his coffee. They were silent for a moment then Flynn held his cup over the table and grinned.

"There're some first-rate sauvignon blanc and semillon vines on that block," he said. "And after Theo's accident with the poison, we've got room to try another variety."

"Surely we'd replant with semillon."

Flynn held his gaze. "I've been doing some research and I'd like to plant a different variety, something we haven't tried before."

"What about pinot noir then? We don't have a sparkling."

"Maybe, but I've got an idea for something else."

Euan felt a quick stab of annoyance then swallowed his pride at the excited look on his son's face. It wasn't going to be easy to give Flynn more control but he had to try. "What did you have in mind?"

"I've been searching for something unique. A wine that no one else grows in our region. I've been reliving my time in Europe, the wines I enjoyed there…"

"And?"

"I'd like to try albariño."

Euan almost choked on his tea. "Unique alright. It's probably not even albariño, it's savagnin. Lots of growers lost money trying to make that variety work. Surely it's not worth the risk."

"The true albariño vines are growing in Australia now." Flynn met his look with a steady gaze. "I've been talking to my mate in South Australia. The one who offered me a job."

Euan's jaw clenched. He waited.

"They grow the true albariño at his family's winery in the Adelaide Hills and…" Flynn's eyes lit up and his face split in a wide smile. "They'd be happy to let us take some cuttings to get started."

Euan hesitated. The look he saw on Flynn's face reminded him of his own when he and Lucy started Levallier Dell. He nodded his head. "Why not? It would be a new challenge."

"We could do it together and I've already got an idea for a label."

"That's counting your bottles before you've grown the grapes, isn't it?"

"Maybe." Flynn's look turned cagey.

Euan didn't press him but lifted his mug instead. "Whatever we plant I'd say the future of the family business is looking good."

Flynn tapped his cup against Euan's. "Here's to the future."

CHAPTER
36

Keely knocked on the door of Maggie's apartment. It would be good to see her again, before she caught the bus the next day. Now that she'd made her travel plans, she was feeling quite excited about the prospect of finally heading north.

"Hello, Keely. Come in." Maggie stood back and waved her through an entrance hall and into a magnificent high-ceilinged sitting room.

Keely took in the elegant decor. It was as if she'd stepped into a home magazine. "What a beautiful apartment."

"I'm very comfortable here." Maggie led the way across the room. "I thought we'd sit out on the balcony. It's a glorious afternoon."

Keely was glad she'd worn her skirt. She'd only bought it that morning. It was made of soft pink crimpy fabric and flowed down to just above her ankles. She'd topped it with a lacy white blouse. It felt good to be out of jeans for a while. She sat in a patio chair decked out with pretty cushions in pinks and greens and took in the view of the Swan River and the city on the opposite side.

"You've had your hair cut," Maggie said.

"I've been a bit indulgent this morning." She ran her hand softly over her hair, which still reached below her shoulders. The hairdresser had praised her for not succumbing to a fringe. He'd raved over her bone structure and brushed her hair back from her face. She'd liked what she'd seen in the mirror. "It's just a trim. I thought it might be easier to manage for the heat up north."

"You're still planning on going?"

"Yes. I've booked a seat on a bus for tomorrow. I'm going to the Pinnacles first."

"I am glad you're going ahead with your trip. Kat is travelling as well, did you know? Only she's off overseas. Did you get a chance to see her before she left?"

Keely stared at Maggie. What did she mean? "No. I mean yes… at least I saw her yesterday and she said goodbye, but I thought she was farewelling me."

"She flew home to Melbourne this morning. I think Flynn said she had another week before she left for Singapore to be with her boyfriend."

"But…" Keely didn't understand. Wasn't Flynn her boyfriend?

A mobile rang from somewhere behind them in the apartment. "Excuse me a moment." Maggie went inside.

Keely frowned at the beautiful vista in front of her. Kat was with Flynn. She'd seen them together the day before. There'd been some remark about them all starting something new and Flynn had said Kat had given him wonderful news and he'd see her again at the flat.

None of that made sense with what Maggie had just said. Maybe she'd misunderstood.

Maggie stuck her head through the open doors of the sitting room. "I've just realised I'm totally out of milk for our coffee. There are some magazines on the table. I won't be long."

"Maggie, are you sure Kat is going to Singapore?" Keely asked.

"Quite sure. Flynn was here yesterday and told me all about it."

"And Flynn's not going with her?"

"Good heavens, no." Maggie smiled. "Flynn had to tend to some urgent business back in Margaret River. Theo is selling him some land. Now you make yourself comfortable. I'll be right back."

Keely stood up and leaned on the balcony rail, staring at the river. What was it with her and water? She seemed to have spent a lot of the last few weeks simply staring at it. She still couldn't comprehend what Maggie had said. Keely had seen all the signs. Kat and Flynn were together and yet, if what Maggie said was true, they couldn't be.

A brief flutter of hope stirred inside her and then she banished it. Her Margaret River adventure was over. It was time to move on.

The wind strengthened and goosebumps prickled her arms. She stepped back into the sitting room and heard the front door close.

"Maggie, I'm here. It's all done."

Keely stopped at the sound of Flynn's voice. She brushed her hands down her sides, smoothing her skirt.

"Maggie?" He paused mid-stride when he saw Keely.

"She's not here."

Flynn ran his fingers through his hair. "But I spoke to her on the phone a few minutes ago. She wanted me to…" He shook his head.

"She's gone to get milk. I was out on the balcony." Keely nodded over her shoulder. "It got chilly."

Flynn continued to stare. Keely looked around frantically trying to think of something to say.

"She shouldn't…"

"She won't…" They both spoke at once.

Flynn smiled at Keely. "There's a shop just down the street, she shouldn't be long."

"No." Keely poked her toe at the pattern on the floor rug.

"You staying in Perth long?"

"I'm heading north tomorrow."

"I guess you're glad to be on your way at last."

"Yes."

They were both silent. Keely glanced around Maggie's beautifully furnished room.

"I'm going to make myself a late lunch," Flynn said. "Would you like something?"

He began to move towards another door. Keely guessed it led to the kitchen. "No. I've eaten, thanks."

He paused, looking at her again. Keely held her breath until she felt as if she would burst.

"Look, I'd better get going." She picked up her bag from the side table. "Say thanks to Maggie. I've got a few more things to organise before I leave."

"Are you sure? She shouldn't be much longer."

"I'll keep moving."

He followed her to the door. "Keely."

She stopped with her hand on the doorknob. She sensed rather than heard him step closer behind her.

"Thanks for everything you did. I…well, Euan and I appreciated your support. If you're ever back this way…well, you're welcome."

She opened the door, went through, then looked back at him. Her heart thumped and she forced the corners of her mouth into a smile. "I enjoyed my time in Margaret River. Levallier Dell is a special place. I hope everything works out for you and Euan." Then with every bit of her strength she walked away.

* * *

Flynn was sitting at the table eating a sandwich when he heard his aunt's key in the lock. He quickly opened the newspaper and lay it out in front of him.

"Keely?" she called. "Flynn?"

"In here, Maggie."

She came through the door and looked around. "Where's Keely?"

"She left about a half hour ago." He turned the page of the paper. "Said she had things to do."

"Did you talk to her?"

"Briefly. She was in a bit of a rush when I arrived. I don't think she expected to see me."

"You shouldn't have let her go without offering her some refreshments."

"I did but she declined." Flynn had a flashback to the image of Keely, framed in the patio door. She had on a long flowing skirt and the light from behind silhouetted her legs. She'd looked beautiful, with surprise written all over her face, and he had let her bolt – again.

Maggie put a magazine down on the table and started to clear up the things he'd left out.

"Why did you want me to phone you when I was leaving the solicitors?" he asked.

"I was worried about you."

"Why?"

"I'm allowed to worry. You've done a lot of driving in the last twenty-four hours and you've had a huge amount on your plate."

"You needn't have worried. I'm fine."

A soft snort came from behind him.

"Where's the milk?" he asked, as he turned another page of his paper.

"Pardon?"

"Didn't you go out to get milk?"

"Oh...how silly of me. I got talking to the fellow down at the shop and forgot all about it."

"Could have saved yourself the trouble, then."

"What do you mean?"

Flynn grinned at her but she turned away quickly, snatched up a cloth and began wiping down the bench top.

"There's a full carton in the door of the fridge. You must have missed it."

He turned back to his paper and something soft and wet hit him on the back of the head.

CHAPTER
37

Keely strolled along the beach in the late afternoon. At last she was heading north. The bus trip from Perth had been uneventful and she'd arrived in Cervantes the day before with plenty of time to check in to the backpackers' accommodation and book herself a place on the sunset tour to the Pinnacles. It had been worth it. The strange limestone formations were spectacular and it was amazing to watch them change through a range of colours she'd never seen before as the sun went down. Now she was walking the beautiful white sand of Jurien Bay, a little further up the coast.

She stopped to watch the waves of the Indian Ocean pound in on the beach. Travelling alone, after the company she'd been keeping, was too quiet. Each day she was putting more kilometres between her and Margaret River and…She didn't even want to think his name.

She'd stopped at Jurien Bay with no particular plan and she felt restless with nothing to do but wander. She had a strange sense of loss and, if she was honest, she knew she was lonely.

There weren't many people on the beach. A family group stood together playing and chasing the waves at the water's edge and a couple walked arm in arm further along. She turned to head back to the guesthouse. The wind was quite strong and whipped her hair onto her face. It was still long enough to wear up. Perhaps she'd try that tomorrow.

She brushed at the hair across her eyes and caught a glimpse of a tall figure striding in her direction. She stopped, held her hair firmly away from her face and stared. The walk was familiar. It couldn't be Marty, he and his mates would be much further north. Just for a moment, she imagined the man walking towards her looked like Flynn. She'd have to take herself seriously in hand or she'd become miserable.

The man held up an arm and called out. The wind blew the sound away but it could almost have been her name. She stared hard and the figure waved again.

"Flynn?" She half raised her arm. Was she seeing things? What would Flynn be doing here?

He came striding towards her waving something in his hand. As he got closer, she could see it was a bottle of wine. He stopped just a step away from her. She continued to hold her hair to the side of her face and stare at him.

He gave a slight bow. "A something more wine," he said in a pompous voice, "the Scarecrow label is produced by one of Margaret River's long-established wineries."

She frowned at him. More like something in the wine. Either he'd lost the plot, or she had.

"That was how the judge described it." He grinned and waved the bottle under her nose. "Scarecrow won. Levallier Dell's new Haystack label...Scarecrow Dry White...won a trophy for best white blend. They rang me this morning."

Keely looked into his eyes and saw just a flash of hesitation. "That's great," she said quickly.

"I tried to get you on your phone but I kept getting your message so I thought I'd come and tell you…in person."

The hand holding the bottle dropped to his side and they both stood in silence for a moment. The waves crashed on the beach beside them and the wind was loud in Keely's ears, so she almost didn't hear him when he spoke again.

"Keely, I'm sorry." Flynn took a little step closer and pinned her with his mournful look. "I let my annoyance at Maggie stop me from saying what I should have said to you the other day. I tried to ring you that night but your phone wasn't answering and I had no idea where you were staying. By the time I got to the bus station in the morning, you were gone. I'd almost convinced myself to let you go but then I got the phone call about the wine winning first prize and I…" His voice faltered and he looked down.

She'd seen the missed calls on her phone but had wanted to put more space between them before she talked to him again. "You drove all this way to tell me?"

"I wanted to share the moment with you. You believed in me."

"How did you find me?"

"Persistence." He gave her a little grin. "When I explained you'd won a prize and didn't know about it, the guy at the backpackers at Cervantes told me you'd moved on. There aren't that many places the bus stops."

Keely looked at him, still hardly daring to move in case she woke up to find that she'd been dreaming.

"I'm glad you came," she said.

His smile widened and he held the bottle up in front of her. "The wine is chilled but I forgot the glasses. We can drink a toast from the bottle or…from the container I had the ice in." He lifted his other hand, which held an empty butter tub.

"Let's use that." She let herself smile. Surely if she was dreaming he would have produced crystal glasses.

They sat down in the sand and Keely watched steadily as Flynn unscrewed the cap and poured the wine into the tub. Then he stood the bottle in the sand in front of them and offered her the makeshift glass.

"Thanks for coming up with the name…and the label."

She took a sip. "Thanks for coming up with a very good wine," she said. "Which, by the way, won without the name or the label."

He took the tub and drank from it. "Just as well it's a good wine. The drinking vessel doesn't do anything for it."

His gaze locked with hers. Keely's heart was beating so hard in her chest that she thought he would be able to hear it.

He put the container down. "I've missed you. Last weekend was great."

"Everything worked out well."

"It wouldn't have mattered if it hadn't. I like being with you."

Keely glanced down at the tub of wine between them. The look in his eyes made her feel as if she were melting and yet all they could do was make polite conversation. "I like being with you, too," she said softly.

"I can't believe how stupid I've been." He gave his leg a slap. "I thought you didn't like me but Maggie says you were giving me space, because you thought I was with Kat, even Euan did. Not that I was ready to listen to anything Maggie had to say, after that terrible attempt at getting us together the other afternoon."

Keely felt the heat spread across her cheeks and then the touch of his hand as his fingers gently lifted her chin so that her lips were level with his. He leaned forward and kissed her. Not a quick brush of the lips this time, but a long, slow kiss that left her in no doubt about how he felt. He pulled her gently to him and she reached around his neck and kissed him back.

Finally, they took a breath. Flynn kept his face close to hers and ran his finger softly over her lips. Tingles ran up and down her spine.

"I've wanted to kiss you for a long time," he said.

"I've been waiting a long time." She kissed the tip of his finger.

"I was going to suggest a toast but…"

They both looked at the butter tub. The wind had blown sand into it and combined with the wine to make a gritty paste.

"To heck with it." She laughed. "Let's drink from the bottle."

Their arms went around each other as they kissed again and clung together for a moment. His body was warm and firm and she loved the feeling of being held by him. She had waited so long for this moment. She exhaled slowly. She wasn't going to hold her breath waiting anymore.

Flynn reached for the bottle and kept her cuddled up with one arm while he unscrewed the cap.

"A sip of Levallier Dell's award-winning wine?" He offered her the bottle.

"Made by the most talented young winemaker."

She already felt intoxicated as the sharp taste of the wine filled her mouth. Flynn gripped her tighter as he took a mouthful of wine and together they watched the sun disappear into the Indian Ocean.

8 MONTHS LATER

Keely peered at the numbers on the overhead panel and stopped beside the man in the aisle seat. His head was back and his eyes were closed. His face was covered in freckles and it was topped by wisps of faded gingery hair. She grinned. If he had a straw hat he would have made a good scarecrow. The attractive woman with auburn hair beside him smiled and nodded.

"Are you going to find our seat, Mrs Levallier?" a voice murmured in her ear.

She gave Dianna a little wave. Euan opened one eye and winked at her before she moved on to the seat behind.

"You're in a rush," Keely said as Flynn strapped himself into the aisle seat beside her.

"I want to have you to myself. We've hardly been alone all week, with wedding preparations, meeting all the rellies, entertaining the visitors, then the whole big wedding day..."

"Which was wonderful," she chided him.

"Which was wonderful." He kissed her.

"Considering we had to do most of the organising over the phone from Margaret River, it all went well."

"Your mother had everything under control."

"Yes." For once Keely was glad of her mother's ability to organise. Working on the wedding together long distance had somehow brought them closer together. She found it so much easier to talk with her mother now, not just about the wedding but in general.

"Even down to getting a cake, the one you wanted, at the last minute."

"That was pretty amazing, even for my mother." Keely recalled their panic when Maggie had arrived from Perth without Anna's cake, three days before the wedding. Anna had insisted on making a traditional fruit cake with white plastic icing and paper flowers. She hadn't asked Flynn or Keely what they would like, and Keely had hated it. Neither she nor Flynn liked fruit cake. She'd wanted something more modern with shards of chocolate and fresh flowers to match her bouquet. It was just like Anna to go ahead assuming she knew everything, as usual.

"It's a shame though," Flynn said. "Anna couldn't be at the wedding and she wanted to do something special for us."

Keely felt guilty at her uncharitable thoughts. "Do we have to tell her?"

"Euan will smooth it over. His idea of holding a repeat wedding dinner at Margaret River once we get back is a good idea. He's even agreed to Theo being there."

"It's good to see Theo's made a full recovery both in health and business. And I'm so glad he and Euan have buried their differences."

"Buried is the right word. I think it's a difficult truce. Either of them could reignite their feud at any time."

"Hopefully not at our wedding celebration."

"I'm glad Euan suggested the dinner. We can invite people who couldn't make it to Adelaide and Anna will be happy. She can cook up a storm." He frowned. "I still can't understand how Maggie could leave the cake behind. It's unlike her to be so forgetful."

Keely had wondered about that herself. Maggie had been the only one she'd told about the kind of cake she would like to have and Keely's mother had taken it all in her stride when Maggie arrived without Anna's cake. Something like that would normally have sent her into a tailspin. When it came down to it though, it wouldn't have mattered what the cake was. They were all too busy having a great time to notice. Bec had delighted in her role as Keely's only attendant and had also caught the bouquet. She was planning to come over for a visit as soon as they were back from their honeymoon.

Keely looked at Flynn and smiled. "It doesn't matter. It really was a very special day."

"Last night was even better," he murmured in her ear.

Keely felt the warmth spread across her cheeks and down her neck. They'd spent their first night together as husband and wife in a beautiful hotel overlooking the sea at Glenelg. She didn't recall getting much sleep.

"I love it when you do that," he said.

"What?"

"Get that pink glow." He leaned in closer and peered inside the neck of her shirt. "It spreads all over you," he whispered with a lecherous look in his eyes.

"Flynn, stop it," she pleaded. People were crowded in the aisle next to him, still looking for their seats.

He sighed. "How long till we get to Broome?"

"We'll be there in time for dinner tomorrow night."

"I thought your mother was never going to stop hugging us goodbye and now to have to share our honeymoon flight with my father…"

Keely laughed at him. "We'll go our separate ways once we get to Perth. Anyway, what can you do on a plane?"

"These seats are very close, aren't they," he said.

"Excuse me." A man stood in the aisle waving his hand at the window seat beside her. "That's my seat."

Keely grinned at the frown on Flynn's face as he stood up to let the man past.

★   ★   ★

"I can't believe I'm here." Keely sighed. The late-afternoon Broome sun was delightfully warm after the cold winter climate of Adelaide. She gripped Flynn's hand and spun around to face him. "It's nearly a year since I first left home to travel north via Perth and I'm finally here."

"It's much better at this time of the year," he said. "Lucky I stopped you at Jurien Bay last time."

"And lucky you decided to come with me this time." She hugged him. "You weren't really going to call in at Levallier Dell, were you?"

"I could have made it there and back in time to catch the flight."

"Flynn." She pulled away from him. When they'd landed in Perth the day before there'd been a call from Hugh. Flynn was overheard saying he could drive down and take a look but both Euan and Dianna berated him for even thinking about it.

"Just kidding. Euan will be able to keep an eye on things while we're away. As long as he doesn't meddle with my blends."

They sat down on the sand and watched the water. Keely leaned her head on his shoulder.

"Wherever we go, we always have to live near water, either the sea or a river," she said.

"We can't get much closer to the water than the studio. Do you think we should move?"

"No. I can't imagine not living at Levallier Dell and we'll be very happy in the studio, but I'm just letting you know that I think water has been lucky for me."

"I thought I was your lucky charm." He draped an arm across her shoulders and cuddled her close.

"You're my number one lucky charm."

"We might need some luck to get through the next few years. It's a risky venture you've joined."

Keely noticed the little frown lines across his forehead as he stared out to sea. "Are you worried about the loan?" she asked.

"Things will be tight for a while."

"But the vintage went well."

"Yes, and so did you." The frown disappeared into a smile. "That's when I really knew I couldn't do without you."

"You hardly saw me."

Keely recalled the hectic times they'd just lived through. Flynn and Euan had been flat out. There were vintage workers to organise at Levallier Dell where everything was handpicked, and contractors at the Haystack Block where the grapes were harvested by machines. Keely and Dianna had been kept busy organising food, running errands and helping where they could in the sheds. Levallier Dell had been a hive of activity from early in the morning till late at night.

"At least you know what kind of life you've let yourself in for," he said.

"I love it."

The vines were just shooting when she'd first come to Levallier Dell and she'd stayed on and been a part of the whole process, right through the vintage. Flynn had been accurate when he'd said she'd find work. She had a few customers already for her fledgling design business and the cellar door kept them busy. Euan had agreed to it after Keely had suggested they turn the old shed by the river into a standalone cellar door so strangers didn't come to the house yard. Work had begun on the conversion and although Euan was still prone to mutter about hordes of tourists and the cost of licences he was taking a keen interest in the construction.

Keely had even done a bit of relief teaching and, while she was comfortable with it, she knew the winery was truly where her heart was now.

"Country life is portrayed as slow paced but there's always something to do in a winery," she said.

"You're a quick learner," Flynn said. "I think you must have been born under a winemaker's star. Although I'm a bit offended you haven't acquired a taste for my Whipcracker red yet."

She ignored his dig at her lack of finesse when it came to red wine. "I hope you'll make a better job of the albariño."

"It'll be a few years before we can try that. But you'll love it. It reminds me of warm evenings in Barcelona. I think we'll have to go there and try it so you'll know what to expect."

"A trip to Spain!" Keely couldn't believe her ears. "I'd love it. And it would be an opportunity to come up with a name for it."

"I've got an idea for the label."

"You really are getting ahead of yourself."

"Something that involves a sketch of you."

Keely shook her head.

"Yes, you'd be perfect for it. I'd call it the River Nymph."

She laughed. "We'll see."

"And while we're travelling we'll go to Greece, sample this assyrtiko Theo has mentioned. Who knows, we might plant a Greek variety here one day and Theo could be on the label. It would be a nod to his and the wine's Greek heritage and also a reminder that we wouldn't have the extra vineyards without his help."

Keely's heart melted. "You really are a good man, Flynn Levallier. You know I can't believe I wasted all that time worrying about teaching. When I came west last year, I was desperately looking for something. It turns out the something was the lifestyle at Levallier Dell. And the bonus was, I found the someone as well."

She giggled as she had a brief recollection of the evening she'd arrived at Levallier Dell and Euan had stopped to look at the newly painted sign. "Did you know Levallier Dell rhymes with so many things, including bloody hell? Maybe instead of River Nymph you could call the albariño Levallier Dell's Bloody Hell."

Flynn looked at her and shook his head. "Come on, Mrs Levallier Dell, I think you've had too much sun." He stood up, took her hands and pulled her up beside him. "I need to get you back to our room and loosen those clothes."

Keely took his hand and they walked back along the beach. In a few days' time they were heading for Derby, then they would begin the journey towards home again. South to the magical river and Levallier Dell, and with Flynn by her side, what else did she need?

ACKNOWLEDGEMENTS

Sixteen years ago I made my first journey to the Margaret River Wine Region in Western Australia and was immediately captivated by its special magic. This work of fiction grew from that first visit. I self-published it in 2006 as *River Magic* and since that time a lot has changed in both Margaret River and the wine industry. It has been an absolute pleasure to work with my publisher Jo Mackay and editor Annabel Blay to revisit this story and bring it to readers in 2019 as *Something in the Wine*.

The people who helped with wine and vine research for my original story have moved on but when I visited the region earlier this year to retrace my steps with a new list of questions I found a familiar face. John O'Connor, who runs a local tour company called Wine for Dudes was very helpful. John was just starting out when I first met him at the original Margaret River launch for *River Magic* and since then his company has gone from strength to strength. Daryl and I had a great day out visiting the wineries John had specially selected to help with my research. If you're ever in Margaret River and want to take a down-to-earth tour that allows you to experience the pleasure of wine without all the hype that sometimes goes with it, I can highly recommend Wine for Dudes.

And thanks to friends Andrew and Joy Hilder who travelled with us and put up with my wanderings in search of information.

In my original acknowledgements I also thanked the team of readers who support my work and keep me going. They are as valuable as a drop of fine wine. I mentioned Kathy Snodgrass, Sue Barlow, Sue Hazel and Mem Westbrook who still support me today along with my cyber writing pal, June Whyte, who sent the encouragement to hang in there and still does.

Now I also have the fabulous team at Harlequin to thank for bringing *Something in the Wine* to life. I am so grateful to Jo who wanted to bring the story to my readership, to Annabel for her editing skills and for helping me to see how much times had changed since the original version and to proofer Kate James for casting an eagle eye over everything. The cover designers have once again excelled. I always think they can't do better than the last cover they created and yet each new cover is unique. Thanks Michelle Zaiter, I love this one. And to Darren Kelly and the sales team and Adam van Rooijen and the marketing/publicity team and the rest of the gang who do so much for my books, my thanks for your dedication.

Just for you, dear readers, I take my research very seriously and, in the case of this book, I sampled some new and different varieties of wine that I'd like to share with you in thanks for your support. In the course of updating this story I came across two wine varieties, assyrtiko and albariño, which were new to me and to Australia as it turns out. My story is set in Western Australia but I managed to slip in a nod to the South Australian wine industry and in particular, Jim Barry Wines in the Clare Valley and Artwine in the Adelaide Hills from where I got the inspiration. Assyrtiko is a Greek wine variety that is now grown and bottled in Clare Valley thanks to Jim Barry Wines. Albariño is a wine variety from Spain and has been successfully grown and produced in the Adelaide Hills thanks to Judy and Glenn Kelly from Artwine. If you like white wine I can recommend both of these varieties.

I am also very grateful to Smokey, my friend in the Force, who was able to help me with police procedure. However, you all know I never let the truth get in the way of a good story so any variations are my own and that includes the finer details of wine making.

When I wrote a book set in Coonawarra wine country, called *Between the Vines* and published in 2015, I acknowledged my son Jared and said if you ever planned to write a book set in a winery it's handy if you have a son who's a winemaker. Jared and I got to work closely on that book and now we've had the chance to do it again with *Something in the Wine*. How lucky am I?

He not only helped me with the wine research but he also has an eagle eye when it comes to proofreading. Thank you, Jared, for the many emails and phone calls we had editing this book and for your support of your mum. I appreciate it more than words can say.

This book is dedicated to my daughter, Kelly, and that is a small acknowledgement for the huge support she gives me. Kelly has been in my corner since I first began to write seriously. She reads all my first drafts and gives feedback, she encourages me to keep writing with regular messages, sometimes just telling me to pull my finger out and get cracking. We chat about plot and characters and nothing's ever too much trouble for her. Thank you, Kelly, I'm truly grateful for your part in my writing journey.

It's so hard to single out two children when my whole family are always there for me. When *River Magic* was published I wrote this –

Daryl, Kelly, Steven, Dylan and Jared – we started the journey together in Margaret River. Your continued support has seen the story come to life. My thanks and love always.

That still holds true today of course but now I can add two daughters-in-law, Sian and Alexandra, and two grandsons, Harry and Archie, to my team and what a team they make.

And to you my readers, thank you for reading my books. I hope you've enjoyed your visit to Margaret River and I look forward to bringing you another story soon.

Turn over for a sneak peek ...

Come Rain
or Shine

by

TRICIA
STRINGER

Out Now

CHAPTER
1

Paula removed the protective hand she'd placed over the imperceptible bulge of her baby and lifted the magazine higher. The two women in the seats opposite had acknowledged her with quick smiles when they came in but now they had forgotten that she was sharing the doctor's waiting room with them and their conversation had turned personal.

"What will you do in the city?" one asked the other.

"I hope I can get an office job. I'm pretty rusty but I think I'll get something."

"What about Pete?"

"He's the one I'm worried about." Her voice wavered. "He's only ever known farming."

"You've had some help from the counsellor, haven't you?"

"Yes, but Pete is so hard to read. I'm on edge watching him all the time."

"Surely you don't think he'd...harm himself? Now that you've made the decision to leave, it must be a relief."

Paula couldn't help a quick glance over the top of her magazine. Pete's wife took the tissue offered by her friend. Tears rolled down her cheeks. She had a neat, tidy appearance and could have been about forty, but it was hard to tell. Her face was taut and she looked worn out.

"Yes and no. Pete still stews over it." The woman sobbed openly now. "He thinks we've failed."

Her friend put an arm around her. "You haven't failed, Sal. But if it doesn't rain, what can you do?"

Paula pressed herself into her chair, wishing she could disappear and give the women some privacy. Only last week the front page of the city paper had shown a family leaving their farm after years of drought. The report came from another part of the state and Dan had reassured her things weren't that bad here but the women she'd just overheard must live somewhere in the local district. Then there were the Watsons, their neighbours to the east. They'd recently gone through bad times, and she'd initially assumed that was because of Ted's mismanagement, but Dan had explained it was a combination of things out of Ted's control, market fluctuations and the weather being the main offenders.

"Paula?"

She jumped and the magazine slipped from her fingers.

"Sorry, I'm running a bit late today." Dr Hunter stood at the door, smiling at her.

Paula could feel the interest of the two women turn to her. Quickly she bent to pick up her magazine, then jumped to her feet. The room spun.

"Steady up." The doctor put his arm under hers.

Paula clapped her hand over her mouth. "I'm going to be sick."

★ ★ ★

At the sound of a vehicle Rowena gripped the edges of the kitchen bench and took a deep breath. She let it out slowly, switched on the kettle and glanced back into the sunny eating area where her small round table was set for two. Her gaze focused on the letter she'd left by her plate. It was the reason she'd asked her nephew Dan to call in for lunch. How she was going to break the news to him she still wasn't sure, but the worry of it had kept her awake half the night.

She moved through the arch into the little sunroom and sat down at the table, unable to resist the urge to pick the letter up and look at it again. Just when there was so much to look forward to, the past had come back to smack her in the face.

How she wished Austin was home instead of interstate. She would have been tempted to jump in the car and drive the couple of hours to Adelaide to talk things over with him. It was all too complicated for a phone call but she would talk to him once he was back.

Austin had become her rock and her confidant over the two years since she'd met him through a mutual friend. After so many years on her own, at first she'd resisted the idea of marrying him and moving to Adelaide but now that Dan was married and had someone to support him, Rowena had given in. She loved Austin and enjoyed sharing her life with him. No doubt some would think her foolish to marry at her time of life – she was approaching fifty-seven – but she wasn't one to dwell too much on what others thought.

Dan and Paula's wedding day flicked through her mind. Even though it had been a struggle for the new bride, fresh from the city, to adapt to country life, they seemed happy. Rowena hoped Paula would cope with the looming bombshell. Perhaps a country girl would understand the situation better but Dan had made his choice.

There was a clang as the garden gate closed and footsteps crunched along the path. Rowena hurried to take the sausage rolls from the oven and put them on the table beside the sandwiches. She wanted to give Dan a decent lunch. It was another of the things she did from time to time just to make sure they were eating properly. Paula wasn't fond of cooking.

Once again Rowena picked up the letter and unfolded it. She had to be strong. This wasn't Austin's problem, it was hers and it affected Dan and Paula and their unborn child. Dan's voice reached her as a low rumble from the back door. He must have the dog with him. She looked down at the letter again and brushed away the wisp of hair that fell forward over her face. How did life become so complicated?

*   *   *

"Everything's fine, Paula, and hopefully you won't have too much more nausea."

Paula gave the doctor a sheepish smile. She'd managed to make it to the toilet before she brought up her breakfast. "I thought I was over doing that."

"Nausea can come and go throughout pregnancy. Have you had a busy morning? You probably just stood up too quickly and the dizziness set you off. Your blood pressure is fine."

Paula slipped on her shoes. Lachlan Hunter appeared to be only a few years older than her. His youthful looks made it hard to tell but she didn't care how old he was. It was his confidence that reassured her.

He'd dealt very capably with Dan's Aunt Rowena when she'd had a bad bout of flu a few months ago. Anyone who could organise Rowena against her will was a miracle worker in Paula's eyes. When Paula had been hospitalised with the same virus, Lachlan had kept a close eye on her recovery. She had also seen his handiwork with their neighbour Bruce after his accident with the auger.

Then there was his patch-up job on Dan after he rolled his car. She gave an involuntary shiver when she recalled how easily she and her friend Jane, Bruce's wife, could have become widows. There was such a variety of things for a country GP to do and Paula had full confidence in Lachlan Hunter.

He looked at the computer screen on the desk in front of him. "Dr Markham has sent your notes from Sydney and with your recent ultrasound results we can be confident your March due date is correct."

Paula couldn't resist putting her hand on her stomach. Was she imagining a slight bulge there already, even though she was only twelve weeks along? She certainly couldn't stand to have anything tight around her middle. That was something that did make her feel sick.

"I've been a bit nervous. I was still taking the pill when I conceived. I've been worried it might have affected the baby."

"There's no need to worry. We'll send you for another ultrasound at twenty weeks but you're fit and healthy. No reason to think the baby is otherwise. How are you feeling in general? Apart from this morning, you said the nausea is easing."

"I thought I would have to start the day with a cup of tea and cracker biscuits forever." She gave the doctor a wry smile. "I still feel a bit queasy at times but this morning was the first time I've been sick in a while. Both my sisters were the same but they felt fine for the rest of their pregnancies."

"Country South Australia is a long way from your family in Sydney. How are you settling in?"

"Until I met Dan I'd never given farm life a thought but I'm very happy here." She smiled. "My sisters wonder what I do all day. They can't imagine how I keep busy without shops and movies and nightlife."

"I know what you mean."

She watched the doctor tap at the keyboard and wondered if there was a Mrs Hunter. "Are you from Sydney?" she asked.

"No. English father and Chinese mother who raised me in the leafy suburbs of Adelaide – a world away from here. I only came for a brief country experience a few years ago and I'm still here."

"I guess we're not that far from the city but I find the local community provides most things I need."

"There are some gaps, unfortunately." He turned to face her. "Like where you should give birth. You can book in at the regional hospital…"

"That's a long drive." Paula recalled the weekend she and Dan had spent in a tiny cabin at Wallaston, the seaside town that was the biggest in their region. It had taken well over an hour to get there. Between Paula's bouts of nausea and Dan's dozing in front of the football on television, it wasn't what you would call the romantic getaway as described in the caravan park brochure. So much had happened since their May wedding, they had both been glad of the opportunity to relax. Paula smiled at the recollection – the weekend hadn't been all nausea and sleeping.

Lachlan handed over some papers. "Or there's a choice of hospitals in Adelaide. Quite a few mothers from here choose one of them."

That was even further away. Paula took the pamphlets without even looking at them. "But you said everything's fine. I'm quite happy for you to deliver our baby here."

"Not an option, I'm afraid. The local hospital isn't able to do obstetrics and that suits me. Babies are unpredictable and I'm on call enough as it is. One of the downsides of living here is that you have to travel to have your baby."

Paula looked down quickly as tears brimmed in her eyes. She bit her lip. Where had they come from? "But how will I know…what if…?"

"You'll have plenty of time, especially with a first baby. But if you're worried you can always stay down in Adelaide for the last few weeks so you're closer to the hospital. Have you got someone you could stay with? Miss Woodcroft will be living there by then, won't she?"

"Well, yes...but..." Paula frowned. The thought of spending any longer than a day with Dan's aunt was not one she cared to entertain. Rowena Woodcroft was a woman used to doing things her way. Paula admired many of Rowena's qualities and had even come to like the woman who was both mother and father to Dan but, even so, she could only tolerate her in small doses.

"You discuss it with Dan." Lachlan walked her to the door. "You've got a bit of time but you should book in somewhere soon."

Paula was amazed; the excitement of her healthy pregnancy overshadowed by the idea of travelling away to have the baby. She thought of Jane on the neighbouring farm with her two little boys. They were both born before Dan and Paula had married but she had assumed they had been delivered at the local hospital. She'd have to talk to Jane about it. Maybe tonight there'd be a chance over dinner.

Deciding where to have her baby was forgotten once she was inside the supermarket propelling her trolley along the aisles. It was only September, the baby wasn't due till March and right now she had a dinner party to prepare.

Dan had been suggesting they invite Ted and Heather Watson over for a meal for some time. Now that Paula was feeling better she had finally given in but only with the proviso that they could also invite Bruce and Jane and her friends from town, Dara and Chris. Glancing from her list to the shelves, Paula cursed her insistence.

She was confident at cooking light meals but her lifestyle in Sydney had meant she'd eaten out a lot. Since marrying Dan, she'd had several cooking fiascos and their entertaining had been limited to casual 'everyone bring a plate' meals or barbecues. It was easy when the blokes cooked chops and sausages and the occasional piece of chicken, while the women all brought salads.

Dan had offered to do that tonight but Paula had been determined to have a proper sit-down meal, all provided by her. The Watsons on their own had been too awkward to contemplate and she'd insisted on inviting the others, but now that she had to cook for eight, she was worried she might have stretched her capabilities.

She picked through the potatoes trying to find several the same size and her thoughts turned to Heather Watson. With four children and a full-time job she was always on the run and Paula rarely saw her, while Ted was regularly at their farm helping Dan with the sheep. The two men had become partners in a new stud ram.

Dan got on well with Ted and even though Paula often found herself cringing at his crude remarks and insensitive comments she had grown to tolerate their neighbour. She wondered yet again how someone as gentle as Heather ended up with someone as boorish as Ted.

The supermarket was busy and around every corner she ran into someone she knew. It was hardly five months since she'd married Dan and moved to this rural community, yet she felt very comfortable most of the time. It was pleasant to have people smiling and calling you by name when you shopped instead of the dash and grab she used to do, or waiting for her Woolworths online delivery to arrive.

Paula consulted her list again. It was all very well to stop and chat but she still had lots to do and making sure she had everything on her list was very important. It was too far to pop back to the shop if she left off a vital ingredient.

Her mobile phone beeped. She read the brief message from Dan. He wanted her to collect something from the stock and station agent on her way home. That would mean a detour to the other side of town and she was already on a tight schedule. It was a nuisance but after the conversation she'd overheard in the doctor's waiting room it was strangely reassuring to get his message. She sighed. If only he'd thought of it earlier, she could have called in before her appointment.

She glanced at her watch. At least the chicken breasts wouldn't take a lot of preparation but the nibbles she'd planned were a bit of a fiddle and the dessert was only half made. She sent a brief 'OK' reply, shoved her phone and her shopping list in her bag and headed for the checkout.

* * *

Rocket lowered himself onto the old blanket Rowena kept for him by the back door. Dan watched him drop his head to his paws and slowly close his eyes. The poor old dog still tried to keep up with Dan wherever he went. Rocket had been with them for fifteen years, a long time for a working dog.

"You rest up, old boy." Dan should have trained a new pup a couple of years ago but he'd never got around to it. Now he didn't want to put Rocket through the indignity of a young pup nipping at his heels and gobbling his food. He bent down and gave the dog a gentle pat on the head. "You've a bit of work left in you yet, eh Rocket?" The dog opened one eye and his eyebrow went up with it, then he let out a long sigh and closed his eye again.

Dan slipped off his boots and walked through to the bathroom to wash his hands. It was strange how quickly he felt like a visitor in the house he had lived in all his life. When he and Paula had married they had moved into the old house at the other end of Dan and Rowena's farm, called Wood Dell. It had been built by his great grandparents early in the last century and it had been empty for many years. Now that Rowena was marrying and shifting to Adelaide she had tried to talk Dan and Paula into moving into her more modern house. The main machinery sheds were here beside the newer place, but they had begun to make the old house comfortable and it felt like their home.

This house, where he'd lived with his aunt before he married Paula, had been built for his parents when they married. He didn't remember his mother. She'd been killed in a car accident when he was young and his aunt had moved in to look after him and his father.

Dan thought of Rowena as his mother. She was the only family he had left. That was another reason the baby that he and Paula were expecting was so important to him. He'd grown up an only child with a father who'd never recovered from the loss of his wife. Rowena had worked hard to make their home a happy one and he was very grateful for that. But Dan was determined that this baby, his and Paula's, would be brought up without the gloomy shadows of the past. Wood Dell gave them a fresh start.

They'd had a rough patch not long after their wedding when Paula thought he'd had a child with his ex, Katherine. Paula had returned to her parents in Sydney and he'd been terrified she'd left him. Her pregnancy had come as a big surprise considering they'd each thought the other didn't want children. They'd done a lot of talking since then, opened up to each other and everything was fine now. They both hoped there would be more children.

He wiped his hands on an old towel. Rowena had work towels and bathroom towels and he wouldn't dare use the wrong one. Paula didn't care which towels he used but he still kept an old one in the laundry at their house. He couldn't bring himself to wipe his hands on the new pale towels Paula filled the bathroom with.

He walked in his socks through the kitchen into the sunroom where his aunt had laid out a lunch of homemade sausage rolls and sandwiches on the cosy little table. She was sitting near the window, frowning over a letter.

"This looks good," he said. "Thanks for the invite."

Rowena glanced up and waved him to his old seat. "Help yourself. I'll make a pot of tea." She folded the letter and slipped it under her plate. "How are the crops looking?"

Dan took some sausage rolls and poured sauce on to his plate from the little china jug provided. He hated the daintiness of it. He never knew how to hold it. Paula used the sauce straight from the bottle, which suited him fine. "We'll be lucky to get half our annual yield," he said through a mouthful. "That bit of rain at the end of August wasn't enough. It'll be hardly worth getting out the harvester."

"Everything all right with that?"

"So far. There are a few tight bearings on the harvester wheels. Tom is getting better at pulling things apart and putting them back together."

"I'd forgotten he was with you today. I should have offered him lunch."

Dan watched Rowena push at a wisp of hair that had fallen across her eyes. He had been surprised when she had asked him in for some lunch. These days he usually went home to Paula. Tom was almost part of the family too. He'd worked for them for a couple of years now and he'd thought it was odd that Rowena hadn't extended the invitation to include him.

"I've sent him home anyway. Told him to rest up. He's playing in the footy final this weekend. I can finish the rest by myself."

"And Paula's gone into town?"

"Yes. She had a doctor's appointment."

Dan looked up in surprise as the cup Rowena sat on the table in front of him rattled precariously on its saucer. "She's all right?" Rowena said. "There's nothing wrong with the baby?"

He noticed worry lines on his aunt's face. "Everything's fine. This is just a check-up. Evidently she's supposed to have one every month."

"Of course." Rowena mopped at the drops of tea that had slopped over the edge of his cup. "And these days there are so many tests they can do. Often couples even know the sex of their baby before it's born."

"Paula and I have talked about that."

"Have you?" Rowena's sharp gaze locked on his.

"We'd rather it was a surprise."

Rowena sat but instead of putting food on her plate, she pulled the letter she'd been reading out from under it and held the folded paper in her two hands. "It may be more of a surprise than you'd bargained for," she said. "I've just received a letter from my cousin, Beryl."

Dan looked quickly at Rowena. The sausage roll pastry stuck to the roof of his mouth. He was an only child. His father and grandparents were dead. Maybe cousin Beryl was like Uncle Gerald. He had been a friend of Dan's grandfather and had become known as 'uncle'. It was a form of politeness children used for family friends. No blood connection existed. To Dan's knowledge, Rowena was his only living relative on the Woodcroft side.

"Who is cousin Beryl?" He washed down the pastry with a slurp of tea.

"She's only a cousin by marriage. Your grandfather had a brother. Beryl married his son, Alfred – my cousin."

Dan frowned at his aunt. "Alfred?"

"We always called him Freddy."

That name was more familiar to Dan. "He was named as the other executor of Dad's will, but he died not long after Dad, didn't he? I didn't even know he was married."

"Your father was closer in age to Freddy. I hardly knew him myself."

"How is it that you've never mentioned Beryl before?"

"I didn't like her." Rowena flicked some crumbs from the table. "While your father and Freddy were still alive I would occasionally hear about what she was doing and sometimes Beryl would write about Jacinta…"

"Who's Jacinta?" Dan's head was starting to whirl.

"Freddy and Beryl had a daughter…Jacinta."

"You mean there are more of them?"

"They only had one child, Jacinta."

"Are you telling me I've got distant cousins I've never met, never heard a murmur of? Why haven't you mentioned them before?"

"We weren't close and after Freddy died I had no reason to keep in touch. Beryl lives in Brisbane. She was always such a snob, thought herself better than the rest of us. Your father liked her though. He spent time with Freddy and Beryl after your mother died."

"I guess that was why Dad made Freddy one of the executors of his will. You're the other one so it's in good hands." Dan watched Rowena tap the letter against her other hand. Unease tingled in his chest. "Why now?"

"What do you mean?"

"Why are you telling me about Beryl now?"

"Because of this." She waved the pages slowly in his direction.

Dan looked from the letter to his aunt's face. There were dark shadows under her eyes he hadn't noticed before. He had rarely seen her like this. She was a strong woman and she'd had to deal with many things over the years. Very little fazed her like this letter seemed to have. He watched her take a sip of her tea and waited for her to reply.

"The letter is all about Jacinta. The poor child was so cosseted and spoilt she never stood a chance. Beryl made her into a piece of work. From the bits I heard, Jacinta turned into a right little madam in her teenage years, went off the rails and led a fairly wild life and now this…" She paused and looked at the letter she held in her hands.

Dan didn't know what to make of it. He didn't understand why Rowena was telling him all this out of the blue. It was a surprise to learn he had distant relatives but that still didn't explain Rowena's agitation. Maybe she was feeling guilty she hadn't told him before and now something had happened to them.

"Are they all right?" he said.

She kept staring at the letter.

"Rowena?"

"Oh yes. They're fine." She flipped the pages open. "Beryl is crowing. After all these years she's going to be a grandmother. It seems Jacinta's settled down. She's met the most wonderful man. He's off the land but a third son and there's not enough work for him on the property. He's working for another farmer and they're trying to get enough money together to get their own place. Jacinta has married him and they're having a baby."

Dan studied Rowena, waiting for her to continue. What was the matter with her? Surely she couldn't be jealous of a distant relative she didn't like. She wasn't his mother but his child would be her grandchild in every sense of the word.

"You'll be able to tell her our good news." He gave her a reassuring smile. "It's nice to know that, here and in another part of Australia, the Woodcroft blood line will continue on."

Rowena's eyes locked on his. "When is Paula due?"

"March, we think."

"Are you sure?"

"Well, that's what Paula's doctor in Sydney said."

Rowena waved the letter at him. "Jacinta's baby is due in February."

Dan frowned. Why was Rowena so agitated over a baby's due date? "Good for her."

"She's had a test. The baby is a boy."

Something niggled at the edge of his memory but Dan pushed it aside. He was more worried about Rowena. She'd shoved back her chair and now she was pacing the narrow galley kitchen.

"That's nice for her..."

Rowena came through the arch and stopped right in front of him. "Paula's got to have that test," she said firmly. "We've got to know."

"Now hang on, Rowena. I've already told you, Paula and I are happy to be surprised when the baby is born."

"Surprised!" She spat the word at him. "It will be a surprise all right. The surprise will be when Jacinta gets this place, or at least a cut of it because she has a son before you."

Dan could feel his jaw drop open. He forced it shut as the recollection thumped into his head — his father's will.

"You turn thirty in a few months, which is the vesting date for you to inherit and any claims must be made before then. Your father made it quite clear if there was any dispute that preference should be given to the person with the oldest male Woodcroft child. Jacinta's baby will be that. She may be married but Beryl made it clear Jacinta has kept the Woodcroft name and so will her son." Rowena lowered herself back into her chair. "Don't you see, Dan? We need to know if the baby Paula is carrying is a boy. If it is, she'll have to have it early. They do that kind of thing all the time these—"

"No."

"Dan, your future...your baby's future could depend on this."

"No!" He had rarely before raised his voice to his aunt. "I am not putting my wife and our baby through that. I don't want Paula to worry about anything but having a healthy baby."

"But, Dan." Rowena reached across and placed her hand on his arm. "If Paula's having a boy it's important that it's born before Jacinta's or you could lose everything."

"That's ridiculous, Rowena. I'm here farming as Dad wanted. Jacinta can't take over just because she wants to. You're the executor. You can stop it from happening."

"I can't stop her from making a claim. Even if she doesn't get Wood Dell, she could cause a lot of problems for us financially."

"No more." Dan pushed back his chair. "I won't add to Paula's concerns. She's worried enough about the baby. Boy or girl, it will be born when it's due. You're not to mention this."

"But, Dan, she's got to know."

"No, Rowena. Promise me you won't mention this to Paula."

"But, Dan…"

"Promise me," he snapped.

They glared at each other across the table.

"All right," Rowena muttered, "but I…"

"Woodie Two, calling Woodie."

Dan jumped as he heard Paula's voice crackle from the two-way radio. She didn't like the radio and rarely used it. He followed his aunt's gaze to the shelf above the cupboard where the radio sat.

"Woodie Two, calling Woodie. Dan, are you on channel?"

In spite of the distortion he thought he could hear agitation in Paula's voice. In two steps he was at the radio.

"Yes, Paula. I'm at Rowena's. Where are you?"

"Just at the end of our driveway." There was a brief pause. "Dan, I need help."

"I'm coming."

He threw the handpiece onto the shelf and without another look at Rowena he ran for his boots.

BESTSELLING AUSTRALIAN AUTHOR

TRICIA STRINGER

*Warm-hearted rural romance
from the voice of Australian storytelling.*

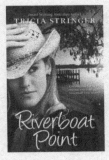